The DEVIL
and
MRS.
DAVENPORT

The DEVIL and MRS. DAVENPORT

A Novel

PAULETTE KENNEDY

LAKE UNION
PUBLISHING

Text copyright © 2024 by Paulette Kennedy
All rights reserved.

No part of this book may be reproduced, or stored in a retrieval system, or transmitted in any form or by any means, electronic, mechanical, photocopying, recording, or otherwise, without express written permission of the publisher.

Published by Lake Union Publishing, Seattle

www.apub.com

Amazon, the Amazon logo, and Lake Union Publishing are trademarks of Amazon.com, Inc., or its affiliates.

ISBN-13: 9781662514883 (paperback)
ISBN-13: 9781662514876 (digital)

Cover design by Kimberly Glyder
Cover image: © CSA Images / Getty; © Watcharaphimchan / Shutterstock

Printed in the United States of America

*For all the girls who have disappeared. And those who
lost themselves for love . . .
May you always find your way back home.*

Chapter 1

September 1955

The first day of autumn brought the fever, and with the fever came the voices. Loretta fought the fatigue until it got the best of her—until her bones ached so deeply she thought her legs might snap. She took to her bed, shivering under mounded quilts, only to toss them off in a sweat hours later. The distant sounds of Peter and the children stirred her guilt—their footsteps on the stairs, pattering past her door. Pete wasn't good at handling things on his own.

This was what it would be like for them if she died. She couldn't die.

On the third day, Loretta blinked away her delirium, her eyes adjusting to the dim light. Her limbs weighed heavy, as if her body had grown taproots, anchoring her to the bed. A fly buzzed near her face, sluggish and loud. The window was open—Pete must have done that. His side of the bed was empty. He'd been sleeping on the sofa, as he did when they argued.

She sat up slowly and switched on the lamp next to the bed. Her reflection startled her in the vanity mirror. A stranger with mousy, unkempt hair and bleary eyes, her slip sliding down one pale shoulder. So thirsty. She reached for the glass of water on the nightstand and took a drink. It tasted of wet leaves. Stale. She shuffled two aspirin from the bottle next to the lamp and swallowed them dry.

She turned off the light and lay back on the sweat-soured pillow. She'd get up later, have a shower, dress properly, then go downstairs and make breakfast. See Pete off to his classes and walk the kids to the bus stop.

She closed her eyes. The darkness settled over her like a fog.

Didn't mean to. Didn't mean to.

Loretta's heart stuttered. Someone had spoken. The voice—a girl's, soft and tentative—sounded like Charlotte's. But Charlotte was in her bed, down the hall.

The filthy, stale taste flooded Loretta's mouth again, choking her. She clawed at her throat, reached for the glass of water, knocked it to the floor. It broke with a loud crash.

She didn't mean to!

That voice. Louder now, ringing through her head like a pealing bell.

Footsteps echoed up the stairs. Pete flung open the door, his thick glasses crooked across his nose. "I heard a crash. Everything okay?"

"I thought someone was in here. I heard a voice." She motioned to the window. Only the curtains hung there, blowing gently. A cardinal's song threaded into the room, greeting the dawn. *Cheercheerprettyprettypretty.*

"There's no one else here." Pete sat next to her on the bed. "You were probably just dreaming." He pressed the back of his hand to her forehead and frowned. "Did you take some aspirin?"

"A few minutes ago. Am I feverish?"

"You're a little warm."

"Maybe I should go to the doctor."

"I'm sure it's only the flu." That thoughtful frown again. A sigh.

"What's wrong, Pete?"

He reached for her hand, turned it over to trace the faint lines crossing her palm. "You haven't been yourself lately. Even before you got sick. I'm worried it'll be like the last time."

"What do you mean?"

"Like it was after Charlotte . . ."

Yes, after Charlotte. When she could barely drag herself from bed and everything—even her next breath—seemed impossible. Loretta listened as Pete quietly recounted her failings: She'd been sleeping too much. She served leftovers to his colleagues last Friday. They hadn't made love in months. She'd gained weight. Even the children had noticed her mood swings.

She let him finish without interrupting, then squeezed his hand. "It won't be like last time. I promise. I've prayed about it. I'm trying, Pete. I am."

He adjusted his glasses, cleared his throat. "Just get to feeling better. I need you. The kids need you." He coaxed her back against the pillows and pulled the quilt to her chin, tucking it around her. He kissed her forehead with cool lips. "Rest. I'll bring you breakfast before I go."

"You're working today?"

"I have to. The deans are meeting this afternoon and I've already missed two days of classes. I'll leave the car for you, though."

"All right."

He swept the broken glass on the floor into the wastebasket and left, closing the door soundlessly behind him. Loretta knew he was unhappy. The years had stretched them thin. Made them strangers. It hadn't always been that way. She'd been little more than a child when they met at a revival during the war. Pete's poor eyesight had kept him from serving in the military, so he'd thrown himself into local missionary work instead, and she'd gotten caught up in his magnetic pull, a planet in orbit around the sun. He was handsome. Intelligent. Five years older and more mature than the boys her age. He'd admired her clever mind and quick wit—made her feel like she could be more than a farmer's daughter. The summer of her sixteenth year held fond memories of river baptisms; sweet, stolen kisses; and heady promises made in the humid dark.

They'd married that fall. Daddy was relieved—Pete had taken his biggest burden off his weary back. She fell pregnant with Lucas right away, and Charlotte came shortly after. Somehow, eleven years had passed. Eleven years of supporting Pete in his ministry. In his education. And what did she have to show for it? A two-story clapboard house with swaybacked floors she could never quite get clean, on the respectable west side of middling Myrna Grove, with a tumbling bush of white hydrangeas by the front porch. She'd wanted to be a journalist. Had edited her school paper and wanted to travel the world someday, writing about the people and places she read about in her mama's old *National Geographic*s.

Instead, she had the privilege of being Mrs. Peter Davenport.

She mustn't ever forget that.

⁕

Loretta surfaced from sleep. The house was quiet. Pete had seen the kids off to school, then. A plate with eggs, bacon, and toast sat on the nightstand, grease congealing. Her stomach turned. She threw off the covers and ran for the hall—made it to the bathroom, just in time. Nothing came up but bile and water.

She descended the stairs on shaky legs. Dirty dishes lined the kitchen counters and filled the sink. Milk glasses sat in a row, with gummy dregs stuck to their bottoms. She'd asked the kids countless times to rinse their dishes. She pressed her face against the refrigerator door, listened to its soothing hum.

Why was everything so overwhelming?

She poured tepid coffee from the percolator and sat at the kitchen table, gathering strength for the day as she sorted through the mail Pete had stacked there. Bills. A card from a travel agency, advertising flights to Cuba.

She went out to the porch to fetch the paper. It was Wednesday. The grocery sales circular and coupons would be inside. She'd make a list, get dressed, and go to the store. Tonight, she'd fix Pete one of his favorite dinners as penance for her days of neglect.

She went back inside and unrolled the paper. The front page featured a picture of a teenage girl with long hair and sweetly inquisitive dark eyes.

Myrna Grove Girl Missing

Loretta read on, her hand going to her mouth. The girl lived only a few miles away, on the outskirts of town, where the houses weren't so neat and tidy and the streets gave way to dirt roads. Darcy Hayes. A high school senior. Loretta thought of Charlotte and Lucas, safe at school, and a twinge of guilt ran through her. That poor mother.

She hurriedly turned the page, drawing out the sales sheets. The bright, cheerful photos of Jell-O salads and festively dressed hams were a pleasant distraction from the news and stirred her appetite. Consumers Market had the best price on meat this week. She'd do the shopping, then tackle the mess in the house.

She showered, brushed her long hair into some semblance of order, then pinned it into a prim bun at her nape. Pete didn't like her wearing trousers—he thought them immodest—so she chose one of her many dresses. Pete was right: she had gained weight. The dress was snug, even with her best girdle. She needed to take better care with her portions. Get more exercise.

Loretta gathered her nightgown and Pete's dirty clothes from the floor and placed them in a laundry basket to wash later. As she moved to the bedroom door, a sudden wave of nausea washed over her. Weakness flooded her limbs. She'd done too much too soon.

She dropped the basket and lowered herself to the edge of the bed just as darkness crowded her vision. That same swampy filth from before filled her mouth. The floor fell away like an elevator with a snapped cable, and Loretta fell with it.

She squeezed her eyes shut, anticipating an impact that never came. When she opened them again, she was outside. It was nighttime. The sky stretched above her, a sliver of crescent moon hanging low, peeking through the trees. How had she gotten there? She tried to sit up and found herself paralyzed. Panic surged through her.

Water gurgled in the distance, undercut by the whine and squeak of machinery. Footsteps approached. Gruff voices. Men arguing. A shovelful of dirt and wet leaves fell over her face. Then another. She couldn't breathe. She couldn't scream. She couldn't move. And in that moment, with certainty, Loretta Davenport knew she was going to die.

Chapter 2

Loretta gasped, her eyes snapping open. Above her, last week's laundry hung on the line—Lucas's bedsheets, with their cheerful blue and red stripes. She'd forgotten to bring the laundry in before she got sick. She'd have to wash everything again. The sun shone weakly through the clouds. A drop of rain hit her cheek.

Confusion sank between Loretta's eyes like a stone. She sat up, her head swimming. She remembered getting dressed, gathering the dirty clothes, and then fainting in the bedroom. The feeling of falling. The terror of being buried alive. But she had no recollection of anything that happened after. No memory of coming outside.

Loretta got to her knees, gripping the clothesline pole as she stood. Chigger bites itched and stung her legs through her nylons.

"Loretta! There you are!"

Loretta turned toward the sound of Phyllis Colton's shrill voice. Her neighbor was crossing the fenceless divide between their yards. Phyllis was kind, but she was also the neighborhood busybody—a retired telephone operator who loved to pry into everyone's business.

"I've been worried about you. Haven't seen you for a few days."

Loretta patted her hair back into place as Phyllis approached. "I've been sick. Some sort of stomach bug. Thankfully Pete and the kids are fine."

Phyllis frowned, pursing her wrinkled lips. "Well. Peter should have told me. I might have helped."

"It's all right. I'm better now."

"You look peaked. Have you had anything to eat today?"

Loretta hadn't, and hunger clawed her belly like an angry cat, threatening to make her sick again. "No. I was getting ready to go to the store. Came out to check on the laundry first," she lied, eyeing the sky, where gray clouds were slowly gathering. "Looks like we might get a storm later."

"I suppose we need it." Phyllis pushed her rhinestone-studded glasses up her nose. "I just took some monkey bread out of the oven. Come on over. Sit on the back porch and have a cup of coffee with me. It's been too long since we talked."

It had been only a week, but Loretta relented and followed Phyllis across the yard. Phyllis *was* a good cook. And she needed to eat something.

She settled herself on one of Phyllis's patio chairs as the older woman fussed around her. The elm tree in Phyllis's yard was just beginning to turn, green leaves rimmed with gold. Fall was usually Loretta's favorite season in the Ozarks—the changing leaves; the bright, clear blue of the sky; and after autumn, the promise of the holidays. But lately, she found little joy in anything.

Phyllis brought out the monkey bread, which gleamed with a glaze of melted sugar. Loretta politely waited for Phyllis to serve her, then tucked in, the bread's warm, yeasty sweetness pleasant on her tongue.

"Shame about that Hayes girl," Phyllis said, lifting her coffee cup. "Did you see?"

The missing girl. The sweetness in Loretta's mouth soured. "Yes. I saw."

"She was on her way to her aunt's house. That's what the news said last night." Phyllis shook her head. "What kind of world are we living in? Young folks used to be able to go for a walk without having to worry about some pervert snatching them up."

"There have always been evil people. Don't you think?"

"It was never this bad. Times are changing."

Loretta smiled tightly and braced for one of Phyllis's bigoted speeches. She took a drink of coffee. It was too weak, as always. She'd stay a few more minutes, then go. She had plenty of excuses.

Phyllis delicately dabbed at her mouth with a napkin. "I just wonder about that man down the way. In the old Robberson place. You never see him out during the day. Only nighttime. And that yard. It's a shame to let the grass get as high as he does."

The Robbersons' nephew had moved in after Mrs. Robberson passed last winter, just months after her husband died. While it was true that the house was neglected, it'd been in such a state for years. The couple had aged well beyond the capability of keeping such a large house. "Just because someone neglects a house, it doesn't make him a suspect," Loretta said. "And perhaps he works nights."

"Well. The police need to start somewhere. They should look at the coloreds, too."

Loretta flinched. "That's unchristian."

"All the same. They should. With all the changes lately." Phyllis tsked. "Shame what this world is coming to."

Loretta found Phyllis's bigotry far more shameful than the long-needed changes sweeping the nation. She lifted her coffee cup to her lips to hide her frown and took a drink. She gagged. Choked. Her head went woozy. She looked in the cup. The bottom was clotted with wet leaves and dirt. As she watched, a slick-backed beetle crawled to the rim, antennae waving. She let the cup fall. Coffee spilled across the tablecloth.

Only coffee.

FinleyRiverFinleyRiverFinleyRiverFinley . . .

The missing girl. That's where she was. A strange, compelling certainty rang in Loretta's consciousness. How on earth did she know that?

"Loretta! My heavens." Phyllis swiped at the spilled coffee with a napkin. "Are you all right?"

Loretta stood, knees shaking. "I'm sorry. I have to go."

She rushed back across the yard to her house, ignoring Phyllis's startled exclamation. She flung open the back door, flew down the hall, and snatched up her pocketbook from the kitchen table.

Ten minutes later, she stood outside the Consumers Market on Olive Street, her hand shaking as she put a dime in the pay phone by the entrance, dialed the operator, and asked for the police. On the other end of the line, a woman answered. "Myrna Grove Police."

"Yes, hello. I think I know where she is. The Hayes girl."

There was a pause on the other end. A scrabbling sound. Papers being shuffled. "Can you give me your name, please?"

"I . . . I'd prefer to stay anonymous. Look by the Finley River. In Ozark. Near the mill."

Loretta hung up, her pulse roaring in her ears. She took a deep breath to compose herself, pulled a shopping cart free from the row lining the entryway, and went inside. She'd make meatloaf for dinner. Pete's favorite.

⛬

Loretta barely had the groceries unpacked and put away before the kids came rushing in, fresh from school. Lucas hung his book bag on the back of one of the kitchen chairs and sat, red-faced and out of breath.

Charlotte strutted in after him, her blonde pigtails bouncing. Pete had parted her hair crooked, but at least he had tried. "We raced all the way from the bus stop! Luke won, but only by a little. I'm getting faster."

"You're both fast as lightning." Loretta went to them, pressing kisses onto the tops of their heads. She inhaled their sweaty-sweet child smell and her earlier annoyance over the dishes faded. After all, some mothers would give anything to wash their children's dirty dishes one more time. Her throat clenched, thinking of Darcy Hayes, and she sent up a silent prayer for the girl's family.

"Are you feeling better, Mommy?" Charlotte asked.

"Yes, a little. Still tired, but I did the shopping today. Would you like some graham crackers with honey and peanut butter?"

"Yes, ma'am!" Lucas answered. Loretta smiled. Her Luke, always ready to eat. Pete swore the boy would be a ball player someday, but Loretta saw their son's softer side—how he much preferred reading and drawing to tussling over a ball.

"Teacher conference is tomorrow afternoon," Luke said, gulping down the glass of milk she offered.

"I haven't forgotten. Mrs. Roush, isn't it? Your teacher?"

"Yes, ma'am. She's really nice."

"I'm glad you like her."

"Can we get a dog, Mommy?" Charlotte interrupted.

"You know what I've told you—it's up to your father."

After the kids finished their snacks, they went upstairs to play. Loretta washed and dried the dishes, then sat on the couch and took up her knitting—a few stolen moments for herself before preparing dinner. She soon lost herself in counting her stitches, and looked up only when a low rumble of thunder caught her attention. The skies outside the picture window had gone a sickly bluish green.

She glanced at the clock. Five. Pete would be home in an hour. Loretta stood, fishing a single dollar bill and the grocery receipt from her dress pocket. She hid the money safely at the bottom of her knitting basket, covering it with her yarn. She had stashes of money hidden throughout the house, in places Pete would never think to look. Each time she went shopping, she wrote her checks for slightly over the total and kept the change for herself. She'd managed to save well over $200 this way, with Pete none the wiser. She'd learned from her mother that a woman needed to save some pocket change for a rainy day, just in case. After the Depression, Daddy had been tightfisted, just like Pete. Mama's hidden money had financed little treats throughout Loretta's childhood—from butterscotch sticks at the five-and-dime to pretty ribbons for her hair.

Loretta switched on the television and turned the volume up so she could hear it from the kitchen. She opened the fridge and poured herself a glass of iced tea, tentatively sniffing it before drinking. It tasted sweet and bitter, the way tea ought to taste. Perhaps the strange tastes earlier that day had only been an odd, lingering symptom of her illness. But illness couldn't explain the voice she'd heard in her room—or that peculiar knowing that had come over her concerning the missing girl. Her frenzied phone call to the police wasn't like her. But she'd felt strangely compelled to do what she'd done.

She prepared the meatloaf and placed it in the oven, then washed her hands, drying them on her apron. The theme song for the local news filtered through the kitchen. Loretta's ears perked as she heard the newscaster mention Darcy Hayes. She leaned against the arched doorway dividing the living room from the kitchen to watch the news. The first drops of rain knocked hard against the windows. She'd forgotten to bring the laundry in from the line. There was no use in rushing out for it now.

Pictures of the missing girl flashed onto the screen—pretty, dark eyes, and dark hair. A chill walked across Loretta's skin. She crossed her arms and rubbed the gooseflesh away. Charlotte's laughter trickled downstairs. Her own children were safe. Sound. She shouldn't feel guilty for thinking such a thing, but she felt guilty all the same.

The picture cut to footage of men walking slowly and methodically through the woods, leashed dogs at their sides. So, they'd taken her call seriously. Loretta was surprised. She prayed they'd find the girl alive. It had been only three days since she disappeared. They might.

Lightning blazed through the picture windows, followed by a sharp crack of thunder. Charlotte shrieked and came clattering down the stairs. She ran to Loretta's side for comfort. The rain went from a patter to a roar.

"It's all right, baby," Loretta soothed, running a hand over Charlotte's crooked pigtails. She glanced at the clock. Six fifteen. And still no Pete.

The power flickered once, twice. Then went out. The television continued to glow for a moment, eerily illuminating the room. "Help me gather the oil lamps, Char."

"Mom?" Luke called from upstairs. "Why is it dark?"

"It's only the storm. Come on down, and we'll play like we're pioneers."

Loretta placed one of their kerosene lamps on the kitchen table, removed the glass chimney, and lit the wick with a match. The flame danced merrily, casting shifting shadows over Charlotte's face as she brought another and set it next to Loretta's.

Lucas sat at the table, watching as they moved to the living room and lit the lamps on the sideboard, hands folded beneath his chin.

"Dinner will be done soon," Loretta said, going to the stove. She flicked a burner on, set a pot of water over the flame, and began peeling potatoes. "We'll eat, and then I'll read you a story before bedtime. Daddy must be working late tonight." Pete didn't have the car—he'd left it for her and walked to work, which meant he might be caught in this deluge. The thought troubled her.

Perhaps he'd stayed on campus until the storm passed. Loretta went to the phone. Thankfully, no one else was on their party line. She hurriedly dialed his office. It rang four times. Just as she was about to hang up, his secretary, Cinderella, answered. "Bethel University, Professor Davenport's office."

"Hello, Cinderella. It's Loretta."

"Oh, Loretta. How are you?"

"I'm good. You all must be working late tonight. Is Pete still there? I'm worried about him with this storm."

There was a pause. Cinderella cleared her throat. "Professor Davenport's gone. He left over an hour ago. Thought he'd be home by now. I'm still here, on account of J. R. He got called in to repair some lines, and he has our car. I may end up spending the night here, given the weather."

An hour was more than enough time for Pete to walk home, even in the rain. "All right, Cinderella. Thanks all the same."

"You take care now, ma'am. Call me back if he doesn't come home soon."

Loretta hung up. Charlotte caught her nervous look and smiled, dimples showing. "Stop worrying, Mommy. You worry about everything."

"Do I?"

"Yes," Lucas chimed in. "Dad says you're gonna worry yourself into an early grave."

Loretta rankled. How thoughtless of Pete to say something like that, even in jest! "I don't plan on dying for a good long while. Not until you're both old yourselves."

"Nobody can know that," Luke said ominously. "Young people die all the time."

Loretta thought of Darcy Hayes once more. She turned to her cooking to put an end to the grim conversation, warming a can of mushroom sauce for the potatoes. The oven timer dinged. Just as she pulled the meatloaf out, she heard Pete's key in the lock.

"Something smells delicious," he said as he entered, setting his briefcase by the door.

Loretta went to greet him. "Meatloaf."

"How long has the power been off? All the streetlamps are out down the block, too."

"Just an hour or so. I called your office. Cinderella said her husband was already out repairing lines, so it shouldn't be off long. I was worried when you were late." Pete shrugged out of his sweater. Loretta took it and hung it on the coatrack. Apart from a few speckles of rain, it was dry. "Did you get a ride?"

"Yes. Earl McAndrews brought me home."

"How was the meeting?"

"Boring. But we discussed implementing a new student code of conduct. We've had issues with the students going off campus and drinking at honky-tonks. The board decided on a one-strike policy to curtail things. The president just needs to sign it into action. He will."

"That's a little harsh, don't you think? Shouldn't they get a warning, at least?"

"These young people . . . they think they're bulletproof. All it would take is one accident to ruin their lives. They need to learn their lessons before they begin their ministry."

Loretta ducked her head, hiding her frown. "I suppose you're right."

Charlotte came running down the hall and jumped into Pete's arms. "Daddy!"

"My goodness. How's my princess?"

"I got an A on my spelling test!"

"Aren't you a smart girl?"

"I am! Can I have a puppy?"

Pete groaned, lowering Charlotte to the floor. "We'll talk about it later."

"Well, come get settled," Loretta said with a smile. "Food's going cold, and I promised them a story before bed."

Pete leaned toward her, pressed a kiss to her cheek. "It's good to see you well again, Loretta. It's been hard without you."

Chapter 3

The police found Darcy Hayes the next day. The Finley River had crested with the storm, as it often did, its muddy banks heaving up Darcy's body in the aftermath. Loretta learned the dismal news outside the school that afternoon, waiting for Lucas's conference. The other mothers huddled together in groups, some of their voices filled with a kind of grim glee, while the more conscientious among them spoke in hushed voices, as if they'd just come from a funeral. They cast occasional glances in her direction, but not in an inviting way. It was always like this, during school functions, where her modest clothes and unfashionable hairstyle set her apart. She imagined how they must see her—lumpy hips hidden beneath a long, pleated skirt, a faded pink sweater pilling from wear. An unremarkable, round face with piggy, small blue eyes.

Loretta tried to tune out their morbid conjectures, humming under her breath. When that no longer worked, she went around the side of the building until their voices faded, replaced by the sounds of playing children.

She'd been right about Darcy's whereabouts. Somehow, she had known, as if it were a prophetic message.

Although Pete had baptized Loretta in water early in their marriage, she had never received the other baptism of their faith—the baptism of the Holy Spirit. Though she'd prayed fervently for the gift at every altar call, hands raised in supplication, longing to be filled with Pentecostal fire, nothing had ever happened. She'd given up hope years ago.

But was *this* finally to be her calling, made manifest? If so, why now? It wasn't at all how she had imagined such a thing to be. It was terrible. Horrific. The dreadful vision she'd been given was more nightmare than blessing.

She shook her head to clear it. A flock of starlings took flight from the maple tree in front of her, wheeling into the sky, their movements hypnotic as they formed different shapes in the air. Murmuration. That's what it was called. She'd read an article about starlings once. They weren't supposed to be here, in America. They were invasive. Just like Loretta, they didn't belong.

"Mrs. Davenport?"

Loretta startled and turned toward the voice. A young woman stood peering at her from the corner of the school, a clipboard pressed against her chest. "I'm Mrs. Roush. Luke's teacher? Are you ready?"

"Yes. I'm so sorry. Am I late?"

"Not at all," Mrs. Roush said warmly. She might have been Natalie Wood's twin, with her wide-set brown eyes and polished brunette bob. No wonder Luke was smitten.

She followed the teacher up the school steps, the gossiping women parting to allow them entry. Inside, the pleasant scents of freshly sharpened pencils and lemon floor polish greeted Loretta. She secretly craved these conferences. They made her feel important. She missed being in school—that promising creak of a new textbook, the sense of mastery when she conquered a bit of challenging math. She'd dropped out when she married Pete, at the beginning of her senior year. It was one of her greatest regrets.

Mrs. Roush motioned to an open door, its window decorated with red and green paper apples. Loretta spied Luke's name on one of them.

The classroom was neat and orderly. Small desks lined up in three rows, facing a freshly washed chalkboard. Mrs. Roush took her place behind her tidy desk. Loretta sat across from the teacher and cradled her pocketbook on her lap.

"The children are all out on the playground. You'll be able to fetch Lucas and his sister after our conference."

"My Luke says such nice things about you," Loretta offered.

"He's a bright boy. You must be so proud of him."

"I am."

"I'm happy to tell you, I don't have many concerns—he's a good student. Well behaved and affable. But lately, I've noticed him floundering a bit in math. And he's been drawing some strange things during our art lessons."

"Oh?"

Mrs. Roush opened a manila folder and pushed a piece of paper toward Loretta. At first glance, it looked like a cheerful family portrait: Peter, tall and gangly as he was in real life, a broad smile on his face. There was Charlotte, with her pigtails and cute snub nose. Luke had drawn himself in his favorite striped shirt. And next to him stood a woman, her face blotted out with a nest of red crayon scribbles. Was this meant to be her? In the background, a massive black hole marred the landscape. Half of their house had fallen into it, the roof bent and buckled like a fun house shanty. A row of tombstones lined the horizon—he'd even drawn the cemetery on the next block. One of the graves bore Loretta's name. She shuddered.

"Children sometimes draw fanciful things. Especially when they're troubled," Mrs. Roush said softly.

"I'm not sure what to say. He's never drawn anything like this before." Loretta pushed the macabre drawing away.

Mrs. Roush steepled her fingers, then knit them together, leaning forward. "Luke mentioned you were ill. Perhaps he was bothered by it more than he's let on. Boys are often taught to hide their emotions."

"My husband sometimes says careless things. He told Luke I'd worry myself into an early grave. He was only kidding around, but with my being sick, Luke might have taken him literally."

"I'm sure that's all this is."

"I *do* worry a lot about dying, I suppose. Their grandmother died young. Not of sickness, though. It was an accident."

Mrs. Roush's perfectly arched eyebrows drew together. "I'm so sorry to hear that."

"It was long before the children were born."

"I see."

"I also wonder if Luke saw the news. About the Hayes girl."

"It's a possibility. Some of the children were talking about it." The teacher sat back, her shoulders falling. "I had both Hayes girls as students. Darcy my very first year of teaching, and then her little sister four years ago. Dora. They're a good family. The news was devastating."

"I'm so sorry." An uncomfortable silence descended between them. At the mention of Darcy's name, the foul, muddy taste intruded, heavy on Loretta's tongue.

"Back to Lucas," Mrs. Roush said, gently touching Loretta's wrist. "I'd like to tutor him, if you wouldn't mind him missing the bus on Tuesdays and Thursdays. His only deficit is in math—long division— and I don't want him falling behind. Things get harder after this year, and it's best to work on potential weak spots early, before they progress."

"Yes, of course. I struggled with math myself."

"Have him do his times tables at home. The sooner he memorizes multiplication, the better he'll do with everything else." Mrs. Roush stood. "It was a pleasure to meet you, Mrs. Davenport. And please try not to worry about Lucas. Children go through their little phases. I'm sure his will pass soon."

⚜

Loretta pinched the edges of her diaphragm and removed it, then washed it and secured it in its zippered case. She carefully hid it behind the rows of soaps and cleansers beneath the sink—another place Pete never looked. A good wife shouldn't lie to her husband about such things, but Loretta's pregnancy and long labor with Charlotte had worn her through. The malaise that came on afterward had nearly consumed her and left a lasting mark on their marriage.

There would be no more children if she could help it. She was lucky she had an understanding doctor, who had written the prescription for the diaphragm without Pete's knowledge.

She went back to bed and settled in next to Pete. He stretched an arm over her. "That was wonderful. Almost felt like we were newlyweds again."

"Mmm," Loretta hummed. "It *was* nice. I'm sorry it's been so long."

"Things will get better," he whispered. "This is a good start."

Loretta rolled toward him, welcoming the gentle kiss he pressed to her forehead. She lay against his chest, listening to the steady cadence of his heartbeat. He had been her first and only love—the velvet-voiced young man who had wooed her with quotes from the Song of Solomon and lifted her from her grief over her mother's death with talk of destiny and purpose. Loretta had never even gone to church before that hot summer night when she'd wandered into a Pentecostal revival tent on a whim. Pete had been one of the ushers. After the fervent hum of the meeting was over, they'd spent all night talking about scripture, and he'd led her in the salvation prayer. Doing the Lord's work had bonded them in the early days of their courtship and marriage. Loretta longed for the kinds of conversations they'd had back then. They had been happy once. They could be again. Their lovemaking tonight had proven that.

Outside, the cicadas droned their evening chorus. They'd all be dead soon, with the first frost, leaving only their brittle husks behind. Loretta listened to the rasping song and thought for a long moment before opening her mouth, knowing once the words left her tongue, there would be no retrieving them. "Do you think prophecy is real, Pete?" she asked tentatively. "I mean, in our modern times."

"The Bible says so. There's that verse, in Acts: 'Your young men will see visions, and your old men will dream dreams.'"

"Is it only for men, then, that gift?" Loretta propped herself on her elbow, gazing down at Pete.

He blinked at her with sleepy blue eyes. "Why?"

"Because something strange happened to me yesterday. After you left for work. I had a vision. I truly think that's what it was. One moment, I was gathering the laundry, and the next, I was fainting. The floor fell out from under me. It was horrible. I felt as if I were being buried alive—only it didn't seem like a dream, or a hallucination. It was *real.*" Loretta could hear the growing shrillness in her voice. She didn't know whether she was trying to convince Pete or herself of the truth in her words.

"And then . . . then somehow, I was in the backyard. I don't know how I got there. Phyllis saw me, invited me over for coffee, but things only got worse. A bug crawled out of my coffee cup! That part wasn't real, though. And then that voice came into my head—the same one I heard when I was sick. It told me where the missing girl was. Darcy Hayes. I called the police, gave them a tip. And I was right. She was exactly where the voice told me she would be! I don't know what to think about it."

"Voices? You didn't tell me you were hearing voices." Pete stared at her, his eyes widening. He sat up, fumbled on the nightstand for his glasses. "That's not prophecy. Or of God. It's delusional, Loretta. You've heard people give a word of prophecy in church. If it's real prophecy from the Holy Spirit, it's always given in tongues first, and then an interpreter translates it for the congregation. It's for the edification of the faith. What you're talking about . . . is . . . well, it's not the same thing. At all."

He rose, paced the floor, switched on the light. Loretta blinked against the sudden brightness. "Why are you upset at me?"

"I'm not upset. I'm worried about you. Hearing voices, seeing things? Are you sure you're okay?"

"It's a little concerning, how quickly it all came on, but mightn't it be a blessing? Might God be using me in a way I'd never imagined?

He once made a donkey speak, after all. And then there was Deborah, the prophetess."

"Yes, but that was different. What you're talking about . . . it's not of God. The Holy Spirit doesn't work that way. It was probably just the fever. A hallucination."

"How do you know for sure? The police took me seriously. Darcy was where I *knew* she would be. How could I make something like that up, all on my own? It didn't come from me. It couldn't have."

"It was only a coincidence. To think it anything else is to tread on some shaky spiritual ground, Loretta. The occult." Pete pawed through the nightstand drawer and pulled out his father's Bible. He thumbed through the thin pages and pointed to a line in the book of Leviticus. "Read this."

She took the Bible from him and squinted to read the cramped text: *"As for the person who turns to mediums and to spiritists, to play the harlot after them, I will also set My face against that person and will cut him off from among his people."*

"There's more in Deuteronomy as well."

"Yes, I see what you're getting at. But I didn't invite this. And I suppose I don't understand the difference between being given a word of prophecy in church and being given a word of prophecy over coffee with a neighbor. Isn't that limiting God?"

Pete sighed, took the Bible from her, and closed it. "I'll try to explain it all better tomorrow. Let's go to sleep. Your imagination goes off the rails sometimes. That's all this was. And please don't say anything about this to anyone else. Especially the children."

Loretta lay back. Pete turned away from her and switched off the light. In the darkness, thoughts crawled through her head like insects, probing her logic and sense of reality. Perhaps it *had* all been her imagination. Perhaps Pete was right.

But if that were the case, why had they found Darcy Hayes exactly where Loretta knew she would be, miles south of where she lived?

Chapter 4

Loretta lit her candle using Pete's flame, then turned to the kids, lighting theirs in turn. Over a hundred people had gathered to remember Darcy Hayes—mostly women and children, although a few families from their church were present. Pete greeted the men solemnly as Loretta made stilted conversation with their wives. Pete had resisted going to the vigil at first, pleading an excess of work, but relented when Loretta told him she didn't feel safe without him—not with a killer still on the loose in Myrna Grove. He'd agreed. A week had passed since Darcy's body was found, and there were still no leads in the case. Loretta spent her nights reading her Bible and pacing the floor, ears alert to any strange sound. She wrestled with the fear that Charlotte or Lucas might disappear next and now took them to and from school herself instead of having them ride the bus. Darcy had been snatched up less than a mile from her aunt's home. Who knew when and where the killer might strike again?

The silence on the town square was deafening, although the sea of flickering candles made for an eerily beautiful sight. After all the candles had been lit, a few of the townsfolk went to the bandstand at the center of the square to recount what Darcy had meant to them. One woman mentioned that Darcy had been a Salvation Army bell ringer every Christmas since she was ten years old. Loretta recalled seeing her now, her sweet face wreathed in a fur hood, in front of the Ben Franklin. The Hayeses' next-door neighbor, a wizened man who walked with a cane, said that Darcy mowed his lawn every summer, and asked for nothing more than a cold glass of lemonade in return.

Mrs. Roush came forward next, her face wet with tears. "Darcy was one of my favorite students. Always kind and thoughtful. She made everyone feel welcome at school and took the shy students under her wing. She wanted to be a teacher and would have been a good one. It's not fair that she'll never get the chance."

Luke looked up at Loretta with a sad smile. She squeezed his hand as Mrs. Roush murmured a quiet thank-you and stepped down from the bandstand.

A cold wind, wet with the scent of autumn leaves and rain, stirred Loretta's candle flame. She clutched her sweater tighter against the chill. The crowd gently parted, and a reed-thin woman with an air of quiet dignity stepped to the microphone. "Good evening, everyone. I'm Thelma Elliott, the choir director at First Baptist, where Darcy and her family attended church. As we gather to remember Darcy, I'd like to lead us in song. We'll begin with 'Amazing Grace.'"

Thelma hummed the opening note, then began to sing, her robust alto filling the chilly autumn air. Others joined in, and Loretta hesitantly raised her voice. It sounded weak and thin. Music seemed a hollow comfort in the circumstances, but it was far better than silence.

Thelma led them in two more hymns and then, as if unsure what to do next, rejoined the crowd. The uncomfortable silence descended once more, broken by muted sobs. A few people extinguished their candles and shuffled slowly to their parked cars.

"Let's go home, Retta," Pete said gently. "It's getting cold."

They blew out their candles and joined the stream of people leaving the square. As they passed the empty fountain, Loretta's eye fell on a woman sitting on its edge, her face pale and weary. A teenage girl sat next to her. A prickle of knowing tingled in Loretta's chest.

"That's Darcy's mother, isn't it?" Loretta whispered.

Pete's jaw clenched. "I'm not sure."

"It is. I saw her on the news. Shouldn't we go say something to her, Pete?"

"What did you have in mind, Loretta? You don't want to say the wrong thing in these situations."

"Well, I can't just ignore her."

Loretta handed her spent candle to Lucas and crossed the square. At her approach, the girl wrapped a protective arm around the woman, her manner wary. She must be Dora, the little sister Mrs. Roush had mentioned.

"Mrs. Hayes?" Loretta said gently.

"Yes," the woman said, lifting her head.

"I saw you sitting here and felt a pull to come over, although I must confess I don't know what to say, other than I'm very sorry." Loretta knelt at Mrs. Hayes's side and offered her hand.

"Thank you. You're the first person, apart from our church friends, who's spoken to me all night." Mrs. Hayes took Loretta's hand and clung to it. "Everyone else just stared."

Loretta took in Mrs. Hayes's worn dress and scuffed shoes and wondered if it had to do with the side of town the Hayes family hailed from. People in Myrna Grove liked to think of themselves as kind and welcoming, but Loretta had experienced her share of shunning. Especially early in her marriage, when Pete's family had treated her like a bumpkin fresh off the hay wagon.

Loretta squeezed Mrs. Hayes's hand. "I think people want to speak to you. But I suppose they're afraid they might say the wrong thing. Make things worse."

"But that doesn't help at all. My husband died in the war. Darcy and Dora, they're all I had left. And now with Darcy gone . . . where am I?" She shook her head sadly. "If I hadn't been working that night—with John gone, I must work, you see—Darcy wouldn't have had to walk to my sister's. There are so many things I would have done differently if I'd only known . . ." She turned away, leaning into her daughter's shoulder, sobbing.

"Mama, it's all right." Dora soothed her. She shot a scathing look at Loretta and then turned back to her mother. "You don't have to talk to this lady if you don't want to."

Loretta rose. "I'm so sorry. I didn't mean to intrude." Pete was right. She shouldn't have come over—she'd only stirred things up. "Just please know, Mrs. Hayes, and Dora—you're both in my prayers." She turned to go.

"It's Ramona. Ramona Hayes. Please . . . what is your name?"

"Loretta," she replied, looking over her shoulder. "Loretta Davenport."

Ramona Hayes stood on shaky legs, her eyes beseeching. Suddenly, the same impulse that had driven Loretta to call the police days before overtook her. Before she could think better of it, before she could stop herself, Loretta closed the distance between them and enveloped the woman in an embrace. Ramona's shoulders shuddered as she fell into Loretta's arms with a desperate sob.

"I know a mother's heart," Loretta said. "How we blame ourselves for everything that happens to our children. But Darcy knew you loved her. And this wasn't your fault. Never doubt that."

Loretta closed her eyes. Suddenly, every inch of her skin began to tingle. A white light grew behind her eyelids, and faded to a fuzzy gray. She opened her eyes. She was no longer in the square. She was lying on her back, looking up at the ceiling in a room filled with sunlight. Above her, a simple mobile turned, playing a thread of tinkling music. A chubby pink elephant, a long-necked giraffe, and a smiling lion dangled from the mobile's strings.

A woman appeared at her side, looking down at her with adoring eyes. Though she was several years younger, Loretta recognized her as Ramona Hayes.

Realization coursed through Loretta. It was happening again. Somehow, she was feeling what Darcy had felt. Seeing what Darcy had seen. Only instead of fear and darkness, this time Loretta felt love and happiness. She pulled in a deep breath. When she opened her eyes, she was in the square again. Ramona was looking at her, tears streaming down her cheeks.

"Thank you for seeing me and coming over," she said. "You knew just what I needed to hear."

"I did see you. And her."

"What?" Ramona's forehead wrinkled in confusion.

Loretta grasped Ramona's hands, desperate to share what she had seen. "Darcy was a happy baby, wasn't she? She liked the pink mobile . . . the one with the giraffe, and the lion, and the pink elephant."

Ramona's face blanched. "How . . . how could you know . . . ?"

"I saw it. I saw her—like in a scene from a movie. I can't explain how."

Ramona stepped back and sat on the fountain's edge, dazed.

"What did you say to her?" Dora asked, her eyes accusatory. "Mama? Are you okay?"

Pete stalked toward them, grasping Loretta by the elbow. "My condolences on your loss, Mrs. Hayes. I'm sorry my wife bothered you."

"She didn't," Ramona said, tears glistening in her eyes. "Not at all. I—"

"Loretta, let's go," Pete interrupted, pulling on her arm.

"I'm so sorry," Loretta said. "I have to go. But if either of you need me, for anything, even if it's just someone to listen, I live in the third house from the corner of State and Mt. Vernon. The white house, with the porch swing."

A look of understanding passed between Ramona and Loretta as Pete steered her away from the square. The kids stood next to the Chrysler, impatiently waiting.

"Why did you tell that woman where we lived? I don't know what's gotten into you lately." Pete's tone had grown harsh "What else did you say to her?"

"Something is happening, Pete. I can't explain it, but that strange feeling I was telling you about came over me again, just now, while I talked with Mrs. Hayes. I *know* things somehow."

"Well, whatever it was, you made a scene, fawning all over that woman. She probably thought you were crazy."

They reached the car. As Loretta grasped the door handle, a wave of dizziness overtook her. Bile crawled up her throat. She sank down onto the curb, cradling her head in her hands.

An ocean suddenly roared in Loretta's ears and crashed over her. "Oh, Pete. I don't feel so g—"

꧁

The doctor leaned over Loretta, a bright penlight in her hands. Dr. Dixon was embroidered on her lab coat above the Burns Protestant insignia. "Look straight ahead, Mrs. Davenport. At the tip of my nose."

Loretta stared at the tip of the doctor's rather large nose as she shined the tiny flashlight into one eye and then the other.

"Now track my finger, from left to right."

Loretta did as she was told. Next, the doctor sat her up, listened carefully to her heart and lungs, then took her blood pressure again.

"Good. You can lay back now. Your responses and reflexes are all normal, as are your vitals, so I think we can rule out a stroke or anything major."

Loretta let out a sigh of relief.

"Have you been having these fainting spells often?"

"Only once before. I was sick, a week or so ago. It started then."

"I see. What were your symptoms?"

"Fever, nausea, and vomiting. And I saw things—heard some strange things, even. I've been lethargic, fatigued."

Dr. Dixon frowned. "The fainting and hallucinations, the lethargy could be due to lingering dehydration. The fluids we gave you will help with that, but make sure to drink plenty of water. Have you been under any pressure lately?"

Loretta laughed. "No more than usual. It all gets to be too much sometimes, doesn't it? The kids, the housework . . ."

"I know exactly what you mean," she said, smiling. "My children are grown now, but I remember what it was like to be a young mother. I think you may be suffering from a mild case of dysphoria, on top of your other symptoms."

"Dysphoria?"

"Depression. Melancholia. Sometimes anxiety can create these fainting spells, too. It all becomes too much for the body to handle, and your nerves rebel."

"What can I do for it?"

"Try to rest when you can. Take time for yourself while your children are at school—go for a walk or do some light calisthenics. And you might consider seeing an analyst."

"An analyst?"

"Yes. A psychoanalyst. Someone who specializes in psychology or psychiatry."

"You mean a head shrink."

Dr. Dixon shrugged. "Some people call them that. There are some real quacks out there, but I have a colleague I can recommend. He's conservative when it comes to treatment, and the women I've referred to him feel safe under his care. Dr. Curtis Hansen. He's holding a lecture at the Carnegie Library tomorrow morning. I believe it's for something related to metaphysical studies instead of psychology, but you might go see him. He's an engaging speaker."

"Metaphysical studies? What does that mean?"

"Some call it parapsychology. In his spare time Dr. Hansen studies people who claim to have psychic visions and telepathic powers."

"How interesting." Perhaps this doctor might be able to explain what was happening to her. She needed to know whether the strange sensations and visions originated from her mind or elsewhere. "Thank you."

"Of course. Go ahead and get dressed. I'll have the nurse phone your husband. Come to the nurses' station for your discharge papers once you're ready. I'll include Dr. Hansen's telephone number. When you call, tell his receptionist that Ida Dixon referred you."

"And you're certain there's nothing wrong with me?"

"I am quite certain there's no physical cause for your symptoms, Mrs. Davenport."

The doctor drew the curtain around the bed and left. Loretta stood, shedding the hospital gown. Her bare skin prickled in the chilly hospital room. She hurriedly dressed, then went out into the hall. The sharp scent of disinfectant assaulted her nostrils. Someone was moaning in pain down the corridor. She abhorred hospitals in one sense and worshipped them in another. They were a powerful reminder of her own mortality—of the human body's inherent frailty. Yet tonight the hospital had brought her a great deal of comfort. She wasn't dying. At least not yet.

She went to the nurses' station and waited as a friendly blonde nurse finished tapping out the discharge instructions, then handed them to her. Dr. Hansen's number was listed on the final line. She'd never considered going to a psychiatrist before. When she'd had her depressed time after Charlotte's birth, Pete insisted it was a matter of faith, that if she truly believed, she could pray her way out of the sadness and emptiness.

Faith hadn't worked, though she pretended it did.

Instead, she tucked the darkness away behind sewing projects and halfhearted attempts at cooking. All the while the darkness had lain in wait, growing, determined to claw its way to the surface no matter how hard Loretta tried to deny its existence.

"Mrs. Davenport?" The nurse was staring at her, a look of concern creasing her forehead.

"Yes?"

"I asked if you had any questions about your discharge notes."

"I think I have it. Rest, plenty of sleep, balanced meals, light exercise, and follow up with Dr. Hansen."

The nurse smiled. "Yes, that's it. I hope you're feeling better soon."

Loretta went outside to wait for Pete. She hoped he'd gotten the children to bed. She was secretly glad he'd left her alone at the hospital. His presence only intensified her anxiety.

The night had grown bracingly crisp, cool. Loretta gathered her sweater tighter and paced back and forth along the dimly lit walkway, humming softly to herself. Pete pulled up a few minutes later. He hopped out, opened her door, and settled her inside the car. Loretta rubbed her hands in front of the heater vents.

"Well, what did they say?" he asked.

"I'm fit as a fiddle. The doctor couldn't find a thing wrong with me. She thinks it may just be my head."

"She?"

"Yes."

Pete made a dismissive sound at the back of his throat. "And what's the matter with your head?"

"I'm not sure that anything is *wrong* with it, but she referred me to another doctor. A psychoanalyst."

"A shrink." Pete went silent, staring straight ahead as he pulled out onto the street.

Loretta's eyes went to the floorboard, where Pete's thermos stood propped against the seat. "Did you bring coffee?"

"No, it's empty. I took some of your soup to work this morning."

"Are the kids asleep?"

"Yes. Although Lucas fought going to bed—he was worried about you."

"He's always worrying."

"He comes by it honestly, doesn't he?" Pete's lips twisted in a wry grin.

"Say, I could really use a cup of coffee. Can we stop by Anton's on the way home?"

Pete sighed. "Retta, I'm beat."

"Only for a cup of coffee. It's been too long since we've done anything together, just the two of us. I miss talking to you."

"Oh, all right."

Pete turned from Division onto Glenstone and headed south. He switched on the radio. That new singer Elvis crooned his rocking brand of blues. Pete abruptly shut the radio off, just as he'd switched off the television the night he'd caught her and the kids dancing to Bill Haley and His Comets on *Ed Sullivan*. "Rock and roll isn't edifying," he'd said. "Listen to the Carters if you want good music."

Well, Loretta liked the Carters just fine, but she liked the new rock and roll sound, too. So she'd taken some of her hidden money to the Ben Franklin the next day, bought a small radio that she hid in her dresser, and brought it out only when Pete wasn't home.

They rode the rest of the way in silence. The sign for Anton's Diner shone cheerfully ahead, the oversize ice cream cone perched on its roof lit up with neon lights. Only one other car sat out front. Pete parked next to it, rolling his head back with a sigh. "One cup of coffee."

Inside, fry grease scented the air. A pair of teenagers sitting at the counter turned their heads to watch as they entered. On a date, from the looks of it. Pete led her to a booth near the back. He shrugged out of his cardigan and folded his lanky form onto the bench. Loretta sat across from him.

"This doctor, this head shrink. Is it a woman, too?" Pete scowled, scanning the menu with disinterest.

"A man. Dr. Curtis Hansen. He comes highly recommended. He's holding a lecture at the library tomorrow. I'm thinking of going."

"We don't have the kind of money for you to run off to doctors all the time, Retta. And I don't like the thought of you going to a shrink. Some of them take advantage of their patients, behind closed doors. I've heard stories."

"If I found a woman doctor, would you feel better?"

Pete smirked. "That would be even worse. Women doctors don't know what they're talking about."

"I disagree. What about Madame Curie?"

"She was a physicist, not a medical doctor."

"Still."

Pete grunted. "I've invited Earl and his wife over this Saturday for dinner."

"Oh?" Pete was ever inviting people over without asking her first, and it always had her in a mad scramble. "That's fine, I suppose. Earl's wife is Gladys, right? Petite. Blonde hair. Talks a lot. I remember her from the faculty wives' luncheon." The spring luncheon had been dreadfully dull, even though they were served four kinds of fancy cakes and tea topped with orchids. The cakes were good, if a bit dry, but the tea tasted like cheap perfume and the linens held stains from the last luncheon. Like everything else in Myrna Grove, the Bethel Ladies' Auxiliary pretended to be better than it was.

"She wears Earl out with all that talking," Pete said with a grin. "He comes to work to escape."

If Earl complained about Gladys, Loretta wondered what Pete said about *her* within the walls of Bethel University.

An exhausted-looking waitress shuffled over to take their order. "What'll it be?"

"She'll have a cup of coffee with cream and sugar."

"And for you, sir?"

"Nothing, thanks."

"Not even a cup of coffee?" Loretta asked.

"I'd like to sleep tonight, Retta. It's almost ten o'clock, and I have a meeting in the morning."

The waitress trudged away, with a slight shake of her head, no doubt anticipating a measly tip to go along with their measly check.

"About the doctor. He might be able to help me, Pete. If there's nothing wrong with me physically, maybe it'd be worth looking into my head? I can't keep having these fainting spells. They're horribly disorienting. What if I had one while I was driving? It could be something serious—like narcolepsy."

"You always have something going on, Retta. Mostly an overactive imagination." He turned to look out the window, the headlights streaming down Glenstone reflected in his glasses. Loretta noticed the scruff of beard shading the crisp line of his jaw. He hadn't shaved that morning. "You're not cracking up, darling. You're just bored. What you really need is to get back into serving at church. You might try teaching Sunday school again. You were so happy when you were doing that."

"I did like it. But it takes so much energy, trying to teach first graders about Jesus when they'd rather climb the furniture. Our kids keep me busy enough. I need something for myself."

Pete frowned. "Don't you think you're being a little selfish? I don't ask for much, Retta, and neither do the kids. You have the whole day to yourself, but sometimes you haven't even bothered to get dressed or clean the house by the time I get home. I'm making life as easy as I can for you."

"I know. And I'm grateful, Pete. I am. But it's not that simple. I . . . I can't explain it. I'm feeling a little lost. That's all. Sometimes I get overwhelmed and lonely, stuck in that house all day. I want to clean, I want to make myself presentable for you, but sometimes I just can't."

Loretta sat back against the vinyl banquette. Tears threatened behind her eyes. The waitress brought her coffee. Thankful for the distraction from Pete's tacit criticism, she drank it so fast it scalded her tongue. It tasted bitter—hours-old coffee. She cast an eye to the teen-agers at the counter, their ankles wrapped together, and remembered when she felt that same giddy excitement with Pete. He'd been so much fun, once. They'd gone to carnivals and movies and weekend revivals. He'd helped her escape the monotony of the farm and her daddy's silent, solemn indifference. But being married had only replaced one form of monotony with another. Once they'd taken their vows, Pete had slowly made his career the great love of his life, leaving her in the dust of his ambitions.

"No one's forcing you to stay at home," Pete said, taking her hand. "You have neighbors to visit with. There are plenty of women at church who would love to take you under their wing. You could make friends if you'd just try."

Loretta nearly laughed, thinking of Phyllis Colton's judgmental, bigoted ways. Always worried about the Russians and desegregation. The women at church were hardly better. They were polite, but Loretta knew her place in their pecking order. "I think I'd like to see that doctor. What would it hurt, Pete? Just for one visit. You can come with me if you're nervous about it."

Pete sighed. "We'll pray about it. Now, finish your coffee so we can go home."

She knew what "we'll pray about it" really meant. It meant no. He'd brush her wishes aside just as he did when Charlotte asked for a puppy. To Pete, she would always be a naive sixteen-year-old girl with childish notions.

Loretta gazed inside the coffee cup. No leaves, no mud, no beetles crawling to the rim. Only her shadowed reflection, staring back at her.

Chapter 5

Loretta didn't like lying to Pete. It never came easy, though she was doing it more and more nowadays. After he left for work the next morning and she dropped the kids at school, she dressed in her best skirt and cardigan and drove to the library.

The soothing, warm scent of books greeted her in the lobby, with its high coffered ceilings and lovely polished oak desk punctuated by green-shaded brass lamps. Loretta loved libraries as much as she loved schools. Places of learning were her favorite kind of church—made sacred by the knowledge within their walls. She approached the desk, and the librarian looked up. "May I help you, miss?"

"I'm here to attend Dr. Hansen's lecture."

"Oh, it's already begun. But you can still go up. He's in the Rothschild Room. Third floor."

"Thank you."

Loretta hurried to the elevator and punched the button for the third floor, her nerves quivering with anticipation. She imagined Dr. Hansen as a sonorous-voiced, elderly man with gray hair and a beard who favored bow ties and sweater vests. A bit like a scholarly Santa Claus mixed with Sigmund Freud.

The elevator doors opened with a soft chime, and Loretta stepped out. A semicircle of chairs sat in the middle of the room, arrayed in rows. Most of them were filled. A man stood before the audience, swinging a glass pendulum back and forth. Surely this wasn't Dr. Hansen. If so, he looked much younger than she had expected, with soft, medium-brown hair curling over his ears and an animated demeanor. The only thing she'd been right about was the sweater vest. Loretta quietly made her way to the back row and sat near the end.

"It is a known fact that the subjective mind is more easily accessed during altered states of consciousness," he intoned. "Sleep. Hypnosis. Coma. During this time, the will is subject to suggestion, but a person will never do anything under hypnosis they wouldn't do while conscious. Hypnosis, when performed by a responsible practitioner, is perfectly safe for the subject, and holds many benefits—among them the retrieval of repressed memories. These repressed memories can create a traumatic response throughout the body. Hypnosis brings trauma to the surface so that it might be dealt with therapeutically, through analysis. Talk therapy."

Dr. Hansen swung the pendulum upward, catching it in his other hand. "What then, of the metaphysical, and its relation to hypnosis and altered consciousness?" He perched on the edge of the reference desk, considering the audience with his piercing blue eyes. "Any single one of you might possess psychic abilities. ESP. Many of you might not even be aware that you've had a psychic experience. Have you ever had a gut feeling? Known who was on the telephone before answering it? Had a dream that seemed more than a dream? All those things can be considered extrasensory perception." Dr. Hansen tapped his temple with his finger. "I myself am a skeptic, a science-minded person who takes great solace in the order of nature and numbers. But in my studies as a psychologist, I've encountered things I cannot explain with science alone. At least . . . not yet. The human mind is capable of much more than we think."

In the front row, a man raised his hand. "But is there any *proof* of these things?"

"That's an excellent question. During my time at Duke, I often participated in and observed Dr. J. B. Rhine's experiments at the parapsychology lab. There, I witnessed firsthand the capabilities of those with psychic sensitivity. Subjects who could accurately guess the hidden images on cards, over and over. I saw people move objects with no more than a focused thought. Twins who knew what the other was experiencing, half a world away. People who claimed to be able to communicate with the spirits of the dead."

Loretta's breath caught.

"That particular ability," Dr. Hansen said with a smile, "is very rare indeed. I've only ever met one true medium in my life. In Morocco. Although there are plenty of parlor practitioners who would be happy to take your money in exchange for their clever theatrics."

A low rumble of laughter came from the audience.

"I'm currently at work on a book about the paranormal," Dr. Hansen said. "I'm always open to hearing from those who have witnessed paranormal phenomena, and especially those gifted with what they believe to be psychic abilities. If that's you, please stay after the short film I'm about to present and speak to me in person."

A cart with a reel-to-reel projector was wheeled out and pointed at a blank wall behind the reference desk. Someone dimmed the lights and switched on the projector. A thread of wavery string music emanated through the room. An image of a large Gothic chapel flashed onto the white wall. Loretta sat, enraptured, as the narrator began describing the parapsychology lab at Duke University. To think, there was an entire scientific laboratory dedicated to studying the exact sort of thing she was experiencing!

After the film was finished, Dr. Hansen thanked his audience and received their applause. Loretta wished she'd gotten there earlier. She rose, tucking her pocketbook beneath her arm. A line formed—mostly women eager to speak to the doctor. It was no surprise, given how charming he was. Loretta wavered. She wanted to approach him. Would like to tell him what she had experienced, but her natural shyness got the better of her. Pete wouldn't like her being here. Not one bit.

Loretta rocked back and forth on her heels for a moment, watching awkwardly from the back of the room, before finally leaving, her thoughts running wild.

When she got home, she paced the floors, thinking about Dr. Hansen's talk. What if *she* were a medium? Wouldn't he want to study her? He said he'd only ever known one other person who could communicate with the spirits of the dead, after all. Was that truly what she was doing? Communicating with the dead?

Loretta made lunch for herself—a Cobb salad that she rushed through eating, barely tasting a bite, and then she tried to read a bit from a novel but found her thoughts drifting back to Dr. Hansen's lecture.

"Stop being so ridiculous," she chided herself, aloud. She fished around in her pocketbook for the discharge papers from the hospital, scanning them for Dr. Hansen's number. Before she could talk herself out of it, she went to the phone and dialed, her hands shaking.

After one ring, a pleasant female voice answered. "Dr. Hansen's office. Barbara speaking."

"H-hello. My name is Loretta Davenport. I was referred to Dr. Hansen by another doctor—Ida Dixon at Burns Protestant. I also attended his lecture this morning, at the library."

"Oh, yes."

"I was wondering how I'd go about getting an appointment with the doctor. There are some things happening to me that he might be interested in hearing about."

"Oh? Could you perhaps tell me a bit more?"

"I've been having visions. Hearing voices." Loretta paused. "I know that sounds ridiculous."

"Not at all. Let me check his schedule, see what he has available. Could you hold for a moment, please?"

"Yes. That's fine." Loretta's nerves ratcheted up. She was doing this. She was going to see this doctor, against Pete's will. It was the most rebellious thing she'd ever done. The radio, the hidden money, perhaps those counted, too, but they were small things. Besides, Pete hadn't *strictly* forbidden the doctor. Not really. He'd only said they'd pray about it. But they hadn't. And Loretta was tired of waiting for Pete to pray over things he had no interest in.

She heard a rustle on the other end of the receiver. Hushed voices talking, then a crackle in the line. She prayed Phyllis Colton or one of their other neighbors hadn't picked up during her call.

"Mrs. Davenport?"

"Yes?" Loretta's heartbeat accelerated.

"Dr. Hansen happens to have a cancellation for this afternoon. At two o'clock. Could you come today? He's very anxious to meet with you."

"Oh. I wasn't expecting to see him so soon. How long will the appointment take?"

"Only an hour."

She'd still have plenty of time to make it to school to pick up the kids at three thirty. Pete had left the car with her since Lucas had his after-school tutoring lessons with Mrs. Roush. "Yes. Two o'clock will work."

"Very good. Do you know where our office is located?"

"No, could you give me a moment to get a pen and paper?" Loretta strung the phone cord out from the wall, as far as it would reach, and found a scrap of receipt on the kitchen table and a pen to write with. "All right."

"We're at 346 East Walnut. The big stone house with the circle drive."

"And how much will it be?" Loretta bit her lip, thinking of her hidden cache of money.

"Well, you're inquiring about his work with ESP, correct? You don't need therapeutic care?"

"I'm . . . I'm not sure yet. Maybe I do."

"His usual session fee is ten dollars."

Loretta's shoulders sagged. No wonder Pete was against it. Ten dollars was a lot of money. Still, she needed to find some answers. Perhaps one or two appointments with Dr. Hansen might do the trick.

"All right. I'll be there at two."

"Very good, Mrs. Davenport. We look forward to meeting you."

⚜

Loretta stared up at the imposing mansion. This wasn't at all what she'd imagined a psychologist's office to look like. It was grand yet welcoming at the same time. Stone urns filled with yellow chrysanthemums accented either side of the portico, and a fountain sat in the center of the circle drive—a berobed Grecian maiden balancing a pitcher of water on her shoulder. A nervous tickle ran through Loretta's stomach as she left the car at the curb and walked to the door.

She rang the bell and heard it chime indoors. A few moments later, a tall, slender woman with icy blonde hair and a smart blue dress answered. "Hello. You must be Mrs. Davenport."

"Yes."

"I'm Barbara Miller, Dr. Hansen's receptionist. We spoke on the phone this morning."

"Yes." It seemed to be the only thing Loretta could say.

"Please come in. He's finishing up with someone else, but you can wait in the parlor. Would you prefer coffee or tea? Perhaps some water?"

"Just water, thank you."

Loretta ducked her head shyly and followed Barbara inside. The entryway smelled pleasant, calming—sage, lemon verbena. Perhaps a hint of lavender. A round table stood in the center of the foyer, holding

41

a vase of plumed sedge. Photos of a handsome, weather-tanned Dr. Hansen engaged in all sorts of interesting activities were scattered artfully on the table's polished surface, their edges labeled with captions. Loretta leaned close to read them.

Dr. Hansen visits the Dalai Lama in Tibet

Dr. Hansen shops at the souk in Morocco

Dr. Hansen at Cambridge University

"The reception parlor is in there." Barbara motioned to a gracefully arched doorway framed by potted palms. "I'll fetch your water. Please make yourself comfortable."

The room was furnished warmly, and decorated with what she assumed were artifacts from Dr. Hansen's travels. She smoothed her skirt behind her thighs and sat gingerly on the edge of a leather sofa, crossing her legs at the ankles. She felt underdressed in this house, with its grand high ceilings and walnut-paneled walls. She scanned the stacks of magazines on the coffee table before her: *Ladies' Home Journal, LIFE, The New Yorker*. She chose a recent issue of *LIFE* with Joan Collins on the cover, perched in a swing, wearing a glamorous pink dress.

Barbara emerged with a glass of water on a tray. "Here you are."

Loretta took the water with a quiet thank-you and Barbara departed again. Loretta admired the crisp sound of her high heels on the wooden floors. She glanced down at her humble lace-up oxfords and tucked them farther beneath the sofa. Perhaps she'd ask Pete for a pair of high heels when he got paid again.

A clock struck the hour somewhere down the hall, and a moment later, she heard a door opening. "I'll see you next week, Mrs. Dexter." She recognized Dr. Hansen's voice immediately. In this setting, it sounded even deeper—warm, cultured, and rich. A voice to match the photographs in the foyer. Loretta's arms prickled in a mix of anticipation and nervousness.

She placed her half-empty glass on the coffee table and leaned forward as Dr. Hansen's patient passed the parlor doorway. She was a woman, modestly dressed, much like herself, with graying brown hair tied back at the nape. Loretta wondered how many women crossed this threshold every day to leave their worries at the feet of a stranger. She imagined it was a bit like going to confession.

Suddenly, a huge ginger cat darted into the room and made a bee-line for Loretta, jumping onto the sofa and butting his head against her arm. "Oh, hello," she said, laughing. She scratched beneath the cat's chin. He nuzzled against her, purring, and rolled onto his back, gazing up at Loretta with large amber eyes.

"Ah, I see you've met Ollie." Loretta raised her head. Dr. Hansen was leaning against the doorway watching her, arms crossed, the toe of one cowboy boot anchored against the floor, an unlikely but becoming contrast to his tailored trousers, sweater vest, and necktie. She hadn't noticed the boots earlier. His blue eyes crinkled at the corners as he smiled at her. "You must be Mrs. Davenport. Didn't I see you earlier today, at the library? You came in late, I believe."

"Yes. I'm so sorry I was late." Loretta stood awkwardly, picking up her pocketbook. The cat wound between her ankles, still purring. "I enjoyed your lecture very much. It's the reason I called you."

"You're not allergic, are you? To cats? If so, I'll have Barbara keep Oliver out here while we meet."

"No," Loretta said. "I love cats."

"Shall we get started? My office is just down the hall."

"All right."

Loretta followed Dr. Hansen, her anxiety ticking higher and higher. What on earth would she talk about for an hour? She'd never talked to anyone for that long, apart from Pete, much less a stranger. The cat trailed them into the office, which was both elegant and cozy. Loretta admired the rows of books, neatly arranged by spine color, and the array of healthy, green plants basking in the wide picture window's light. Outdoors, rosebushes and neatly trimmed hedges beckoned. A pair of wrought-iron park benches stood beneath an oak tree. Gravel paths sprouted in all directions.

"We could go outside, to the contemplation garden, if you prefer," Dr. Hansen said, noting her gaze. "It's important that you're comfortable. Some like to sit in here during their sessions. Others prefer to walk outdoors."

"In here is fine," Loretta said, sinking into a wingback chair by the empty fireplace. Ollie jumped onto her lap, kneaded the fabric of her skirt for a moment, then settled. "I wasn't expecting this. I feel like I'm in someone's living room."

Dr. Hansen went to his desk and sat on its edge. "What were you expecting?"

Loretta shrugged. "Something more like a doctor's office."

"I see. I find a homelike environment is much less intimidating. This house is where I grew up. After I finished my doctoral studies at Duke, I came back to start my practice in Myrna Grove. I feel most comfortable doing my work at home, and I hope you will be comfortable here as well. Where did you grow up, Loretta?"

"Here. Well, in Marshfield, actually. On a farm."

"Really? What kind of farm?"

"Hogs, mostly. We had chickens and cows, too. A few crops."

"Did you like living in the country?"

"Not really."

"And why was that?"

"I was lonely. It was just my father and me, after my mother died. He was always working."

Dr. Hansen took a notepad and pen from his blotter and settled in the matching chair opposite hers. He pulled a pair of glasses from his shirt pocket beneath his vest and put them on. "How old were you, when your mother died?"

"Twelve."

"That's a difficult age to lose your mother."

"Yes." Loretta gazed into the fireplace. "But is there ever a good age to lose your mother, Doctor?"

"No. There isn't. I was twenty-five when I lost mine. Cancer. I don't think I'll ever get over it. Before we get started, I should tell you that it's all right to talk about anything you'd like within this room. Doctors like me—psychologists—take an oath of confidentiality. Anything said here is never spoken of to others."

"Never? You're sure?"

"I promise." He looked at her curiously. "What are you afraid of someone else knowing, Loretta?"

"Well, for one thing, my husband doesn't know I'm here."

"Do you keep secrets from him often?"

He asked the question gently, without a hint of accusation, only curiosity. Still, Loretta's hands clenched on the chair's arms. "No. I don't," she said, a bit too defensively. "It's just that he doesn't believe in psychology—or the things you spoke about at your lecture. He only believes in God. And prayer. But I've been praying, for years and years. And nothing ever really changes. But that's not really why I'm here." Loretta bit her lip as Dr. Hansen scrawled something on his notepad. She needed to be careful what she said. What if he *did* go to Pete and tell him everything? He was a man, after all, and men tended to stick together.

"Let's go back to your childhood," he said, smiling at her softly. "What did you want to be when you grew up?"

"A journalist. A writer."

"I see. And did anything get in the way of that?"

"I dropped out of high school."

"Oh?"

"When I married Peter. My husband. Then I got pregnant."

Ollie nudged her hand, and she buried her fingers in his soft, long fur, scratching his neck. He trilled and resettled in her lap.

"Do you ever think about writing now?"

"I don't have time. I have two children to take care of. And the house is always a mess. Some days I feel so overwhelmed I can't even find time to shower or brush my hair. I wouldn't know where to begin with writing. And I lead a boring life, on any account. No one wants to read what a housewife has to say."

"You might be surprised about that. What does your husband do?"

"Do?"

"For a living."

"He's an assistant professor at Bethel University. He teaches history of the Bible. He's up for tenure this year, even without a doctorate."

"He must be very accomplished. And you support his aspirations?"

"Yes, of course."

Dr. Hansen frowned thoughtfully, steepling his hands beneath his lower lip. "Can you tell me what brought you in? Barbara mentioned you were having visions. Hearing voices?"

"Yes. Sometimes." Loretta paused petting Ollie and he jumped down to bat at the shattered sunlight winking on the floor. "I've been having fainting spells, too. And that's when the visions happen. I lose time. Feel like I'm out of my body."

"And there's no apparent physical cause for these spells? Did you have a fall? Hit your head, perhaps?"

Loretta shook her head. "No. But it all started after I got sick with the flu."

"Have you seen your doctor for a workup? A physical?"

"No. But Dr. Dixon, the doctor at Burns Protestant who referred me to you, says I'm healthy as a horse."

"I see. Tell me what happens when you have one of these spells. Exactly."

"I get a little dizzy. And I hear the voices. Well, *a* voice. Only one, so far. A girl's voice."

Dr. Hansen's pen paused. He glanced at her over his glasses. "What does the voice say?"

"Sometimes I can't make any sense of it. The first time, it said they 'didn't mean to do it' or something like that. It was very confusing."

"Is the voice menacing? Does it tell you to do things you wouldn't normally do?"

"No, it's not like that. It's hard to explain." More scrabbling with the pen. Loretta's hands tensed in her lap. What if she *were* crazy? What if the voice was a sign of something like schizophrenia? "I've never had anything like this happen before. I've always had strange sensations of knowing, though, like you mentioned in your lecture. Premonitions, I suppose. But this is all new. The voice. The visions. Do you think there's something wrong with me, Doctor?"

Dr. Hansen looked up at her, blinked twice. "I can tell you're very nervous, Loretta, but please try not to worry. I must ask you all sorts of questions, to rule certain things out. Do you understand?"

"Yes."

"Do you ever have thoughts of harming yourself or others?"

"No, not at all." Loretta crossed her arms over her belly, as if Dr. Hansen might have X-ray vision and be able to see through her clothing. "I would never . . . no."

"Good." More scratching and scrabbling. Loretta could only imagine what he was writing down.

"If it helps, some of the visions seem to be connected to Darcy Hayes."

A line appeared between Dr. Hansen's brows. "Darcy Hayes? The young woman who was recently found murdered?"

"Yes. The voice told me where she was buried. I called in a tip to the police. They found her where I said she would be."

Dr. Hansen raised his head, blue eyes suddenly piercing. "Really?"

"Yes. I saw what happened to her in a vision. Or what I think happened to her. Well, some of it." Loretta pulled her eyes from his and focused on the wall behind Dr. Hansen's head instead, where his professional certificates hung in a neat row. "It was as if I left this dimension and fell into another. Does that even make any sense?"

He nodded, pen scratching wildly across the notepad. "Go on."

"Then it was as if I were being buried alive. I tasted leaves, mud. When I came to, I was lying in my backyard, but couldn't remember how I'd gotten there. And then later, when I was having coffee with my neighbor, the words 'Finley River' came into my head, over and over. I had an overwhelming urge to call the police, to tell them that's where they'd find Darcy. So I did. And they found her there the next day, after the storm. I can't explain it." Loretta paused. "I'm afraid you'll think I'm crazy, Doctor. Pete thinks all this is just in my head. That it's my imagination gone wild."

"Oh?"

"Yes. He says I should focus on serving at church and be more attentive to the house and kids. I've given my mind too much space to wander, I suppose."

"Sometimes a mind needs to wander, Loretta. It's nothing to be ashamed of. And I don't think you're crazy. In fact, I abhor that word." The doctor looked at her steadily, in a way she'd never been looked at before—with an engaged sense of curiosity and interest. "You mentioned that you've prayed for things to change. Can you tell me a bit more about that? What sort of things do you want to change?"

"Well, I tend to have moods . . . They come and go. The worst one happened after my daughter was born. My husband is concerned I'm slipping into a blue phase again. I've been praying about it. We attend church regularly as a family. At Myrna Grove Assembly."

"I see. Do you ascribe to the faith-healing aspects of your denomination? Miracles and such?"

"I'd like to hope those sorts of things can happen, yes. Are you a religious man, Dr. Hansen?" she asked.

"I used to be. Very. I was raised a Catholic, and I suppose I still believe. Only it's not the same blind faith I had in my youth. I've traveled the world and opened my mind to many other possible ways of looking at religion and spirituality. Psychology and its connection to spirituality are endlessly fascinating. But I no longer consider myself religious."

"Have you ever heard of the gifts of the Holy Spirit?"

"You're talking about Pentecost? Speaking in tongues and such?"

"Yes. And prophecy. I've wondered if that's what this is."

"The voice and visions?"

"Yes."

Dr. Hansen took off his glasses and regarded her quietly for a moment. "There are many mysteries in this world, and even though I remain a skeptic at heart, the seeker in me enjoys investigating phenomena that might, at first, seem to exist outside rational science. Things like life after death. Reincarnation. Astral projection. Prophetic visions and glossolalia—speaking in tongues—I find it all fascinating. There are some things that simply cannot be explained by science, or psychology, or by any singular religion. Believe me, my studies have gotten me laughed out of lecture halls, and many of my colleagues think it's all a farce. But psychoanalysis was once laughed at, too. Even the great Carl Jung believes in the value of studying the metaphysical."

Loretta let out her breath. "So you're saying what's happening to me might be real, and not just my imagination?"

"If you're experiencing it, it's a part of your reality. It's the *why* I'm most interested in, Loretta."

"Well, I certainly can't explain what's happening to me. Or why. Maybe it's God. Maybe it's something else. It's more than a little frightening. But I'm just as curious as you are, Doctor."

"I think, perhaps, together, we might figure things out." He smiled at her, and Loretta felt herself relax into the chair, some of her apprehension melting away. "Now, let's go back to when all this started. You said you had the flu?"

Chapter 6

Loretta hummed to herself as she finished preparing dinner, her mind lighter than it had been in months. She'd even slept better. Her session with Dr. Hansen had awakened her curiosity in ways she was still contemplating. But most of all, the power of being listened to—of truly being heard—had restored Loretta's sense of hope.

Earl and Gladys McAndrews would arrive any moment. Pete and the kids were in the backyard, soaking up the last flare of warm weather. She wore her most flattering dress—pale-pink gingham with a full skirt and a nipped-in waist. She had even taken her mother-in-law's china out of the hutch, dusted it, and set the table with proper linens. Things looked as nice as they could, though she wished their house had a formal dining room for such occasions. Two roasted chickens sat in the center of the table, ready to be carved, and an apple pie was browning in the oven.

These social occasions always felt like a performance on which she'd be judged for days afterward. She never felt comfortable around Pete's colleagues. Even though they didn't mean to, they had a way of making her feel small—less intelligent. But tonight would be different. Tonight, she'd be the perfect hostess and make Pete proud. Besides, she liked Gladys. She seemed fun. Carefree.

From the kitchen, she heard a car pull up in the driveway. She went to the door. The McAndrewses' two-toned Buick sat next to their car. It had a dent in its right fender, marring the smoothness of the green paint. Gladys emerged from the passenger side, her petite, almost cartoonishly curvaceous figure swathed in a vivid yellow dress that accented her blonde hair. She took Earl's arm and walked up the drive. He reminded Loretta of a fish, with his fleshy lips and heavy jowls. They were such an odd couple—he with his serious, stuffy personality and Gladys with her girlish effervescence.

"Hello, Gladys, Earl," Loretta greeted them, stepping out onto the porch. "You're looking well."

"Oh, gracious, so are you, Loretta! That dress is lovely."

"Just something I got off the sale rack at Heer's last year." Loretta ushered them inside.

"Something smells wonderful," Earl said, craning his neck toward the kitchen.

"Yes, roast chicken with all the fixings. Make yourselves comfortable at the table. Sit wherever you'd like. There's iced tea in the pitcher. Pete and the kids are out back. I'll call them in."

Loretta left them and went to the back porch. Pete was pushing Charlotte on the swing set, her dress flying up over her knees. Luke sat on the grass, looking forlorn and contemplative. "Dinner's ready!" Loretta called.

Pete ambled to the door, the kids in tow. "Mr. and Mrs. McAndrews are in the kitchen," Loretta said. She distractedly smoothed Lucas's cowlick and brushed nonexistent dirt from Charlotte's dress. "Go say hello while I freshen up. Remember your company manners. I'll just be a minute."

Pete frowned. "You seem nervous. What's wrong?"

"Do I? It's just that sometimes I just don't know what I should or shouldn't say to your work friends. I know these dinners are important to you."

"Just be pleasant and let me lead the conversation. If Gladys gets too chatty, which she probably will, find some reason to excuse yourself." Pete leaned close to her ear, his voice a rough whisper. "I didn't want to say anything before—I didn't want to make you nervous—but

Earl and I are on the same tenure track. Only one of us will be chosen in January. I don't want to give him any reason to get ahead of me or have him thinking anything here at home is less than perfect." Pete straightened his tie in the hallway mirror and gave her a smile. "You look very pretty tonight, Retta. You should wear that dress more often."

He steered the kids toward the kitchen, and Loretta went to the powder room and switched on the light. It flickered. A moth was trapped within the light fixture, desperately trying to free itself. Loretta stood on tiptoe and unscrewed the tulip-shaped globe. The moth flittered out. Loretta replaced the globe and then gazed at her reflection in the mirror above the sink, staring herself in the eye. "Don't be shrill. Be calm. Don't talk about politics, or the news, or God or the Bible," she murmured. "And smile."

She ran cold water over her hands to shock her nerves back into place, dried them, and went into the kitchen. Pete and the kids sat at the table with their guests, backs straight, elbows at their sides.

Gladys looked up at her entry. "Would you like any help with anything, Loretta?"

"I just have to take the pie out of the oven to cool, and then we can eat."

"Pete was just telling us about your upbringing. I'd no idea you were a farm girl. My mother was as well." Gladys smiled. She had a dimple in her left cheek and sharp little white teeth. "What kind of farm was it?"

"A small one. We raised pigs."

"Oh my." Gladys laughed. "I bet that was something on a hot summer's day."

"If you're implying it stank—yes. It certainly did."

Pete cut a glance her way. Shook his head, ever so slightly.

"And what kind of farm did your mother grow up on, Gladys?" Loretta asked, knowing the question was expected of her.

"Oh, we had a pecan grove. But we raised some cotton, too. Down in Arkansas."

"How nice." Gladys probably thought pecans and cotton were far above hogs. But Loretta refused to compete with other women. She'd never been able to compete as a girl and saw no purpose in doing so as an adult. She imagined Gladys's family "farm" was really a large plantation like the one Daddy had worked on as a sharecropper, alongside the children and grandchildren of former slaves. The things he witnessed and experienced as a boy in the Arkansas delta had made him determined to farm his own land. At the harvest and at butchering time, when he needed to hire outside hands, he always paid—and treated—his farmhands fairly. Daddy's principles and work ethic were something she was proud of, even though it meant she and Mama hardly saw him during the growing season.

Loretta donned an oven mitt and retrieved the pie. The crust was just shy of being burned. "I hope you all like apple pie."

"Yummy, Mommy!" Charlotte crowed. She could always count on Charlotte's enthusiasm. Loretta would get through dinner as best she could, then excuse herself to put the kids to bed with a long bedtime story.

Loretta took her place at the end of the table, across from Pete. "Shall we pray?" he asked. Loretta offered her right hand to Lucas and her left to Gladys, then bowed her head.

"Heavenly Father," Pete intoned, "we thank you for this food, and for its blessing to our bodies, so that we might have the strength to carry on your work. May we ever be grateful for your bounty. In Jesus's name, amen."

"Amen," Loretta echoed. Her left hand, still encased in Gladys's, tingled as if it had gone to sleep. She pulled her hand away and offered the breadbasket to Gladys, but she waved it away. Watching her figure, no doubt. Pretty women like Gladys were always watching their figures. Loretta passed the basket to Luke without taking a roll.

"Earl and I had lunch with Dean Matthews today," Pete said. "The revised student guidebook is going out this week."

"Oh?" Loretta asked. "The one with all the new rules?"

"Yes," Earl said. "We put several new policies in place. There's to be no more going to movies, or restaurants that serve alcohol. If a student is seen at a bar or a honky-tonk, it will result in immediate expulsion. If any alcohol or tobacco items are found in a dorm room, the student will be given a firm warning on the first offense, and if it occurs again, expulsion."

Loretta raised her glass to her lips and took a drink of iced tea. "Will the same rules apply to the faculty?"

Pete frowned. "Well, of course. That's understood. It doesn't have to be stated."

Loretta only hummed and nodded.

"These young people. It's a shame, really. Sneaking off in the middle of the night to drink and carouse." Earl shook his head. "Sometimes I'm thankful we haven't had children. They get out of hand as they get older."

Loretta's eyes darted to Lucas and Charlotte, but they seemed oblivious to Earl's thoughtless words. Luke was happily tucking into his green beans, and Charlotte was gazing up at the chandelier, watching the moth Loretta had rescued from the powder room. It knocked desperately against the lights.

"Did you happen to catch the final game last night?" Pete asked Earl. "Yankees fought hard, but they couldn't pull out of that slump."

Earl nodded. "It was good to see the Dodgers win for once. I like to see the underdog come out on top. Don't you?"

"If they deserve to win."

Loretta glanced at Pete. At first, she wondered if Earl's remark about underdogs was a thinly veiled reference to their rivalry for tenure, but as the men began discussing batting averages and baseball plays, she thought herself silly for considering such a thing. Pete was competitive, but not maliciously so. Her gaze drifted out the window, where the setting sun was tracing a slow orange fade of color across the kitchen counters, but a shimmer of movement caught her eye, right over Gladys's right shoulder.

A woman stood there.

Loretta blinked. Shook her head. Blinked again.

The woman remained, smiling softly. She had blonde hair, marcel-waved and accented with a jeweled headband. She was very pretty, with aquiline features and a tiny Cupid's bow of a mouth, painted red. She wore a beaded white dress that caught the light, sending out a myriad of kaleidoscopic sparkles. The woman rested a hand on Gladys's shoulder. Gladys was oblivious. She continued smiling and chattering with the men.

Tell her everything will be all right. Tell her to name the baby Katherine, after my mother.

The woman's voice, sweet and rich with southern wealth, entered Loretta's head, as clear as if the woman had whispered the words into her ear.

Loretta looked at Pete. Looked at Earl. Looked at the kids. Lucas stared at her, his eyes wide. "Mom?" he asked. "What's wrong?"

Loretta leaned close to Luke. Her head went into a spin. "Do you see her?"

"Who?"

"That *lady*," Loretta hissed. "In the white dress."

Luke frowned in confusion. Shook his head.

Loretta's pulse quickened. A man and another woman, this one older, had joined the lady in white. They were dressed in similar clothing, their features slightly hazy, flickering in and out, like a poor signal on a television screen. Voices crowded into Loretta's head, all talking at once.

The man was very angry. He was shouting a name—*Bedingfield*—over and over. Loretta's temples throbbed at the sound of his voice. So loud. She resisted the urge to clap her hands over her ears.

The older woman shook her head, rapidly, so rapidly it was a blur. *No no no no no.*

Nausea crested in Loretta's stomach. She broke out in a cold, clammy sweat. She pushed the heel of her hand against her eyes, then reached for her iced tea and found a glass of champagne instead. Her familiar kitchen faded from view. She was at a party—a big one, at a dance hall. People flowed around her, dressed in movie-star finery. Paper streamers hung from the high ceiling, and a crystal chandelier winked overhead. A band played from an elevated stage, a woman's velvet voice crooning over muted horns. The lady in the white dress was dancing with a man, his hair slicked back with glossy pomade. He guided her clumsily as they danced. They suddenly broke apart, the woman gesturing in frustration. The man grasped her by the wrist, leading her from the dance floor. They brushed past Loretta. The woman's eyes met Loretta's. They were a stunning dark blue, glossy with tears. *Tell her everything will be all right. Tell her it's not her fault.*

Bedingfield!

It was the angry man again. He pushed through the crowd, following the young couple, his teeth clenched. Loretta felt his rage tumble through her body. The older woman—his wife, she was sure of it—trailed him, still repeating the word "no," over and over.

Loretta pinched her eyes shut. Willed herself back to reality. When she opened her eyes, she was in her kitchen. Silence greeted her. Gladys McAndrews was staring at her, her fork poised over her plate, a single green bean speared in its tines. "How did you know my name?"

"What?"

"My name. My maiden name."

"I . . . I'm sorry. I don't know what you're talking about."

The moth knocked against the chandelier.

"You were whispering it, just now. I heard you. Bedingfield." Gladys looked to Earl. "Did you tell her my name?"

"Now why would I do that, Gladys?"

"Loretta." Pete nudged his chin toward the stairs. "The kids are finished eating."

"I should probably put the children to bed," Loretta said, pushing back from the table. "Come along, Luke. Charlotte."

"But I haven't had any pie yet," Charlotte whined.

"Daddy will save you a piece. I'll let you have pie for breakfast tomorrow morning, just this once." Loretta stood, her knees shaking. "I'm so sorry to be such a poor hostess."

"Nonsense!" Gladys said, blinking rapidly. "I can see you're not feeling well. I'll clean up the kitchen before we go. Perhaps we can meet for coffee next week? Talk more?"

"All right. I'd like that," Loretta lied. She gently guided the kids from the table and up the stairs, past their gallery of smiling family portraits. Her head floated somewhere above her, unmoored from her body, like a balloon.

"Loretta's been having these sickly spells," she heard Pete say as they reached the landing. "The doctors can't seem to figure out what's wrong with her."

"I'm so sorry to hear that," Gladys said, her voice low. They continued talking, and Loretta strained to hear what they said about her. She heard a sudden burst of male laughter. Gladys's girlish titter followed.

"Mommy, can we have the story about the poky puppy?" Charlotte asked, tugging on Loretta's hand.

"Yes, honey."

Once she'd read the story to Charlotte twice, her eyelashes finally fluttering closed, Loretta went to tuck Luke in, then to her room to change into her nightclothes. She could still hear their company downstairs through the closed door—the clatter and clink of dishes being washed, the occasional laughter, Pete's steady, rumbling voice. They were having more fun without her. She wouldn't be missed, but she didn't mind.

As for the others, those strange people she'd seen in the kitchen— the spirits—they were gone. Their coming and leaving had her wrung out like a washrag. It was an altogether unpleasant feeling. Her head still swam slightly as she knelt by the edge of the bed and pulled out the small suitcase she used for weekend trips. She'd tucked the book Dr. Hansen had given her yesterday inside the shoe pocket. He'd wanted to hear her thoughts on the book at their next session. Loretta drew out the antique, leather-bound volume with care. *The Law of Psychic Phenomena.* She'd only skimmed it briefly, parked along the curb in front of the school, waiting for the kids.

The text was complex, old-fashioned, and wordy. It was difficult to follow. Instead, Loretta found her eye wandering to Dr. Hansen's copious notes in the margins. His handwriting was smooth and slanted to the right. He seemed to be particularly keen on the passages about hypnosis. She settled in, back against the headboard, determined to read the book from cover to cover.

She'd just finished the first chapter when she heard Pete's footsteps on the stairs. She hurriedly shoved the book beneath her pillow and lay down, pretending to be asleep.

The door creaked open. Pete came to her side. She could feel him looking down at her. "Already asleep." He sighed, softly reaching out to caress her cheek. "What am I going to do with you, Loretta?"

Loretta didn't react. She kept her breathing steady, her eyes closed. Pete switched off the lamp, gathered his pillow, and left. He was upset with her. She'd disappointed him again.

As she lay there in the darkness, she dreaded the morning and Pete's thinly veiled ire—the days of silence after—his quiet way of punishing her. She would have to extend the olive branch, eventually, as she always did. Either with some artfully concocted meal or with her body. And she would. She knew she always would. For the children's sake. For the ease of the days that followed and the brief reclamation of the love that had drawn her to marry Pete in the first place. They could be happy again. For a few days, or even weeks, if she only tried harder.

Chapter 7

Loretta watched Dr. Hansen watching her. Blue eyes, shaded behind horn-rimmed glasses. Up close, she could see his wavy brown hair was streaked with gray and just beginning to recede on either side of his forehead, although it did nothing to diminish his attractiveness. A wedding ring—a simple gold band—adorned his left hand. A ring, but no wife she'd seen. Not in the pictures that lined his desk nor bustling about in the halls. Only Barbara, who was his cousin, a fact Loretta had learned after her last session. They had the same long limbs, the same easy way of moving. Dimpled chins. Eyes that creased at the corners when they smiled. Family traits.

Loretta's curiosity about the doctor grew more intense with each weekly visit. He seemed out of place in Myrna Grove—like a denizen of the last century, worldly and wise beyond his years. And he was generous. At the second session, when she tried to pay, producing her secret money from her jacket pocket, Dr. Hansen had waved it away. "I can't take your money, Loretta. Not for this. Your being here is just as much a benefit to me."

They were playing the card game again. Only it wasn't poker or bridge. Dr. Hansen touched one of the cards in the row turned face down on his desk. "Tell me what you see."

Loretta closed her eyes. "It's a red suit. Three of diamonds."

Dr. Hansen flipped over the card and smiled. Three red diamonds. "Very good. Now this one?" He touched the card beneath it.

"The joker."

He laughed softly as he revealed the card. "You are remarkable."

Heat flooded Loretta's cheeks, ran down her neck. No one had ever called her remarkable.

"You've gotten every single card right today. That's never happened before," he said, gathering the cards into a neat stack. "Your abilities are growing stronger, Loretta."

"Thank you."

"Now, let's see if you might be able to move things with your mind."

Loretta raised a brow. "Is that possible?"

"Very much so. It's something we studied in the parapsychology lab, with some success." Dr. Hansen lined up several objects on his desk: A pen. A dime. A small rubber ball. A paper clip. "Now, concentrate on each object."

Loretta aimed her eyes at the paper clip because it was the lightest and seemed the easiest to move. Nothing happened. Next, she tried the pen. Nothing.

"Should I try again?" she asked.

He shrugged. "Perhaps another time. Psychokinesis tends to develop with time and practice, and not everyone has the capability." Dr. Hansen gathered the items from the desk and put them away. "We have thirty minutes left. Would you like to go out to the gardens?"

"I would."

Loretta stood, smoothed her skirt, and followed Dr. Hansen out of the study and down the hall. Her new high heels clicked on the wooden floors—an indulgence, a prize, a good-wife gift Pete had bestowed after Loretta let him make love to her three times in one week and managed to behave properly at a faculty luncheon. She was better. She'd been praying, and her moods were under control.

The crisp late October air greeted Loretta as she and Dr. Hansen stepped onto the stonework terrace behind the house. The maple trees were just beginning to bare their limbs—dark, skeletal arms held high against the gunmetal sky, their leafy canopy now at their feet. The days were shorter. Colder. Tomorrow was Halloween.

Luke and Charlotte never went trick-or-treating. Pete had long ago declared the holiday, and everything it stood for, evil. Loretta was fine with not celebrating, mostly, although memories sang bittersweet from her childhood. Mama had always liked harvesttime. Every year, she'd decorated their farmhouse with colorful gourds from the garden, strung popcorn garland from corner to corner, and hung Indian corn from the porch rails. Loretta remembered autumn as a firelit time of spiced cider, hayrides, and cozy bedtime stories about headless horsemen and witches.

"What are you thinking about?" Dr. Hansen asked.

"My mother. She loved this time of year."

"Mine did, too."

"She always told me Halloween was when the veil between the spirit world and our world was at its thinnest."

"There could be some truth to that. The pagans certainly thought so—the early Christians, too."

"Really?"

"Yes. Many of the church's rituals were taken directly from the pagans. To make it easier to convert people, you see. Beltane, Samhain, Lughnasa—they all correspond to Christian holidays. It's not a coincidence. Belief systems and religious philosophies tend to be circular— or like an ouroboros, a snake eating its own tail. Human beings have always longed to connect with the spirit realm. That longing can take on many forms."

They walked past the stand of maple trees, and farther on to the hedge garden, where a circular labyrinth stood at the center. The roses were going dormant, petals frost-browned and limp, their scarlet rosehips poking out like rounded berries. Beyond, the shuttered guest cottage stood like a yellow doll's house at the edge of the gardens.

"I've been seeing them more often lately. The spirits," Loretta said. "Sometimes it's very clear and obvious when they come—like it was that night at dinner with Gladys McAndrews. Other times, it's a bit like radio static. Voices. In and out. The sense of someone standing behind me or watching from the shadows. It's unnerving."

"Remember what I told you about envisioning a door inside your head. If you want them to come, open the door. If not, close it up tight. Sometimes, they might resist, try to come in through the cracks in your psyche—mostly while you're sleeping. But always remember, you are in control, Loretta. They are your guests. And just like unwanted guests, you can tell them to leave."

"I'm trying." Loretta shrugged in exasperation. "I still don't understand why this has happened to me. I've always had strange sensations and pricklings of knowing—simple things, like knowing who was calling before I picked up the phone. And on the day my mother died, I had a bad feeling something terrible would happen. But this, with the spirits . . . it can be frightening, Doctor. Some of them are angry."

"The gift you possess is a rare one. As you know, I've only ever met one other true medium in my lifetime. The rest have been shams—charlatans who prey upon the grieving. Quite frankly, your psychic ability astonishes me. With time, and with focus, you'll learn to control it. When you gain control, the fear will lessen. You might even come to enjoy your abilities."

"I hope so."

"Have you told Pete about our sessions yet?"

Loretta stopped on the path, shoved her hands deep in her pockets. "I haven't."

"Why not?"

Loretta had said very little about Pete or her marriage during their sessions. She had only mentioned his academic and professional accomplishments.

She turned to Dr. Hansen, met his eyes. "I haven't told him, Doctor, because if he ever found out, it's very likely he wouldn't let me come back here."

"I see." Dr. Hansen blinked thoughtfully. "And what would you do if that happened?"

Loretta sighed. "I don't know. I only know our sessions . . . *this*"— she gestured at the gardens—"is the one thing I look forward to. A thing that's only for me. And I don't want to give it up. Even though I don't understand why all this is happening to me, I'm learning so much about myself. And I feel like there's a purpose to my life again. Beyond motherhood. Beyond being Mrs. Peter Davenport. I was Loretta Connor for sixteen years of my life. Sometimes I wonder what might have happened if I'd remained Loretta Connor." Loretta bit her lip. She'd said too much. Even if it was honest.

"I think it's normal to consider those sorts of things, Loretta. But right now, in this moment, even as Mrs. Davenport, you still have choices. You're young. You have so much living ahead of you. I'm glad our sessions have given you a sense of purpose—they've certainly done the same for me. You mentioned you always wanted to be a writer. Perhaps you might consider writing again. About anything. They always say to write what you know. You could start there and see what happens."

Loretta smiled. "Maybe I will."

❧

Loretta stared at the blank yellow page in front of her. She flexed her fingers around her pen and began again.

At first, she tried a few lines of poetry—about sadness, about loneliness—but they were nothing more than vague feelings, written down in free verse. She ripped the page from the tablet and crumpled it. It joined the others at her feet. She sighed and looked out the window, at the elm's pointed, golden leaves. She'd moved a small console table from the hallway into her room after her session with Dr. Hansen, placing it beneath the window as a makeshift desk. She liked having a view while she wrote.

Dr. Hansen had told her to write what she knew.

Well, she knew all about being a wife and a mother.

She began again, and this time, the words streamed forth as she shared her simple, day-to-day frustrations.

A mother lives in a world of magical thinking . . . the belief that somehow, some way, if she packs the perfect lunch, she might be granted the perfect child in return at the end of the school day. This kind of domestic witchcraft rarely yields the desired results. Children have infinite ways of thwarting the clever bargains their mothers make.

Two hours later, she'd filled her yellow tablet with anecdotes and humorous personal stories. She read through her writing, smiling to herself. Perhaps, through her writing, she might escape the humdrum and become the woman she wished she *really* were—a charmingly frustrated, well-groomed mother with a loving, if hapless, husband and children whose traits were endearing and honest.

Perhaps.

She glanced down at her watch. It was nearly four o'clock. She sprang from her chair. She was late to pick up Charlotte and Lucas. She hastily secreted the legal pad in the suitcase under the bed, threw the wadded-up failures into the trash, and tied a scarf over her hair. She shrugged on a light jacket and went out to the car.

"Loretta!" Phyllis waved at her from the other side of the hedge. She had a pair of pruning shears in her hands. "Goodness, your yew is overgrown again. Have you ever thought about digging it up? It keeps pushing over into my yard. I'm allergic. Did you know that?"

"Can we talk about the yew later, Phyllis? I need to get the kids. I'm already late." Loretta opened the car door and placed one foot inside.

"You're always rushing off." Phyllis adjusted her glasses. "You look pretty today. Been taking more care with your appearance lately, I've noticed."

"Oh, I don't know about that."

"You've lost some weight, too."

"Have I?" Loretta hated it when people commented on her fluctuating figure—as if her body had value only when it was diminishing.

Phyllis smiled shrewdly. "Why don't you come over later, for a cup of coffee. Catch up?"

"I can't. Not tonight." Loretta folded herself into the Chrysler and, before Phyllis could reply, shut the door. She started up the car and backed out of the driveway. Phyllis stood staring at her with a bemused expression. Loretta waved, rattled by her neighbor's intrusive tone and manner. Such a busybody. Perhaps she'd make Phyllis the subject of her next writing session. There was certainly plenty of inspiration there.

A few minutes later, she pulled up to the school. Lucas and Charlotte sat out on the front steps. Loretta parked the car, silently scolding herself for being late. Anything might have happened to them. A flurry of coppery leaves fluttered by, kicked up by the wind as she rolled down her window and waved to them. "I'm so sorry," she called. "Mrs. Colton caught me outside and made me late." It was a half truth.

As the kids got in the car, Charlotte chattering a mile a minute, Loretta studied Luke in the rearview mirror. Something was wrong. He sat slumped next to Charlotte in the back seat, a sullen expression on his face.

"Luke, honey, is something the matter?"

He didn't answer, only groaned, and turned toward the window.

"Are you sick?"

Another groan.

"Let's get some ice cream on the way home, since I was late."

"Ice cream!" Charlotte squealed, bouncing in her seat.

After all, it was Halloween. Every other child in the neighborhood would have a sugar belly at the end of the night. It wasn't fair for her children to not get a treat of their own.

"Mommy, why don't we ever go trick-or-treating?" Charlotte asked, as if she'd read Loretta's thoughts. "Kitty told me that she's dressing up as a witch. Can I dress up as a witch?"

Loretta sighed. "No, honey."

"Halloween is against our religion," Lucas said. "That's why we don't do it."

"I'm sorry. Does it make you sad that we don't do anything special?"

"Yes. We *never* get to do anything fun," Charlotte said, pouting. "I hate religion."

"Charlotte May!" Loretta frowned at Charlotte in the mirror.

"I do, too," Lucas said. "Church is boring."

Loretta glanced at her watch again. It would get dark around five. Pete typically worked late on Thursdays, when he held his evening office hours. He'd be at Bethel until at least six o'clock. If they hurried, perhaps she could cobble together some costumes and take the kids for a short walk around the neighborhood.

"Do you really want to go trick-or-treating?" Loretta asked.

"Yes!" Charlotte squealed.

Lucas sat up in the back seat. "We don't have any costumes."

"I bet we can come up with something. We won't have time to get ice cream if we go trick-or-treating, though. Is that okay?"

"Trick or treat!" Charlotte said.

"Luke?"

He cracked a small smile and Loretta's heart soared. "I guess so."

"All right. But this has to stay our secret. No telling Daddy."

Loretta's list of secrets was growing longer by the day. She only hoped none of them came spilling out, else she might end up losing the best secret of all.

Chapter 8

Loretta rushed the kids into the house, her excitement equal to theirs. She led them upstairs and began rummaging through dressers and closets. "I have an old felt hat that you can wear, Char. We'll shape the top into a cone, make it look more witchy."

"Can I have a wart, too? Right on the end of my nose?" Charlotte's eyes gleamed.

"I don't know if I can do that, with the time we have, but witches can be pretty, too. Wouldn't you rather be a pretty witch? Like Glinda?"

Charlotte sighed and shrugged. "I guess so."

"Luke?" Loretta asked. "What would you like to be?"

Luke thought for a minute, eyes to the ceiling. "A pirate."

"Oh! With all your stripes, that'll be easy."

An hour later, the kids were dressed in a hodgepodge of motley garments. Ink-pen whiskers dotted Luke's chin and upper lip, and a hastily sewn eye patch covered one eye. Charlotte's loose, golden curls gleamed around her shoulders. She wore one of Loretta's old, filmy nightgowns over her school clothes, tied with pastel ribbons, and held a paper star fastened to a fallen switch from the yard. Her magic wand. The makeshift witch's hat was a little lopsided, but no one would notice. It was nearly dark, and the point was to have fun.

Loretta gathered a grocery bag to hold the candy, and they went out. A low-hanging fog had drifted in after sunset, adding spooky ambience.

The air smelled of woodsmoke. Loretta drew in a long breath, savoring the fragrance. It reminded her of the bonfires Daddy made at the end of the harvest. The brisk weather set a spring to her step as Loretta led the kids away from Phyllis Colton's house—her porch light was off anyway—and toward the long end of the block, where they knew fewer people.

A smattering of children roamed about—miniature ghosts, more witches, and even an adorable vampire. Their mothers trailed behind them. Charlotte and Luke chattered excitedly as they made their way up the street. Loretta kept her head down, her scarf tied over her hair. They stopped in front of a friendly-looking house, its wide front porch bedecked with dried corn stalks and jack-o'-lanterns.

"What do we do?" Luke asked in a broken whisper. His voice was already beginning to change.

"Go up to the door, knock, and when they answer, say 'trick or treat.' Sometimes they might ask for a joke in exchange for the candy. Do you know any good ones?"

"Knock-knock," Luke answered, with a sly grin.

"Who's there?"

"Luke."

"Luke who?"

"Luke, who's at the door!"

Loretta giggled. "Very good, honey."

Charlotte bounced on her heels, impatient. "Let's go. I want some candy!"

The kids rushed up the brick walkway, and a smiling woman opened the door to them, waved to Loretta, and dropped a generous handful of sweets into the waiting bag. Charlotte skipped back to Loretta's side, waving her magic wand. "That was fun!"

"Was it? Shall we hit the next house?"

"*That* house has a light on," Charlotte said, pointing across the street. "Let's go there!"

Loretta turned to look. It was the Robberson house. The bare-bulbed porch light cast a shallow cone of yellow across the sagging porch and overgrown yard. The house's dark upper windows winked forebodingly. "I don't know about that one, Char."

"Why not?"

Loretta remembered Phyllis's gossiping and conjecturing about the man who lived there—that he might have had something to do with Darcy's kidnapping and murder. She thought of the man—she didn't even know his name, only that he was the Robbersons' nephew—tall, pale, thin, and balding. The few times she'd seen him, he'd put her in mind of an undertaker. *Might* he be capable of the crime? As a light came on upstairs, and she saw the man's shadow move behind the curtains, Loretta felt ashamed that this unkind part of herself had reared up. She reasoned with herself to slake the shame. She was only being protective. Not judgmental like Phyllis.

Pete would be home soon. They needed to hurry. She took Charlotte's hand and gently coaxed her forward. "There are three more houses on this side of the street. We'll go to them and then head home. You need a proper supper before you eat this candy. How about tomato soup and grilled cheese?"

⚜

Three hours later, Loretta stood gazing out the living room window at an empty driveway. Pete was late again. It was after eight. She'd rung the office, but this time, no one answered. After putting the kids to bed, she took to pacing back and forth through the house, her head spinning with grim scenarios.

She turned the TV on as a distraction, keeping the volume low. *I Love Lucy* was on. Television Lucy and Desi always seemed happy. Loretta wondered if it was all an act. Perhaps their real marriage was just as fraught with the kinds of troubles most couples had. No one really knew what happened behind closed doors. People often assumed smiles meant happiness. But smiles could be masks, too. Better than any made of plastic or paper.

Loretta ceased her pacing and sat heavily on the couch. She rolled her head back. A slight headache was just starting between her temples, a slow, steady pulse of pain. She'd eaten a fair bit of sugar herself—peanut butter kisses from the kids' stash. The brief burst of energy had worn off quickly. A bone-deep weariness settled in, and before she knew it, she was drifting off to sleep, her eyelids weighted with a leaden fatigue.

Loretta

Her eyes snapped open. Someone had said her name.

The flickering TV cast bouncing shadows around the room. Loretta's ears pricked, listening. She sat up, and the wary feeling intensified, as if she were being watched. She had the strange compulsion to look behind her. She refused the urge, her heartbeat ratcheting higher.

Loretta? Honey? Can you come here?

There it was again—softer, tentative, like a question. It was a familiar voice—one Loretta hadn't heard in many, many years. She slowly turned.

Her long-dead mother stood on the threshold between the kitchen and the living room.

Loretta squeezed her eyes shut and opened them again. The chandelier above the kitchen table winked off and then back on. One of the bulbs died with a soft fizzle. Mama stood there, smiling, looking much the way she had on the day of the accident. Her shining, thick chestnut-brown waves fell around her jawline. She wore her favorite housedress, the one printed all over with cherries and daisies, made from the flour sack fabric they'd collected during the Depression.

"Mama?" Loretta slowly rose from the couch, her knees weak as jelly. "Is that really you?"

Mama just smiled again and dipped her chin.

Fear and curiosity and love warred within Loretta, spinning like the inside of a snow globe. Loretta shook her head, rubbed her eyes. Mama still stood there, but the closer Loretta got to her, the more liminal she became. Loretta could see the hulking outline of the Frigidaire through Mama's shoulders, the window above the sink through the top of her head. "Are you really here?"

Mama nodded. "I am. You've opened the door."

"The door?"

"You'll see," Mama said cryptically. "We're all here, just on the other side."

"The other side." Loretta's skin goose-pimpled.

"Yes. And one day, we'll be together again."

"What's it like?"

"Like a beautiful dream. The most beautiful dream you've ever had."

Mama began to fade, until she was a faint silhouette shining with pale light. Loretta panicked. There was so much she still wanted to say. Wanted to know. How many times had she wished she could talk to her mother one last time. To apologize for the way things ended. No. This wasn't enough. "Wait! Don't go!"

I'm always here, Loretta. I always will be. Here and there, and every-where, all at the same time.

Mama's faint voice lingered in the kitchen for a moment, a soft whisper of sound, and then she was gone. Loretta reached out with desperate hands. A ragged cry tore from her throat. Hot tears burned behind her eyes. "No! I need you. Mama, I need you! Don't leave me!"

Just then, the front door swung open. A cold bullwhip of air lashed at her legs, whisking the hem of her housecoat. Pete crashed against the doorframe, his body sagging. He grimaced, his mouth a pained rictus. "Retta, help me."

Chapter 9

Somehow, Loretta managed to get Pete to the couch—half carrying him, half dragging him across the floor. She took off his shoes and propped his head to the side just in case he vomited. The smell of liquor rolled off him, cutting through the scent of his aftershave, which he'd no doubt slathered on to disguise the scent. She hovered over him, disappointment and pity flooding her veins with agitation.

They'd been here before.

She had thought it was over.

He'd told her it was.

She hadn't found any hidden flasks or bottles in years—not since Charlotte was little. But she'd always suspected he might be hiding his habit—that the long nights at the office might have been something other than his working late. Loretta eyed his briefcase near the door, where it had fallen when he collapsed. She lifted it and sat in the chair next to the window, springing the clasp. Inside, Pete's plaid thermos lay nestled against a passel of paperwork. Loretta unscrewed the lid. Sniffed it, and grimaced. Coffee, mixed with the warm bite of whiskey.

The thermos had been in the car the night she'd gone to the hospital. Had he been drinking then, too? He claimed to have used the thermos to bring soup to work for lunch. Loretta's eyes narrowed. Rage bubbled up through her. She wondered just how long he'd been drinking on the sly. Whether he'd ever stopped in the first place.

Her guilt over her secret visits with Dr. Hansen faded. *Her* secrets did no harm.

Loretta thought of the new student policies Pete had so proudly helped institute a few weeks ago. He was ever portraying himself as a beacon of Christian temperance and virtue—especially to his students. The hypocrisy grated on Loretta more than the drinking.

Pete groaned, flinging a hand over his forehead. Loretta hurriedly shut the briefcase and set it on the floor next to the chair. She rose and went to her husband's side. His skin was a sickly shade of green in the pale light leaching through from the kitchen. "Are you all right?"

"No." He groaned again. "Water."

Loretta went to the sink and poured a glass of water. She rolled her head back on her shoulders to ease the tension in her neck. She saw a crack in the plaster, right above the window, slender and spidery. That was new. She brought the glass of water to Pete, helped him raise his head to drink. "What happened, Pete?"

"I must've caught the same bug you had. It's going around," he slurred. "Lotsa kids at school have it."

Her flu had passed weeks ago. Did he really think she'd believe such a thin lie? Loretta turned her head, bit her lip. On the television, Lucy and Ricky cavorted around their living room, silently laughing.

"That's too bad," she said. "Hopefully it won't last long."

Pete leaned onto his elbow, wincing. "Could you bring me a couple of aspirin, honey?"

"Sure thing." Loretta stood, her body wound tight as a spring. She wanted to slap him. To shame him into confessing his indiscretion. But the last time she had confronted him about his drinking, he'd lost his temper and driven his fist through the plaster, right next to her head. She'd been so frightened of him she cowered like a child. The message was clear. Next time, it would be her. Next time, she would suffer.

Loretta silently padded to the upstairs bath and switched on the light. She opened the medicine cabinet and pulled out the half-empty bottle of Bayer. She shook two aspirin into her palm. As she passed into the hall, Charlotte peeked through a crack in her door.

"Mommy, I can't sleep. There was a lady in my room."

"What?" Loretta's hair prickled along her arms.

"A ghost lady."

A ghost. Had Mama visited Charlotte, too? And if so, why was her spirit restless after all these years? "I'll come back up in just a second. Daddy's sick."

Charlotte nodded, brushing her mussed waves out of her eyes. "Okay."

Loretta went back downstairs, avoiding the soft spot on the last step, so as not to wake Luke.

Pete sat up when he saw her. "Retta, what's wrong? You're pale as a sheet."

"I . . . I'm fine. Just tired. Charlotte had a bad dream. Can't sleep." She handed Pete the pills. He gulped them down. "I think I'll go back up, check on her. Will you be all right?"

"Sure thing. It's just a little stomach bug."

Loretta turned away, ducking her head. "Of course it is," she whispered.

Pete raised an eyebrow. "What did you say?"

"Nothing. I'm very tired, honey."

Pete frowned and stretched out on the sofa. "Oh. Well, good night. Could you turn off the TV and the kitchen light, please? It's shining in my eyes."

Loretta flicked off the television, then the kitchen chandelier, plunging the house into darkness. She felt her way to the stairs. Charlotte's door was open. A cone of yellow light blanched the floorboards in the upstairs hall. Charlotte was lying across the bed, on top of the covers, one hand over her eyes. Loretta reached across the bed and switched off the lamp, then snuggled close to Charlotte. She reached out, cupping her hand around her daughter's cheek.

"I'm here, baby," Loretta soothed. "What happened?"

"I woke up, and she was standing at the end of the bed. The lady."

"What did she . . . look like?"

"I couldn't see her face, but she had long hair. She was crying."

Mama never had long hair—the longest her hair had ever gotten was to her shoulders. "Did she say anything to you?"

"No. She just stood there, then she faded away. I thought I was asleep. But I wasn't. I could hear you downstairs, talking to Daddy."

Loretta absentmindedly stroked Charlotte's back. "I'm sure it was just a dream. Sometimes dreams can linger a bit, even after you wake. If it ever happens again, you'll tell me, won't you?"

"Mm-hmm." Charlotte yawned and nestled close, her head tucked beneath Loretta's chin.

As Charlotte drifted back to sleep, Loretta lay there in the darkness, her mind wheeling. It was one thing for the spirits to visit her. For her to have to deal with their presence. It was another thing entirely for them to visit her children. The spirit in Charlotte's room didn't sound like Mama—it sounded like someone else. And that worried her.

"Whoever you are," Loretta whispered to the shadows, "leave my children alone."

⚜

Loretta scratched Oliver beneath the chin, coaxing a low, rumbling purr from his chest. Dr. Hansen sat at his desk, making notes as Loretta told him about the spirit in Charlotte's room and the visitation from her mother. And then there was Luke. She'd found more strange drawings in his room when she went to fetch his laundry that morning—images of the same woman in the drawing he'd made at school, her face a mass of scribbles.

"I'm concerned about my children, Doctor. Luke has been so troubled of late. And now, with what happened with Charlotte . . . what if my abilities have somehow influenced the children in a negative way? I'm not all right with my children seeing ghosts."

"I don't blame you." He removed his glasses and set them on his blotter. "The spirit in Charlotte's room might not be malevolent, only desperate. Sometimes, if a spirit doesn't feel heard by the medium, they begin acting out in other ways. Poltergeist activity, scary manifestations. A bit like a child throwing a tantrum."

"Things feel out of control. I don't like that feeling. I don't know why this is happening to me. And I don't know what these spirits want. Seeing Mama was one thing . . . it was comforting. I only wish she had lingered longer. There's so much I wanted to say."

Dr. Hansen fixed her with his gaze, searching her face. Sometimes, she felt he could see right through her. "There's something I'd like to try, with your permission. But it requires a great deal of trust."

Loretta ceased petting Ollie. He looked up at her and blinked slowly. "All right. What did you have in mind?"

"You've been reading the book I gave you? About hypnosis and altered consciousness?"

"Yes."

"I'd like to try hypnosis with you, Loretta. When you spoke about your mother—about seeing her spirit—I sensed unresolved feelings. Guilt. You've mentioned that you had a premonition before her death."

"Yes. I didn't know that's what it was, at the time. But I woke that morning with an intense feeling of dread, as if something terrible were about to happen. And it did."

"I believe your psychic abilities have been present for a very long time. Since childhood. But they were repressed—perhaps due to your self-imposed guilt over your mother's accident. The virus merely opened up a pathway for your abilities to take a greater hold. Fever is a type of altered consciousness. The brain, on fire. Neurology is full of mysteries, and how the brain functions under duress is an area of study that scientists are just now pioneering. When I was at Duke, we studied several people whose abilities manifested after head injuries or car accidents. One supposed medium's abilities came on after a fall from a ladder."

"And what does this have to do with the spirits and their manifestations?"

"I'm wondering if your mother's spirit came through because she knows about your guilt and doesn't want you to carry that burden anymore. I'm wondering, if we take you back to that day and give you the chance to say all the things you'd like to say to her, through hypnosis, if it might help you more than you know."

"Is it dangerous?"

"Not at all. Not with me. While it's true that a person is more vulnerable to suggestion while they're in a hypnotic state, a responsible practitioner will always protect the psyche of their patient. You can trust me, Loretta." He smiled gently. "Even though our sessions have benefited my research immensely, I still care about your psychological health a great deal. Your unresolved trauma is just as important as studying these spiritual manifestations."

Loretta closed her eyes. The thought of going back to that awful day terrified her, but perhaps he was right. Even though it would change nothing about what had happened, it might be a balm to her own spirit. With everything else happening in her life—the kids, Pete's return to drinking—perhaps doing this one thing might help her get a grip on all the rest.

"All right, Doctor. I trust you. Let's try."

INTERLUDE

Remembrance

Loretta dreams of a time before. A time when she was still Loretta Connor, twelve years old, with gangly limbs and crooked teeth. As the heavy mantle of unconsciousness settles over her, the scene behind her closed eyes unfolds like a movie. Dr. Hansen's calm voice is still somewhere in the background, but soon it fades away, overtaken by the buzz of summer cicadas and the steady creak of Mama's rocking chair on the front porch. Her hands move quickly, breaking beans with a crisp crack-crack while young Loretta reads the latest Nancy Drew mystery at her feet, legs crisscrossed, skirt pulled tight and tucked under her knees. Out beyond the stand of hedge apple trees, Daddy's tractor rumbles over the pasture. It's early August, and Loretta remembers how hot it was that day—much too hot to be inside. Even now, in whatever form she's taken, the humidity clings to her skin like a wet dress.

Mama lifts her eyes from her work, gazes out over the lawn, past the gravel road, where the sky meets Tom Howell's cornfield. Clouds boil high in the distance, their tops lit with sunlight, their bottoms heavy and dark. A fork of lightning strikes, silver flashing against shadow. "Storm's brewing up fast, over yonder," she says. "I'd best head into town. Get to the store before it hits."

"Can I come?" young Loretta asks.

"Of course you can, baby."

A few minutes later, they're rambling toward Marshfield in Daddy's Model A. Loretta watches herself and her mother from the back seat. An unseen passenger. The sky is closing in now, blue blotted out by a dismal greenish gray. Thunder crackles. Young Loretta cranks down the window, pulls in the earthy, damp air. She's always hated storms—remembers the bad feeling that settled in her belly when dawn first cracked open like a yellow egg. Yet she stays silent about the bad feeling, even as Loretta wills her younger self to say something. To say anything. But the past has already been written, no matter how much Loretta wishes she could change it.

She wonders if this feeling of helplessness is why the spirits come to her. If it's the reason some of them are so desperate, especially if they were taken suddenly like Mama.

As they turn onto the state highway, the skies let loose. Rain beats heavy against the roof. Mama switches on the windshield wipers, though they're flimsy and little use against the sheeting water. Outside, the trees blur, the road a barely visible gray line through the gloom. Wind rattles the car.

Even though Loretta knows she's safe inside Dr. Hansen's office, and that this is only a memory playing out in her mind, her heart tumbles with the knowledge of what is about to happen.

"Mama? Shouldn't we turn around? Go back home?" Young Loretta's eyes are wide. Afraid.

"We're almost there." Mama swipes a hand at the fogged-up windshield. "Safer to keep going than to turn around."

The rain gives over to hail. It pings against the hood, bouncing like mothballs shot from a cannon. Young Loretta hunkers low in her seat, covering her ears. It's so loud. "What if there's a tornado?"

"There ain't gonna be no tornado, Retta May." Mama clutches the steering wheel. Her knuckles have gone white. "We're almost there. We can wait things out at the store."

Suddenly, the hail stops, as if God turned off a spigot in the sky. A hard push of wind comes out of nowhere, shoving the car from side to side.

Loretta hears herself crying, somewhere in the future. Feels the soft brush of a hand on her forehead. Dr. Hansen's voice floats up. "If it's too much, we can stop, Loretta."

"No," Loretta whispers, shaking her head. "Not yet."

Another snatch of wind throttles the car. Mama curses and wrenches the wheel. Suddenly, the world outside goes topsy-turvy. Loretta screams in unison with her younger self. Tree limbs and brush thrash angrily against the car. Mama's head slams against the driver's-side window. Glass shatters.

The Ford rolls to a stop, right side up again. There's a hiss of steam. Young Loretta raises her head. She puts a hand to her temple. Loretta remembers how much it hurt, as if a thousand hammers were pounding away inside her skull. It's raining again, drops pattering on the roof and splashing off the dash. The windshield is broken, the sharp glass scattered all over the seats, Loretta's lap, the floorboards.

"Mama?" young Loretta asks. Mama's blood-streaked arm is thrown over her head. There's so much blood. When an answer never comes, she gently nudges Mama's shoulder. Her arm falls to the side, limp. "Mama?"

"She can't answer you," Loretta whispers. "She's dead."

"No! No!" young Loretta screams, as if she's heard her. Pity wells up inside Loretta as her younger self claws her way loose from the car, cutting her fingers on the broken glass, then tumbles out onto the wet ground. Loretta follows the girl—because that's all she is, a precious little girl—as she makes her way to the road on coltish, unsteady legs. She falls when she gets to the road, catches herself with her hands. Loretta still has a mark where the gravel cut into her flesh, right above the wrist. A tiny scar, white and spoked like a star. No one knows about the other scars. Not even Pete.

Headlights shine around the curve. Young Loretta waves, weakly rising onto her knees. It's Daddy, in the farm truck, fresh-baled hay in the back, covered with oilcloth. He eases the truck onto the shoulder and runs to Loretta. She points down the ditch, where the Model A lies like a twisted, broken toy. "Mama's hurt. Real bad."

ToolateToolateToolate

"Oh, Lord help us." Daddy rushes off, young Loretta stumbling behind him.

"No, no, no. Don't go down there," Loretta pleads. She already knows what her younger self will see. Nightmares. Half of Mama's skull gone, a slick ooze of pink, sightless blue eyes staring heavenward. Things her child brain will never forget. Things that will haunt her for the rest of her life. She claws at young Loretta's dress, trying to hold her back. But it's futile. Her fingers only close on air.

This has already been. This can never be again, anywhere else but in her mind.

At the bottom of the gully, Daddy hauls Mama out of the car. He falls to the ground, legs splayed as he rocks Mama in his arms, his mouth a pained grimace.

She watches, helpless, as young Loretta begins to wail. She wills herself forward, not wanting to relive this moment, but knowing that she must.

When she gets to the bottom of the gully, she reaches out, touches Daddy's head, his hair waved back with Brylcreem, rain beading on the ridges his old black comb made that morning. He cries over Mama's broken body, a long keening *heeeeee* that seems to never end.

"Daddy, I'm sorry I didn't know how to help you." Daddy doesn't hear her, just goes on rocking and howling. "It's not your fault Mama died."

"Tell *her* that, Loretta. She's the one who needs to hear it."

Loretta looks up at the sound of Mama's voice. Her spirit is there, behind Daddy, her hand on his shoulder, looking just as she did that night in Loretta's kitchen. "Tell her, Loretta," Mama urges. "Tell her everything she needs to hear. That's why you're here. For her. For *you*. Not for me. Or your daddy."

"I'm sorry I didn't tell you about the bad feeling."

Mama smiles, her eyes full of love. "How could you have *ever* known what would happen, baby? It was my time, that's all. Some people are lucky. They just go to sleep and never wake up. But for some . . . it ends like this. We can't know until it happens. Not a one of us. We just got to live our lives and not think about dying all the time."

Loretta's shoulders shake. Tears fall. She reaches out to Mama. "I miss you."

"I love and miss you, too. Now go talk to that little girl. Tell her it's not her fault."

Mama's form begins to fade, until she's gone from view. Loretta looks for young Loretta. She finds her sitting on a fallen tree, her back turned to the grisly wreck, holding her knees and rocking, her braids drenched with rain. Loretta longs to hold the child she once was. She longs to reach out to her, to comfort her, but she approaches carefully, as if her child-self is a small animal prone to startle. When she gets to the tree, she kneels on the wet grass. She has a cut on her chin, from the glass, beading blood. That one hadn't left a scar.

"Loretta?"

Young Loretta's eyes widen.

"Can you see me?" Loretta asks.

Young Loretta nods. "Who are you?"

Loretta thinks about telling her the truth, just for a moment. "I'm . . . someone who knew your mother."

"She's dead, isn't she?"

"I'm afraid so. I'm sorry."

Young Loretta's lip trembles. "It's my fault. I knew a bad thing would happen today."

"Yes. But you didn't know *what* it was."

"I should have said something."

"I don't think it would have changed a thing. I think it was just her time. I know that's hard to accept."

"I guess." Young Loretta's eyes narrow thoughtfully. "Why are you all glowy?"

"Am I?"

"Yes. You're shining. Are you an angel?"

Loretta laughs. "No. But your mother sent me to talk to you because she loves you. She doesn't want you to blame yourself, because none of this was your fault. It doesn't feel like it right now, but everything is going to be all right. You're going to grow up, get married, and have children of your own someday. And you'll love them just as much as your mama loved you."

"How do you know?"

Loretta reaches out, and her younger self takes her hand. She can feel the warmth from the little girl's touch, even though it's only a figment of her imagination—a memory constructed from suggestion and the pain of her past. "I know because I *know*. You'll see."

Chapter 10

"Loretta, Loretta. Can you hear me?"

Loretta opened her eyes, emerging from her trance. Dr. Hansen knelt at her side, next to the sofa. His hand was in hers. Warm, comforting. A scholar's hand—a callus on the second knuckle of his index finger from the pressure of his pen. Up close, he smelled crisp and cool. Like cedar mixed with bergamot. Loretta pulled away. Sat up. The intimacy of being this near to another man flooded her face with heat.

Dr. Hansen looked down, abashed by her embarrassment. "I'm sorry if I overstepped. You were reaching out for someone, and I didn't want you to feel rejected in such a vulnerable state."

So, it had been Dr. Hansen's hand she'd felt when young Loretta had taken her hand during her trance. "It's all right."

"How are you feeling?"

Loretta patted her hair, turned away from his depthless blue eyes. "I'm not sure." Her head spun a little as she looked around the room, recentering herself in the here and now. A fire crackled in the grate. Oliver was stretched out on the rug in front of the hearth, belly up. She could hear him purring, even from her place on the sofa. Her eyes leaped to Dr. Hansen's books, his desk, his array of plants on the windowsill, then back to him.

He smiled at her, then stood and went to his usual chair in front of the hearth. Loretta let out her breath. As if startled by the sound,

Oliver ran from his place before the fire and jumped into Dr. Hansen's lap. "What you said was beautiful. I heard you speaking to your mother, but at the end you were speaking to your younger self, weren't you?"

"Yes."

"That's good. Very good, in fact. There's a child within all of us— the child we were when our formative trauma occurred. In some ways, even as we grow older, our inner self can remain 'stuck' at that age. How did it feel, talking to your younger self?"

"It was comforting and difficult at the same time. I felt very tender toward her—like I would if it were Charlotte or Luke who were hurting."

"Yes."

"I knew I couldn't take away her pain—my pain—but perhaps I might help soothe it, a bit." Loretta shook her head. "And it gave me empathy for the spirits. Watching that accident unfold once more, knowing I couldn't do a thing to stop it . . . that's how they must feel when they see their living loved ones hurting. No wonder some of them grow desperate and begin clanging pots and pans. I've never felt so helpless."

"Yet, by going back, you *did* help."

"Who?"

"The most important person of all, Loretta. Yourself."

⚜

Loretta drove home in a contemplative mood. Her session with Dr. Hansen had given her much to think about, and she was eager to peruse the new books he'd given her before they parted. One was on hypnosis, and the other on tapping into psychic consciousness. No matter how apprehensive the spirits made her, there was no sign her sensitivity to their presence would abate. While fear and uncertainty had made her hesitant to fully pursue her gifts, she was eager to learn as much as possible about controlling and honing her abilities. If she could help someone in the same way Dr. Hansen had helped her today—if she could hasten the spirits' rest into eternity and give comfort to their loved ones here on earth, then who was she to deny this calling?

Because, despite Pete's protestations otherwise, she knew that's exactly what this was.

Her calling.

The thought of Pete made Loretta clutch the steering wheel, her leather driving gloves tight over her knuckles. She hadn't spoken of his drunken episode. If he sensed that she knew about the drinking, he didn't seem bothered by it. Perhaps it had been a one-time mistake. Perhaps it would never happen again. He'd certainly been attentive and loving to her and the kids lately—overly so. But this was a cycle Loretta knew too well, and she dreaded the shadows that often came after the sunshine. She could only hope that this time might be different. If she were patient, and attentive to Pete's needs, and didn't react when his moods soured once more, perhaps she could redirect the course of the tide.

As she turned onto State Street, the clouds opened, and it began to sprinkle. She pulled into the driveway and hurried to the porch, cold rain biting at her face.

"Loretta!" Phyllis's voice pierced the frigid wind channeling between their houses.

Loretta paused at the door, her key in the lock. She could go on in, pretend she hadn't heard. But as she glanced over her shoulder, she saw Phyllis already making her way up the drive. She sighed and turned with a hurried wave. "Hello, Phyllis."

"Goodness! I'm glad I caught you. The weather's supposed to turn. Ice. Best go to the store before tonight if you need anything."

Loretta smiled tightly. "I just went shopping the other day. We have all we'll need, I think."

Phyllis squinted at Loretta through her glasses. "There was a girl here, earlier. Looking for you."

"A girl?"

"I told her you're usually not home on Thursday afternoons. Wherever you go, it must be special, because you're always so dressed up." Phyllis smiled slyly.

Loretta felt the blush creep up from below her collar. "It's just a Bible study. What did the girl say? Did she give you her name?"

"Yes. She left her phone number." Phyllis dug in her coat pocket and produced a slip of paper. She handed it to Loretta. "She was in a hurry. Just like you always are. You young people need to slow down. Take time to visit."

Loretta nodded, ignoring Phyllis's words, and unfolded the paper, studying the girlish, looping handwriting. *Dora.* Why was that name so familiar?

"Thank you, Phyllis. I'll give her a call." Loretta turned the key in the lock, and a rush of warmth beckoned from inside. "It's so cold. I think I'll go in now. Warm up before I get the kids. Call if you need anything, with the storm."

"Oh, I'll be fine. I was raised in the mountains. A little bit of ice never scared me." Phyllis crossed her arms, looked Loretta up and down, her eyes landing on the books clutched to Loretta's chest. "I just worry about *you*, Loretta. Doesn't take much to fall, especially if you don't mind your feet."

"I'll be careful. I promise."

Loretta went in, shutting the door behind her and locking it. As she made a pot of coffee to fight the chill, it came to her. Dora was Darcy's sister. Loretta remembered telling Mrs. Hayes that she could contact her anytime she liked—had even told her where she lived. Maybe Dora had been listening. But if so, why would Dora seek her out instead of Mrs. Hayes? And why now?

Loretta poured a cup of coffee and sat at the table, studying the phone number before she went to the telephone. She picked up the receiver. Their party line was open. She dialed quickly, listening to the distant ringing. On the fifth ring, she heard a soft click on the other end.

When there was no greeting, Loretta prompted, "Hello?"

"Hello?" The voice sounded young, hesitant. Nervous.

"My name is Loretta Davenport. I'm calling for Dora."

"This is she."

"Hello, Dora. My neighbor said you'd been by my house and wanted me to call you."

"Yes. But I can't talk right now," the girl said, lowering her voice. "Can you meet with me tomorrow morning?"

"I can, after I take my children to school," Loretta said. "Where and what time?"

"With the ice storm, there might not be school tomorrow. Can I just come to your house?"

Loretta hesitated. She wasn't sure why. Dora knew where she lived and had already been there, after all. "That will be fine. What time?"

"Ten o'clock. It's about my sister."

There was another click, and the line went silent.

Chapter 11

Loretta dressed, pulling a half slip over her belly, where the network of pale, raised scars crosshatched against one another. She donned a thick sweater, then a heavy tweed skirt over her winter stockings. Cold light streamed in through the window. Ice gleamed on the elm tree's bare branches, enrobing them in crystalline brilliance.

She cast an eye to the bed, where Pete lay, his mouth open, a steady snore rumbling from his throat. It was nearly eight o'clock. She went to his side of the bed and shook his shoulder gently.

He opened his eyes, smacking his lips. "What's wrong?"

"I'm worried you'll be late for work. Shouldn't you be getting up?"

He yawned, brushing a hand over his face to block out the light. "We canceled classes for the day. I forgot to tell you last night."

Loretta blanched. It was one thing for the kids' school to be canceled—which surely, with the ice, it would be—and for them to be here during Dora's visit, but she wasn't sure how she'd manage if Pete were home, too.

"So you're not going in?"

"I am," he said, sitting up. "I'm just going in late. I have papers to grade."

"Oh, good," Loretta said, a bit too eagerly. "I'll drive you. That way you won't have to worry about walking on this ice."

"Sure."

"What would you like for breakfast? Pancakes? Eggs and bacon?"

"Would both be any trouble?"

"No trouble at all," Loretta said, forcing a smile.

She went down to the kitchen, switched on the news to listen for school closings, and began assembling her ingredients for breakfast. A few moments later, she heard the upstairs shower start. Good. If they left by nine, that would give her plenty of time to drop Pete off at Bethel and get back to the house before Dora arrived.

As she was making coffee, Loretta looked up at the ceiling, her eyebrows knitting together. Another hairline crack stretched across the ceiling above the sink, barely visible, joining the crack above the window. It hadn't been there yesterday. She was sure of it.

A few minutes later, the sound and scent of frying bacon roused Charlotte and Lucas. They came trundling down the stairs in their pajamas. "No school today," Loretta said. "I heard so on the morning news."

Lucas let out a whoop and Charlotte clapped her hands. "I'm going to play with my dollies all day long!"

"You can do whatever you like," Loretta said with a smile. "Just do Mommy a favor and stay in your rooms this morning, after you've had breakfast. I need to drive Daddy to work, and then I'm having company."

After their hurried breakfast, Loretta and Pete went out to the car. A treacherous glaze of ice shone on the front steps, and icicles punctuated the porch's overhang in a jagged line. Loretta wound her arm through Pete's to keep from slipping as they shuffled out to the Chrysler. The doors were frozen shut, but after a few taps with the steel corner of Pete's briefcase, the driver's-side door cracked open. Loretta climbed in and opened the passenger door from the inside. Pete angled himself in the door and sat, arranging his briefcase at his feet.

They waited in silence as the Chrysler's engine idled and the heater roared. The ice began to melt, dissolving into islands that floated down the windshield.

"It won't happen again," Pete said, breaking the silence. "I'm getting help."

She continued to stare straight ahead. "I'm not sure what you mean."

"Don't play dumb, Loretta. I know that you knew. About my slipup. Why didn't you say anything?"

"The last time I did . . . Your temper."

Pete sighed. "I know."

Loretta looked down, listened to the car's steady rumble.

"I've started going to AA meetings. At St. Agnes."

"Is that where you've been? At night?"

"Yes." Pete reached out, resting his hand on the back of her neck. "I love you. I do. And the kids. I don't want to be that man again. I messed up one time, and it scared me."

"Your slipups scare me, too, Pete."

"Just . . . don't say anything to anyone, Retta. Please. I could lose my job. My standing at church. Everything."

"I've been keeping your secret for a very long time, Pete. Years."

"I know. And you shouldn't have to."

"I am glad you're getting help." Loretta smiled tightly. "Hopefully things will work out this time."

"They will. You'll see."

Loretta put the car in gear. The tires crunched over the ice, crackling like broken glass on the driveway as she slowly backed out. The street looked like a scene from a fairy tale—the sun sparkled on the ice-shrouded trees, and everything seemed cast in crystal, turning the most mundane objects into things of fragile beauty. They drove at a snail's pace to the college, engine in low gear over the hills and inclines. When they reached Bethel, Loretta turned into the circle drive in front of

Meyer Hall, Pete's building. The handsome cluster of buildings around the commons, with their brick facades and climbing ivy, seemed out of another century, even though Bethel was relatively new, having been constructed in the 1920s. Still, it had the prestigious Ivy League charm that looked good on postcards and made the parents of the school's well-to-do students proud.

Pete leaned over, gave her a peck on the cheek. He tested the slippery ground with his oxfords before stepping out. "Pick me up around six?"

"All right. Be careful. I love you."

Loretta watched him go up the steps, then flicked the radio on. Elvis was singing. She turned the volume up as high as it would go and drove away. The rest of the day was hers.

⁕

The knock came at her door just minutes after she returned home. Loretta hung her coat in the hall closet under the stairs and went to answer it.

Dora stood on the porch, her long brown hair drawn back into a ponytail. She was dressed in blue jeans and a well-worn navy peacoat buttoned to the collar. A smudge of pink lipstick colored her lips. Her dark eyes were large and wary as Loretta greeted her and ushered her in out of the cold.

"Would you like something to drink? Coffee? I suppose you're old enough for that, aren't you?"

"Yes," Dora answered with a shy smile. "I like cream and sugar, if that's all right."

"Certainly. Make yourself comfortable in the living room. I'll be right back."

Dora hesitantly crossed to the sofa, unbuttoning her coat. Loretta went to the kitchen. She poured herself a mug of black coffee, then poured another in Charlotte's special cup, decorated all over the inside with yellow stars. She topped it off with milk and brought the coffee, along with the sugar dish and a spoon for Dora.

"Thank you," the girl said. Beneath her coat, she wore a simple white sweater with a strawberry embroidered over the left breast. She was a pretty girl, like her older sister had been.

"I'll bet you're happy school was canceled," Loretta said, easing into the armchair across from Dora. "My kids are. They're upstairs, playing."

"I guess. It's hard to be happy about anything, really." Dora shrugged. "I skip school a lot these days. My grades are slipping. I just can't bring myself to care."

"I'm so sorry."

Dora sighed. "It'll work out, I guess. I have junior year to pick up the pieces." She added two spoonsful of sugar to her cup and stirred, then lifted it to her lips. "Good coffee."

"Thank you. It's only Folgers. I add a little bit of salt to the grounds, to help cut the bitterness."

"Smart." Dora sat back against the cushions, crossing her legs. "Maybe I'll try that when I make the coffee tomorrow. I'm doing everything right now, at home. Mama can barely get out of bed unless it's to go to work. And she has to work even more now, with Darcy gone. Her job helped pay the bills." Dora shook her head. "What a mess."

Loretta didn't know what to say, so she made a sympathetic hum at the back of her throat, as Dr. Hansen often did when she spoke to him of her own troubles.

"That night, at the vigil . . . I'm so sorry I was rude. It's just that, right after they found Darcy, the reporters and the busybodies wouldn't leave us alone." Dora fiddled her fingers over her knee. Loretta noticed the girl's cuticles were red and raw. "I got a little protective. I had to be."

"I understand," Loretta said, leaning forward. "I lost my mother when I was young. Suddenly. Tragically. The death of someone you love is difficult to deal with in the best of circumstances. But when an accident—or worse—happens, it can make the grief seem overwhelming."

"Yes. I feel like I haven't even had a chance to mourn Darcy. Because of everything else." Dora's lip trembled. "I miss her so much. She was always there, you know?"

Loretta nodded. "Yes."

"Mama told me what you said to her—about the pink giraffe and the elephant. That mobile hung over both our cribs. There's no way you could have known about it unless you'd been to our house when we were little. And you never knew my mother, did you?"

"No. That night at the vigil was the first time we'd met."

"Then how did you know?"

Loretta eyed the clock above the sofa nervously. She had never spoken of her abilities to anyone outside Dr. Hansen's office, apart from her failed attempt to tell Pete. But if she were going to truly help people—to make herself and her gifts available as she felt called to do, she supposed she must. She wasn't ready to hang a shingle by her door like a palm reader, but hiding her light—this gift—with all its terrible, wondrous beauty, wouldn't help anyone, either.

"Have you ever had a bad feeling about something, before it happened, and it turned out you were right?"

"I . . . I guess so. Maybe."

Loretta took another sip of coffee, considering her words. "Well, I have something called ESP, Dora," she began, softly. "Extrasensory perception. I don't fully understand it. But somehow, I'm able to know things and see things. Both before they've happened, and after."

"I think I know what you're talking about," Dora said. "One of the men in my dad's platoon had a bad feeling the day the bombers came. He warned Daddy to stay in his foxhole that morning. But he didn't. He was out fishing when the bombers flew over. His friend feels guilty—like he should have done more."

Loretta pinched her eyes shut, remembering the day her mother died. "Yes. It can be a terrible burden, this knowing. Sometimes you only know a little. A fleeting impression. An uncomfortable feeling that you can't put words to. But even this gift, if that's what it is, can't prevent the inevitability of death. I suppose that day is marked by God for all of us."

"Well. I certainly don't think it was God's will for Darcy to die." Dora's mouth hardened. Angry tears sprouted from the corners of her eyes. "She was only eighteen, Mrs. Davenport. How can that be right?"

"I know. I'm so, so sorry."

Loretta had often questioned the justness of a god who allowed so much pain and suffering to happen to innocents. Dora was right. It wasn't fair.

"And it's the way she died that hurts the most." Dora's jaw clenched. Her anger was so raw, so near the surface that Loretta could almost taste it in the air. "The way she was murdered. She had bruises all over her body. Her back and one of her legs was broken. I wasn't supposed to know that, but the detective went to the bathroom when I was at the police station and left Darcy's folder open. She smothered to death. Asphyxiation. I know what that means. She was probably still alive when they buried her."

Buried alive. There was a loud whoosh in Loretta's head. Suddenly, the floor fell out from under her feet, just as it had before. She was back in the pit—Darcy's grave—the muffled arguing of the men a low hum in her ears. Darcy's panic crowded her tongue, her mouth, the taste of dirt and rotten leaves overwhelming her senses. She clawed and clawed, fingers desperately trying to find purchase in the loamy ground. There was no light. No air. No hope.

Loretta came back to the present, sucking in a deep breath. Her heart was beating so fast she thought it might burst from her chest. Dora sat staring at her, wide-eyed. "What just happened? Your eyes rolled back in your head. I thought you passed out."

Loretta clutched at her collar, unbuttoning it with frantic fingers. "I . . . I had a vision."

"You saw what happened to my sister, didn't you?"

"Yes." Loretta's voice shook. "Yes. A little."

"What did you see?"

"There were two men. They were the ones who . . . buried her. I don't know much else." Loretta would keep the rest locked inside herself for Dora's sake. Darcy's fear, her pain, her panic—none of that would help to salve her sister's wound.

"Two men! That makes sense." Dora sprang from the couch, her face animated. "We have to tell the police! They're just looking for one guy."

"Do you think they would believe me?"

"I don't know. But we have to try." Dora crossed the room and gripped Loretta's shoulders. "Please. Won't you help me?"

Loretta gazed into the girl's eyes and saw her own hurt and grief reflected—her guilt over Mama, and all the years of pain that followed. "All right. I'll try."

Chapter 12

Loretta stood in front of the police station doors for a long moment. There would be no going back after this. Her fears crowded around her. They might think she was a deluded crackpot. Or worse yet—that *she* had something to do with Darcy's murder. If she was arrested, what would Pete and the kids do?

"Are you okay?" Dora asked, nudging Loretta's elbow. "Shouldn't we go in now?"

Loretta stiffened. The cold air whisked around them. "Maybe I should talk to a lawyer first. Just in case they think I had something to do with this."

Dora frowned. "I know you didn't."

"But that won't matter to them. This looks suspicious, doesn't it? My coming in here with information out of the blue."

"But you don't know that much. Not really. Besides, you're just a housewife. And you're meeker than a mouse. No one would ever think you were a murderer."

Just a housewife. Loretta's face fell. Dora's chiding hit close to the bone. It reminded her of the smooth, beautiful girls she'd known in high school, who'd teased her for her hand-knitted sweaters, her homely looks, and her shyness.

"Come *on*," Dora pleaded, tugging on Loretta's coat sleeve. "The worst they'll do is ask you a few questions, just like they did with me. I lost my sister. She's never coming back. Please?"

Loretta nodded. "All right. But if things turn and they arrest me, promise me you'll go to my husband. He works at Bethel University. Peter Davenport. He'll know what to do."

"I promise. Now get brave, and let's go in. It's freezing out here."

Dora swung open the door and ushered Loretta inside, following after her. The lobby was too bright—garishly lit with fluorescent lights. A gray-haired woman sat pecking away behind the L-shaped front desk, pince-nez glasses perched on the end of her bulbous nose like an after-thought. She looked up at their entrance. "May I help you?"

Dora stepped forward. "I'm Darcy Hayes's sister. Dora. Maybe you remember me? I was here in September."

The secretary, whose name badge read NANCY FOSTER, sucked on her teeth with a hiss and nodded. "Yes. I remember. So sorry. How is your mother doing?"

"Not well. But the reason why we came in is because Mrs. Davenport, this lady right here, has a lead on Darcy's case."

"Oh?"

Loretta's palms itched and sweated. She clenched her fists until she could feel the bite of her nails in her palm. The pain calmed her. Gave her focus. "Yes. I'm Loretta Davenport. I have some new information that might be useful."

"All right." Nancy Foster stood, removing her glasses. "I'll go get a detective. The two of you can wait in that room, over there." She motioned to a room with a tiny window centered in the door.

"That's the same room where they talked to me," Dora said.

Loretta followed Dora into the room, which held a table, three chairs, and a water cooler stacked with paper cone cups. Another door stood opposite the first. The only thing on the wall was a large mirror that reflected Dora's and Loretta's images.

"It's not really a mirror," Dora whispered. "It's a one-sided window, so the other cops can see in, and watch."

"You probably shouldn't have told me that," Loretta said. "I'm nervous enough as it is."

"I watch *Dragnet.* That's how I know these things."

A few moments later, the door on the other side of the room opened. A middle-aged man dressed in plain clothes entered, carrying a manila folder, his shirtsleeves rolled to the elbow. "Richard Eames, Myrna Grove PD. I'm the lead detective on the Hayes case." He flashed his badge at them, then quickly pocketed it again. "Please sit down, ladies. Can I get you some water?"

"No thank you." Loretta sat, her spine rigid, her pocketbook balanced on her lap. Dora sat next to her, slouching in the chair as if she had done this a thousand times.

"Nancy said you had a tip for us?"

"I . . . maybe." Loretta fiddled with the clasp on her bag. Detective Eames didn't seem the type to suffer fools, and Loretta felt quite foolish being there.

"She does," Dora said, confidently. "Tell him what you saw, Mrs. Davenport."

"I know this may sound ridiculous, Detective, but I have had visions about Darcy's murder."

Detective Eames tilted his head, raising one bushy, black eyebrow. "Come again?"

"Visions."

There was a long beat of silence. The detective studied her, his eyes boring into hers so intensely she had to look away. "Visions?"

"I . . . I see things. Get impressions. Sometimes they're only vague feelings—notions. But with Darcy, I've had two visions that were so clear I almost felt as if I was there when she died, watching it happen." Loretta's fingers tightened on her purse strap. "I've been working with a psychologist to understand things more. He can vouch for me. Dr. Curtis Hansen."

"I see," the detective said with a slight smirk. "And what did you see in your visions?"

"I saw Darcy, being buried alive. There were two men with her, arguing. I couldn't make out what they were saying—it was garbled. But one of them was very angry."

He opened the folder and scratched inside with a pen. "Anything else? What did these men look like?"

"I . . . I couldn't tell you. I never really saw them. They were only shadowy figures."

The detective sighed, ceased writing, and leaned back in his chair.

He didn't believe her. Loretta could see that much. Instead of frustrating her, though, his disbelief emboldened Loretta—made her want to prove herself. She sat up straighter, steeling her voice so it wouldn't quaver. "I'm the one who called in the tip. The anonymous tip that led to the search party. I knew she was buried near the Finley. Because I could hear the mill and the river . . . in my vision."

Eames nodded. "Interesting."

Dora sat up, uncrossing her legs. "She *does* know things. At Darcy's vigil, she told my mother about a mobile that hung over Darcy's crib when she was a baby and described her nursery. She couldn't have known that. There's no way."

Detective Eames sighed wearily. "I've seen this type of thing before, Miss Hayes. You're vulnerable. Grieving. And this woman saw an opportunity. How much have you paid her?"

Loretta's anger began to simmer, then, like a slow pot boiling. "I have not received one red cent from Dora, or her mother, sir. I wouldn't take their money, even if they offered it. Dora came to me, wanting my help. That's why I'm here."

"Well. I'm a very busy man, Mrs. Davenport." He steepled his fingers and peered at her. "I don't have time for witchy nonsense. What you've told me today, even if it were true, won't get us any closer to solving this case."

"But it will! You're only looking for one killer, and there are two!" Dora stood, her face blazing. "My sister deserves justice, and the way I see it, you all are just sitting on your asses and not doing a damn thing to solve her murder."

Detective Eames stood, crossing his arms over his chest. "Please sit down, Miss Hayes. I understand you're upset, but you must see our side of things. We have limited resources. Our investigation hasn't turned up anything new. Until we have something concrete, our hands are tied."

"I know what you're really saying. You're saying my sister doesn't matter. Well, she matters to me!"

Dora yanked open the door, storming out. Loretta followed her, murmuring an apology to Detective Eames and the stunned secretary. She caught up to Dora outside. She found her crumpled against the wall, beneath the blocky silver letters that read MYRNA GROVE POLICE DEPARTMENT, fists tangled in her hair as she banged her forehead steadily against the bricks. Her breath fogged the frigid air as she wailed. Loretta knelt next to her, gently easing her away from the wall. "Come on now. You'll hurt yourself, doing that."

"I don't care! I don't care about anything anymore."

"That's not true. You care about Darcy."

"Darcy."

The girl wilted into Loretta, and Loretta held her, rocking her gently as she cried. "There, there. It's going to be okay. We're going to find out what happened to your sister, one way or the other. I promise."

❧

Loretta watched as Dora walked alone down Chestnut Street, shoulders hunched forward, hands shoved deep in her coat pockets. She'd offered the girl a ride home, but Dora had declined. Loretta understood. For many months after she lost her mother, she'd taken long walks on their farm, round and round the pastures and the pond. It was the only time she allowed herself to cry. Daddy didn't know what to do with her tears. They only seemed to anger and frustrate him more.

Sometimes solitude was grief's best friend.

Loretta sighed and turned to the car. As she opened the door, she caught sight of a man crossing the parking lot. Though young, he leaned heavily on a cane as he came toward her, walking with a slight limp. He was bundled up in a tawny camel coat, a homburg cocked jauntily on his head. "Mrs. Davenport?" he called. "Could you wait a moment, please?"

Loretta closed the car door and faced him. As he approached, she caught sight of the badge pinned to his lapel. Another detective. "Yes. But I don't have long. I need to see to my children."

"I understand." He closed the space between them, huffing steam into the cold, sun-bright air. He was rather handsome, with broad shoulders and a neat blond mustache. "I'm Detective Steven Pierce. I was on the other side of the glass when Eames had you in the interrogation room. I heard everything you said."

Loretta crossed her arms defensively. "I suppose I wasted everyone's time today."

"No. Not at all. That's why I'm glad I caught you."

"Really?"

"Yes. I know Dr. Hansen. I consulted with him on a case a few years back—a cold case that turned up no leads. Paula Buckley. Maybe you remember her?"

Loretta scraped her mind. Yes. The young woman who had gone missing after a New Year's Eve party, three years ago. She'd left her friend's house on the north side of town, near Dearing Park, and had never been seen again. "Yes, I remember Paula."

"It's still unsolved."

"That's unfortunate. Seems to be that way with a lot of missing girls, doesn't it?"

"Yes. Well, everyone seems to have forgotten about Paula, but I can't. She was my first case when I became a detective, and you never forget your first." He shook his head. "There were just too many loose ends and inconsistencies. I have sisters. If one of them disappeared, I'd go to the ends of the earth to find out what happened to her. I understand why Dora's so angry."

"What does this have to do with me?"

"Well. I'm not supposed to be working on Darcy's case. Since I couldn't track down Paula . . . they took me off missing persons and murder cases."

"I'm sorry."

Detective Pierce shrugged. "I'm a junior detective, Mrs. Davenport. We get shoved to the sidelines unless we prove ourselves early and often."

"I'm not sure I understand where you're going with this, or how I can help."

He sighed, took off his hat, and ran a hand through his close-cropped hair. "I'd like to interview you. Test the limits of your abilities, with Dr. Hansen's help."

"Oh. I'm not sure, Detective. I don't know what else I could do to prove myself. I told you all where to find Darcy, and she was where I said she would be. That wasn't enough for Detective Eames to take me seriously, and I doubt it's enough for you." Loretta rubbed her arms. The cold had seeped into her skin and burrowed its way through to her bones. She thought of Charlotte and Luke, home alone, babysat by the television. Guilt threaded through her. "I'd better be going."

"Look. Eames is an old-school detective. By the book and jaded as hell. But I've heard of situations where so-called sensitives were able to assist in cold cases. I'm open to the possibility." He reached inside his coat and handed her his card. "I won't keep you, but if you're willing, I'd like to talk to you again. If you could possibly help me with another case—say the Buckley case—it might go a long way toward lending credence to your skills."

Loretta considered what Detective Pierce said, her interest piqued. "I think I understand."

"Call me, whenever you're ready to talk more."

As Loretta drove back home, she thought of all the missing girls out there. Girls who had once had bright futures, only to have them stolen away. If she could prove herself and help bring peace to Darcy's family—or stop her murderers from killing again—the disturbing visions might prove to be worthwhile, after all.

Chapter 13

"That lady was in my room again last night," Charlotte said, running her spoon through her Malt-O-Meal. Loretta froze, her coffee cup halfway to her lips. A chill danced between her shoulder blades.

"She won't stop crying. It keeps me awake." Charlotte lifted another spoonful of cereal, then let it pour back into the bowl.

"Don't play with your food, darling."

"She says you won't let her in."

"Let her in?"

Charlotte nodded. "She scares me, Mommy."

Loretta's own fear curdled in her stomach. She had to find out why this spirit was haunting Charlotte. Perhaps the new books Dr. Hansen had loaned her might have answers.

Luke came clattering downstairs in his Sunday best, cheeks scrubbed pink, followed by Pete.

"Let's talk about this later," Loretta whispered to Charlotte. "You can stay home from church with me. We'll play dolls."

"You're not going to church?" Pete asked.

Loretta silently cursed Pete's perfect hearing. "No. I have an awful headache. Kept me up half the night." It wasn't a lie. Not entirely. She did have the beginning of a headache, throbbing behind her eyes. This sudden cold snap, likely. But the real reason she wanted to stay home from church was to catch up on her reading. Dr. Hansen's books were a much more seductive draw than Brother Webb's meandering sermons.

Pete sighed and went to the coffeepot. Dark circles sat below his eyes. He'd been out late again. He hadn't gotten into bed until long after midnight. "You missed church two weeks ago, too. Are you getting sick again?"

"No. Only my nerves. You know how it is."

"Yeah? Try living my life for a day, Loretta."

As if he had any idea how difficult it was to be a wife and mother! Loretta bit back her words and worried the skin between her eyes with her fingertip. It wouldn't do to argue with Pete. He always had to be right.

"They're going to hold special healing services at Bethel," Pete said, settling into his favorite chair. "Sort of like a winter revival. They're bringing in an evangelist from Georgia. Reverend Mountjoy. He travels all over the country."

"Oh?"

"Yes. They'll hold the first service for the faculty at the Christmas gala, then another for the students, before holiday break. With all your troubles lately, I'd like you to go."

"I don't know . . . Surely there are people sicker than me."

Pete's eyes scraped over her. "There are lots of ways to be sick, Loretta."

"In that case, maybe you should go, too," she shot back. "Were you at St. Agnes again last night? I didn't realize the meetings ran so late."

Pete set his mug down hard on the table. Coffee splashed over the side. Loretta recognized the gesture for what it was—a warning.

"Who's St. Agnes?" Charlotte piped up.

"No one, honey." Pete stood with an air of finality. "Now go get ready for church."

"Mommy said I could stay home with her!"

"Charlotte," Lucas intoned wearily. "We *have* to go to church. You know the rules."

"I hate church!" Charlotte pushed back from the table and stormed up the stairs.

"This is your fault," Pete said, leaning over Loretta. "You're supposed to be setting an example. Get her under control, Retta. Or I will."

Pete touched his belt buckle and Loretta winced, remembering the time he'd whipped Lucas so hard he had welts on his legs for a week. "I'll make sure she's dressed. You and Luke go on to the car and I'll send her out."

He pressed a kiss to the top of her head. "Good. Get to feeling better. No more missing church. We can't let the Devil get a foothold in this house."

❧

Loretta waited until Pete had pulled out of the driveway before making a fresh pot of coffee. Stronger, the way *she* liked it. She poured herself a mug, then went up to the bedroom. She pulled out the suitcase where she'd hidden Dr. Hansen's books and the yellow tablets she used for writing her stories. She had written five essays about family life in the past month, stealing moments when the kids were busy with homework or by rising early, when the house was quiet. When she was writing, she became someone else—someone with a sparkling, wry wit and a rich social life. Someone she would never be. The escape her writing provided was intoxicating.

As she read over what she'd written, she wondered what Dr. Hansen would think. More and more, Loretta found herself wondering what Dr. Hansen would think. Perhaps she would show him her writing. Someday.

She took the borrowed books from the suitcase, placed her writing tablets inside, and slid the suitcase back under the bed, then curled up against the headboard and considered the two newest books Dr. Hansen had given her. One was about ESP, and the other was a slim volume on channeling spirits. Loretta perused the latter, scanning the table of contents before deciding to read it from cover to cover. There seemed to be several methods for encouraging spirits to communicate. Hypnosis was one of them. Other methods employed the occult. Ouija boards. Pagan rituals. These methods made Loretta nervous. She'd been taught in church that divination was dangerous, although lately she'd begun to question everything she'd been taught. There were so many inconsistencies in her faith, after all. Even in the Bible, where their supposedly loving God could turn on a whim and slaughter thousands in the name of justice.

Loretta turned the pages until she found a chapter on energetic vibrations and employing meditation to make oneself more sensitive to psychic energy. That seemed reasonable. Meditation was close to prayer. The Bible even referred to it as a tool for contemplation.

Perhaps, if Loretta could learn to put herself into a meditative trance, as this book instructed, she could better control her gift, and choose when and how the spirits manifested. If she gained more control over her abilities, then she could direct them in a way that might better help others. She'd been thinking about what Detective Pierce had proposed. She still had his card tucked safely away in her wallet. She'd been tempted to call him, but she was wary. She wouldn't meet with him until she knew for certain she could prove her abilities. She wouldn't make herself look foolish twice. Better yet, if she could connect with the spirit who had been haunting Charlotte, perhaps it would leave her daughter alone.

Dr. Hansen had told her to practice her skills and hone them. This morning provided the perfect opportunity to do just that.

He had used his crystal prism when he hypnotized her. The bright, spinning orb and his soothing voice had quickly put her into an altered state of consciousness. But the book said any object would do—the object was merely a tool to focus the mind and allow the subjective consciousness and extrasensory perception to emerge.

Loretta went to her dresser and opened the second drawer, where she stored her hosiery and scarves. Buried beneath the mounds of silk, she found the small wooden coffret where she kept her mother's jewelry. Inside were three pairs of simple screw-back earrings, a necklace, her mother's wedding band, and a brooch with a translucent amber cabochon. She sat on the floor, her back against the footboard to prevent the dreadful falling sensation she'd experienced before. She cupped the brooch in her hands, took several deep breaths, and fixed her eyes on the oval-shaped stone at its center.

As she stared at the brooch, Loretta visualized the doorway in her mind, as Dr. Hansen had instructed her. At first, the door remained firmly closed, but as Loretta relaxed into her breathing, it began to open, until a sliver of white light shone through. She concentrated on the light until it grew and became all encompassing, bathing her in the most remarkable feeling of warmth and love.

Suddenly, she heard a slight, soft ringing, like a distant bell, and her mother's spirit materialized before her.

"Mama? You're here again?"

"Yes. Always. Just on the other side of that door, Loretta. There are others here, too."

"Others?"

"Yes. I can help you with them if you'd like. Sometimes they feel safer if they have a guide to help them. There's one wanting through now. Can you see her?"

"No."

Mama turned slightly, looking over her shoulder, where a shimmering curtain of white light flickered like the aurora borealis. "It's all right, Darcy. You can come through. My Loretta wants to help you."

Darcy. Loretta's heartbeat ratcheted higher.

There was a shudder within the curtain of light, and then a figure emerged: a young woman, with shining, dark hair and brown eyes. She was crying.

"Darcy? Darcy Hayes? Is that you?" Loretta asked, her voice pitching higher.

The spirit wavered, like the reflection on a pond's surface. She was afraid. Loretta felt her fear like an ache in her own gut.

"It's all right," Loretta gently urged. "No one can hurt you now. Not anymore."

"She's not afraid for herself." Mama reached for Darcy's hand. "Darcy, can you tell her?"

"It's Joan . . ." Darcy said, softly. "Joanie."

Loretta's brow wrinkled. "Who is Joan?"

Darcy shook her head. "My friend. He'll hurt her. Like he hurt me."

Loretta's pulse quickened. "Who hurt you, Darcy?"

"I can't tell you."

"Why not?"

"They know the secret. Joan knows, too."

Darcy bowed her head, her dark veil of hair falling forward as she wept.

Mama reached out to her, laid a hand on her shoulder. "It's all right. You can tell us."

"I can't. Tell Joan to leave. Before he hurts her."

"Where is Joan?"

"Ashley."

"Is that her last name?"

"I'm going now." Darcy's spirit flickered and then faded from view.

"Wait!" Loretta cried, reaching out.

". . . can't."

Darcy disappeared, but Mama remained, her eyes sorrowful. "The new ones . . . they aren't very strong yet. It takes time for them to accept that they've passed, especially if it happened suddenly. She'll likely come through again, but it might be a while. Takes a lot of energy to communicate with the living. She's been going to Charlotte instead, because children have an easier time seeing us and hearing us."

The weeping lady in Charlotte's room. It was Darcy.

"She's frightening Charlotte."

"I know. She understands that now. She heard you and Charlotte talking this morning. Darcy was just trying to find a way to get through. She's desperate. Charlotte has your gifts, too, Retta. So does Luke."

Loretta thought of Luke's disturbing drawings. Was this the way *his* abilities manifested?

"Do you know who hurt Darcy, Mama?"

"No."

Frustration ebbed inside Loretta. "Joan Ashley. I have no idea who that is, nor how I should find her."

"In time, Loretta. You're new to this, too. Have patience."

"But if he's going to kill again, we may not have much time!"

A harsh banging intruded on Loretta's consciousness. She jolted out of her trance. Heavy footsteps echoed down the hall. The bedroom door flew open. Pete stood there, staring down at her. "Who were you talking to just now?"

Loretta shook her head, stunned. Her fingers closed over the brooch, tightening until the metal clasp bit her palm. "You're home. I thought you went to church."

"We did. We've been gone all morning. It's eleven thirty."

"Really? Goodness." She unfolded her cramped legs and stood. Perhaps time slowed down, somehow, when she was in that altered state of consciousness. It had seemed like only a few minutes. Or perhaps she'd merely gone to sleep and dreamed it all.

"What were you doing down there?"

"I was just going through my dresser drawers. Sorting some of Mama's old things. I suppose I dozed off here. You must have heard me talking in my sleep." She placed the brooch back in its box and closed the drawer.

"Are you feeling better?"

"Yes, I am. The nap did me a world of good."

Pete frowned, his eyes landing on something over her shoulder. "Were you reading?"

The books. Oh God. The books.

Her mouth went dry as Pete crossed the room and picked them up. Stupid. So stupid. She should have put them away before she went into the trance. It was too late now.

"What is this, Loretta?" He lifted the book she'd been reading, flipping through the pages. "Occult rituals? Summoning spirits?" He threw the book on the mattress like it was a hot coal. Loretta picked it up, held it protectively against her chest.

"Is this what you've been doing while I've been gone?" he demanded, his voice rising as he came toward her. "You never read when you have a headache. You weren't sick this morning, were you?"

"Pete, please. The children can hear us." She backed against the dresser, her heart hammering.

"I cannot believe you've brought books on witchcraft into this house, Loretta!"

"It's not witchcraft," she said, willing her voice to stay calm. "One of them even talks about Jesus. About his healing ministry. There are pages and pages at the end."

"Where did you get these? Did someone give them to you?" He wrenched the book from her grasp and opened it. His eyes landed on the bookplate pasted to the inside cover, engraved with Dr. Hansen's name. Loretta's gut filled with lead. "Curtis Hansen. Who is this?"

"He's a doctor. The psychologist I told you about."

Realization dawned behind Pete's eyes. "The one I didn't want you to see." His jaw clenched. "You've been going behind my back."

"Only because he's been helping me!"

Pete turned away from her. He shook with anger. Loretta steeled herself for what was to come, her body tense as a coiled spring. "I'm sorry I lied, Pete. I am. But he's helping me to understand myself. Can't you see I've been happier? That *we've* been happier?"

"How often do you see him?" Pete's voice was preternaturally low. Almost a growl, as if he were speaking through clenched teeth.

"Once a week."

Pete turned, his breath huffing as he closed the distance between them. He shook the book in her face. She flinched as the corner grazed her cheek. "These books? They're of the Devil, Loretta. They're evil. And this man—this Dr. Hansen—is his instrument."

"No. He's a good man. A wise man. He's helping me . . . he's helping me to understand my gift."

"Your *gift*?"

"Yes. My gift. The visions. The voices. I tried telling you, and you told me they weren't real. But they are, Pete. They are! At first, I was afraid of them. But Dr. Hansen is helping me to understand they aren't anything to fear. I can use my gift to help people. To solve crimes, even. There's a detective—"

Pete slammed his hand against the wall next to the dresser, sending the picture frames rattling. One fell—Charlotte's baby portrait—and shattered. Loretta whimpered and sank to her knees, as if making herself smaller might cause him to stop. "Please don't."

Pete knelt next to her, grasped her wrists, and pulled her hands from her face. "You're never to see that man again. Do you hear me?"

"But he's helping me! It doesn't even cost anything."

"So, he sees you for free." Pete laughed. A drop of spittle landed on Loretta's forehead. He released her wrists. "And I'm supposed to believe he wants nothing in return? Maybe I need to pay your doctor friend a visit."

Pete's implication was clear. "No! It's not like that. He's married. He would never . . ." Loretta fought desperately for the right words to placate Pete. Her brain was on fire with frustration. "I'm helping him with his research. He's writing a book."

"No more, Loretta. No more." He picked up the volume on channeling spirits from the floor, stalked over to the bed, and gathered the other books she'd left there.

"What are you doing?" Loretta scrambled to her feet.

"Making sure you never read these again."

Loretta ran to him, pulled on his arms, trying to pry the books free. He pushed her, sending her sprawling. Her head smacked against the footboard so hard stars exploded behind her eyes. Loretta gasped and put a hand to her head. It was the first time, in all their arguments, that he had ever hurt her. He'd gotten close enough before—throwing things, punching walls—but *this* had been intentional.

Pete shook his head at her in disgust and walked out. Loretta shakily pulled herself back to her feet. Her ears rang as she made her way down the stairs, gripping the banister for balance. When she reached the downstairs hall, she found Lucas standing there, still in his church clothes, his eyes wide. "What's going on? Why is Dad so mad?"

"I don't know, honey. Where did he go?"

"He went outside. Out back."

Loretta made her way to the back door and opened it, her head pounding. The piercing cold air hit her, full in the face, sobering her delirium. Pete was near the fence row, piling sticks and dry leaves into a heap. She saw no sign of the books, but knew they had to be somewhere in the pile. He was going to burn them.

She flung herself down the porch steps, just as Pete touched a match to the pile. A plume of smoke rose as the fire caught. Everything slowed down. "No!" Loretta screamed. She ran toward Pete. "Those aren't yours! They aren't yours to burn!"

Rage poured over her like a cloak of ice. She hurtled herself at the fire, stomping and kicking in a futile attempt to put it out. Heat flared around her knees. Too late, she realized her skirt was on fire.

Pete charged her and wrestled her to the cold ground, rolling with her to snuff out the burning fabric. "You little idiot!"

"How could you!" Loretta cried, shoving against Pete's chest.

"I'm trying to protect you!" Pete said, pulling her to her feet.

"I don't need protecting! They're just books!"

"You might think you're just reading a book, but the Devil lies in wait, Loretta. Watching for weakness. Books like these change your mind about things, make you turn your back on God."

"It's not like that. I still have my faith! Can't you see that? I have it now, more than I ever did before. God is calling me, Pete." Loretta raised her hands in supplication.

"You're bleeding."

"What?"

"Your hand. You must have hurt yourself."

Loretta looked down. At the center of her right palm, blood had pooled and now ran down her arm. "Oh." She must have been clutching Mama's brooch harder than she realized. She hid her hand in her skirt pocket. Her head pulsed like a drum. She cast an eye to the small bonfire, where Dr. Hansen's books were burning to ash. "You hurt me. Upstairs. If you'd pushed me any harder . . ."

"I didn't push you. You fell. You shouldn't have lied to me about seeing that doctor, Loretta. It makes me wonder what else you've been up to."

"You *did* push me! And I only lied because you lord over me! You manage every bit of our lives. Our money. My time. Even my body and what I wear on it! My sessions with Dr. Hansen were for me, Pete. Me. Don't you think I should have one thing in this life that's only for me?"

"You're being selfish." Pete motioned to the house. Charlotte and Lucas stood watching them through the screen door. Charlotte was crying. "Look at the children. What about them?"

Loretta closed her eyes, gathered her arms about herself to control her seething. Of course he'd use the children as leverage. Of course he would. "I didn't want this. I didn't want any of this." She turned and walked back to the house.

Inside, the walls seemed to convulse around her. The claustrophobic feeling grew as she made her way down the hall. The kids had gone upstairs. She could hear Charlotte crying. She would go up in a moment—comfort them both. But for now, she needed to be alone.

Loretta went into the kitchen. She leaned over the sink, with its perpetual dirty dishes, elbows locked as she clutched the counter and looked up at the ceiling. The crack there had grown longer just since that morning, and joined with the crack above the window, twisting together like a river through the plaster.

The faint scent of smoke drifted from her clothing as she began sorting the dishes.

He had burned her books.

Hot tears spilled from the corners of her eyes. She heard Pete open the back door. His steps creaked across the floor. She turned to face him and put up her hand as he came toward her. "I'm tired, Pete. Leave me alone, please."

"Loretta—"

"I said, I'm *tired*," she growled through clenched teeth. The anger flowed out from her center and flooded her limbs with incandescent rage. If he came any closer, she might hit him.

"Don't talk to me that way. You know better."

"And what about the way you talk to me?" Loretta's hands fisted. The dirty dishes rattled in the sink. "You don't want a wife, Pete. You want a dog. I'm tired of it."

Pete's face hardened. He crossed the narrow space between them, grasped her by the wrist, and twisted. She cried out in pain. He pressed her hips against the counter, trapping her. His breath was hot on her face. "What? You thinking about leaving me, Loretta?" His hand tightened on her arm. "I've been good to you. You know I have. You think anyone else will treat you better?"

Loretta trembled. He could snap her wrist, easily, with just a twist of his hand. Behind her, the dishes rattled again.

"I've spoiled you. That's the problem."

"Stop, Pete, please." She tried to wrench away from him, but he held her fast. She gasped as the counter dug into her lower back. He pressed his hips against her. He was hard. Their fight had excited him. Revulsion crept up her throat. "No. Not here." She pushed against him. "What if the children come down?"

"Turn around." Pete reached behind her, turned on the faucet. "Do the dishes."

"No."

"Turn around, Loretta."

Loretta slowly turned. She fixed her eyes on the water running from the tap. She didn't have her diaphragm in. If he did this to her here, like this, she might get pregnant. She heard Pete fumbling with his zipper, then felt the heavy press of him behind her as he lifted her skirt. His fingers tore at her stocking clasps as he tried to undo them from her girdle. "Dammit."

"Can't we go upstairs?"

"Just do the dishes and hush up."

Loretta braced herself on the edge of the sink, shaking with anger and fear as her stocking clasps finally gave way, betraying her. Pete nudged her legs apart. Rage boiled inside her as he rutted against her, trying to claim her body in anger and dominance instead of love.

In the sink, one of the faceted orange juice glasses caught the light. Loretta focused her eyes on that point of light and willed her mind somewhere else. Anywhere but here. Suddenly, the glass fell against the other dishes and shattered.

Pete continued moving against her. "Can't you be more careful?" he panted in her ear.

"I didn't do anything."

Loretta looked at the broken glass. *Had* she done that? She hadn't been able to move the objects on Dr. Hansen's desk, but perhaps . . .

A loud crash echoed through the kitchen. "What in the hell?" Pete said, releasing her. Loretta quickly smoothed her skirt over her hips and turned to see what had caused the commotion.

Two china plates lay broken on the floor, their remains strewn across the linoleum. Somehow, they'd fallen from the hutch. As Loretta watched, three more followed suit, tipping forward and tumbling over the edge of the top shelf, one after another, as if knocked by an unseen hand.

"What the hell?" Pete said again. "What did you—"

"Wasn't me." Loretta faced Pete, her eyes blazing. "Must have been an earthquake. I hear we have those sometimes." She considered his slack-jawed face. His crooked glasses. His fading erection. From somewhere, a bubble of joy floated up. She began laughing. She laughed so hard she doubled over with it, clutching her belly, her woolen stockings pooling around her knees.

"Mommy, what's so funny?" Charlotte's voice floated down the stairs.

"You're crazy, Loretta. You know that?" Pete hastily zipped his pants, his face flushed with embarrassment.

"*I'm* crazy." Loretta laughed. "I didn't do a thing." She laughed for joy, there in the kitchen, with a broken pile of blue and white china on the floor and the sink overflowing with water.

Chapter 14

The jangle of car keys woke Loretta. "I'm taking the car."

Loretta lifted her head from the pillow. Pete's reflection glowered at her from her vanity mirror. He pocketed the keys and shrugged on his jacket.

She sat up, swinging her feet onto the floor. Her head swam. The radiator *ticktickticked* like a bomb. "I can drive you to work. Just give me a moment to get dressed."

"No." Pete's lips thinned. "I don't think so."

Realization dawned on Loretta. He was *taking* the car. Not just to work. But *from* her.

"But when we bought the car—"

"When *I* bought it."

Loretta started to speak and stopped herself. He was right. He had bought it. It was his. Just like this house. She was no more than a servile, flinching maid charged with taking care of all the things Pete's money had bought them. Nothing belonged to her.

"I'm only taking the car for your own good. That killer is still on the loose. Until he's caught, I don't want you leaving this house, unless it's to walk the kids to and from the bus stop."

"That's not why you're doing this. We both know it. It's because you don't trust me."

"Well." He gave a tilted smile, walked to her side, and kissed her on the head. "I have a full day. I need to go."

After he'd gone, dread and desperation settled in Loretta's gut like a stone. No more visits to Dr. Hansen. No more trips to the five-and-dime. No more long drives around town, just to listen to music and feel the wind on her face. Even Daddy, strict as he was, had let her drive. Had taught her first on the tractor, and then on his truck.

In time, perhaps Pete would relent. In time, perhaps she could soften his ire with her body, with her good-wife behavior. But for now, she was trapped. The domestic monotony had her skin crawling with anxiety. The same sounds, over and over. The red clock on the kitchen wall, with its half-hitch hesitation every five seconds. The milkman's knock on the window each Friday at ten. (Why did he knock on the window instead of the door? It startled her so.) The sharp, bright way the sun shone through the windows right before collapsing into the bleak, shadowed houses across the street.

Pete had taken away the one salve for the sameness in her life. But she'd *let* him take everything over the years, in the name of security. Her education. Her books. The car. Her freedom.

Loretta stood on weak, shaky legs and went to the vanity. She undid her long braid and drew the brush through her waist-length hair, wincing as it snarled in the tangles. She'd wanted to cut it many times. But Pete had forbidden that, too. *Your hair is your glory,* he said.

Her head still pounded. The morning light hurt her eyes. Like as not, Pete had given her a concussion when he'd pushed her during their argument. But he refused to admit he'd pushed her. Refused to take her to the doctor. It was probably for the best. They'd ask too many questions.

Loretta wound her hair back into the prim bun she always wore, pinned it into place, and stood. She shed her flannel nightgown and looked at herself in the mirror. The old scars remained, taunting her. She skimmed her fingers across her belly, feeling their cross-stitching.

She had chosen her belly for two reasons: her clothes would hide the marks, and her belly was where the bad feeling had started. By cutting her skin, she had foolishly hoped, as a girl of twelve, that she might cut it out. Might cut through the guilt. Might cut through the numbness and feel something other than her heavy, smothering grief. The brief, sharp pain had centered her. The temporary high had sustained her. Had kept her alive. The cutting had been a balm for Daddy's neglect and her loneliness. The only other person who had ever seen the marks was the doctor who had delivered Luke and Charlotte. He'd asked her about them once, as he guided his stethoscope over her skin, but she claimed she'd fallen through a broken window as a girl, and that was the end of things.

Loretta closed her eyes. The temptation was still there, even now. Especially now. To take anything sharp—a safety pin, a nail file, even the tines of a fork, and bring a brief rush of relief. She'd done it just the other day, after all, with the brooch. Without even realizing what she was doing.

She shook off her bad memories and dressed. She was supposed to see Dr. Hansen on Thursday.

She longed to talk to him—to tell him about her vision of Darcy, as well as what had happened in the kitchen, with the broken dishes. She had no explanation for it, and no psychokinetic abilities that she knew of, but if she had actually made the plates crash to the floor, it was terrifying. If she didn't learn to control it, she might accidentally hurt the children. She wished she'd had more time to read about such things in Dr. Hansen's books. But the books were now nothing but ash. Dr. Hansen deserved to know about that, too.

She went downstairs to call Barbara, her feet heavy with the finality of it all. When she picked up the receiver, she could hear someone on their party line, laughing and chattering away. Loretta hung up. She'd wait thirty minutes and try again.

She turned on the TV, parted the curtains on the same scene she saw every day, and took up her knitting to pass the time. But she couldn't concentrate. Her mind was addled by thoughts of Darcy and Dora, their faces alternating on a loop. Dora's distress over Darcy was heartbreaking. And then there was Darcy's friend, the mysterious Joan Ashley. Who was she? Did she know she was in danger? Without Dr. Hansen's guidance, Loretta felt powerless to help any of them. She was only just beginning to understand the depth of her abilities and how to direct them. Everything was such a mess now. Because of Pete.

After she had knitted a few rows and torn them out again when she lost count of her stitches, she went back to the phone. This time, the line was blessedly quiet. She quickly dialed Dr. Hansen's number. Barbara answered, her warm, friendly voice sending a bittersweet twinge of longing through Loretta. This would likely be the last time they'd ever speak.

"Hello?" Barbara prompted.

"Yes, good morning, Barbara. It's Loretta. Davenport. I'm afraid I'll have to cancel my session with Dr. Hansen."

"But it's only Monday. Are you sick?"

Loretta paused. It would be an easy lie to tell Barbara that she was ill. But then, what of next week and the week after? She couldn't keep canceling. Dr. Hansen deserved to know the truth. None of her wishful thinking would change reality.

"I can't see Dr. Hansen anymore." She pushed the words out in a rush.

"What? Why not?" Barbara paused for a moment. "Is something the matter, Loretta?"

"I . . . I had an argument with my husband. He didn't know I'd been seeing Dr. Hansen." Loretta's voice wavered. "Well, he found out. Now he's taken the car from me."

"I see. Oh dear. Could you hold for a moment? Dr. Hansen just finished with his patient, and I'd like to speak with him."

"Yes, I can wait."

Barbara put down the receiver. Loretta heard muffled voices in the background. One of them was Dr. Hansen's—though she couldn't make out any words, she could sense his agitation. He was upset.

She heard a click. Loretta stiffened. One of the neighbors had picked up on their party line. She cleared her throat. "Hello?" she said. "I'm on a call. I'll be off shortly."

Silence followed.

"Hello?" she said again.

"Loretta?" It was only Barbara. Loretta let out a sigh of relief.

"Yes?"

"I've spoken to Dr. Hansen. We've found a solution if you're willing."

Loretta's heartbeat picked up. "A solution?"

"Yes. I'll come pick you up myself."

Loretta's breath left her lungs. The thought was thrilling. But dangerously so. "You can't come to the house. The neighbors are nosy, and if Pete ever finds out . . ."

If Pete ever found out, she would pay dearly.

"I've thought of all that. I won't pick you up at your house. I can meet you at the closest intersection. Would that work? Is it walkable?"

Loretta's pulse quickened. "Yes."

"You do want to continue your work with Dr. Hansen, don't you?"

"Of course!"

"It's settled, then!" Barbara's voice was chipper, resolute. "Tell me the closest intersection and I'll meet you there at twelve thirty on Thursday."

"State and Mt. Vernon."

"It's a date, dear."

On Thursday, Loretta stepped outside, into the bracing air. The temperatures had risen slightly after last week's ice storm, but it was still cold for November. She glanced furtively at Phyllis's house as she passed. The curtains were drawn and Phyllis's car was gone. Good. She'd come up with an excuse if Phyllis questioned her about where she was going—a student/teacher conference at the school—but she was relieved she wouldn't have to lie.

She walked to the corner at a brisk pace, bundled in her coat and scarf. She checked her wristwatch when she got to the corner. Twelve twenty-eight.

At twelve thirty on the nose, a sleek black Cadillac Eldorado pulled up to the curb. Barbara emerged from the driver's side, her blonde hair wrapped in a fuchsia scarf. "Go ahead and get in, dear. It's cold."

Loretta opened the passenger door and slipped inside, arranging her coat over the seat and perching her pocketbook on her lap. The car smelled of rich, oiled leather and Barbara's perfume. Loretta couldn't resist pressing her hand to the lavish burlwood trim on the dash.

"It's nice, isn't it? This is Curt's car," Barbara said, folding her long limbs into the vehicle. "So glad you're still coming." Barbara smiled at her. "We were really worried about you when we heard what had happened. Curt—Dr. Hansen—especially."

"I'm sorry to be such a bother."

"You're not a bother at all, Loretta. Don't ever think that." Barbara pressed her hand to Loretta's quickly, then put the car in gear.

They drove across town, the Cadillac riding like silk over the pavement. Barbara was a confident and courteous driver, her perfectly manicured hands elegantly guiding the car through turns and smoothly coming to a stop at intersections. Loretta already missed driving so.

"I didn't learn to drive until five years ago," Barbara said, as if reading Loretta's mind. "After my divorce. When I heard what your husband had done, it reminded me of what my husband did to me. He never let me learn to drive."

"I'm sorry."

"He was controlling. In many ways." Barbara shook her head. "I married him when I was only eighteen. The summer after my parents had my coming-out party. My and Curt's parents—they were very old world, as you've probably gathered from the house. All potted ferns and walnut paneling. Our grandmother claimed to have descended from Norwegian royalty." Barbara laughed. "Just a silly story she invented to impress the Myrna Grove Junior League."

Loretta found Barbara's past fascinating. She'd never met a divorcée. She was surprised that this vibrant, glamorous woman had experienced heartache and mistreatment. "How long were you married?"

"Eight long, miserable years." Barbara's scarlet lips drew together tightly. "He finally divorced me when he found out I was having an affair."

Loretta sat in stunned silence.

"He couldn't even look at me after that. It was such a relief to sign those papers. At first, I thought my life was over. But it was just beginning. My parents were disappointed, of course. Once I told them some of the things he'd done to me, though, they were relieved as well. There are worse things than divorce. I'm just thankful we never had children."

Loretta looked away. "Yes. Children make everything more complicated. A person can feel as if they have to make things work. For the children."

They pulled up to a stoplight, and Barbara turned to Loretta, fixing her with her cool Grace Kelly gaze. "Pardon me if I'm speaking out of turn, Loretta, but does it really help the children to stay in an unhappy marriage? Won't they just repeat the same sort of thing when they have a family of their own?"

Loretta sat back in her seat. It was as if Barbara had punched her in the stomach. A brief flare of defensiveness rose up, but she throttled it back. Because Barbara was right. Already, she could see some of her own traits mirrored in Luke. His submissiveness. How he cowered under

Pete's temper. His need to protect her. A child shouldn't feel the need to protect his own mother. She should be protecting *him*. And the thought of someone hurting Charlotte the way that Pete had hurt Loretta on Sunday sickened her. She swallowed to push back the stinging sensation in her throat. "I suppose you're right."

"I realize I don't know you that well, and so this may be awfully bold of me to say. But you look like a whipped dog, with your tail tucked beneath your legs, Loretta. I don't mean that unkindly. I only know because I was once a whipped dog, too. Do you have any friends? Anyone you could stay with, should you need to leave?"

Loretta closed her eyes. "I can't leave, even if I wanted to. I don't have enough money. I've been trying to save as much as I can. Skimming here and there. If I left, I'd need to find work. But there's nothing I'm good at. I'm just a housewife. I have no real skills."

"You are not *just* a housewife." Barbara's tone softened. "If worse comes to worst, you can come stay with me. Vera won't mind at all. She works nights, and sleeps most of the day."

"Vera?"

"My friend. We live together."

"That must be nice. Living with another woman. I'm sure things are neat as a pin."

"They are. It's lovely." Barbara grew quiet. A faint blush colored her cheek. "Well. We're almost there." The light changed, and Barbara turned left onto Walnut. As they passed the stately Victorian homes lining the street, Loretta wondered about the families who lived inside them. She wondered whether money and comfort had brought them happiness, or if they suffered in old-world marriages like Barbara's. How lucky Dr. Hansen's wife was! Wealth, comfort, and a husband who surely treated her like a queen. It was hard for Loretta not to be envious. As they neared Dr. Hansen's house, her curiosity about his marriage got the best of her.

"What about Dr. Hansen?" she asked. "He married happily, I hope."

Barbara nodded. "Curt and Esther were lucky. She was from an old Myrna Grove family, so she ticked all the right boxes with our family. But they genuinely fell in love with one another. They met one summer when Curt was home from college."

"I've never seen her at the house. Does she work?"

"No." Barbara cleared her throat delicately. "I don't think he would mind my telling you. She's no longer alive. She died years ago. In France. She was away on a long holiday when it happened. A train derailed. Their son died in the accident, too."

Loretta kept herself from gasping, but only just. So he was a widower. That's why the ring but no wife. And the son . . . she couldn't imagine the depths of such grief. "How terrible. I'd no idea."

"Yes. It was awful. But Curt keeps it hidden from his patients. He doesn't want them to know."

"Why?"

"Because patients occasionally fall in love with their doctors, dear. It would be unprofessional if they ever thought he might reciprocate their feelings."

"I suppose you're right." Loretta's cheeks suddenly flamed. She cranked down the window and let in a brief scream of cold air. She wondered what kind of woman Esther Hansen had been. Was she beautiful? An angelic presence who still held dominion over Dr. Hansen's home and heart? And the little boy . . . how heartbreaking. She wanted to ask Barbara more, but it felt intrusive, so she quietly inspected the scratches on her wedding band instead.

A few minutes later, Barbara pulled into the drive. Loretta checked her reflection in her pocketbook mirror before getting out of the car. She looked pale, her features wan. She wished she had some lipstick— anything to brighten her face. With a resigned sigh, she joined Barbara at the side entrance.

"Dr. Hansen's cleared his calendar for the rest of the day, Loretta. You can stay as long as you'd like."

"That's generous."

"Well, as I said, he values the work the two of you have been doing. Very much."

Loretta's heart lifted. "I'm happy to hear that."

She followed Barbara inside, reveling in the house's comforting warmth. Dr. Hansen came out of his office to greet them, Oliver wending around his ankles. His face lit up in a genuine smile, his eyes crinkling at the corners in a way that made Loretta's pulse quicken. "I'm so glad you're here," he said. "I have something I'm excited to share with you, Loretta."

"Oh?"

"Come in. Get settled. Barbara, can you bring us some tea?"

"Certainly," Barbara said. "Anything else?"

"Are you hungry, Loretta?"

"I'm famished."

"Perhaps two of those blueberry scones. Thank you, Barb."

Dr. Hansen motioned Loretta into his office. He shut the door with a gentle click and turned to her, his cheerful demeanor suddenly gone sober. "I have to tell you something. And I want you to listen to me as a friend and someone who cares for you very much."

A friend? He considered her a friend. "Yes?"

"I'm concerned about your well-being, Loretta. I have been for weeks. But as I'm not seeing you as a patient, I didn't want to overstep my bounds. Your husband's behavior is concerning." Dr. Hansen held her eyes. His tone was gentle, yet firm. "When Barbara told me what he'd done—taking the car and forbidding you to come here—it made me quite upset. I've been worried about something like this happening. When you told me you were afraid to tell him about our sessions, that said more about your marriage than you could ever imagine."

"It's not that bad, Doctor. We've had these kinds of arguments before."

"I'm sure you have. But what's happening at your home isn't at all normal, or good, and you need to know that. Things only seem normal because you're used to them and don't know any different."

Loretta let out her breath. "Barbara told me about her husband. What he did."

"Yes. Her situation, and yours, are not unique. I've seen this sort of thing over and over with my patients. Dissatisfied wives, kept under their husbands' thumbs. First, it begins with control—finances, freedom, time. Then it gets more extreme. It can become deadly, Loretta. You should know that. I lost a patient last year to spousal battery. I don't want that to happen to you."

"Our argument started when he found your books. He burned them."

"Did he?"

"Yes."

Dr. Hansen loosened his tie and unbuttoned his collar. He went to the window, looked out at the dormant gardens. Loretta had the urge to go to him, to rest her hand on his back, to lean into him. Instead, she stood there awkwardly in the middle of his study.

"I can pay for them . . ." she said, wringing her hands. "I'm sorry."

"You say that a lot. Do you realize that?"

"What?"

"I'm sorry."

"Oh. I never realized."

"It's not your fault he burned the books." Dr. Hansen turned to her. "You don't need to pay for them, but most importantly, you don't need to fear me, Loretta. You don't have to soften me with apologies or be meek and deferential. You're safe here. Always."

A soft knock came at the door, and Barbara pushed through with a tray loaded with pastries and a tea service. She set it on the table in front of the hearth and left them.

Loretta sat in her usual wingback chair, poured herself a cup of tea, then added milk and sugar. Her wrist shook as she lifted the teacup to her mouth. "I was petrified when he did that. When he burned the books. He was so angry. He's always had a temper. And I found out recently that he's been drinking again and hiding it from me."

"I see."

"I still hope that he might change—that we might be able to make things work. He's been going to AA."

"Alcoholics Anonymous has helped many people." Dr. Hansen joined her in front of the fire, seating himself in the chair across from hers. "One of my mentors at Duke—J. B. Rhine—is a close friend of the founder. It's a wonderful organization."

"I've heard that." Loretta shook her head. "I hope it helps him. I feel so sorry for Pete. His father was a minister but drank as well. Pete poured himself into religion to cope with it all."

"That's understandable. One addiction is often replaced by another. It may be a long road, Loretta. Addiction is a complex issue. His recovery could take years. He may have relapses. It's an issue with the mind and the body. The underlying causes must be addressed."

"I understand."

"In the meantime, you need to protect yourself. If he gets violent with you or the children, you must leave. Immediately. You can stay with Barbara, or in my guesthouse. It needs some repairs and a good cleaning out, but there's plenty of room for you and the children there."

Loretta looked down, remembered the fear she'd felt when Pete shoved her. She couldn't tell Dr. Hansen about that. Or about Pete forcing himself on her, after. He'd tell her she needed to leave. And she wasn't ready. She needed time. And there was still hope. If Pete followed through on what he learned in AA, they could be happy again. If she were calm, and patient, and understanding . . .

"Do you have money?" Dr. Hansen asked gently.

"A little. I've been able to skim a bit from our grocery budget every week. He doesn't know about that."

"Good."

"I can't keep doing that, though. Now that he's taking me to do the shopping, he's the one writing the checks."

"I see. You need another way to make money, then, in a way he won't know about."

"I don't have any skills, Doctor."

"Please, I wish you'd call me Curt or Curtis, Loretta. I'm not seeing you as a patient, after all." He smiled at her, and Loretta's world tilted. She couldn't imagine calling him by his first name. It felt too intimate. Curt. It was such a strong, abrupt name for such a gentle man. She preferred Dr. Hansen.

"And you absolutely have skills. What about your writing? Have you been doing any of that?"

"A little." Loretta thought of the yellow legal pads hidden in the suitcase under her bed. At least she had left her writing there on the morning he found the books, or her work would have likely gone into the fire as well. "Nothing much. Just essays about family life."

"Have you considered submitting them anywhere?"

Loretta laughed. "They're not that good. No one would want to read them."

"You might be surprised."

"I don't have a typewriter. They're handwritten. I'd need to type them in order to send them out, and I haven't the first idea who would want to publish them."

Dr. Hansen smiled cheekily and stood. "I can solve one of those problems." He went to a cabinet behind his desk and rummaged around. A few moments later, he hefted an ancient Remington typewriter onto the desk with a grunt. Ollie startled at the sound, flattening his tufted ears. "Here we are. It'll need a new ribbon and a few of the keys have to be struck with great determination, but it works."

Loretta grinned. "Well."

"No more excuses, then. By next week, you'll have submitted your work. Somewhere. Anywhere." Dr. Hansen came around his desk, took off his glasses to polish them, and then sat across from her again. "And now, for what I was excited to tell you about. A friend called me last week. Said he'd met you."

Loretta brightened. "Was it that detective?"

"Yes. Steven Pierce. He said you'd come to the station, with Darcy Hayes's sister."

"I did. Dora came to my house after our last session. She sought me out, because of something I said to her mother at Darcy's vigil." Loretta shrugged. "I don't think I helped much at all. The detective in charge of Darcy's case didn't believe me, and Dora ended up even more upset than she was before."

"Detective Pierce was intrigued by you. He'd like to come to one of our sessions. Observe our work. Would you be all right with that?"

"Of course. I want to help. I'm just not sure how I can. And besides all that, I'm afraid Darcy's killers may strike again."

"Oh?"

"I put myself into a meditative state, as you did with me last week. During my trance, I had another visitation from my mother . . . and Darcy's spirit." Loretta shook her head. "She was very frightened. She kept saying another girl's name. Joan. She said *he* would do the same thing to her. But there are two men, not just one. I've seen that very clearly, in my visions."

"Perhaps one of them is the killer, and the other the accomplice."

Loretta nodded excitedly. "That would make sense. Darcy said something about them both knowing the secret. And that they were ashamed."

Dr. Hansen thought for a moment. "It may have been an accident. Her death. Shame is a powerful impetus for people to cover up their mistakes. To hide things."

"She was still alive when she was with the killers. In my visions, she's being buried alive. She's conscious—she knows what's happening. But she can't move. Or speak. Dora saw the coroner's report. She wasn't supposed to see it. Darcy smothered to death. She asphyxiated. But the report also said there were bruises—contusions—all over her body. And several broken bones."

"It sounds like a car accident. It would make sense, given where she disappeared."

Loretta sat up, her heart pounding. "Yes! It would. Maybe the murderer and his accomplice hit her when she was walking to her aunt's house. It's a dark, curving stretch of road. And then, to cover things up, they buried her, not realizing she was still alive."

Dr. Hansen smiled. "You'd make a better detective than half the police force, Loretta."

Loretta ducked her head. "Oh, I don't know about that. I just want to find answers. Dora and her family deserve them."

"You will," he said gently. "With your gifts, it's only a matter of time."

"I hope so."

"So it's all right if I tell Detective Pierce to come next week?"

"Yes. He seemed sincere. He mentioned I might help him with another disappearance."

Dr. Hansen nodded. "Paula Buckley. There are several loose ends with her case. Detective Pierce sought me out because he'd heard about my research—read an article I wrote about psychic forensics. He hoped I might know a medium who could help with Paula's case. At that time, the only true medium I had ever met was half a world away." He leaned forward, fixing Loretta with his gaze. "And then, here you come. Enlivening my work and my life with new meaning."

Heat crawled up Loretta's neck, under her prim collar. The way he looked at her, she felt she could do anything. That there was more to her boring, tedious life. It was almost like the lavender haze of falling in love, this purpose. This calling. And to know that it meant the same to him . . .

She remembered what Barbara said about patients falling in love with their doctors. This wasn't that. It was admiration, mutual respect, a meeting of minds.

Loretta cleared her throat. Shook herself free of her silly thoughts.

"Are you all right, Loretta?"

"I'll be fine. Just a little warm." She tugged at her sweater and reached for her tea, gulping the tepid liquid down.

"What I mean to say is, will you be all right at home?"

Loretta's spirit plummeted from its lofty height. She had to go home again, didn't she? Had to leave this room, with its comforting velvet furniture and its soft, warm light. Had to leave the man who made her feel safer than any other person had in a very long time.

"I'll be fine," she reassured him, with a tight smile. "I have to be."

Chapter 15

"Why are you still in bed?"

Loretta rolled over, blinking. Pete stood over her, arms crossed. Rain beat a steady tattoo on the roof. "I'm tired, Pete. Leave me alone."

"It's Sunday. Church is in an hour."

"I'm not going. I don't feel well."

"You didn't feel well last week, either. We both know that was a lie." Pete crouched next to the bed. The whites of his eyes were bloodshot. He hadn't been sleeping. Or he'd been drinking again, late at night, after she and the kids had gone to bed. Just like the old days. Things had begun to slide downhill again, as they always did. Pete's good moods had gone, fast as a flash of lightning. Every morning that week, Loretta had combed through her words like wool, choosing them carefully to avoid his anger. Today, avoiding his anger meant going to church.

Loretta gave a resigned sigh and slowly sat up, putting a hand to her sleep-swollen face. "Give me a moment. Please. I'll come down in a bit."

"All right. But be snappy about it, Retta." He sent a sharp look over his shoulder as he shut the door.

Loretta stretched, considered her closet and the drab clothes therein. She hurriedly dressed, her body rebelling against the chill in the room. Pete had turned the boiler down again to save money. The house was freezing.

All three were already outside, in the car, by the time she made it downstairs. Loretta switched off the lights, donned her coat, and plucked her pocketbook from the sofa. Pete honked the horn.

"I'm coming, dammit," she muttered.

She had barely seated herself in the car before Pete put it into gear. She glanced at the clock on the dash. Nine forty-two. The church was only ten minutes away. They had plenty of time before the service. But not for Pete—he liked to be there at least thirty minutes early to glad-hand with the elders and the other deacons.

By the time they arrived, the rain had stopped, and the congregants were milling around the entrance, their breath clouding the air as they exchanged smiles and handshakes. Loretta waited for Pete to open her car door. He only ever acted the gentleman in public. To make a show of things. *Such a good husband,* she imagined the elderly ladies of Myrna Grove Assembly whispering whenever Pete helped her with her coat or offered her his arm. *A true gentleman.*

Inside, a blast of organ music greeted them. Loretta took Charlotte's hand and led her to her Sunday school classroom. Luke preferred sitting with them in the main sanctuary and went with Pete to take their usual place near the front.

Loretta was making her way back down the hall when she caught a glimpse of Gladys McAndrews near the coat room. She was crying, dabbing at her heavily mascaraed eyes with a tissue. Her husband—Earl—was nowhere in sight. Gladys took a seat on one of the padded benches lining the church foyer. Her usually perfect bottle-blonde bouffant was flat on one side, as if she'd just gotten up from lying down. She raised her head as Loretta crossed the foyer.

"Are you having as rough a morning as I am?" Loretta asked with a smile.

Gladys smiled in return, straightening her spine. "I suppose so. I can't seem to stop crying lately. My doctor says mood swings are to be expected. With the hormones."

"Oh?"

"I'm pregnant. Only three months along. I thought you might have known. Earl is very excited. I'm sure he's told Pete."

"They don't talk about us, I don't think. At work."

"Oh. Well. Probably not."

"Congratulations, though," Loretta said. "It's wonderful news."

"We've tried for so many years. I'd given up. But God's timing is perfect, isn't it?"

"Yes."

"I think it's a girl," Gladys whispered, putting a hand to her still-flat belly.

Loretta remembered the night they'd hosted Gladys and Earl for dinner, when the frightened woman's spirit had appeared next to Gladys, and the vision of the glamorous party had followed. She still didn't understand the shouting man, or why the spirits attached to Gladys had sought her out, but some of the words the woman had said came back to her now. "Do you have a name picked out yet?"

"Not yet, no. Earl likes Matilda. I'm not so keen. Matilda McAndrews is a bit much."

"You could call her Tilda, I suppose. But what about Katherine? You could call her Katie, for short."

"Katherine." Gladys's eyes widened. "That was my grandmother's name."

"Was it?" Loretta said, playing coy.

"You're coming to the Christmas gala next month, aren't you?" Gladys asked, brightening. "I'm on the planning committee. We're deciding on the menu now. The Bethel Girls' Choir is going to perform a special program. It's going to be marvelous."

It wasn't even Thanksgiving yet. Loretta marveled at the boundless energy women like Gladys seemed to possess, even while pregnant. It made her envious. "Pete would like it if I came. I'll be there."

Everything was about making Pete happy these days.

"Good. We'll be sending the invitations next week."

The organ blasted out the opening bars of "Shall We Gather at the River?" Gladys stood, smoothing her smart woolen dress. "I suppose we should go in now."

"Yes, Pete will wonder where I've gone."

Gladys offered Loretta her hand, and she took it. "Look. I know you're a little shy, Loretta. I once was, too, if you can believe that." Gladys laughed, the dimple in her left cheek deepening. "But I'd like to be your friend. Bring you out of your shell a bit. We women need one another. You know?"

Perhaps that's what she needed: a friend. Someone besides nosy Phyllis Colton. She could invite Gladys over for coffee while the kids were at school. It would break up the monotony of her days and hasten the time between her sessions with Dr. Hansen. Seeing Gladys once or twice a week would give her a reason to get up in the mornings, neaten the house, and take more care with her appearance. Loretta squeezed Gladys's hand before releasing it. "I'd like that."

⸎

"I saw you talking to Gladys McAndrews," Pete said as they drove home after church.

"We're going to try to get together this week. Have coffee."

"She's coming to the house, then?"

"Yes." He had to subtly reiterate his rule, didn't he? She wasn't to leave the house without him, except to walk the kids to and from the bus stop. "You said I needed church friends, and Gladys is a church friend."

"Did I say that? If you want to have her over, that's fine. Just be careful what you say to her. She's a gossip. And don't let her influence you."

"What do you mean?"

"She looks like a floozy, for one thing. That bleached hair. All those cosmetics. That ridiculous figure of hers." Pete's lips narrowed. "She draws too much attention to herself with how she dresses."

As if Gladys could help the way she was shaped! And she was pregnant. Loretta's bust had grown exponentially with both babies. Her hands clenched.

"Daddy, what's a floozy?" Charlotte asked from the back seat.

"Just a silly word," Loretta said. "A nonsense word."

"I think Mommy's friend is pretty. *I* want to look like a floozy when I grow up," Charlotte said cheerfully.

Loretta stifled the giggle bubbling up in her throat before it could break free.

"Charlotte, hush up," Pete said firmly. He was quiet for a moment, then cut a scathing look at Loretta. "You know the real reason I don't like her? Gladys? She reminds me of Donna."

Donna. Loretta's stomach sank, remembering. Donna was her childhood best friend—her only friend. But Pete didn't like her bold ways. Said she was a bad influence, with her string of beaus and her brash personality. And Donna hadn't liked Pete. At all. Tired of the tug-of-war between her best friend and her husband, Loretta slowly abandoned their friendship. Neglected it. Until Donna would no longer even look at her if they passed on the street. She wondered about Donna, now. Last Loretta heard, she'd married a dentist she met while serving in the Women's Army Corps and moved with him to Des Moines.

Looking back, Loretta could see how foolish she'd been to let Pete tear them apart. She'd let him take so much from her over the years. She could feel the tears threatening, like an ocean, ready to break over her like a wave. She bit the inside of her cheek to quell them and changed the subject. "Let's stop by Howard Johnson's and get a burger. I'm famished. I didn't have breakfast."

"There's plenty of food at the house."

There was. Food that *she'd* have to cook.

"All right. I suppose I can make sandwiches with the leftover ham from last night. Is that okay?"

"I want a hamburger!" Charlotte whined.

"Me too," Luke echoed. "And a shake."

"You have stout genes, like your mother, Luke. You need to eat healthy to be a good ballplayer. No more junk."

"I don't want to play baseball, Dad." Luke sighed. "I'm not good at sports."

"Don't get fresh with me, son."

"He isn't being fresh," Loretta said, trying to smooth things over. "He's just telling you the truth."

"This is your fault, Loretta," Pete muttered. "Giving him sweets all the time. Encouraging his scribbling. You're turning him into a fat sissy boy."

"No, Pete. Luke is who he is." Anger welled up inside Loretta. Pete could insult her, try to control her, but when it came to the children, she'd had enough. "Sports or the military are the only two things you think he should do. And *you* did neither. Maybe he wants something besides what you want. Did you ever think of that?"

Pete went silent. Ominously so. She had gone too far. Said too much. The stoplight turned green. The Chrysler's engine revved as he accelerated. They jolted forward at a breakneck speed. Loretta braced herself, fingers splayed against the dash. Her heartbeat careened as fast as the car. "Pete! Please! Slow down!"

"Daddy!" Charlotte cried.

"You're scaring the children!"

Pete suddenly swerved into the left lane, narrowly missing another car, then slammed on the brakes. Loretta screamed, pitching forward as the car skidded and spun in a circle in the middle of the road. Horns blared all around them. Loretta shut her eyes in anticipation of the inevitable crash. A thousand horrific images crowded her head at once:

Charlotte, mangled and bleeding on the pavement. Luke, his skull caved in. Herself, staring at the sky with sightless eyes like her mother.

The crash never came. Loretta waited, huddled against the dash, her trembling hands gripping her ears. She sensed the car turning, slowly, and then accelerating smoothly. She looked up. By some miracle, there had been no accident. Pete was driving normally, his face a mask of calm, as if nothing had ever happened. As if he hadn't just tried to kill them all.

She turned to check on Charlotte and Lucas. Charlotte was crying silently, tears dripping from her chin. Luke wrapped his arm around her shoulders, drawing her close. "It's okay, Char. You're all right."

Loretta reached out her hand. Luke took it. His eyes held a haunted, vacant look that she recognized. It was the same look that met her every time she saw her own reflection in a mirror. Numbness. Hopelessness. A tired, resolved acceptance that *this* was her life. And nothing would ever get better.

Chapter 16

On Monday morning, after Pete left the house and the kids were at school, Loretta went out to their detached garage. She unlocked the padlock, pushed open the door, and pulled the chain on the bare bulb hanging from the ceiling. Dim yellow light bathed stacks of unpacked boxes from their move five years ago, and the dusty, unused sports equipment Pete bought Lucas every Christmas.

She went to the far corner of the garage, where Pete stored the camping supplies, and lifted the folded layers of tent fabric. The Remington typewriter Dr. Hansen had given her sat there, perched on a box. When Barbara had dropped her off at the corner after her last session, Loretta had lugged the heavy typewriter home and hidden it. Her arms ached the next day. But now, with her newfound sense of resolve and spite, she hefted it easily.

She would find a way out of this marriage. She had to. For the children. He might have killed them all on Sunday. Loretta had been hanging on to hope—dreaming that things might get better. But she knew in her gut and in her spirit that they never would. Their happily-ever-after was only a made-up story in her mind.

Loretta kicked the garage door shut behind her and brought the typewriter into the house. She needed a place where Pete wouldn't go, where she could be alone and hide her secret from him. The bedroom wouldn't do. She'd learned that the hard way when he'd discovered her books.

Loretta paused for a breath in the kitchen, resting the typewriter on the table. The basement might work. No one ever went down there unless there was a bad storm. It wasn't ideal, but it would suffice for now. Loretta went to the small half door in the downstairs hall and unlatched it, peering into the darkness. Dank, stale air greeted her. She reached for the flashlight they kept on the rickety first step and switched it on. A network of cobwebs shone in the narrow cone of light.

An hour later, with her hair and clothes covered in dust, she had a makeshift office. In the recesses of the basement, she'd found an abandoned, wheelless bar cart that now served as her desk, the typewriter perched on its mirrored surface. A chair with a broken slat back sat in front of it. It was cold and uncomfortable, and she'd have to tuck her knees to the side of the bar cart to sit at the desk, but it would do.

By the light of a kerosene lantern, Loretta wound a sheet of yellow paper through the typewriter's roller carriage and pressed a key. It snapped upward with a satisfying clack. To her surprise, the ribbon still held plenty of ink. She tested more keys, her excitement growing. Dr. Hansen was right: some of the keys were sticky—the T and the K especially—but they still marked the paper when she struck them with gusto.

In Lucas's room, she gathered a few sheets of the white bond he used for drawing paper, and rushed back to the basement. She propped the legal pad on her knees to begin transcribing the first handwritten story and stared at the blank paper in contemplation. She needed a name. A pen name. Something that no one would ever guess was her. A name to reflect the woman in her stories.

Loretta thought carefully. And then it came to her: Daphne, for her favorite author, and Harrington, because it sounded important and elegant—two words no one would ever use to describe her. Daphne Harrington. Loretta bit her lip, her body thrumming with excitement and possibility. This, like her sessions with Dr. Hansen, was something for only her.

By that afternoon, Loretta had transcribed three stories and written a cover letter, in which she fully embraced her alter ego. Daphne was involved with the PTA, volunteered with several philanthropic organizations, and enjoyed playing tennis and gardening in her spare time. She imagined Daphne was the type of woman Dr. Hansen's wife had been—polished, worldly, and kind. The sort of woman she would like to be.

It felt ridiculous, pretending to be someone else, but it was fun, too.

She folded the papers neatly, then sealed them into an envelope addressed to the *Myrna Grove Focus*. On her walk to the bus stop to pick up the kids, she dropped the letter into the blue mailbox at the corner of Main and High.

Her heart had never beaten so fast in all her life.

What *if*? What if she could write herself out of one life and into another?

༺ঞ৵

The next day, a newfound confidence had Loretta rising early. She dressed for the day, made breakfast for the kids and Pete (he was in a good mood, thankfully), and then set about neatening the house, seeing to all the repetitive, relentless tasks she'd neglected. After all, Daphne Harrington would never be content with a messy house. She'd just finished folding the laundry when the telephone rang.

"Hello?"

"Good morning, Loretta. It's Gladys. Wondered what you had on the docket for today. Would you like to have coffee?"

"Oh, hello! Yes. I would."

"Meet me at Anton's? Say, in an hour?"

Loretta paused, gripping the phone cord. She could walk to Anton's or take the bus. But that would complicate things. The more often she left the house, the more likely it would be that Pete would find out, and she needed to be wary of Phyllis Colton's prying eyes.

"I . . . I can't. I don't have the car. Pete has it."

"Oh. Well, then I'll come pick you up."

"Could we just visit here? I've made a fresh pot."

"Sure thing," Gladys answered. "I'll be over in a jiffy!"

Loretta hung up, put the folded towels in the linen closet, and hastily cleaned the downstairs powder room. She was dusting the high, overhead windowsill when her fingers brushed against something, sending it to the honeycomb-tiled floor. It was the moth she'd seen weeks before. It was dead. Loretta's heart panged in sympathy. In solidarity. The moth had only wanted out—had felt just as trapped as she did now.

Loretta gently scooped the little brown moth into her hand and wrapped it in a tissue. After Gladys left, she would bury it out back, in her lily garden.

If Loretta felt like a moth, Gladys was a butterfly. She bounced through the door an hour later, dressed in a dazzling purple coat with a matching A-line frock that skimmed her curves, her smile as bright as the sunlight streaming in the windows. Loretta fought back her envy. "You always look so smart," she said. "Where do you get your clothes?"

"Savage Juliet. Downtown. I know the owner, and she gives me a discount. I worked there when I was going to Bethel."

Loretta had never set foot inside that store, or any other boutique, for that matter. The rush she felt the few times Pete had taken her to shop at Heer's had been heady enough. She made most of her clothes at home, with the same antique Singer treadle machine she'd learned on, and knitted her own sweaters.

"We'll go there sometime," Gladys said, taking off her gloves and folding her coat over the sofa's arm. "I can help you choose something for the Christmas gala if you'd like."

"Yes. I'd like that," Loretta said. "I'm hopeless when it comes to fashion. I'll fetch the coffee. Do you take cream and sugar?"

"Always. I'm not as mindful of my figure these days."

"You look like you're feeling better."

"I am! I'm not nearly as tired."

"I always felt better about four months in, as I recall," Loretta said over her shoulder as she went to the kitchen. "The tiredness comes back at the end, but by that time you're almost done, and the end is in sight."

Loretta poured two cups of coffee and brought everything out to the coffee table, as she had when Dora came to visit. Loretta had thought of her often in the days that followed their ill-fated trip to the police station. She had considered calling, after her vision of Darcy, but until she understood more about what Darcy's spirit had tried to convey, she didn't want to burden the girl and open her wounds. And then there was Joan. Loretta had called the list of Ashleys in the phone book yesterday evening—there were only four families with that name in Myrna Grove—but had no luck. One woman had angrily hung up on her, stating that her dead sister's name was Joan, and Loretta had given her a fright.

Each night, she watched the news, fearful that Darcy's killer would strike again, although everyone else in Myrna Grove seemed to have gone back to life as usual.

Loretta turned from her grim thoughts, settled herself on the sofa, next to Gladys, and added a dab of cream to her coffee.

Gladys lifted her coffee cup and blew across it. Her full lips were painted a bright rosebud pink. "I've been wondering something, Loretta."

"Yes?"

"That evening we had dinner with you, I heard you whispering a name. It was my maiden name. Bedingfield. How did you know it?"

Loretta cleared her throat. "I . . . I'm not sure how I knew. Perhaps Pete mentioned it to me, once."

"But you said yourself that our men don't talk about us at work. Besides, Earl wouldn't have told him that. In fact, I've told him never to mention my maiden name to anyone. It was a relief to be rid of that name when I married Earl." Gladys pressed her lips together. "You saw the papers, somehow, didn't you? It was all over the news the year I was born: 1923."

Loretta wrinkled her brow in confusion. "I don't follow."

"The Bedingfield Standoff." Gladys took a quick drink of her coffee. "It happened on New Year's Eve. My father held the Fayetteville police at gunpoint for most of the night. He shot my mother. And then he killed himself."

Loretta sat back. Her breath caught. Of course. It all made sense now—her vision of the roaring twenties party. The frightened woman had been Gladys's mother.

"My grandparents raised me. They said Mother married low. Daddy was a bootlegger and a gangster, with a rap sheet a mile long. I don't even know how they met, with as strict as my grandparents were." Gladys's eyes dipped. "They'd always fought, apparently, but they had a particularly nasty argument that night."

"I'm so sorry."

"It's terrible when your only memory of your parents is a bad one."

"I understand, a little. I lost my mother in a car accident when I was young. I was there when it happened. I blamed myself."

"Oh, Loretta. Why?"

"Because . . ." Loretta choked on her words. She was close to telling Gladys her secret—too close. But with the way Detective Eames had reacted, she was wary of telling anyone else. "I think people always blame themselves when someone they love dies."

Gladys nodded. "Yes. I've often thought that if only I'd been sick that night, my parents wouldn't have left me with the nanny and gone to that party." She shook her head, gave a sharp laugh. "As if I could control that. I was only a baby. And then sometimes, I think, perhaps I shouldn't have been born at all. My mother was pregnant with me when they got married. I think they were just having a fling, and I was the unwelcome, uninvited guest. Having me must have made things worse for my mother. You know?"

"Don't say that." Loretta laid her hand on Gladys's arm. "It wasn't your fault. I think your mother would want you to know that. Carrying that kind of unfounded guilt—holding something like that inside—it can poison a person." Loretta thought of the scars on her belly and wondered how many scars Gladys might have hiding behind her lovely hazel eyes, fashionable clothes, and perfectly made-up face.

"I'm so glad I told you, Loretta." Gladys smiled. "I haven't spoken about it in years. You have a way about you, you know? You shouldn't hide your light under a bushel."

Once again, the urge to tell Gladys about her gift butted up against her common sense. As much as she was growing to like her new friend, she needed to be careful. Gladys was a gossip, after all. Or was she? Only Pete had ever said as much. Loretta thought of Donna, and how Pete had used her friend's flaws—both real and false—to tear them apart. She wouldn't let him do that again with Gladys.

Suddenly, the phone rang, breaking their companionable silence. "Excuse me," Loretta said. Her anxiety rose with the next ring. Something was wrong. The bad feeling roiled in her gut. "I should get that."

"Of course."

Loretta crossed to the kitchen in three strides. "Hello?"

"Mrs. Davenport?"

"Yes?"

"It's Mrs. Roush. Luke's teacher. He's been in a fight. You need to come get him."

Loretta nearly dropped the receiver. "A fight?" Lucas had never been in a fight in all his life.

"Yes. Now please come. Lucas is upset, and he has a bloody nose. He's in the nurse's office."

"I . . . I'll be right there."

Loretta hung up and turned to Gladys. "It's my son. He got into a fight at school. Would you mind taking me to get him?"

"Oh goodness. Not at all."

Ten minutes later, they pulled in front of the school in Gladys's green Buick. Loretta rushed to the steps on wobbly legs. Already, she was wondering what she would tell Pete. He'd find some way to blame her for this, no matter what she said.

When she reached the nurse's office on the third floor, she was out of breath. Flustered. She knocked gingerly on the door. Nurse Frederick opened it a moment later, her starched cap perched proudly atop her salt-and-pepper hair.

"He's right in here, Mrs. Davenport. A little banged up, but I got the bleeding to stop. I've packed his nose with cotton. Try to leave it in for another hour or so. I'll go get Charlotte for you. That way you won't have to worry about coming back later to pick her up."

"Thank you." Loretta rushed into the spare office. Luke was lying propped up on a cot. He had a black eye, and his nose was unnaturally swollen. She went to him, giving him an awkward hug. "Oh, Lukie. What happened?"

"I dunno. I lost my temper, I guess. I hit Johnny Newhall."

Loretta stood there, stricken. "You started it? The fight?"

"Well, I threw the first punch."

"Lucas James!" Loretta stared at her sweet, normally mild-mannered son, aghast. "We do not start fistfights."

He shrugged. "I didn't figure you'd care. Nobody cares what I do."

"That's not true at all!" Loretta could hear the needling tone in her voice and softened it. "Do you really feel that way?" A deep wave of sadness welled up in her core. "Luke . . . I wish you'd talk to me."

"Can we just go home?" he asked wearily.

As they were leaving the office, Charlotte and Nurse Frederick met them in the hall. Charlotte's eyes looked like saucers as she took in Luke's swollen face.

"He'll be fine," Loretta said, placing a firm hand on Charlotte's shoulder and gently steering her toward the stairwell.

"Principal says Lucas can come back to school tomorrow, Mrs. Davenport," Nurse Frederick called. "He'll just have to remain in the in-school suspension room until Friday. But if this happens again, I'm afraid he'll be expelled."

"I understand. It won't happen again, will it, Luke?"

Luke shook his head.

Outside, Gladys waited for them, one hip propped against the Buick's rear fender. She was smoking. Loretta blinked as if Gladys were one of the apparitions in her visions.

"Filthy habit, I know," she said, dropping the cigarette and grinding it into the pavement with her shoe. She exhaled a final plume of smoke. "Earl doesn't know I do it. Please don't tell Pete."

"Oh, I certainly won't."

"Mama, is that your friend? The floozy?"

Loretta squeezed Charlotte's hand. "Don't say that word, Char. Please." Thankfully, Gladys didn't seem to hear. Loretta ushered the kids into the car.

"That's quite a shiner you're going to have, Luke," Gladys said, putting the car in gear. "A cold steak over the eye. That's what helps the most. I got in a fight once at school, too."

"Gladys!" Loretta said, aghast. "Really?"

"Remember what I told you earlier? Kids can be cruel. I got tired of it. I'd bet you got tired of something, too, didn't you, Luke?"

"Yes. They make fun of me. Johnny's the worst."

"Why do they make fun of you?" Gladys asked.

"Lots of reasons. But mostly 'cause I'm fat."

"Why, that's nonsense. You'll grow into your weight. You might even be a football—"

"Let's stop by Dairy Dream," Loretta said a bit too loudly, interrupting Gladys. "I could do with a shake and some fries, couldn't you?"

The kids echoed one another in a chorus of excited yeses.

As they pulled into the Dairy Dream parking lot, Loretta caught a glimpse of a blue Chrysler Saratoga rounding the corner onto College Street. She sat up, leaning forward. It was their car. The whitewall tires Pete had splurged on gave it away. She had thought the tires foolish— Pete's ridiculous bid to try to look young and hip in front of his students.

"There went Pete," she said aloud. "I wonder what he's doing."

"They probably went out to lunch, I'd say. He and Earl. They do that sometimes."

Loretta sighed. "It must be nice, to be able to do whatever you'd like, without anyone's permission."

Gladys's lips quirked up at the corner. "Aren't we doing what *we* want? Right now?"

"Yes. I suppose we are."

"There's always a way to do the things you want, Loretta." Gladys held her gaze for a long, meaningful moment. "Let's have something sugary and naughty, kids. My treat."

Chapter 17

Loretta paced the living room floor, waiting for Pete to get home. She'd gone over what she was going to tell him about Lucas's fight a thousand times. A full dinner sat on the kitchen table, in wait, with some of Pete's favorites. Even though she wanted out of the marriage, eventually, she needed to bide her time until she had enough money to leave. Keeping Pete happy would help ensure that she and the kids stayed safe until she could get a plan in place.

She had never thought she'd be a woman contemplating divorce. But a lot had changed since she and Pete first met. *She* had changed. So had he. Gone was the hopeful young man with an earnest smile and a passion for ministry and serving others. The winds had shifted. It was obvious that all Pete cared about was himself and furthering his career. She and the children were a necessary burden to make himself look like a wholesome family man in front of his colleagues.

Lucas's sudden turn to violence was more than concerning. It was frightening. Barbara's words about setting an example for her children haunted her. She would not let her gentle, kindhearted boy turn into a man who solved his problems with his fists.

Loretta startled as a sweep of headlights lit up the darkened room. He was home. And he was late again. He'd never told her which day of the week his AA meetings were on. She had a sinking suspicion he wasn't even going to the meetings.

She composed herself as his key turned in the lock, ready with a smile. He opened the door, carrying a bouquet of roses so deeply scarlet they looked like blood.

"What's this?" she asked.

"It's our anniversary!" Pete said. "That's why I'm late. I stopped by the florist on the way home."

Loretta blanched. *Was* it their anniversary? She mentally checked her inner calendar. Yes. It was.

"Oh! You remembered," she said, taking the roses. "I'll put these in a vase, and we can admire them while we have dinner. They're beautiful."

Pete never remembered their anniversary, but she always had. Until this year. It was telling of how far she'd slipped away from their marriage. She no longer cared.

"I know I've forgotten most years, but I'm trying to be a better husband, Retta." He came up behind her as she filled the vase at the sink, wrapping his arms around her waist. Loretta froze, every muscle in her body tensing.

"We never finished what we started last week," he murmured against her cheek.

Loretta wriggled free, forcing a tight smile as she turned. She held the vaseful of roses in front of her, like a shield. "Later, after the kids are asleep. I've made some of your favorites for supper. We wouldn't want it to get cold."

Pete sat down at the table as Loretta placed the vase in the center, her hands shaking. "Kids," she called. "Supper's ready!"

Charlotte came bounding down the stairs, like a puppy. "Mmm, macaroni and cheese!"

Lucas followed, slowly, his eyes downcast. His nose had gone almost back to normal, and she'd soothed some of the swelling with a cold steak, as Gladys had instructed, but the bruise around Luke's right eye had deepened in color.

Pete glanced up as Luke took his seat. "What happened?"

The words shot through the room like bullets. Loretta flinched.

"I can explain," Loretta said hastily. "Luke was in a fight at school. But it wasn't his fault. I thought about calling you, but it happened in the middle of the day, and—"

"Why don't you let the boy tell me about it, Loretta?" Pete's face was stony, impassive. Unreadable. But Loretta could sense the anger threatening beneath his calm facade. "Luke, what happened at school?"

Loretta knotted her hands together beneath the table. Charlotte had paused eating her macaroni. Lucas cleared his throat and finally spoke. "I . . . um . . . I hit Johnny," he stammered. "He was making fun of me. Called me a fatty Patty."

Pete grunted. "Who threw the first punch?"

Lucas shifted in his chair. "I guess I did."

"Well. It's about time." Pete beamed. He jostled Luke's shoulder. "Proud of you, son."

"Pete!" Loretta said, shock roiling through her. "He could have been expelled. There are other ways Lucas could have handled it."

"I don't know. Sometimes a fist works better than anything. Sounds like old Johnny got what was coming to him."

Luke smiled bashfully. "I don't think he'll bother me anymore."

"He came out of it worse than you did, I hope?"

"He sure did!"

"Sounds like you have a future in boxing instead of baseball, son. I'll buy you a punching bag for Christmas. We can turn the garage into a boxing gym." Pete jokingly punched the air, left and right. "Lucas Davenport, heavyweight champion of the world!"

Loretta sat back, aghast, as Pete and Lucas laughed. Had she overreacted about the fight? Was this merely a rite of passage for all boys? She'd never felt so out of her league. Sheer joy bloomed on Lucas's face. All he'd ever wanted was his dad's approval, and now he had it.

The thought should have made Loretta happy. Instead, it horrified her.

❧

Loretta stared at the crack in the bedroom ceiling. Like the cracks in the kitchen, it had somehow emerged without her noticing until now. It was at least the width of a pencil. She gripped the sheets as Pete drove into her, willing him to finish quickly, thinking of a million things she'd rather be doing.

Thinking of someone else.

Loretta closed her eyes and turned her head. She imagined Dr. Hansen in Pete's place. Imagined the words he might whisper in her ear. Imagined the slow, gentle glide of his hands over her skin, the scent of his sandalwood cologne. His mouth teasing her and tasting her in ways she'd only read about in romance novels. Her body began to respond as it hadn't in years. Her hips rose, and she arched her back, her pulse thudding between her legs.

Pete cried out and collapsed atop her, just as her wave was beginning to crest, then rolled off, panting. Loretta squeezed her legs together, wanting to touch herself, wanting to bring the rising tide to shore and let it break over her. But the last time she had touched herself after he'd finished, Pete had shamed her so terribly that she wouldn't chance it ever again.

"That was worth the wait," Pete said, laughing softly. "You felt so good."

He stroked her back through the flannel fabric of her nightgown. She'd never been naked in front of him. Ever. Sex had always been the same, from their wedding night onward—nightgown pushed up above her hips, with the lights off. Anytime his hands wandered to her belly, where the scars stood out from the smoothness of her skin, Loretta would roll away or direct his hands elsewhere.

Now, with her own pleasure denied, his touch only served to irritate and emphasize the ache of emptiness inside. Tears threatened, and she forbade them, swallowing against the sting at the back of her throat. How had she not realized how truly unhappy she was? How had the years gone by so quickly when they were so maddeningly similar? She'd settled and bargained with the denial of her own desires—her body her only currency in a marriage to a man who seemed to resent her very presence most days.

"What's wrong, Retta?"

"Nothing," she lied. "I'm just tired."

"All right. I need to tell you about something, then I'll let you go to sleep."

He'd *let* her.

"I'm going to be out of town next week. I'm leaving the day after Thanksgiving."

"Oh?"

"I have to go to a conference, in Saint Louis."

"How long will you be gone?"

"Ten days."

"That long?" Loretta feigned disappointment. She felt the exact opposite. The thought of ten days without Pete's domineering presence was almost exhilarating.

"Yes. It's an opportunity I couldn't turn down."

"Of course not. I understand." Perhaps, if she buttered him up, he might leave her the car.

"You do?"

"Yes. The kids and I will be fine." She bit her lip. "Are you driving or taking the train?"

"Driving. I'll take you to the store before I leave to make sure you have everything you and the kids will need." He wrapped his arms around her once more, tightening them. "I'll let Phyllis know I'm leaving, too. She'll help keep an eye on things."

The threat in his words was implicit. If she did anything she wasn't supposed to do while he was gone, he'd know. He'd find out, through Phyllis.

Well. No one would keep her from her sessions with Dr. Hansen. Even if she had to slip out through the back alley, she would find a way.

Chapter 18

Loretta studied the objects arrayed on the desk in front of her. A sweater clip. A toy train. A strand of pearls with a broken clasp. A garnet ring. Dr. Hansen sat across from her, next to Detective Pierce, watching as she picked up each object in turn and held it, closing her eyes.

At first, she felt nothing—only texture and shape. But when she went back for another pass, the garnet ring captured her attention longer. She slowed her breathing, concentrating. The ring almost seemed to vibrate in her hand. An impression of a girl with shoulder-length brown hair and gray-blue eyes came to her. The girl had gotten the ring for her high school graduation, from her father. She hated it—the large stone and gold filigree weren't her style. He'd bought it for her only because it was showy, and he liked people knowing that he made a lot of money.

"It's this one," she said, placing the ring back on the desk. "This was Paula's ring."

Detective Pierce nodded. "You're right, Loretta. It was."

"Her father gave it to her. She didn't really like it. She only wore it to make him happy. She preferred dainty, delicate things."

Detective Pierce jostled Dr. Hansen's shoulder. Loretta caught the look that passed between them. So, she had proven herself, at least a little. A thrill of pride went through her.

She cleared her throat, gathered herself, and motioned to the other objects on the desk. "Let me try again with these. Just for curiosity's sake."

She picked up the sweater clip. After a moment, an image of an elderly woman with regal features appeared in Loretta's mind, the silver sweater clip fastened to a pink cardigan.

"This clip belonged to a Millie or a Mildred. I can't quite make out which."

"Mildred." Detective Pierce beamed. "My dad always called her Mil or Millie. My aunt."

Loretta's eyebrows drew together. "She says you were very sick as a child."

"Wow. Yes. I had polio. I nearly died. That's why I walk with a limp. You really are the real deal, aren't you?"

Dr. Hansen smiled at her. "Yes, she is, Steven. She's fantastic."

Loretta ducked her head, unable to hold Dr. Hansen's gaze. Her sinful fantasies about him were more embarrassing than titillating in the light of day. Besides, a man as sophisticated as him would never want someone like her, even if she were free. And she wasn't, which she needed to remember.

Besides, it was obvious that Dr. Hansen was still devoted to the memory of his wife. If not, he would have already remarried. Men like him—wealthy, accomplished, handsome—didn't stay single for long. Loretta turned from her thoughts to focus on the work at hand.

"This method seems to be the easiest and fastest way for me to communicate with the other side. When I held my mother's brooch, the same sort of thing happened. She came to me, just like that." Loretta snapped her fingers.

Dr. Hansen nodded. "Even though we've seen no evidence of telekinetic ability in our sessions, I had wondered whether psychometric abilities might be within the realm of possibility. You seem to have a particularly strong sensitivity to the residual psychic energy found in objects."

For a moment, Loretta thought of telling Dr. Hansen about the broken dishes after her argument with Pete but decided against it. With

Detective Pierce in the room, she didn't want to reveal too much. She'd wait until their next session when she could express her concerns to him alone.

"How are you feeling?" Dr. Hansen asked, as if he'd read her thoughts.

"A little tired. But excited, too."

"Try again with these," he said, pushing the strand of pearls toward her. "Then we can stop for the day."

She reached for the pearls and closed her eyes, cupping their smooth, round warmth in her hands. But no matter how hard she concentrated and opened herself to receiving a message from the woman who had worn them, nothing came. It was like running into a solid lead wall. A few moments later, Loretta opened her eyes. "I can't form a connection with these. It's almost as if something is standing in the way of my reading them, physically."

Dr. Hansen nodded. A slight shadow of disappointment fell across his face. "That's all right, Loretta. Not all objects carry energy."

"You've certainly done enough today to convince me of your abilities, Mrs. Davenport." Detective Pierce leaned forward. "I'd like to try something if you're game. Paula Buckley disappeared at Dearing Park. We have a few of her personal belongings, including the hat she was wearing that night. I'm wondering if we went to the park, and you held one of her items, whether your impressions of Paula might be even stronger. Enhanced."

"It might be worth trying," Loretta said. "She did come to me rather strongly when I held her ring. There seems to be a willingness on her part to communicate."

"Thanksgiving is next Thursday, but we could meet at the park, week after next, at our regular session time." Dr. Hansen stood, taking off his glasses to polish them. "One o'clock on the first?"

"Yes," Detective Pierce said. "Let's meet by the bridge. That's the last place Paula was seen."

"We'll be there."

The detective shook Dr. Hansen's hand, then turned to Loretta. "Thank you so much, ma'am. You've given me hope that we might yet bring justice and closure to Paula's family—and eventually, Darcy's."

Loretta hoped he was right.

❧

The postman's truck sat idling in front of Phyllis's house when Loretta got home. Even though she felt tired after her session with Dr. Hansen, she also felt invigorated. It had been a good day. She'd proven her abilities. She hurriedly went to the mailbox and opened it, hoping for a response from the *Focus* about her stories. She pulled out two envelopes.

The first was their utility bill, but the next held the return address she most wanted to see.

She ripped open the envelope, right there on the walk, and unfolded the letter, almost tearing the paper in her haste.

Dear Mrs. Harrington,

Thank you for submitting your work to the *Focus*. While we found the pieces entertaining and humorous, please understand that we must be selective. We regret to inform you that we will not be extending an offer of publication at this time.

Sincerely,
Mavis Turner
Editor
The Myrna Grove Focus

Loretta's spirits sank. They didn't want her. She wasn't good enough. Her high-flying dreams of independence crashed to earth like a bird with a broken wing.

"Loretta! There you are."

Loretta tensed at the sound of Phyllis's voice.

"Pete came by, before he left for work. Told me he was going to Saint Louis for a few days after Thanksgiving," Phyllis said, crossing the lawn. "Asked me to check in on you and the kids while he's gone. I told him I'd be happy to."

"Thank you, Phyllis, but I'm sure we'll manage just fine." Loretta pressed her lips together tightly.

"Well. It's difficult to do everything you need without a car. Ten days is a long time. You're doing an awful lot of walking these days. I saw you leave earlier. Did you walk to the store?"

"No, I'm just trying to get more exercise."

"Well, you're wise to mind your figure while you're still young." Phyllis smiled condescendingly. "The pounds do creep on with the years."

Loretta fought to maintain her composure, but it was difficult. Phyllis had a way of goading a person into a reaction, and with the rejection from the newspaper already dampening her mood, she didn't have the patience for Phyllis's needling. She tucked the rejection letter into her coat pocket and turned away. "I'm sorry, Phyllis. I've got an awful lot of housekeeping to do before the kids get home."

"Of course you do. Now don't be shy about asking for help."

"I won't be. I'll let you know if I need a ride."

Loretta unlocked the door and shut it behind her before Phyllis could respond, not caring if she was being rude. From Phyllis's comments, it was obvious she watched everything Loretta did and would report anything suspicious to Pete. She needed to be more careful with her comings and goings. And she needed to find a way to make money. Soon.

Loretta went to the fireplace and rummaged through the pile of newspapers and magazines stacked on the hearth. Pete had several subscriptions: the *Wall Street Journal*, the *Christian Science Monitor*, the *Saturday Evening Post*, and the *Kansas City Star*.

Loretta chose the *Star* and the *Post* and sat at the kitchen table, scanning their fine print for mailing addresses. Once she'd found them, she hastily scrawled the addresses on a sheet of stray paper and rushed to the basement. The *Myrna Grove Focus* hadn't wanted her. But she wasn't finished yet. Daphne Harrington wouldn't be the type to let a single *no* shake her confidence. And neither would Loretta.

Chapter 19

Loretta watched through the front window as Pete drove away. Her every muscle twitched with anticipation and her head brimmed with stories yet unwritten. Ten whole days. As soon as she got the kids settled, she'd tuck away to her basement hideaway. "Wave goodbye to Daddy," she instructed the kids. Lucas halfheartedly did so, and Charlotte followed suit.

"Can we have a dance party later?" Charlotte asked.

"Yes, we sure can. After lunch. Mommy has some things I need to do first. Do you want to watch the Macy's parade this morning? They're running it again on channel three."

"Yes!" Charlotte said, clapping her hands.

"And this weekend, we can put up the Christmas tree."

"Can I have some new colored pencils this year?" Luke asked.

"I think you should ask Santa when we write our letters," Loretta said pointedly, shifting her eyes to Charlotte. Luke had stopped believing in Santa Claus two years ago but had been good about keeping the secret from Charlotte. Her kids were becoming adept at keeping all kinds of secrets—especially the ones she told them to keep from Pete. From the dance-party radio to their Halloween outing, they recognized, just like she did, that life was much easier the less their father knew. Any guilt she felt was assuaged by how their moods seemed to lighten anytime Pete left. Which was why she was that much more determined to find a way out. If she were happier, Luke and Charlotte would be happier, too.

Their Thanksgiving had been dismal. She'd left the turkey in the oven too long, and it was dry and tough, which Pete was all too happy to point out. With only the four of them, it hardly felt like a holiday. Not like the Thanksgivings she had as a child, when Mama piled the table with delicious food, and her aunts, uncles, and cousins came from all over the countryside. After Mama died, it had been just another day, with Daddy facing her across the table, the weight of all the things left unsaid between them.

After helping with the breakfast dishes, Luke went upstairs, and Loretta switched on the TV for Charlotte. The screen showed a gigantic mechanical turkey winding its way through the New York City streets. Loretta had never been to New York. Perhaps someday, once she was free, she'd take the kids and they could experience the parade in real life.

The thought spurred her downstairs, to her typewriter. If she used this time wisely, she could have pages and pages of new stories to pitch by the time Pete got back. Loretta eagerly fed a fresh sheet of white paper into the typewriter and began.

She'd gotten only a few lines written when she heard Charlotte skip past the basement door and then back down the hall, singing to herself. Already bored. While she loved her younger child's exuberant temperament, Charlotte's energy sometimes wore her down. Loretta massaged her temples and tried her best to concentrate through the noise, but between the rank fumes from the kerosene lamp and the constant *thudthudthud* of Charlotte's feet, she felt a headache coming on.

"Charlotte!" Loretta yelled. "Can you please be still!"

"Sorry, Mommy. Where are you?"

"I'm in the basement." She hadn't told the kids about her writing. They kept too many of her secrets as it was, and this was the biggest and most important secret of all. "I'm dusting the preserves."

"Oh."

"If you're bored, go upstairs with Luke."

"All right."

She heard Charlotte clatter up the stairs, and then the house settled once more into blessed quiet. Loretta turned back to her work and had managed to eke out a few more lines of her story when a loud crash came from above, as if something heavy had fallen. A volley of girlish laughter followed.

Loretta groaned. She stalked up the basement stairs, her frustration growing with every step. "Kids! What are you doing up there?"

"Charlotte was jumping on my bed and fell off," Luke said, emerging from his room and peering down the stairs at her. "I told her to stop, or she was going to get us in trouble."

"I'm okay, Mommy!" Charlotte called cheerfully, poking her head around Luke's doorframe, her cheeks flushed.

"You know I don't like you jumping on the furniture. It's dangerous. Now, if you can't find something quiet to do, we won't have our dance party later and I won't give you dessert tonight, either." At Charlotte's crestfallen look, Loretta softened her tone. "Why don't you color or put together a puzzle? I'll just be another hour or so."

"Okay. I will."

Loretta turned to go back to the basement, her pulse clamoring behind her ears. Monday and the kids' return to school couldn't come fast enough. Writing with them in the house was proving to be a challenge, but she was determined to finish at least one article each day Pete was gone, come what may.

She'd just gotten settled back into her chair when the patter of footsteps echoed down the stairs. "Mommy!"

Loretta clenched her fists and knotted them in her hair. "What, Charlotte?"

"Luke won't share his colored pencils."

"Tell him I said to share them, or there's no dessert for him tonight, either."

Charlotte's footsteps departed. Loretta peered at the last few lines of her story, found her place, and began typing again.

"Mom!" Loud steps, above her head. Luke this time.

"What!" Loretta screeched, her tenuous patience spent.

There was another crash, this one much closer.

Loretta flung open the basement door. Luke stood in the hallway, his eyes wide. The antique mirror that used to hang next to the coat-tree now lay broken at his feet, reflecting Luke's frightened expression in bright, sparkling shards.

"Did you do that?"

"N-no. It just flew off the wall."

"Flew off the wall," Loretta said flatly. "By itself."

Luke nodded.

"Are you sure you didn't knock it down?"

"No, Mom. I promise."

Loretta sat on the bottom step, a dreadful thought festering in her head. Had she done this? Just like on the night the dishes fell? If Luke had been just a step or two closer . . .

She had to get a handle on things. Before the kids got hurt.

"I'm sorry I yelled. Go on back upstairs, honey. I'll clean this mess up."

After Loretta had swept the mirrored glass into the trash, she went to the phone and dialed Dr. Hansen's number. It was unlikely he or Barbara would be in the office, given the holiday, but to Loretta's surprise, he answered right away, his voice sending a thrill of relief through her.

"Dr. Hansen. It's Loretta. Something else is happening. Can you see me before next Thursday?"

⁓

Loretta sat next to Dr. Hansen in his Cadillac, the engine purring softly. They were parked in the cemetery at the end of the block, the sun rising over the monuments and grave markers. It felt illicit, sitting in the car alone with him, in a place where Myrna Grove's teenagers often parked to fool around, but she'd been desperate to talk to him. After a sleepless night, spent tossing and turning, she'd sneaked out at dawn, before the kids woke. As she looked out at the gravestones, she thought of Luke's macabre drawing and the way he'd depicted this cemetery and their broken house. If she didn't get a handle on herself, was that coming next?

"And the psychokinesis only happens when you're experiencing heightened emotions?" Dr. Hansen asked, his voice a steady, calming counterpoint to her nerves.

"Yes. I'm afraid. What if I hurt the kids, Doctor? Luke was right there. Anything might have happened."

"But you haven't hurt them."

"No. At least not yet." Loretta bit the inside of her cheek. "I've never told anyone this before, but after Charlotte was born, I fell into a black state of mind. I used to imagine all sorts of terrible things happening to her and Luke. Strange things."

"Mothers often imagine the worst-case scenario. It's more common than you might realize. Some even go as far as to imagine harming their children, even though they never would do such a thing in reality."

"I suppose I'm worried about that sort of thing happening with the psychokinesis. That it might be an outward expression of those ugly thoughts. I was so irritated at the children for interrupting my writing yesterday. I'm ashamed of myself."

"But you'd never *really* hurt your children, would you?"

"No. I've never even spanked them. Not once."

"You're a good mother. Of that I have no doubt." Loretta's limbs relaxed at his words. How often had she longed to hear Pete say such a thing? Instead, his words only served to multiply the doubts she already felt. "We can do more experiments with psychokinesis in the office, but I think," Dr. Hansen said, "that what you need most of all is to do something for yourself. Without the kids, while Pete is away. Something indulgent might relieve some of your stress."

"I have our sessions. And now my writing."

"Yes, and that's wonderful. But I'm talking about something that *feels* truly selfish. Perhaps a manicure or a shopping trip. Or a good meal out, with a girlfriend. Something pleasurable, for pleasure's sake alone."

Loretta's face burned at the sensual way his words evoked thoughts she shouldn't be having. "I've been taught that doing things for yourself is selfish, Doctor. That taking pleasure in indulgent things is sinful."

"Do you really believe that?"

"I—I don't know anymore."

Dr. Hansen went quiet, studying the bare-limbed trees. "Some of my family is buried here. It's an old Catholic cemetery. Our mausoleum is at the center." Loretta briefly wondered if his wife and son were interred here, or if they'd been buried in France. She was tempted to say something—to offer a sympathetic apology about their deaths—in a bid to fill the silence, but it didn't seem appropriate.

"I used to come here with Luke when he was little," she said instead. "To make grave rubbings and such." Loretta shook her head. "He was such a happy child, once. I worry about him—that's he's prone to melancholy, like me. I'm afraid that, even if I do leave Pete someday and we strike out on our own, I've already ruined my children's lives."

"No." Dr. Hansen smiled. "It's not too late. You deserve to be happy, Loretta. And if you're happier . . ."

"The children will be happier?"

"Yes."

"Well, we're all much happier with Pete gone." Loretta felt ashamed, saying the words aloud. But they were true.

"How does it make you feel to say that?"

"Guilty. Selfish. Mean-spirited."

"You're not any of those things, Loretta."

Loretta shaded her eyes with her hand as the sun popped over the trees. "I should go. The kids will be awake soon. I don't like leaving them alone." He probably thought her incredibly foolish, calling him to her side in such a tizzy.

"Of course. Are you sure you won't let me drive you home?"

"I'd better not. My neighbor is nosy. And Pete . . ."

"I understand."

Dr. Hansen walked around the side of the car and opened her door. They stood facing one another, awkwardly. Loretta's eyes bounced about the cemetery. She worried that someone might see them. But the markers and their dead were both silent. There was only the wind, sighing through the trees and rustling the leaves at their feet. Loretta shoved her hands into her pockets. "Thank you for meeting me, Doctor. I'll try not to bother you so much."

"It's no trouble, Loretta. None at all." His glasses fogged with the change in temperature, and he took them off. In the early-morning light, his eyes were two depthless pools she might drown in. If she were a different person, someone made of bolder stuff, she might reach up, push his errant, windblown hair behind his ears, and then kiss him. She imagined what it would be like, in toe-curling detail. His soft lips, on hers. His hands . . .

Loretta suddenly felt light-headed. "I suppose I'll see you this Thursday, then," she said, clearing her throat. "With Detective Pierce."

"Yes. But if you need me before, you can always call me. I'm not seeing any patients until Monday, and I'm up late every night."

Loretta wondered what he did at night, all alone in his great, looming house. She wondered what his bed looked like. What he slept in. She wondered if he dreamed of his wife, or if his fantasies were as forbidden as her own.

"Get some rest," he said, taking her hand in his for a brief, blissful moment. "And try to do something nice for yourself this week."

As she walked back to the house, Loretta thought of Dr. Hansen's perfect words, the thrill of his touch warming her all the way home. She went upstairs, peeked in on the children. They were still fast asleep. She made her coffee and sat at the table. The silence settled over her like a soft cloak. Someday, she vowed, every morning would be like this.

Chapter 20

Loretta woke from her midmorning nap, stretching luxuriously. With Pete still away and the kids back in school, she had embraced Dr. Hansen's advice. Instead of spending her days mired in thankless housekeeping, she indulged in decadent things, like naps and long baths, and wrote for two hours each afternoon before going to fetch the kids from the bus stop. She felt less moody as a result, and there had been no more disturbing happenings since the mirror incident.

Today, she even had a hair appointment—the first in years. When Gladys called and suggested it, Loretta had balked. Pete didn't like her spending time with Gladys. And he certainly wouldn't like her going to the beauty parlor while he was gone. But Pete wouldn't be home from his conference until Monday. She wouldn't let the beautician do anything Pete would notice. Only a trim, to make brushing her hair less of a chore.

After dressing, she went out to the back alley to wait for Gladys, who pulled through a few minutes later, guiding the Buick down the narrow gravel pathway. Loretta quickly got inside the car. What if Phyllis was watching out her back door? Hopefully the thick tangle of blackberry brambles lining the alley would be enough to camouflage them.

"You look nervous, doll," Gladys said. "Is something wrong?"

"No, not really."

"Good. I've been looking forward to this."

"I have, too."

Gladys smiled behind her oversize sunglasses. She had painted her lips a brilliant crimson. "Today will be fun. And next week, we'll go to Savage Juliet and choose your dress for the Christmas gala."

"Pete will be home next week. I suppose I could sneak out while the kids are at school, but he wouldn't like me spending that kind of money. I'd better not."

"Is it really that bad, Loretta? He won't let you go anywhere or spend any money on yourself?"

"He won't let me drive anymore. And he's even got the neighbor spying on me while he's gone. That's why I had you pick me up in the alley."

"That's terrible. Earl has his moments, of course. They all do. But he's never forbidden me to leave the house. Have you ever given him a reason not to trust you?"

Loretta didn't know what to say. On one hand, she had lied about Dr. Hansen, and was still lying, which might justify Pete's actions in Gladys's eyes. But she was desperate. And her desperation had forced her to resort to deception.

"You aren't having an affair, are you?" Gladys asked gently. "You could tell me if you were, Loretta. I won't judge you."

"No. Pete's the only man I've ever been with."

Gladys laughed. "Wish I could say the same about Earl. I was a get-around girl before we met. Even when I was at Bethel. They didn't have all the rules they do now. No one cared if you drank or danced." She shook her head. "We had the best parties at Ashley House back then."

Ashley House. The girls' dormitory at Bethel. A thought niggled at the back of Loretta's mind. She'd had no luck finding the mysterious Joan Ashley. But what if Ashley wasn't the girl's name, but where she lived? The thought followed her all the way across town.

When they entered the salon, the scents of perm solution, hairspray, and setting lotion overwhelmed her senses. Drawings of elegantly coiffured women lined the pink-painted walls. A row of hair dryers sat on one side of the long, narrow room, and on the other side, three beauty operators worked on their clients, setting their hair with rollers. One of them looked up as they entered and gave a cheerful wave. She was slim and stylish, with arched brows and ebony curls piled atop her head in the poodle style favored by Betty Grable. "Good morning, Gladys! Is this your friend?"

"Yes. This is Loretta."

"I'll be right with her, soon as I get Margie finished up."

Gladys sat in one of the upholstered chairs near the front, and Loretta sat next to her, watching the beauticians work.

"Doris is my gal. She's best with the blondes," Gladys said. She motioned toward the first operator, who wore a platinum bouffant like Gladys's. "But Evelyn is just as talented. You'll be in good hands. Do you know what you want to have done?"

"I'm just getting a trim."

"Oh." Gladys studied Loretta. "That's all? You're sure? It's my treat, after all."

Self-consciousness colored her cheeks. She *wanted* to do more. She'd love to look as stylish and put-together as Gladys or Barbara. But Pete would kill her if she came home with short hair. Or bleached hair. It was safer to remain the same, no matter how boring it was.

"Just a trim," she said, nodding with finality. "This is still such a treat, though, Gladys. Truly."

Loretta watched as Evelyn finished her client's roller set and escorted her to one of the cone-shaped dryers. "Loretta?" the operator said. "I'm ready if you are. We'll start at the shampoo station."

Loretta rose and followed Evelyn to the back of the room, where three sinks sat, side by side. "What are we doing today?" Evelyn asked.

"I just need an inch or so off the ends." Loretta sat in front of one of the sinks and pulled the pins free from her hair. It cascaded down the back of the chair.

"Oh my. You certainly have a lot of hair," Evelyn said breathlessly. "I don't think I've *ever* seen this much hair on a person."

"My husband says it's my crowning glory. I haven't cut it in years."

"I can see that." Evelyn guided her to lie back, scooping her hair into the sink. Warm water flowed over Loretta's scalp, and then a delightfully fresh scent wafted into her nostrils as Evelyn began scrubbing her hair with deft fingers. It was so pleasurable Loretta could have purred. After, she applied a cream rinse and then directed Loretta to her workstation.

"Have you ever considered a more current style?" Evelyn asked as she gently combed through Loretta's tangles. "You have a lovely oval-shaped face. It would suit any number of haircuts. And your color—it could also be enhanced. Nothing extreme, of course. But an auburn rinse would flatter your complexion and your eyes."

Temptation warred with Loretta's practical side. A rinse didn't sound so bad. And she'd always liked reddish hair. It wasn't like she would leave looking like Lucille Ball. Pete would probably never even notice. He hardly noticed her looks as it was.

"All right. I'll do the rinse."

Evelyn smiled at her in the mirror. "I think you'll be pleased. I'll go mix it up. And while I'm doing that, here's the latest style booklet. Have a look at it and see if there's anything you might like."

Loretta took the book Evelyn offered her and thumbed through it. She paused on a photograph of a woman walking a dog. She had a pageboy haircut, with the ends resting on her shoulders in a pert flip. The woman looked happy—carefree. Loretta only ever took her hair down to wash and brush it. With this style she could still pull her hair into her everyday bun. Pete would likely never know. She could wear it down during the day and put it back up before he got home.

"I . . . I think I want to cut my hair, after all," she said to Evelyn when she returned with the rinse. "It's so heavy it gives me terrible headaches." She showed Evelyn the photograph of the lady walking the dog. "Would this style work for me?"

Two hours later, a different woman stared back at Loretta in the mirror. Her hair now fell just below her shoulders in bouncy, roller-set waves that gleamed and shone with glints of deep, ruddy copper, like a maple tree in autumn.

Evelyn stood back, admiring her work. "What do you think?"

Loretta regarded herself shyly. "I . . . it's perfect. Thank you."

Gladys came over, her hands flying up to cover her mouth. She bounced on her heels. "Oh, Loretta. You look so beautiful!"

On the way home, they stopped for milkshakes at Dairy Dream. Loretta had a newfound spring to her step, and her head almost seemed to float above her shoulders it felt so light. All that hair had been weighing her down more than she'd realized. Now she felt as pretty and carefree as the lady in that photograph.

As they finished up their milkshakes, Gladys narrowed her eyes and assessed Loretta. "Do you know what you need with that new hairdo?"

"What?"

"Some lipstick."

Gladys rummaged in her handbag and produced a tube of lipstick. She offered it across the booth. Loretta took it and twisted the bottom. It was the same brilliant shade Gladys was wearing. Loretta hadn't ever worn lipstick, or any cosmetics for that matter. She'd been tempted, during the war, when it was rumored that Hitler hated red lipstick, but Pete's admonishments about vanity being sinful had prevented her from going through with it.

"Here's a mirror." Gladys held up a compact. "Go on. Give it a try."

Loretta pressed the lipstick against her mouth and carefully followed the outline of her lips. "Goodness," she said, studying herself. The cool red made her pale skin glow and contrasted with her new auburn hair in the most marvelous way.

"Now. *That's* perfect," Gladys said.

"What color is this?"

"Cherries in the Snow. It's the color Elizabeth Taylor wears. Why don't you keep it, Loretta."

"Are you sure?"

"Yes," Gladys said. "I'm sure."

❧

That afternoon, while the children finished their homework, Loretta called the Bethel switchboard. As the university operator connected her to Ashley House, she contemplated what she would say to Joan. There were so many ways the conversation could go wrong. It seemed ridiculous, in the light of day, to call a young woman she had never met and tell her that her dead friend was concerned for her safety. It was something a crackpot would do. But she wouldn't forgive herself if she didn't at least try.

Loretta listened to the connecting clicks on the line, her pulse racing.

"Ashley House. Susan speaking."

"Hello, Susan. This is Loretta Davenport, Professor Davenport's wife."

The line went silent for a moment, and then came a flurry of muffled girlish giggles. "It's Mrs. Davenport," she heard the girl hiss, as if she were talking to someone else. Loretta remembered the house phones at all the dormitories were located in the first-floor lounge, and the students took turns with telephone duties. She must have an audience.

"Hello?" she prompted.

Susan cleared her throat. "Yes, I'm so sorry."

"I was wondering if I might speak to Joan."

More silence. "Joan?"

"Yes."

"Which one?"

Loretta swore inwardly. She knew nothing about Joan, save her first name. "How many are there?"

"Three." Susan sighed, annoyed. "There's Joan Ward, Joan Everly, and Joan Kirsch. Two of them are here. One is not."

An abundance of Joans. The best Loretta could do was guess and hope the Joan she needed was one of the two girls present. "Joan Kirsch, please."

"Just a moment. I'll have to lay the phone down and go find her."

She heard the sound of heels on hard floors, and then more laughter. A few moments later, a girl answered, out of breath. "This is Joan."

"Hello, Joan. This is Mrs. Davenport."

"Susan told me."

"I won't keep you long. I just have a question. It might seem strange, but your answer is very important."

"Oh . . . okay."

"Did you know Darcy Hayes?"

"No. Who is that?"

Loretta's head fell in disappointment. She had the wrong Joan. "Never mind. I'm sorry to have bothered you."

"It's all right."

Loretta hung up. She could have asked to speak to one of the other Joans. But a thread of intuition told her the girl she needed was the one who wasn't there. And if so, she might already be too late.

Chapter 21

That Thursday, when the Cadillac pulled up to the corner, Dr. Hansen was in the driver's seat, instead of Barbara. As he got out to open her door, his eyes went to her hair. "You've changed your hair."

"I did," she said, smiling. "Do you like it?"

"I do. But mostly, it seems to have made you happy. And that's what I like most of all."

"You always say the right things, Dr. Hansen. Has anyone ever told you that?"

"I'm only telling you the truth, Loretta." He held her gaze for a long moment before closing her door.

"Are you ready for today?" he asked, getting behind the wheel.

"I am. I could hardly sleep last night. I hope I'll be able to help. I'm nervous that nothing will happen, and I'll just waste the detective's time. My abilities seem to come and go."

"Don't put too much pressure on yourself. If you receive any impressions, it will be tremendous. But if you don't, please don't blame yourself or your abilities. The residual energy you sensed in that ring could have only been a stored memory, caught in a loop, like a record. Or a reel-to-reel tape recorder."

"Can that really happen?"

"Yes. I've seen it with some supposedly haunted houses. Wood, stone, plaster—they all absorb the energy around them and store it.

Some of the hauntings I've researched aren't phantasms or ghosts at all, but stored memories. Jewelry is a particularly effective psychic sponge, because of the molecular structure inherent with precious stones and metals."

"How fascinating."

"It is." Dr. Hansen smiled. "I've spent so many years looking for answers to the unexplained, and you're helping me immensely in my work, Loretta. I can't overstate that enough. I just hope it doesn't come at too much of a cost to you. How are things at home?"

"Nothing frightening has happened since I saw you last—nothing crashing down off the walls. I took your advice." She motioned to her hair. "This was part of that—of doing something for myself." She paused before speaking again, wondering if she should tell him the rest. But he was her friend—he'd said so himself. And she might need his and Barbara's help, if it came down to it. Especially if Pete ever got violent again. "I've decided I'm going to leave Pete, Doctor. Eventually. I just need to bide my time for now. Until I have more money saved up and a plan."

"I'm sorry to hear it's gotten to that point. But I'm also relieved you're choosing yourself and your children, Loretta. These things are never easy."

"No," Loretta said, shaking her head. "They're not. But he frightens me. His mood swings, his temper. I don't see things getting better. No matter how much I try to change and be the kind of wife he'd like me to be, we can't seem to make things stick. I need peace, Dr. Hansen, even though I know I'm in for a long, difficult road." Loretta thought of Gladys, and how quickly they had bonded. Earl and Pete were colleagues and friends. As soon as she left Pete, he'd no doubt work to undermine her friendship with Gladys and turn her and the rest of the church against Loretta. She'd be a scarlet woman in their eyes. It was a difficult price to pay, but for the sake of Luke and Charlotte, she would give up anything.

"No matter what happens, you'll have my support, and Barbara's as well," Dr. Hansen said. "I can promise you that. Have you still been writing?"

"Yes!" she exclaimed. "I have. I've written seven new stories, just this week. That typewriter you gave me is a champ. I submitted my original three to the *Myrna Grove Focus*. They rejected them. But I sent them on to the *Kansas City Star* and the *Saturday Evening Post*."

"Not to worry. Even the best writers get rejected. The key is to not give up. My first few academic articles were rejected, too. You'll find a home for your writing, eventually."

"I hope so." Loretta watched the city fly by as they made their way toward the northern city limits, where a hand-painted mural proclaimed THANK YOU FOR VISITING MYRNA GROVE, A GOOD PLACE TO GROW. Eventually, distance stretched between the houses, and they became grander as the highway unspooled. Loretta wondered if Dr. Hansen's wife had grown up in one of these monstrous houses, where the descendants of Myrna Grove's founding elite still lived. The winter landscape held a bleak, desolate beauty, with naked trees clawing toward the gray sky and a blanket of crisp frost on the manicured lawns.

"We're almost there. Have you ever been to Dearing Park?"

"Yes, a few times."

"Then you know about the cave. When Paula disappeared, there were rumors she'd been kidnapped by a satanic cult that held rituals inside the cave. But none of the evidence pointed to that and the cave was searched thoroughly."

"I keep getting the sense that there's something with the father," Loretta said, tapping her knee. "Was he investigated?"

"Yes, but in a rather shallow way. He's an influential businessman in Myrna Grove—owns a paper mill. They live near the park. Detective Pierce was ordered to back off by his superiors, several times. Most of the investigation focused on Paula's boyfriend."

"And he was found innocent?"

"He had an airtight alibi. He was at work the night Paula disappeared."

"All right. That gives me a place to start, but I don't want too much information, just in case it influences my impressions."

"You're becoming adept, Loretta. I'm impressed. You're testing your boundaries—with both your psychic abilities and your everyday life, and that's a good thing."

Loretta smiled inwardly. Despite her modesty, she was pleased that Dr. Hansen regarded her so highly. She was proud of how far she'd come, too. Now if she could just find Joan. Every night, she sent up a prayer for the girl's safety.

They turned down the winding road leading to the park and went through the metal gate with its curling script. In the distance, a Ferris wheel's hibernating skeleton stood above the trees. She and Pete had shared their first kiss on that Ferris wheel—a memory that set her heart aching for the past, when she was flush with the fever of new love.

They approached the arched giraffe-stone bridge. Detective Pierce stood there, looking down at the water. As he heard them arrive, he gave a friendly wave and came to open Loretta's door.

"Good afternoon, Mrs. Davenport. How are you feeling?"

"Excited, but a little nervous, too."

"Don't be nervous. We'll walk down the hill, to the mouth of the cave. That's where we found this." Detective Pierce reached into his coat pocket and pulled something out, smoothing it in his hands. It was a beret, made of loden-green wool. "Paula was wearing it that night."

"Shall I put it on?"

"If you'd like. Or you could just hold it. Whatever you're comfortable with."

"Perhaps we should wait until we get to the cave," Dr. Hansen said, politely interjecting. "Just in case Loretta is overcome by her impressions and needs to sit." He offered Loretta his arm. "The path becomes quite steep."

Loretta wound her arm through his, relishing his closeness. She leaned into the solid strength of his arms as they went downhill, letting him guide her as the paved path became slippery with ice. His warmth bled through the layers of wool separating them. Loretta shook herself out of her adulterous thoughts. They were only friends. Colleagues. Partners in research. Nothing more.

Up ahead, the cave yawned, the spring at its mouth a slow, icy trickle as it ran over the rocks. Dead vines draped the entrance. A park bench sat near the edge of the path. Dr. Hansen led her there and sat next to her, his arm still entwined with hers. Anyone passing by might think they were a couple. He momentarily took her hand and squeezed it. She felt the cold press of his wedding ring as he pulled away.

"I'll be close by, Loretta, should you need me," he said, standing. "I don't want to interfere with your concentration."

Detective Pierce handed her the beret, and Loretta put it on. Immediately, a wave of nausea and faintness overcame her, nearly making her vomit. Loretta forced herself to breathe slowly, placing her hands on the park bench to ground herself in reality as images spilled into her mind and overtook her senses. She tasted alcohol mixed with bile, bitter on her tongue. "She was sick," Loretta said, gagging. "She'd had too much to drink. That's why she left the party early. They wouldn't stop pressuring her to drink."

She closed her eyes and saw the world through Paula's eyes—the silent sketch of the amusement park rides, the reflecting pond with its boats moored and covered for winter. Paula's brown leather oxfords whipped through the dead grass as she made her way across the park, the distant sounds of the party fading, until all she could hear was the rasp of her labored breathing. She was alone. She was afraid. Someone named Toni was supposed take her home, but Toni was drunk, too, busy necking with a boy. Dizziness muddled her senses, made her stumble. She caught herself against the bridge post, tried to steady her breathing. Vomited into the creek.

She was halfway down the hill when she realized she was being followed. She paused to listen, her heart beating like a frightened rabbit's. Another set of footsteps stopped behind her. At first, she thought it might be her friend Toni, come to fetch her and take her home. She turned, calling the girl's name. But it wasn't Toni. It was a man, his hulking figure silhouetted against the sky. Paula whimpered and ran blindly, panic driving her feet. She'd almost made it to the bottom of the hill when her foot caught a stone, and she fell, her ankle twisting beneath her. The man was on her in an instant. Paula flailed in his arms, clawed at him. The moon came out from behind the clouds, illuminating her assailant's face. Disgusting, lurid memories flooded Loretta's mind. Paula's memories. His fingers closed around her throat, stealing her breath. He grunted as she kicked, one of her knees finding purchase in his groin, but he didn't let up. The world faded, the edges of her vision blackening. There was a slight *pop*, and then Paula's spirit was outside of her body, watching as her lifeless corpse was carried into the cave.

Loretta surfaced from the vision, gasping. She tore the hat from her head and threw it to the ground. "It was him. It was him. It was him."

"Who was it, Mrs. Davenport?" Detective Pierce asked.

"Give her a moment, please, Steven," Dr. Hansen said gently. He sat next to Loretta, and she collapsed against him, weeping. "There now, you're here. You're here with me. You're safe."

"He killed her," Loretta said, panting. "He did terrible things to her, over the years. She was going to tell her mother. It would have ruined their marriage. His reputation. So he killed her."

"Paula's father. George Buckley. That's who you're talking about, Mrs. Davenport?" Detective Pierce asked, his voice rising in pitch. "You're absolutely sure?"

"I think so. I had an impression it was him, before, with the ring. But she showed me everything just now. It was horrible." Loretta wiped at her eyes. "You'll find her in the cave. I don't think they went back far enough when they searched for her before."

Loretta leaned into Dr. Hansen's shoulder, and he put his arm around her, his solid strength a comfort. She had the strange, sudden urge to look at the mouth of the cave. She raised her head. Paula's spirit stood there, watching them, her party dress torn, her coat hanging crookedly off her shoulder. A month or so ago, the spirits had startled Loretta—made her almost jump out of her skin. Now she just saw them as they were—hurting people who needed her help. As Loretta watched, Paula's spirit gave a slight nod and then turned away, fading into the darkness of the cave.

"Anything else, ma'am?" Detective Pierce asked, looking up from his notes.

"No," Loretta said, letting out a long breath. "Nothing more about Paula. But there's something else that's been bothering me. There's a girl. Joan. I believe she lives on Bethel's campus, in Ashley House. I don't know her last name. But during one of my visions, Darcy's spirit told me that her killer wanted to hurt Joan, too. She knows the murderer. Perhaps you might go there—interview the girls."

"A student at Bethel?" Detective Pierce cocked an eyebrow. "How interesting."

"You believe me, don't you?"

"You've done enough to prove yourself to me, but I'll say we got an anonymous tip about this Joan, since Detective Eames didn't believe you about Darcy. We'll also get a team out here to search the cave. And if we do find Paula's body, I'll make sure everyone on the force knows it was you who led us to her."

Loretta tensed. If word got out in Myrna Grove that she helped solve a murder mystery with ESP, Pete would find out. Reporters would want to interview her. It could quickly become a media circus, especially if they ended up charging someone as influential as George Buckley for the crime.

"If you wouldn't mind, Detective," Loretta said, "I'd prefer to remain anonymous. It's enough for me to know that I've helped. I don't want, or need, any credit. I'm just happy to be believed."

"Well. If you're right about this, it won't be the last time I call on you. You could prove to be one hell of an ace in the hole, Mrs. Davenport," Detective Pierce said, smiling.

"I'd be glad to help again."

Dr. Hansen stood, offering Loretta his hand. "We should be getting you home, Loretta. You're sure to be tired after all this."

"I am." Even though her eyelids were heavy as lead and exhaustion hung on every limb, Loretta felt exhilarated. She'd used her gift to a good end and helped Detective Pierce. If she was right about Paula, what else might be possible? How many more families might she be able to help? Only time would tell.

✧

That evening, after a short nap, Loretta woke refreshed and eager to make the most of the time she had left alone with the kids before Pete's return. She served baked spaghetti, Luke's favorite meal, followed by chocolate cake for dessert. After, she tuned the radio to KWTO. She turned up the music, and she and Charlotte danced by the light of the Christmas tree as Lucas laughed at their antics. His black eye had faded, with barely a trace of yellow around the socket. The kids were so different when Pete was away. They were all so much happier.

Loretta had just stopped dancing to catch her breath when the phone rang. She turned down the radio, which blasted Jerry Lee Lewis, and went to answer it.

"Hello?"

"Retta? Why are you so out of breath?"

It was Pete. Her good mood fell. Loretta wrapped the phone cord around herself and leaned against the kitchen counter, her eyes going to the ceiling. She spotted another crack forming in the archway between the kitchen and living room. She was beginning to wonder if there was a problem with the foundation.

"I was putting away laundry. I ran downstairs when I heard the phone ring. Didn't want to miss your call."

"Oh."

"How's the conference?"

"It's been swell, but I'm going to come home a little early. Thinking about driving back tonight." Maybe it was only her imagination, but his words seemed to slur together at the end.

"Have you been drinking?"

"Really, Loretta? No. I haven't."

In the background, Loretta heard someone say something to Pete. His reply was muffled, as if he had placed his hand over the phone receiver.

"Is someone there with you?"

"Just Earl. He's wanting to go to dinner."

An uncomfortable wrongness wove through Loretta's gut. That week, when she'd been with Gladys, she hadn't mentioned anything about Earl being out of town with Pete. "Tell him I said hello. Gladys and I are supposed to meet for coffee soon."

Pete went quiet for a moment. "Oh, really?"

Loretta chased the nervous jig in Pete's voice. "Yes. And I saw her just the other day as well."

"Can't you find someone else to have coffee with? You know I don't like her."

She heard more scrabbling in the background. More muffled voices. "Look, Loretta. I need to go. I'll be home by morning, all right?"

She heard a click, and then the line went silent. As soon as the dial tone sounded, before she could talk herself out of it, she dialed Gladys's number. She answered on the third ring.

"Hi, Gladys. It's Loretta."

"Loretta! I was just thinking about you. I have a dress for you. It will need to be altered a bit, I think, so I was going to bring it by to have you try it on and take your measurements."

"That sounds lovely." Loretta paused, her pulse hammering as the question she wanted to ask Gladys waited on the tip of her tongue. *Is Earl there with you? Or is he in Saint Louis with Pete?* But asking in that way would immediately alert Gladys she thought something fishy was going on. She changed her tack. "How is Earl?"

"Oh, he's peachy!" Gladys said. "We've just finished up dinner, and we're sitting down to watch the football game."

A cold chill walked down Loretta's spine. "Oh, well, I won't keep you, then."

"I'll call you tomorrow, okay?"

"Sure thing. Good night, Gladys."

"Good night, doll."

Loretta unwound herself from the phone cord and hung up. She sat at the table, her head in her hands. Pete had lied about Earl. But if Earl wasn't in the room with him, who was? Was he having an affair? She hadn't been able to discern whether the voice she'd heard in the background belonged to a man or woman. And was Pete even in Saint Louis? If she'd been thinking straight, she would have asked which hotel he was staying at, so she could call to see if there was a conference there.

Later, after the kids were in bed, Loretta rummaged through Pete's drawers, looking for any clues to his deception. She found only stacks of perfectly folded undershirts and pants. She went to the closet and checked his suit jackets next, her hand darting into pockets. Nothing. If he was having an affair, he was covering his tracks well.

A thought came to her, as she sorted through his dirty laundry. She'd been able to help Detective Pierce by reading Paula's things. She could try holding one of Pete's objects—to see if she got any impressions, as she had with Paula's beret.

She sat on the edge of the bed, holding a pair of Pete's cuff links. She closed her eyes and stilled her breathing, focusing on the feel of the cool metal in her hands. After a few minutes, the cuff links warmed, and a series of images flashed through her mind: Pete lifting a tumbler of whiskey to his smiling lips. Male laughter. A thread of music. The clink of silverware. Her suspicions were right. He hadn't been going to AA meetings. He'd been going out—drinking on the sly. Lying to her.

A thrill of anger flowed through her. Pete was her husband—the person she was supposed to be closest to, the person she was supposed to trust most. She'd spent years blaming herself for their problems. Years apologizing and trying her best to be a good, godly wife. Only to be betrayed. And if he was drinking, what else might he be hiding? His hypocrisy sickened her. Just like on the day her mother died, the bad feeling in her belly crested and told her something was horribly, terribly wrong.

Chapter 22

Dawn was graying through the windows when she felt Pete slide into bed next to her. He pulled her close, nuzzling her neck with his nose. "Good morning," he murmured. "I've missed you." One of his hands moved to her breast, kneading her flesh roughly. The other reached for the hem of her nightgown.

Loretta tensed and pushed his hands away. She rolled onto her back. "I have my period," she lied.

"Well, that's a fine welcome home."

"I can't help it that I'm bleeding."

"I don't know if I believe you."

He reached for her again. She scrambled across the mattress and out of bed. Pete sighed. "I knew it. That's fine, Loretta. You're lucky I'm tired." He stretched, yawned. "We'll try again later. When I've had some sleep and you're in a better mood."

Loretta eyed the crack in the ceiling above the bed. "I think there's a problem with the house, Pete. Haven't you noticed all these cracks in the ceiling?"

"Cracks?"

"Yes, look." Loretta pointed to the ceiling.

"I don't see anything." Pete squinted.

"Only because you don't have your glasses on."

Pete reached for his glasses, put them on. "There's nothing there, Loretta. Are you seeing things again?"

"No. There's one downstairs, too. Above the sink. And last night, when I was on the phone with you, I noticed one in the archway between the kitchen and living room."

"I'll look later. When I get up."

"All right. How was Saint Louis?" she asked lightly. "Did you and Earl have a good time?"

"It was fine. I'm tired, Retta. If you're not going to come back to bed, let me go to sleep." Pete rolled onto his side, took off his glasses, and closed his eyes. So, instead of telling her the truth, he was going to shut her out. Loretta gathered her robe and slippers and left the bedroom. She'd been tempted to play her trump card. Had almost told him she knew he'd lied about Saint Louis. But she needed to be careful. Needed to bide her time. Angering him now, before she was ready to leave, would be a dangerous mistake.

She went downstairs and filled the percolator with cold water and mounded coffee into the filter basket, her hands trembling. A hard, heavy rain started up outside, beating the roof. Lucas came down a few moments later and sat at the table.

"Are you all right, Mom?"

"Yes, honey."

"You look upset."

"I'm fine. I just need my coffee."

"Dad's home, isn't he? I heard him come in."

"Yes."

Luke frowned. "Is he being mean to you again?"

"No," she lied. "I'm okay. I promise."

"Things are better when he's gone," Luke said, in a near whisper. "You're happier. I wish . . ."

"You wish what, Luke?" Pete's voice cut through the hum of the rain like a blade.

Loretta's heart nearly stopped beating. Pete stood on the stairs, his eyes pointed like twin daggers at the back of Luke's head.

"I thought you were sleeping," Loretta said.

He ignored her. "I asked you a question, Luke. You wish what?"

"N-nothing," Luke said, turning in his chair. "I just said I'm glad you're home."

"That's not what you said, son."

"Yes, it is, Pete. You couldn't have heard him from there."

"But I did. I heard everything. What have you been telling the kids while I've been gone, Loretta?"

Loretta's knees went to jelly. "I haven't told them a thing."

Pete stalked across the room and lifted Luke from his chair by the elbow. "What do you wish, Luke? Tell me."

"I'll tell you, all right!" Luke said, his face reddening. "I wish you'd leave again! I wish you'd go away and never come back!"

"Don't you dare talk to me that way," Pete seethed. He grasped Lucas by the collar of his pajama shirt and backed him into the wall.

"No! Leave him alone!" Loretta tried to sandwich herself between Pete and Luke, but Pete pushed her, hard, and she fell to the floor, her head narrowly missing the table leg. A deep groan came from above. Loretta looked up. The crack in the ceiling above the sink was widening before her eyes. A ruddy, reddish stain began seeping through the plaster. "The crack . . ." she said weakly, rising to her knees. "Pete! Something's happening with the house!"

"Shut up, Loretta!" Pete said, temporarily letting go of Luke to haul her up from the floor. He pushed her into a chair and bracketed her with his arms. His eyes narrowed. "Have you done something to your hair?"

Panic threaded through Loretta. "What do you mean?"

"Your hair. It's red." Pete held her in place and wrested the pins free from her hair. It fell around her shoulders in a tangled cascade. "Where did you get the money to do this? Your doctor friend?"

"Gladys. She wanted to do something nice for me. I told the beautician just to trim it, but she cut too much off!"

"This is why I didn't want you hanging around that woman." Pete twisted his hand in her hair, yanking painfully. Loretta gasped. "You look like a whore."

Luke screamed in rage. He launched himself at Pete, broadside, sending him to the floor. "Leave her alone!"

"No!" Loretta scrambled from the chair, helplessness flooding her limbs. Pete wrestled with Lucas, trying to straddle and subdue him, but Luke was like an enraged wildcat. Pete was taller than Luke, but their son nearly matched him, pound for pound.

Charlotte came running down the stairs, her eyes wide. "Daddy! Stop!"

That unearthly, deep groan came again, like a giant's voice, reverberating through the kitchen so loudly Loretta felt it in her bones. The plaster above the sink began to crumble like a wet biscuit. There was a loud, metallic wrenching. A gout of water burst through the ceiling, soaking the floor. Everything slowed down, as if they were caught in some horrible stop-motion film.

Luke fought his way from Pete and joined Charlotte at Loretta's side. They dived under the table, just as the ceiling joists gave way and the upstairs bathtub came crashing down from above. Wet plaster, insulation, and rotten wood rained down, showering the kitchen with filth.

"Goddammit!" Pete swore. "Why didn't you tell me there was a leak?"

"I've been trying! I told you about the cracks this morning!" Loretta emerged from beneath the table, brushing plaster from her clothes. The bathtub was wedged halfway through the gaping hole in the ceiling, temporarily cantilevered and supported by the upper cabinets. The window above the sink was broken. Cold air stirred the curtains. Rain spat onto the floor.

"This is going to cost a fortune," Pete said, pacing. "Dammit! This is the last thing I need right now."

"I'll . . . I'll call a plumber today. Start getting estimates. Do you think our insurance might cover it?"

"I don't know," Pete said, kicking at the detritus. "I don't know! Everything's a mess. Everything's falling apart." He almost looked like he was going to cry. "I can't fix any of it."

"Why don't you go upstairs. See what the damage is like up there, while I clean this mess up," she said smoothly. "We'll get it fixed, Pete. We're not the only ones this has ever happened to."

Pete trudged up the stairs, grumbling to himself. After he'd gone, Loretta gathered Luke in her arms. "Are you all right, baby? He didn't hurt you, did he?"

Luke shook his head and sobbed against her chest. "I'm so sorry."

"It's not your fault." She lifted his chin, looking him over. He had a small scratch on his cheek, but other than that, it didn't look as if Pete had done any real damage—apart from the emotional scars Luke would likely bear for years. Scars that would never really heal.

"I hate how he talks to you," Luke said. "He's so mean."

"I don't like it when he gets mad," Charlotte echoed softly. "It's scary."

Loretta sat in the ruins of her kitchen. Her scalp ached where Pete had pulled her hair. She put her fingers to the spot, and they came away bloody. She drew her children close, lowering her voice to a whisper. "Can I tell you both a secret? It must stay a secret, or it may never happen. Promise me you won't tell another soul."

Charlotte nodded solemnly, crossing her heart. "Promise."

"And I know you can keep a secret, Lukie."

"Yes. I can."

Loretta took a deep breath, lowering her voice to a whisper. "Mommy is working on something. A way out. For all three of us."

"You and Dad are getting divorced?" Luke asked in a whisper.

Loretta wasn't prepared for that question. But divorce was the logical, eventual outcome to her leaving. She might soften the blow with words like "separation" or "time away," but that wasn't what she wanted. She wanted a clean break. She'd lied to Pete plenty. But she would never lie to her children.

She met Luke's gaze evenly. "I'll have to talk to a lawyer. See what they say. But yes, I think so. Eventually."

He looked away, crossing his arms over his chest. "Good."

"What do you think, Char?"

Charlotte bit her lip, weaving her fingers together on her lap. "I love Daddy, but I don't like it when he's home. He scares me. Would it just be the three of us from now on?"

"I'm not sure. That'll be up to the judge, I think."

"I hope I never have to see him again," Luke said through clenched teeth. "I wish he were dead."

"Oh, honey. You don't mean that."

"Yes. I do."

Loretta shivered at the coldness in Luke's voice. But hadn't she thought the same thing, from time to time? How much easier it might be if Pete died? Instead of a divorcée, she'd be a widow and the object of pity and compassion instead of scorn. The thoughts made her feel ashamed and guilty, but hearing them echoed by Luke set her spine to steel. She glanced at the ruined ceiling and wondered, if somehow, she was to blame.

She had to get out. Soon. Before things got worse.

Chapter 23

Loretta stared at the crack in the bedroom ceiling, at the narrow lines that branched outward from the main artery. "There's definitely something wrong with the foundation, Pete," she whispered in the early-morning darkness. "There are cracks all over the place. Perhaps we should have the workmen take a look when they come."

"I can't afford to have anything more done, Retta. We'll get the leak repaired, and then we'll see. They're charging us more because they're coming on the weekend, as it is. At this rate, I'm going to have to take a second job to keep a roof over our heads."

"I could work," she offered, rolling over to face him. "I could get a part-time job, just while the kids are at school. The grocery store is hiring."

"No." Pete laughed roughly. "I'm not going to have the other faculty wives talking about how they saw Professor Davenport's wife working at the market. It'll get back to their husbands, and then I'll be the laughingstock of Bethel."

It was always about Pete. His reputation. What others might think or say about him. As if any of that mattered to Loretta. She needed money. And she needed it fast.

She'd discreetly scanned the classified section of the Friday paper in the aftermath of the kitchen catastrophe. There were very few job postings for Myrna Grove that she could get to without a car, and fewer still that paid above minimum wage. With the average two-bedroom apartment costing forty to fifty dollars a month, plus utilities and groceries, she'd need to make at least fifteen dollars a week. Few jobs would pay an entry-level worker that.

Loretta could go to Dr. Hansen or Barbara—could lean on their offered charity—but she wanted to do things on her own. Wanted to prove to Pete and everyone else that she could be independent and make a living. And she needed to consult with an attorney. Which would also take money, if she even had a case. Pete's drinking might not be cause enough for divorce. But she had a strong suspicion, given his lie about Saint Louis, that he might be having an affair. An affair would be enough to ensure a divorce—if she could prove his infidelity.

She sighed and focused on the crack. Imagined flowers growing out if it, reaching tendrils of yellow toward her. Even dandelions found a way to grow in the bleakest conditions, pushing up through sidewalks and forcing their way through the hard-packed earth.

Pete was snoring again, sated by their perfunctory lovemaking and oblivious to her thoughts. Her needs. Her everything. She rose and quietly padded across the floor on bare feet. If she was quiet enough, perhaps she could sneak down to the basement and get a few words written before he woke. It was a risk she was desperate enough to take.

Downstairs, Loretta cast a wary eye at the bathtub, still suspended over the kitchen sink. Pink light bled through the sheets of waxed paper she'd taped over the broken window. She had perhaps an hour at best to write in solitude before morning would bring her family out of their beds.

She lit her lamp and felt her way down the rickety basement steps, wincing as the brittle wood creaked beneath her weight. She sat at her makeshift desk, considered the half-finished story about the never-ending nature of laundry, and pulled the paper from the carrier. She would finish it later. Another idea had taken root, as she lay in bed, watching her house crumble around her—something darker. Something horrific and honest.

Something that better reflected her circumstances and the broken world she lived in. Loretta wound a fresh sheet of paper into the typewriter and began.

❦

The plumber scratched his head, eyeing the ceiling. "Job's gonna take at least three days. The water's leaked for so long it's rotted the floor joists under the upstairs bathroom. Whole floor might need to be replaced. I'll have to call in more contractors for the plaster and paint. We don't do that."

"How much will it cost?" Pete asked.

"Oh, rough estimate, about a hundred to two hundred dollars."

Pete exhaled. "That much?"

"It's a big job. You can pull more estimates, if you want, but we're the cheapest in Myrna Grove. And we do good work, too."

"Thank you," Loretta said, taking the man's offered card. "We'll call once we've made a decision."

After the plumber left, Pete paced around the kitchen, swearing and slamming cabinet doors, looking for something to eat. He wasn't even trying to hide his foul moods anymore.

"I'll start lunch, here in a bit," Loretta said. "I can put some soup on."

"I'm tired of soup. I'm going to the diner." Pete stalked to the living room, where Lucas and Charlotte were playing a game of Scrabble. He threw on his coat and hat. "I'm sick of looking at this mess."

"But the other plumbers will be here in an hour, Pete."

"You can talk to them. Just don't hire anyone until I say so."

Pete slammed the front door, and a few moments later, Loretta heard the Chrysler's tires spit gravel as he backed out of the driveway and sped away. Loretta let out a sigh of relief, hoping they'd have at least an hour or so of peace before he came back. She had come to dread the weekends, with their unrelenting tension, like a minefield, where one false step or a word said wrong might set off an explosion.

"Do you want grilled cheese for lunch?" she asked cheerfully, in a vain attempt to hide the tremor in her voice.

Charlotte and Lucas looked up from their game. "Sure!" Luke said. "Make mine with extra cheese, please."

"All right. And after we've had lunch, I want to join your game."

"But you always win, Mommy," Charlotte said. "You think of the best words."

Loretta thought of the writing she'd done that morning. Of all her very best words strung together, like a road—a road that might, some-day, somehow lead her somewhere new.

Chapter 24

Loretta would never forget December 6, 1955. For the rest of her life, she'd remember the way the sun rose brightly that morning and bathed the world in warmth, dancing over the freshly fallen snow and sparkling through the new kitchen window. She clutched the telephone in her hands, her breath stilling as the voice on the other side spoke the words she had prayed to hear.

"And so, Mrs. Davenport, the feature pays twenty dollars a week. If you agree to the terms in our contract, you'll send us a new story each week, to be received no later than Wednesday, to be corrected in time to go to press by Friday. Do you understand?"

"Yes, I do," she said breathlessly. She paced to and fro across the linoleum, silent tears sliding down her cheeks. She wanted to dance. Wanted to shout. Eighty dollars a month. For her silly little stories! And on the months with five Fridays, a hundred. With that, she could afford to rent a three-bedroom apartment. Or a whole house, even!

"These stories will become the exclusive property of the *Kansas City Star* upon receipt. You won't be able to publish them elsewhere. Are these terms satisfactory to you?"

"Yes. It all sounds wonderful. You've no idea how happy you've made me."

"Well, we do enjoy discovering new talent, Mrs. Davenport. We'll send payment for the three stories you've already submitted to us today. You should receive the contract and the check in a few days."

"Thank you. Thank you so very much!"

"You're quite welcome, Mrs. Davenport—or should I call you Mrs. Harrington?"

"Either is fine!" Loretta laughed, then tried her best to compose herself. "I'm sorry. I'm a little giddy right now."

"Of course, of course. Well. We look forward to seeing more of your features. I have a feeling they'll be very popular."

"I do hope so."

"Goodbye, Mrs. Davenport. And congratulations."

"Thank you, sir. Goodbye."

Loretta hung up the phone and stood for a long moment in utter astonishment. She was going to be published—by the same newspaper that had published Ernest Hemingway. A dreamy haze settled over her. She eyed the patch of wet plaster above her head. The repairs were almost finished. The contractors had lived up to their promise. They'd worked diligently, and quickly, repairing floor joists and setting new pipes. Now all that remained was for the plaster to dry and the painters to come.

On Thursday morning, when the promised check and contract arrived, she held the envelope with the kind of reverence she'd only ever reserved for scripture. It was the very first piece of mail she'd ever gotten with her name, and only her name, on it. Loretta walked to the post office to set up a PO box and then to the bank, not caring if Phyllis Colton was spying out her window. No one could tell her what to do anymore. She was the captain of her own fate now.

She whisked into the bank lobby, bouncing with excitement as she joined the line for the teller window. When it was her turn, Loretta presented the signed check and her driver's license. "I'd like to open a checking account with this, please. And reserve a safe-deposit box as well."

The teller looked at her, incredulous. "Is your husband with you?"

"Pardon?" Loretta asked.

"Your husband, ma'am," the teller replied icily. He raised an eyebrow. "Your husband, or another male relative if you're *not* married, must cosign for you. Ladies aren't allowed to open a bank account on their own here. Not outright."

"Oh." Loretta's hopes crashed around her. She certainly couldn't ask Pete to cosign. He'd take every bit of her money—or worse, forbid her from writing her weekly column in the first place.

The teller pushed the check and her license toward her. "Come back with your husband, your brother, your father, anyone else in your family of the male persuasion. When you do, I can issue you an account."

"Couldn't you just cash this, then? Please?"

"I'm sorry, ma'am. I can't. Now, if you'll please step aside for the next customer."

Loretta left the bank, dejected. She had no male relatives, aside from Pete. None who lived close by, at any rate. Daddy had died three years ago, after a stroke, and her only uncle lived in Evansville, Illinois.

Loretta carefully folded the check, placed it in her handbag, and walked home. The Christmas gala was tomorrow, and she hadn't a thing to wear. Pete had forbidden Gladys from coming by and bringing her dresses. He was embarrassed by the thought of Loretta wearing another woman's clothes, and after he'd seen her hair, he told Loretta there would be no more coffee dates or socializing with Gladys, ever again. When Gladys had called, Loretta hung up on her, and ignored the phone's incessant ringing, until her friend eventually gave up and the phone went silent. It saddened her immensely to lose Gladys, but she'd known it would be inevitable, especially once she left Pete.

But she'd never be able to leave Pete if she couldn't cash her own checks.

❧

That afternoon, Loretta sat next to the fire in Dr. Hansen's office, holding Ollie. The old yellow tom purred contentedly in her lap, resting his head on the arm of the chair. They'd had a good, if emotionally taxing, session that day. They'd attempted to trigger a psychokinetic episode through talk of Pete's latest tirade, which elicited a ten-minute-long crying jag from Loretta, but nothing else happened. The objects in Dr. Hansen's study remained blessedly untouched and unbroken. He'd comforted her after with a walk in the gardens, and now he was finishing his notes as they enjoyed their tea by the fire.

"Have you spoken to Detective Pierce since we went to the park?" Loretta asked. She'd often wondered what might be happening behind the scenes with Paula's investigation over the past week, but her domestic struggles since Pete's return had overtaken everything.

Dr. Hansen looked up from his writing. "I spoke to him just yesterday. They've managed to pull extra manpower from the sheriff's office. They'll start searching the cave for Paula's body tomorrow."

"Good. Hopefully they'll find her. Her spirit deserves rest. Has he had any luck finding out anything about Joan?"

"I'm not sure. But knowing Steven, he'll pursue your lead. He's a diligent investigator." Dr. Hansen peered at her thoughtfully. "Do you have something else on your mind, Loretta? You've been pensive all afternoon."

"I . . . have some news. Good and bad."

"Yes?"

Loretta tapped her foot on the carpet. Oliver sensed her agitation and jumped down, crossed to Dr. Hansen, and rubbed against his pant leg. "I'm to be a published author, it seems. The *Kansas City Star* has accepted three of my stories, and they want a new one from me every week."

Dr. Hansen beamed. "Why, that's excellent news, Loretta! How proud you must be."

She exhaled, sitting back in her chair, her cheeks coloring. "Yes, I'm very happy about it. It's the first thing I've ever been paid for." She bit her lip, tap-tapped her foot. "They sent the check this week. Twenty whole dollars for each article, so sixty dollars in total."

"That's wonderful!"

"Yes. For my silly little stories." Loretta paused, counted the tick-tick-tick of the clock on the mantel. "I've decided I'm leaving Pete this summer, after the kids are out of school. If I can write a new article every week, I'll make plenty to rent an apartment or a small house of my own. There's only one problem."

"You can't cash your checks without your husband signing them."

Sometimes she wondered if Dr. Hansen could read her mind. She shook her head. "No. Nor open my own bank account, or even reserve a safe-deposit box. It's ridiculous. I went to the bank this morning. I can't do anything without my husband's permission."

"Or another male relative."

"Yes. And those are in short supply, I'm afraid. I only have one living uncle, and he's in Illinois. I haven't seen him in years." Tears threatened behind Loretta's eyes. "I can't tell Pete about this money. It'll ruin everything."

"Of course not. Well, there's a simple solution. You and I will go to the bank, any bank you choose, right now. I did the same thing for Barbara when she divorced. I'll say I'm your brother and that you're a widow. They'll never know we're lying. Our different last names won't matter. They don't check birth certificates, only driver's licenses." Dr. Hansen stood. "One way or another, you're going to have the money you've earned, Loretta."

Her tears came again, sharp and biting. She seemed to always be crying lately. Loretta turned away, wiping them discreetly. "You'd do that? For me?"

"Of course I would."

Fifteen minutes later, they stood at the teller window of Myrna Grove First Savings and Loan. A different teller was working—a woman this time—who cheerfully welcomed Loretta and her "brother." Loretta signed the paperwork for the account, then passed it to Dr. Hansen, who signed his name beneath hers.

"Now, Mr. Hansen, you'll have to grant permission for the safe-deposit box as well," the teller said. "Your sister will have the main key, but if you'd like, I can give you a copy, too."

"Yes," Loretta said. "I want him to have a key."

"Are you sure, Loretta?" Dr. Hansen asked.

Loretta's breath hitched as their eyes met for a long moment. "Yes, Doc—Curtis. I'm sure." It was the first time she'd called him by his Christian name. Even though circumstances necessitated it, it seemed intimate, personal—both the giving of the key and her use of his name.

The truth was, Dr. Hansen was the only person she trusted. She thought of the stacks of manuscripts back home, in the basement. If Pete ever found them, he'd destroy them. The first thing she intended to do in the morning was to bring them here, to the bank, along with her better jewelry and some of the cash she'd been secretly saving. If something happened to her, Dr. Hansen would make sure Charlotte and Luke would get her things. Pete was unpredictable. Loretta thought of that day after church, when he'd driven like a maniac and nearly killed them. Once she left, he might be capable of anything.

After they'd finished with the paperwork, Dr. Hansen offered Loretta his arm as they went down the bank steps. "How are you feeling?"

"Relieved, mostly. Like a thousand bricks have been lifted off my back."

"You should do something to celebrate."

"I should, shouldn't I?"

"I'll take you wherever you'd like to go."

Loretta thought about it for a moment as he helped her into the passenger side of the Cadillac. What *would* she do with the crisp twenty-dollar bill she'd reserved? If she were being bold, she'd offer to treat Dr. Hansen to lunch—somewhere nice, like the Shady Inn, to express her gratitude. But then people might see them together and assume the wrong sort of thing. Someone who knew Pete. She couldn't risk it. Not with her children in the balance. But she did want to do *something* special to mark the occasion.

As they pulled into traffic, an idea came to her. "There's a boutique downtown. Called Savage Juliet. I've never been, but a friend of mine told me about it."

"Yes. Barbara shops there."

"Could you take me? It wouldn't be any trouble, would it?"

"Not at all." Dr. Hansen smiled. "My next patient won't arrive until four, and it's close enough to the office."

"All right. I'll be quick."

A few minutes later, Dr. Hansen pulled the Cadillac in front of the boutique and parked next to the curb. "I'll wait for you here. Take your time."

Loretta placed a dime in the parking meter, then stood outside the brass-trimmed doors for a long moment, taking in the festively decorated windows. A mannequin wearing a luxurious fur coat stood as the centerpiece, her plaster hand extended and dripping with glimmering baubles.

Her heart thrummed with excitement as she opened the door. A burst of warm, perfumed air greeted her as she went inside. Loretta's eyes widened at the array of gorgeous dresses, coats, and shoes, and the long glass counter that held all manner of jewelry and accessories. It was a feast for her senses. And she had a whole twenty dollars to spend.

A salesgirl looked up from her place behind the counter. "Good afternoon! Were you looking for anything in particular today?"

"I have a Christmas party tomorrow night. And I haven't anything to wear."

"Well. I think we can remedy that." The salesgirl came out from behind the counter and looked Loretta up and down. "I have just the thing, I think. Wait right here."

Loretta perused the goods inside the lit counter while she waited. Cocktail rings mounted on rolled velvet winked at her, their colorful facets gleaming. Farther down, elbow-length gloves made of satin sat next to a bejeweled clutch, a lacquered lipstick case with a mirrored flap, and opera glasses. The placard in front of the ensemble read A NIGHT AT THE OPERA. Loretta longed to be the type of woman who needed elbow-length gloves and opera glasses. She imagined herself, draped in silks and satin, arriving at the Landon Theater on Dr. Hansen's arm. The thought enlivened, then embarrassed her. How silly she was to imagine such a thing!

"Here we are," the salesgirl called. "We just got this in yesterday. When I saw your hair, I thought of this dress immediately. Redheads look wonderful in green." She held up a stunning dress for Loretta. The full skirt, made of iridescent, starched taffeta shifted between gold and a rich olive green. A dazzling Lurex sash gathered the waist. The bodice was enhanced by a shoulder-baring shawl collar. It was like nothing she'd ever worn.

"Would you like to try it on? If so, I can fetch a strapless bra and can-can. You'll need both with this dress."

Loretta hesitated. She knew she wouldn't buy the dress, no matter how much she might want to. It was too attention-grabbing and immodest. And even if it were more demure, Pete would ask too many questions. Still, a part of her thrilled at the thought of wearing something so fine, even if she never got past the dressing room with it. "Sure. I'd love to try it on," she said. "It's beautiful."

The salesgirl nodded. "I'll fetch the undergarments and meet you at the dressing rooms. They're near the coats."

Loretta made her way through the racks, her hand trailing over the myriad soft furs, in all colors and lengths. Astrakhan. Mink. Arctic fox.

She went into one of the curtained alcoves and slipped out of her shoes, rolling her feet on the plush carpet to soothe the ache from the narrow, pointed heels Pete had bought her. The shoes did wonders for her legs, but they were cheap and uncomfortable. Perhaps once she was single, she'd come back to Savage Juliet and buy a new pair that didn't hurt her feet. Only five more months. Summer would come, she would leave Pete, and then she'd dress however she liked. She wouldn't need Pete's permission or money for anything, ever again.

The salesgirl returned a few moments later, with a strapless longline brassiere and an armful of tulle can-cans. "Go ahead and get undressed, and I'll help you with the brassiere."

Loretta hesitated, thinking of the marks on her belly. "Can I leave my girdle and stockings on?" she asked. "It's such a hassle to get them back on."

"Of course."

Loretta unbuttoned her coat, then removed her sweater set and skirt. The cool air hit her skin, setting it to prickle. She reached behind her back and unhooked her bra. The salesgirl averted her eyes and wrapped the longline bra around Loretta's torso, quick as a flash. She did up the clasps at the back and helped Loretta step into the petticoats. Then she lifted the green dress.

"Arms up!"

Loretta raised her arms as the cloud of taffeta settled over her shoulders and fell around her hips. She spared a shy glance in the mirror as the salesgirl did up the zipper. The brassiere hoisted her bosom and whittled her waistline dramatically, giving her figure an exaggerated hourglass silhouette. The dress fit like it had been made for her. Loretta smoothed her hands over her hips, turning to admire the way the back dipped low, between her shoulder blades. A broad smile spread over her lips, her cheeks blazing with color. She felt glamorous. Sophisticated. Like the woman she'd fantasized about becoming.

"It's perfect for you," the salesgirl said. "I knew it would be."

"How much is it?"

"Fifteen, including the undergarments."

Temptation warred with Loretta's common sense. She *could* buy the dress. Hide it. Save it for her eventual exodus. But she wanted to wear it now. It deserved to be seen—not hidden at the back of her closet or in a box beneath the bed.

"I'm afraid that's a little more than my budget will allow," Loretta said, crestfallen.

"Oh. I'm so sorry. If your husband would like to come in with you, he could apply for a line of credit and you could make payments. Is that him, waiting for you outside?"

Loretta shook her head. "No. He's only a friend." Even *that* sounded ridiculous. The salesgirl probably thought she was his mistress—a kept woman. After all, proper married women didn't go around in cars with men who weren't their husbands. "I'm sorry to have wasted your time."

"I could look for something a bit more economical, if you'd like. We have some dresses from last season in the back. They're still lovely."

"I-I'd better be going. My children will be getting home from school soon. Perhaps I can come back when I get my next paycheck."

"Certainly. My name is Pamela. Just ask for me when you come back. I never forget a face."

Pamela helped her out of the precious, perfect dress, then left. Loretta donned her dull woolens and went to the counter, eyes darting once more to the lacquered lipstick case. It was special and lovely, with its gilded scrollwork pattern, twinkling crystal accents, and velvet-lined interior. She thought of the tube of Cherries in the Snow Gladys had given her, and how perfectly it would fit inside the case. It was so small, Pete would never know she had it.

When Pamela returned to the counter, Loretta pointed to the lipstick case. "How much for that?"

"It's five dollars. Those are Swarovski crystals, embedded in the lacquer. It came all the way from Austria. It's very unique. One of a kind."

A thrill ran through Loretta at the thought of owning something so special and frivolous. A tiny treasure, purchased with her own money. Something meant only for herself, to mark how far she'd come. "I'll take it."

Pamela smiled. "All right. I'll wrap it up for you."

As Loretta secreted the small, tissue-wrapped package in her coat pocket, she thought once more how wonderful it would feel to be the kind of woman who wore the clothes in that store. With twenty whole dollars a week—someday, that woman might be her.

Chapter 25

The bad feeling broke over Loretta the next morning—a familiar, deep dread that lodged in her belly and gnawed at her insides all through breakfast. By early afternoon, she had a massive headache but forced herself to walk to the bank to secure her manuscripts, thirty dollars in cash, an extra key to her post-office box, and her best jewelry. As she made her way back home, she decided to plead sickness to avoid going to the Christmas gala that night. She had nothing to wear, and she couldn't bear the thought of facing Gladys in one of her plain dresses after she'd ignored her calls and her kindness. Pete would be angry, but he was always angry with her now, anyway.

When Loretta returned from the bank, she spotted Phyllis Colton in her backyard. Loretta paused in the alleyway behind the house, watching as Phyllis cupped her hands around her face and peered into their back windows, standing on tiptoe.

Loretta crept through the rear gate and cleared her throat, loudly.

Phyllis turned. "There you are! I was worried about you. I've been knocking all morning and couldn't get you by phone, either. I thought you were hurt."

"I was just out for a walk."

"Well, all that walking has you slimming down."

Loretta gritted her teeth behind her smile. "Did you have something important to tell me, Phyllis?"

"Just that I'll be over at six o'clock. To watch the children. Pete asked if I would. Said you had some kind of to-do tonight. I was going to ask you what they might want for dinner."

"Oh. I've decided I'm not going."

"Why not?"

"I've had a horrible headache all day. And I'm sick to my stomach now, too."

Phyllis lowered her gaze to Loretta's stomach. "You're not in the family way, are you?"

Loretta's anxious thoughts multiplied. What if she was? What if her diaphragm had slipped, or failed? The thought sickened her even more.

"I'm sorry, Phyllis, but I really need to go lie down," she said, pushing past Phyllis to the back steps, her key at the ready. "I appreciate your offer to babysit, but I don't think we'll need you."

"Maybe you'll change your mind after you've had a nap." A frown crept across Phyllis's pinched, birdlike face. "After all, you seemed to have mustered up enough energy for a walk."

"I'll let you know," Loretta said curtly, and went inside. She rushed to the powder room as the wave of nausea crested, fell to her knees in front of the toilet, and promptly retched up her breakfast. As she washed her face and hands, a flicker of movement caught her eye in the mirror. She startled. For a brief second, a face appeared in the glass, behind her.

"Is someone here?" she asked. "Do you have something to tell me? It's all right if you do."

Be careful.

The words were nothing more than a shaky, slight whisper that hung in the air for a moment, lingering like the faintest wisp of perfume.

❧

"What do you mean you're not going?" Pete paced their bedroom floor, his agitation visible in every step. "You can't do this tonight, Loretta."

"I've been sick all day, Pete. I'm not exaggerating. I can't keep anything down." Loretta crossed her arms over her churning belly. Something bad was going to happen. The voice had warned her, too. *Be careful.*

Pete looped a silk necktie around his collar and tightened it. "You're always sick whenever it's convenient for you. I'm not having it. Get dressed."

"I don't have anything to wear, remember?"

Pete went to the closet and jerked open the door. He began throwing dresses onto their bed. "This one will work. So will this one. I'm going over to fetch Phyllis. By the time I get back, I want you dressed and ready to go."

"I . . . I think something bad is going to happen tonight, Pete. I really do. I don't think either one of us should go. What if there's a fire while we're gone? Or we get into a car accident. What would the kids do if both of us died?"

"Your imagination is something else. You know that?" Pete slung a suit jacket over his dress shirt, then sat on the edge of the bed to tie up his oxfords. "The kids'll be fine. We'll be fine. This is an important night, Retta. I'm up for tenure review in January. Do you know what that means?"

"Yes."

"I'm doing this for you and the kids. That's why I've been working so hard. Don't let me down."

After Pete stormed out, Loretta considered the three dresses he'd flung onto the bed. She picked up the long-sleeved, modest gray silk shantung she'd worn to a faculty dinner three years ago and prayed it still fit. By some miracle, it did, though the zipper snagged slightly in the middle of her back before completing its path.

Loretta hurriedly exchanged her wool stockings for nylon, tidied her hair, and considered her nearly empty jewelry box. The only pieces she hadn't taken to the bank that morning were her wedding pearls and Mama's amber brooch. She took out the brooch and held it for a moment before pinning it to the pleats at her shoulder, where it added a bit of color to the plain dress. She considered herself in the mirror—her glum expression, the sickly pallor to her skin, the dark circles beneath her eyes. She looked as terrible as she felt.

She switched off the bedroom lights and went downstairs. Lucas and Charlotte sat in front of the Christmas tree, playing with the train set and miniature village beneath. Charlotte looked up at Loretta, a tiny porcelain dog in her hands. The first thing Loretta planned to do once they had a place of their own would be to get Charlotte her longed-for puppy.

"You're going, Mommy?" Charlotte asked. "I thought you were staying home with us."

"Daddy wants me to go with him. Mrs. Colton is going to come stay with you while we're gone. It won't be for long. Only a few hours."

"Oh." Charlotte's face fell. "I don't like her. She looks like the mean lady in *The Wizard of Oz*. The one who took Toto."

Loretta stifled a laugh. "Charlotte, that's not very kind."

"I'm just going to go up to my room and draw while she's here." Lucas shrugged. "You can stay with me until bedtime if you want, Char."

"At least wait until Daddy gets back with Mrs. Colton, Luke. Say hello. No need to be rude."

She couldn't blame her children for their displeasure over Phyllis. The thought of their nosy neighbor being inside their house for hours rankled Loretta, too. She imagined every piece of mail Phyllis might snoop through—imagined her riffling through their drawers and cupboards, looking for anything she might hold over Loretta's head.

Loretta went to the sink and poured a glass of water, eyeing the ceiling. No crack. Only fresh white paint. She took two aspirin, then sat primly on the edge of the couch with her handbag on her lap, watching the kids play. The uncomfortable high-heeled pumps were already pinching her toes. What was taking Pete so long at Phyllis's?

As if summoned, he came through the door a moment later, Phyllis behind him. She cast a nervous eye to Loretta, then greeted the kids effusively. They were polite, if guarded, and allowed her to kneel on the floor next to them and inspect the miniature village and train.

"Are you ready?" Pete asked, his eyes hard as flint.

"Yes." Loretta stood and went to her children, kissing each of them on the top of their head. She closed her eyes for a moment, hoping the bad feeling was just that—a feeling—and then reached for her coat. "Be good, darlings," she said. "I love you."

"For heaven's sake. We're not going to the outer reaches of Siberia, Retta." Pete took her elbow and guided her to the door. "Let's go. We're already late."

As Pete whisked her down the porch steps and to the car, Loretta's eyes went to the corner of the house. The Chrysler's headlights shone against the clapboards. A crack reached up from the ground, just behind the bare limbs of her hydrangea bush, running through the foundation. "Pete, look. There's another crack. I'm telling you, we need to have the house inspected. I'm afraid it's going to come crashing down around us."

"Get in the car, Retta. I'm not in the mood to talk about the house."

"What's wrong?"

Pete got behind the wheel, slamming his door closed. He was angry beyond his earlier irritation at her. Something had happened, at Phyllis's. She'd told him something. The wrongness settled in Loretta's gut, like a slag of lead. She tilted her head to look at the sky, where the stars shone in the bright, clear night, and sent up a hushed prayer before getting inside the car.

Pete began backing out of the driveway before she could close the door, not even giving her time to settle in her seat. He whipped the Chrysler onto the street and changed gears. Loretta gasped, steadying herself with a hand to the dash as Pete sped to the corner. He didn't stop at the intersection—merely slowed down for the briefest of seconds—and then careened onto Mount Vernon.

"Pete. Please. What's the matter?"

"Oh, you know exactly what the matter is, *doll*," he sneered. "Don't you?"

"I have no idea what you're talking about."

"Playing dumb. Like always. You forget we have a party line, Retta."

Phyllis. She'd been listening in on her phone conversations. Loretta remembered the day she'd called Barbara to tell her Pete had taken the car—the series of clicks she'd heard in the background. She'd dismissed her worries. But now, she knew. How many phone calls had Phyllis listened in on, lurking quietly in the background of her conversations?

"I know you're still meeting that man. That doctor. Phyllis heard you on the phone with his secretary. And she saw the two of you together, yesterday. She was at the cemetery decorating graves when he dropped you off at the corner."

"Yes. I've still been seeing him." There was no use in lying. Loretta's hands clenched around her purse handle. Anger flared alongside her fear. She thought of the night Pete called and lied to her, from a hotel room in Saint Louis. With someone who definitely *wasn't* Earl McAndrews. She could spit accusatory words of her own. The temptation was there. It danced on her tongue.

Be careful, the voice warned. She had to think of the children. She had to survive this night, come what may. *Be careful.*

"Are you sleeping with him?" Pete asked. He pulled to an abrupt stop at the light on Chestnut and College.

"Would you believe me if I told you I wasn't?"

"I can't believe a word you say anymore, Loretta. You've broken covenant. In many ways. I could divorce you. Take the kids. Is that what you want?"

"No. You're not taking my children. Divorce me if you must. God knows we're both miserable. But you're not taking my babies from me."

"You're a terrible mother. Sleeping all day. Feeding them junk. Leaving them alone to meet that man. Phyllis told me everything that happened while I was gone. I'll have her testify on my behalf, if necessary."

Loretta flinched. There was something base and horrific about a woman turning against her own sex. And for what gain? For titillation? Did Phyllis hold some bizarre fantasy that Pete might fall in love with her? "Why does Phyllis care so much?"

"Family values, Loretta. Women like Phyllis sacrifice their own needs for their husbands and children."

"Yet her own children never visit her. Don't you wonder why that is?"

"This isn't about Phyllis. This is about us. About your lies."

The light changed. Bethel lay just ahead, on the right, the campus cheerfully lit up for the holidays. Pete took a hard turn into the circle drive, then slowed the car to a crawl, looking for a place to park. "This is why I didn't want to be late. It's going to take forever to find a parking spot. Dinner will have already started by the time we walk in. We'll make a scene."

Always worried about what people would think. Not the fact that his marriage was crumbling and he'd just threatened to take her children. But she wasn't surprised. Pete only saw the world through his own personal lens. No one else mattered unless they had something they might give him. Something that might make him feel more important than he was. Loretta had never been that person. She'd only ever been flotsam in his life—a charity case, excess baggage. A burden.

When they finally found parking, almost a block away from Wilson Hall, which served as the student union and event building, the feeling of dread at Loretta's core sent her guts reeling. She fought the urge to vomit as Pete flung open her door. The night air hit her like a splash of cold water.

"Come on. You've made us late enough." He took her by the elbow and marched her down the street, walking at a fast-paced staccato clip. At the corner, her ankle turned in her cheap shoes. She gasped and came to a stop. Pete yanked on her arm. "What's the matter now?"

"I twisted my ankle."

His heavy sigh clouded the air between them. "I never should have bought you those shoes. You don't even know how to walk in them."

He slowed, ever so slightly, allowing her to lean on his arm as they approached Wilson Hall, where the lights blazed yellow through the floor-to-ceiling windows. It was the newest building on campus—with an arched, sloping roof meant to look modern. To Loretta, it resembled an oversize barn.

Inside, people milled about, their conversations amplified by the soaring ceiling. A magnificent cedar tree stood at the center of the room, decorated with red-ribbon bows and electric candles. Evergreen garlands draped the beams, lending a brisk aroma to the room. It was a lovely display, but all Loretta could think about was how much she wished she were at home. With her children. She should never have left them with Phyllis.

"Ah, Peter. There you are. Wondered when you'd be getting here." Dean Matthews approached, dressed in a natty sharkskin suit with a plaid bow tie.

Pete dropped Loretta's arm to shake his boss's hand. "Sorry to be late, sir. You know how it is with a wife. They take twice as long to get ready."

Dean Matthews smiled at Loretta warmly. "I miss those days, myself. Wish I could have them back. Patsy's been gone for two years, and I miss her the most whenever we have an event like this. She always made me look better. How are you, Mrs. Davenport?"

"I'm well, sir. Thank you so much for asking." She ignored her throbbing ankle and smiled in what she hoped was a becoming way. She didn't belong at these events. Didn't like them. Hated the pretension of men who thought themselves cleverer than her because of the string of letters behind their names. Resented having to play the dutiful, if stupid, wife.

"The other ladies are over by the dessert table, Loretta," Pete said as Dean Matthews turned to greet another late arrival. "Why don't you go say hello?"

"Am I allowed to speak to Gladys tonight? I'm bound to run into her, and I owe her some sort of explanation."

"Be cordial. But not too friendly. Just use your head, Loretta. Don't say or do anything rash. Remember what we talked about in the car. Things are going to change, starting tonight, and they're going to go my way, or—"

"I understand," Loretta said sharply. "I'll see you at dinner."

She took a cranberry spritzer—virgin, of course—from a passing server, and nervously wove through the sea of suits and modestly fashionable party dresses, looking for Gladys. Even though she dreaded explaining herself, Gladys deserved an apology.

Loretta found her by the punch bowl, stirring frozen sorbet into the mint-sprigged, foamy liquid. Gladys was turned out in vibrant red satin, a festive green and red dotted sash emphasizing her still-narrow waist. She glanced up when she saw Loretta. Her mascaraed eyes fell over the plain gray dress and then came back to Loretta's face. Instead of judgment and anger, Loretta saw only sympathy there.

"Loretta. I've been so worried about you," Gladys said, relinquishing her punch bowl duties to another of the faculty wives and coming to Loretta's side. She took both her hands. "Why didn't you answer my calls?"

Loretta glanced left and right, to see if Pete was nearby, watching her. She saw no sign of him. "Things have gotten worse. He wouldn't let me talk to you on the phone."

"Oh no. I wondered."

"There's so much more I could tell you. He's threatened to take the children from me if I don't fall in line."

"What? Why?" Gladys's eyes widened. "Surely he hasn't any grounds for a divorce."

"I can't . . . I can't tell you everything." Loretta thought of Dr. Hansen, and how even though she wasn't having an affair, her affection for him made it feel as though she were. "But he's found out I've been lying to him about leaving the house—our neighbor has been watching me." Loretta patted her hair. "And he isn't pleased about this, either."

"I worried about that. But getting your hair done made you so happy. Surely he wants you to be happy, doesn't he?"

Loretta's throat clenched. Tears threatened behind her eyes. "I don't know, Gladys. I think he only wants me to be happy on his terms. Not my own."

A bell rang cheerfully above the conversational din.

"That's dinner. We'd better find our seats. We'll talk more after the music. I sat you and Pete across from Reverend Mountjoy. He's really something. You'll see."

Oh yes. The healing evangelist from Georgia. Pete would want to impress him. Which meant he would either be extra critical of her every word and action or ignore her entirely. She hoped it would be the latter. She'd do her best to stay quiet and small. The way he liked her.

❦

"Well, you see, spiritual oppression can take many forms. There's outright demonic possession, which usually presents as an aggressive ambivalence to any mention of Christianity and besets the victim with ailments of a physical and mental nature. A certain kind of madness, you might say. But the enemy has several methods in his employ." Reverend Richard Mountjoy dabbed at his plump mouth, taking a sip of water before continuing. "Many times, the attacker will be more subtle. The oppressed might suffer from a lack of sleep, or too much of it. Changes in appetite or mood. A general disinterest in the things a person once enjoyed—specifically the study of scripture and church attendance."

Pete nodded thoughtfully. "And what of the occult? Is a person inviting the Devil in by reading about occult practices?"

Loretta sat stock-still, her fork poised midway to her mouth.

"Oh, naturally," Mountjoy drawled. "It's like opening a door and ushering in all manner of evil spirits. A person who entertains such interests—no matter how innocent their intentions—is sure to soon be utterly beset by oppression." He shoveled another forkful of potatoes au gratin into his mouth. "Why, I once delivered a young woman of twenty demons. All because she had watched a friend receive a card reading by a fortune teller. Merely being in the same room was enough to set the evil spirits upon her, like dogs on a ham steak."

Pete cast a sidelong gaze at Loretta. "How unfortunate."

"Yes. But after a long evening spent in prayer, with laying on of hands and calling on the name of Christ, the young woman was freed of her oppression. She went on to marry a year later and had no further issues. Happy as a clam, with a new baby. She gives her testimony each time I visit her church. It always leads to a resounding altar call."

The bad feeling tangled and tumbled in Loretta's belly, stealing her appetite. She pushed back from the table and half rose from her chair, vomit threatening at the back of her throat. "Pardon me. I need to go to the powder room."

Pete grasped her wrist. "Can't you wait? The girls' choir is getting ready to perform."

Loretta sank back down into her chair and took a drink of water to quell her nausea. Her hand shook as she returned the water glass to the table. A carillon of bells sounded through the room, and a line of girls dressed in white and gold robes entered, each carrying a bell. They swung them on cue, producing a lovely chorus of tones.

They arranged themselves before the Christmas tree in a semicircle, facing the long dining table. The director, a small, mousy woman dressed in a sensible navy suit sprigged with an evergreen corsage, came to the front to address the crowd.

"The Bethel Girls' Choir is pleased to present a special selection of a cappella Christmas medleys for you this evening. Soloists will include Joan Everly and Marjorie Brown."

Joan Everly. Could this be Darcy's Joan?

The director blew on her pitch pipe, and the girls lifted their songbooks in unison, as pure and chaste as a heavenly troupe of angels. They began with "O Holy Night," their voices rising to the rafters and resonating in the large room. On the second verse, a young woman stepped forward, her head a halo of brilliant copper ringlets. She looked very pale and seemed frightened as her eyes darted around the room. Her eyes landed on Loretta briefly, then flinched away. But when she opened her mouth, all her timidity disappeared. Her voice rang out with a confident, crystalline purity, as bright as a winter's day as she soared through the highest, most challenging notes. At the end, she stepped back, taking her place in the line of girls. Loretta smiled when the girl's eyes skittishly danced to hers once more.

The choir moved seamlessly into "O Little Town of Bethlehem" and ended with a rousing rendition of "Hark! The Herald Angels Sing." Loretta rose with the rest of the audience, applauding. The girls bowed and then filed out, ringing their cheerful carillon.

As the sounds of the bells faded, the pains in her lower belly came again in a wave, this time sharper than before. Loretta hunched forward, clutching at her stomach beneath the table. The pain radiated to her right flank, cramping so badly she thought she might cry out. A cold sweat broke out along her forehead. She dabbed at her face with her napkin. What if she had appendicitis? Or worse yet, a pregnancy gone wrong? One of the ladies at church had died of such a thing, just the year before. A tubal pregnancy. Phyllis Colton's words haunted her.

You're not in the family way, are you?

"I have . . . to go . . . to the bathroom," she whispered. "Can I please be excused now?"

Pete peered at her, narrowing his eyes. "What's wrong?"

"I don't know. Something's upset my stomach."

"All right. But come right back. They'll be serving dessert soon, and then Reverend Mountjoy will be giving his message in the chapel."

"I . . . I'll hurry," she said, and stood, her head swimming. When she reached the ladies' powder room, she barely made it to a commode before the urge to vomit overtook her. She knelt on the tile floor and retched into the toilet. Hot and cold chills walked over her skin. *Was* she pregnant? She thought back to her last menstrual cycle. She was a few days late, she supposed. But not by much. This could be anything.

The door to the restroom swung open, squeaking on its hinges. Then the tap-tap of high-heeled shoes. Loretta worked her way up from the floor, using the toilet seat for leverage. How embarrassing it would be for one of the other faculty wives to see her like this!

"Loretta? Is that you in there?"

It was Gladys. Relief washed over Loretta. "Yes, it's me."

"I saw you leave the table." Gladys rushed around the corner. "Are you sick?"

"There's something wrong. With my belly. I've been nauseous for the past two days."

"Honey, you're bleeding. Did you know that?" Gladys motioned to Loretta's legs.

Loretta lifted her skirt and looked down. A thin trail of blood ran down her left leg, staining her nylons. Another wave of relief passed through her. "Oh, thank goodness. I was worried I might be pregnant. Do you happen to have a sanitary napkin?"

"No, remember?" she said, touching her belly and smiling. "But there's a machine. Right over here. It's only a nickel. Go back in the stall, and I'll pass it under the door."

"I don't have a belt with me."

"Oh, it comes with a paper belt. Are you wearing a panty girdle?"

"Yes."

"Well, just put the pad inside your girdle. It'll work, for now."

Loretta went back inside the stall, pulled the swinging door to, and latched it. She heard a metallic cranking, and then Gladys's hand appeared beneath the door, holding a slim cardboard box. "I'm going to wet some paper towelettes so you can wash up. I'll hand them under, too."

"You're so kind, Gladys. I'm grateful."

"Of course! Heaven knows I've been there."

Loretta worked her girdle to the side, as much as she could, and forced the pad into place. It bunched uncomfortably between her legs, but it would have to do. Gladys offered the wet towelettes beneath the door, and Loretta used them to dab the stains from her nylons, then went out to the sink to wash her hands.

"You should make Pete take you home," Gladys said.

"I'll be all right," Loretta said, sitting on the counter to relieve the pressure on her throbbing ankle. "I've had hard periods like this before. I just need to rest here for a moment."

"Well, if you're sure you'll be okay. I'd probably better be getting back, to help with dessert."

"I'm sure I'll be fine."

The outer door swung open once more. The redheaded soloist from the girls' choir glanced at Loretta and Gladys and then furtively ducked into a stall.

After Gladys had gone, Loretta leaned her head against the wall, absorbing the chill from the lime-green tile. Her head pounded from the pressure of throwing up, but her nausea had abated somewhat. Only cramps. She wasn't sick with some grievous disease that might send her to an early grave. She closed her eyes for a moment, thankful to be away from the loud party and Pete.

From inside the stall where the redheaded girl had gone, Loretta heard a wet sniffling. Then a full-on whimper. She was crying. With Loretta perched as she was atop the counter, the girl probably thought herself alone.

Loretta cleared her throat. The crying abruptly stopped. "I liked your singing," she offered gently.

There was a beat of silence. "Thank you."

"Are you Marjorie or Joan?"

"Joan," the girl said softly. She emerged from the stall and went to the sink. She glanced at Loretta, then looked away. Loretta noticed the girl's hands trembling. It was more than nervousness. She was afraid—of something or someone.

The girl switched on the tap. But instead of clear, clean water, mud sputtered from the faucet. Joan seemed oblivious, running her hands beneath the dirt-clotted stream and lathering soap into her palms.

"The water . . ." Loretta said. "Can't you see the water?"

Joan looked at her in confusion. "What?"

Suddenly, the taste of wet leaves flooded Loretta's mouth. She gagged and slowly turned her head toward the mirror. Reflected in the glass, a shadowy figure emerged from behind Joan, her face pale and half-hidden by her hair. Darcy. Realization poured over Loretta.

"Joan," she whispered. "You're Darcy's friend Joan, aren't you?"

The girl gasped, her green eyes widening. "How did you know that?"

Loretta stood, reaching out. Her hand brushed against the girl's dress. In an instant, a thousand images flashed into Loretta's mind. A car's headlights. Squealing brakes. A piercing scream. Darcy's face, streaked with mud, her right leg bent at an odd angle. A sterile, cold room, lit with fluorescent light. A man with ice-cold hands, the lower half of his face hidden by a surgical mask.

Holdherlegs. Holdherlegs.

"Get away from me!" Joan cried. She backed away from Loretta, her eyes wild. "Don't touch me!" The girl turned, fleeing through the restroom door.

"Joan, wait! Please!" Loretta followed, hobbling as fast as she could go. But when she reached the hallway, she saw no sign of the girl. It was as if she had vanished.

"I'll find her, Darcy, I will," Loretta whispered. A cold breeze whispered near her, brushing her bare forearms like a frigid caress. "And when I do, I'll tell Joan she needs to leave. Before he hurts her, too."

Chapter 26

Loretta peered over the crowd of people gathered outside the student chapel, looking for a bright spark of copper hair. She'd searched the library and study rooms during the dessert service but had seen no sign of Joan.

"What are you doing?" Pete asked, grasping her arm.

"Looking for someone."

"Who?"

"That girl who sang earlier. Joan. I wanted to tell her how much I admired her singing," she lied.

"She probably went back to her dorm room. I'll make sure the choir director knows you enjoyed the program." The line forming in front of the chapel shifted. The doors to the chapel opened and a blast of organ music sounded from within. Pete's grip tightened on her arm. "You're going forward for the altar call at the end of the service. Reverend Mountjoy wants to pray with you."

"What? Why?"

Pete looked down at her, his eyes hooded. "You heard our conversation earlier, Loretta. At dinner. About the dangers of the occult. When you left the table, he told me he could sense the oppression surrounding you. That man—that doctor—has beguiled you. Turned you away from God and your family."

"There's nothing wrong with me." Loretta jerked her arm from his grasp, anger simmering through her. "And the only thing that bedevils me is *you*."

"He said you'd be resistant. It's proof of the oppression. You're sick with it."

"I'm not going into that chapel," Loretta said, pushing against Pete.

His hand clamped on her shoulder like a vise. "Remember what we talked about in the car?" he whispered harshly. "Do you want everyone to know what you've been doing? What a bad mother you are, leaving your children alone at home to meet your lover?"

Ice danced down Loretta's spine. *Was* she a bad mother? She'd certainly felt guilty enough lately to have her doubts. She'd lost her temper with the kids the day Pete had left for Saint Louis. And she shouldn't have left the children alone to seek comfort from Dr. Hansen. Even though nothing had happened to them and she was in sight of the house. She had been distracted lately. Neglectful. And no matter how much she wished to deny Pete's accusations, she desired Dr. Hansen. Did desiring someone without acting on those feelings still count as adultery?

No matter what, she needed to play along with Pete's demands. Pretend to be agreeable, at least for tonight and the rest of the weekend. Come Monday, she'd keep the kids home from school, pack their things, and call Barbara. It wasn't ideal. Money would be tight for a while, and she'd have to rely on Barbara's and Dr. Hansen's charity. But the thought of spending the months before summer under Pete's thumb maddened her. If the children were in her custody when she left, perhaps she would have the upper hand in the courts. Their marriage would end—of that she had no doubt—but it would end on her terms. Not his.

Organ music surged as they moved forward, beckoning the crowd into the candlelit chapel. Loretta forced her tense muscles to relax.

Forced a smile onto her face. "I'll try to be better, Pete. I will. I just want us to be happy again."

"There's my good girl," Pete said, brushing his lips against her cheek. She resisted flinching, even though inside, she recoiled at his touch.

He guided her up the evergreen-bedecked aisle as the bad feeling tangled and clawed at her from within, telling her to run. To hide. To leave. Instead, she sat next to Pete in the second pew as Reverend Mountjoy took his place behind the rostrum. After leading them in song, Mountjoy motioned to a woman sitting in the front pew. She rose and came forward, standing next to the minister, her fingers laced primly together.

"Hello," she began, "my name is Thelma Haseltine. I'm here tonight to give my testimony. A year ago, I was consumed by my own vices. I was having an affair. Drinking. I'd gotten caught up in all manner of sinful things." She turned to gaze at the minister with adoring eyes. "And then Reverend Mountjoy came to my church, for a special healing service, just like this one. He told me if I'd believe in the power of the Holy Spirit, all my transgressions would be forgiven, and I'd no longer be tempted to stray. That night, I was delivered of my sins and set free from my bondage."

From the back of the church, someone shouted, "Amen."

Thelma Haseltine stepped down, and two more women took her place. The first was a teenage girl who had made the mistake of using a Ouija board at a party and unwittingly summoned a legion of demons, and the other was a weary-looking woman who had been hooked on barbiturates until she encountered Reverend Mountjoy's miraculous healing touch. While Loretta didn't doubt the sincerity in the women's words, a part of her rankled at how Reverend Mountjoy had chosen only women to give testimony.

"Does he ever deliver men of their afflictions, I wonder?" Loretta asked Pete as the plates for the love offering made their way through the congregation. "To be here tonight, you'd think women are the only ones who ever sin."

Pete's jaw flexed. "It's blasphemy to mock the Holy Spirit or deny the Gifts of the Spirit, Loretta."

"Is it?" Loretta asked under her breath. She didn't recall Pete worrying about denying *her* gifts.

After the women finished testifying, the organ kicked up again with a muted version of "Just as I Am." Reverend Mountjoy grew somber, his head bowing slightly. "In this season of hope, God has called me to offer a message of healing and restoration, as well as salvation. If you've never accepted Jesus Christ as your Lord and Savior, this altar is open. If you need a healing touch, for your body, mind, or spirit, this altar is open. Come sit at the feet of the Master. Come touch His robe and be restored through the power of prayer, brothers and sisters."

People slowly rose and began walking to the front of the chapel. As they knelt at the upholstered benches before the altar, Reverend Mountjoy moved to each one of them, his hands hovering over them as he began to pray, speaking softly in tongues.

"Come on, Loretta," Pete whispered, rising from their pew. "I'll pray with you."

"Can't we just pray here?"

"Going forward will make a statement. It'll show the faculty that you're a worthy helpmate."

A worthy helpmate. So, it was about him again. About what people thought. "I'm not going up there. There's nothing wrong with me, Pete. I've never been closer to God in my life."

"You've been deceived. You can't see it now, but you will."

"I *have* been deceived. But not by Dr. Hansen." She turned to him, her eyes blazing. "I know you lied about Earl being with you in Saint Louis. I called Gladys after I hung up with you. Earl was home with her. You were with someone else. Who was it, Pete?"

"I don't know what you're talking about. I never told you I was with Earl."

"Yes, you did! That night when you called from your hotel room. So if it wasn't Earl, who was it? Was it a woman?"

"That's enough." Pete lifted her from her seat, forcefully pushing her into the aisle. Loretta's heart hammered beneath her rib cage. As Pete marched her to the front, Loretta caught a glimpse of Joan, coming forward at the same time. She was crying, her eyes flooded with tears.

When they reached the altar, Loretta knelt on the carpeted floor, and Pete sank down next to her, wrapping his arm around her back, holding her in place. To anyone else, it would appear he was praying with her like a loving husband. But she could feel the anger and tension rolling off Pete. He was furious at being caught in his lie. He had tried to pass it off as her imagination—that she had made it up—but she knew what she'd heard.

Loretta cradled her head in her hands on the bench, peering beneath her folded elbow, watching as Joan knelt just a few feet away. A few of the congregants moved to the crying girl, laid hands on her, and began praying.

Loretta sensed Reverend Mountjoy's presence before she saw him— smelled his obnoxious musky cologne. Pete stood to speak to him, their voices low. Now was her chance. She could make her way over to Joan. Give her Darcy's warning message, under the guise of prayer.

Loretta rose on shaky legs and backed away from the altar. Pete's head swiveled in her direction, his eyes narrowing. Reverend Mountjoy nudged Pete and they moved toward her, as one. The bad feeling at Loretta's core became a torrent of dread. She willed her feet to move faster, to run to the side door of the chapel and escape into the night. But with her sprained ankle and the pinching shoes, she got to only the edge of the pews before the men caught up to her. Mountjoy took her by one arm, and Pete took her by the other.

"What are you doing?" She locked her knees, rooting herself to the spot as they pulled and tugged at her.

"Only helping you, Sister Davenport," Reverend Mountjoy intoned, his eyes scraping over her. "Now, don't fight us," he said gently, as if he were speaking to a child. "This is for your own good." The minister's grip on her arm tightened. "Deacon Black," he called, "take over the service while we see to Sister Davenport. Brother McAndrews, come with us. We might need more hands."

Panic clawed at Loretta's insides. "No! What are you doing?" She thrashed as the men half dragged her to the passageway leading to the offices behind the chapel sanctuary. The narrow hallway closed in as Pete pressed her forward, forcing her into the first office they came to and shutting the door behind them. He walked her backward until her hips met the edge of the desk, then pushed her onto it. Reverend Mountjoy grasped her wrists and twisted them above her head, until she was lying on her back, looking up at the popcorn ceiling.

She bucked and tried to twist away, but Pete half lay atop her. "Retta, be still. Let him help you."

"I don't need help."

"I told you," Reverend Mountjoy said, chuckling. "Things can get a little wild. Keep hold of her legs, Brother Davenport. Otherwise, you might get a mule kick to the face once we really get started. Brother McAndrews, hold her shoulders. We're in for a fight, I'm afraid."

Holdherlegs

Loretta thrashed as Pete grasped her ankles and Earl pushed her shoulders hard against the desktop. A bead of sweat dropped off the tip of his nose and landed on her cheek.

Reverend Mountjoy took a vial of anointing oil from his jacket pocket and began applying it to Loretta's forehead. Prayer flowed from his lips in an unknown language, the language she'd prayed to receive so many times herself—but instead she'd been given something else.

Something that now had her flat on her back in a cramped college office, accused of blasphemy and consorting with the Devil.

Loretta turned her head to the wall, her eyes locking on a portrait of Jesus, head haloed in Glory as He prayed in the Garden of Gethsemane, the Holy Spirit soaring in the form of a dove in the background.

Forgive them, Father. For they know not what they do.

Reverend Mountjoy ceased his prayers and pressed a hand to Loretta's forehead. The back of her head ground against the desktop. "Tell us your name, demon!"

None of this felt real. How any of this could be happening among so-called intelligent people—college professors, no less—mystified Loretta. She would be tempted to laugh at the ridiculousness of the situation if she weren't so afraid. And worse yet, no one in the chapel had intervened when they took her away. But hadn't she witnessed others being prayed over, during those early tent revivals with Pete, where the impassioned shouts and theatrics held her in thrall? Reverend Mountjoy was just the same as those traveling evangelists—a showman full of himself and convinced of his calling.

As Mountjoy railed at the imaginary demon once more, Loretta clenched her teeth and struggled to free herself. "There is no demon," she said. "The only spirit that resides within me is God's spirit."

"Lies!" Reverend Mountjoy roared, spittle flying from his mouth. "How dare you mock the Holy Spirit. Tell me your name, deceiver!"

Mountjoy struck her, his open hand landing across her lips in a stinging slap. Loretta tasted blood. Tears sprang to her eyes as Mountjoy's hands roved over her, muttering his useless deliverance prayers. He pressed down on her belly, painfully digging in with his fingers. She screamed, arching her back, and managed to kick free of Pete's grasp. She wriggled off the edge of the desk, tried to stand.

"Loretta, be still! Let him help you." Pete wrestled her back onto the desk. One of her nylons ripped as his fingers clawed at her legs, locking her ankles together. A dizzying sickness flooded her at his touch. Her vision spun. She screamed again, but the music soaring from the chapel drowned out her voice.

"Hoo. This one's a wildcat," Mountjoy exclaimed, almost gleefully. "We'll have to tie her down. It's going to be a long night, boys."

"Here. We can use my belt." Earl unbuckled his belt and wrapped it around Loretta's wrists, tightening it painfully. Pete did the same with her ankles, until she was trussed and helpless.

A commotion came from the hallway. Gladys wedged the door open, her sweet, round face washed with a look of disbelief. "What in heaven's name are you doing to her?" she asked frantically, her eyes wild.

"Gladys! Help me!" Loretta cried.

"Now, Gladys," Earl barked, "get on out of here. This is none of your concern."

"We're in the middle of a deliverance, Sister McAndrews," Reverend Mountjoy said soothingly. "Don't you worry. She's gonna be just fine." He pushed Gladys out the door, locking it behind her.

"Call Dr. Curtis Hansen, Gladys!" Loretta called, willing her panic to purpose. "He's a psychologist. Tell him what they're doing to me!"

Pete's hand clamped over Loretta's mouth. She bit him, sinking her teeth into his flesh until it yielded. He yelped and jerked his hand back.

"Call him, Gladys! Go now!"

Earl grabbed her by the hair, wrenching her neck and head back. He shoved something into her mouth. She gagged. Her tongue worked over salty cotton. A handkerchief. He had stuffed his filthy, sweat-soaked handkerchief into her mouth. Loretta retched, turning her head to the side. The vomit forced the handkerchief out, but not before some of it flowed back into her nose, stinging and burning as she fought for breath.

They'd kill her if she didn't get free. She would die here. And they would blame it all on her imaginary demons.

"Emesis is one of the signs we're making headway," Mountjoy said. "Now's not the time to give up, men. Put on the full armor of God. We'll emerge victorious at the end."

Pete wrested her jaw painfully in his hand, forcing her to look at him as he leaned over her. "You bit me. You'll pay for that later, Retta."

"I hate you," she growled, twisting away from him.

Pete climbed atop her, locking her hips to the desk. "Do what you need to do, Reverend. Whatever it takes."

She needed a distraction, something to draw the men's attention away from her, so she might escape. If ever she needed her telekinesis to emerge, it was right now. She focused on one of the pendant lights hanging from the ceiling. The light swayed, ever so slightly, under her concentration. She wondered, if she tried hard enough, if she might break it. She narrowed her eyes, listened to her own ragged breathing. But no matter how much she tried, nothing else happened. The light only swayed in a gentle circle. No one even noticed but her. It could have been anything—the draft from the door. A heater vent. Anything.

"Evil spirit, I command you to leave this woman's body!" Reverend Mountjoy struck Loretta's breastbone with his hand, nearly knocking the wind from her. "In the name of Christ, be gone!"

Loretta closed her eyes, pain lancing through her body as she was held down and abused, her soul flagging. This would be it. This would be how she would die—at these men's hands. At least she knew Mama would be waiting for her, in the end.

Loretta. Open your eyes. Darcy's voice rang out in her head. Above her, half-lit and shimmering, Darcy's spirit hovered. *Let me in, Loretta. I can make them stop. I know what to say to make them stop.*

Fear tangled in Loretta's gut. She'd never given herself over to a spirit. Had never allowed herself to channel in a way that relinquished all her control. But what choice did she have, in this moment, when her prayers went unheard and her own husband held her down while strange men put their hands on her? Pete would likely stand by and watch, even if they killed her.

Loretta locked eyes with Darcy's spirit. And then, Loretta let go.

INTERLUDE

LIMINAL

Loretta is herself but not herself. Every cell in her body has been touched with light.

RiversideRiversideRiverside

A single word repeated over and over, through her lips, but not in her voice. In Darcy's voice. Men shouting. An explosion in her head. Pain, lancing the back of her skull. Stars behind her eyes, then a limitless blackness. Nothing. There is nothing. Only a void.

Chapter 27

Loretta opened her eyes. How long had she been in this bed? In this place? Days? Weeks? Her last memory was walking into a candlelit chapel. Everything after was lost to her.

Her limbs ached. Her head throbbed. Every nerve ending felt blistered and raw. Something had happened. Something bad. Perhaps it was for the best that her mind couldn't remember what her body could.

She tried to stretch. Tried to move. But she couldn't. She was tied down, her wrists and ankles bound to the bed with leather straps. Panic poured through her. A vague memory of being held down. Strange hands on her body.

She screamed.

Footsteps echoed down the hall. The curtain surrounding her bed was yanked back. Two nurses stood there, one middle-aged and stern, the other young and pretty. "Draw up a dose of Thorazine, Vera. Hurry."

"Yes, ma'am."

The younger nurse turned and rushed to the door.

Loretta thrashed uselessly, bucking her hips.

"Calm down, Mrs. Davenport," the older nurse said firmly. "No use getting agitated. If you don't settle down, we'll have to take you to the electrotherapy room again. We're only trying to help you."

We're only trying to help you.

Loretta screamed again, hot tears running down her face.

The younger nurse returned with a syringe. She handed it to the other nurse.

"Hold her arm."

Holdherlegs

She felt a quick, sharp prick to the inside of her elbow. A delicious warmth flooded Loretta's veins. She fell into the warmth, her muscles unclenching.

"There. All better, isn't it?"

"Yes," Loretta slurred, her heavy eyelids closing. "Better."

⁂

She woke sometime later, her head fuzzy, her mouth dry. Sunlight streamed through the windows, illuminating the young nurse—Vera—who sat at her bedside, reading a romance novel. She looked up when she heard Loretta, smiling gently. "Good morning, Mrs. Davenport."

"It's morning? How long was I asleep?"

"Almost twelve hours. I've been sitting with you all night, but I'm going off shift soon." Loretta saw kindness in this nurse's eyes—a softness lacking in her raw-boned superior. "Beverley will be taking over at seven."

"Could I have some water?" Loretta smacked her lips. They were cracked. Raw.

"Certainly. And I'll see if I can find some Vaseline in the dispensary. For your lips."

"Thank you."

A few moments later, Vera returned with a cool glass of water and a small tub of Vaseline. She helped Loretta raise her head to drink, then gently dabbed the balm around her mouth.

"I shouldn't be doing this," she said conspiratorially. "One of the other nurses got the end of her finger bitten off by a restrained patient."

"Don't give me any ideas." Loretta smiled, despite herself. "Where am I?"

"Agape Manor."

The mental hospital. "Why am I here?"

"You had a head injury. A severe concussion. You couldn't remember your name, where you lived, anything at first. Amnesia. The attending physician recommended you come here for further evaluation after they released you from Burns Protestant. Your husband had you admitted."

Loretta pressed her lips together. "Of course he did. How long have I been here?"

"Nearly a week. I know who you are. I'm Barbara's friend. Her roommate."

Loretta's breath caught. "Barbara Miller? She knows I'm here?"

"Yes. And so does Dr. Hansen. After you didn't show up for your last session, Barb was worried about you. She called all the hospitals and found out you were here, with us. She told me all about you. And your husband. But don't tell Nurse Fletcher that I know who you are. She'll reassign me if she finds out.

"Dr. Hansen is trying to find a way to have you released. But since your husband admitted you and this is a private hospital, there's not much he can do. At least until the board of directors reviews your case. I'm sorry."

"And I've really been here nearly a week?"

"Yes."

Why couldn't she remember anything?

A shrill bell rang, piercing the quiet.

"I have to go. That's shift change. I'll be back tonight, though. Try to stay as calm as you can. If you're calm for twenty-four hours, they'll likely remove the restraints." Vera offered a small wave as she went through the door.

Loretta turned her head to look out the window. An iron grate was bolted to the outside. To prevent escape, no doubt. Or patients from jumping. She'd passed by this hospital many times on her way to her appointments with Dr. Hansen. Agape Manor. It was a Catholic hospital for women—established by the Sisters of Mercy. In the Christian faith, "agape" meant "unconditional love"—the highest form of love. The irony was not lost on Loretta as she tugged uselessly on her restraints. She had often wondered about the patients in this hospital. And now she was one of them, concealed behind brick walls, confined to a bed, completely helpless.

Loretta thought of her children and began to cry, tears coursing down her face. By her reckoning, Christmas was in a week, and she wouldn't be home to see them open their gifts. She was under Pete's complete control now. He'd put her here. He'd locked her away. Now, with her in an asylum, he'd have all he needed to take Luke and Charlotte from her. Loretta prayed, silently, hoping that somehow Dr. Hansen would find a way to free her.

⌘

Loretta paced around the exercise yard, counting each pointed picket in the high iron fence that encircled Agape Manor. Her legs ached from the time she'd spent in confinement, muscles already atrophied from lying in bed. She'd been good. Had obeyed her nurses and the gruff staff psychiatrist, Dr. England, who seemed too bored and indifferent to truly care about her health. She'd endured their sedatives and their electroshock therapy without complaint, so that she might have this slender half hour of recreation every day before being confined to her room once more.

If she remained pliant and yielding, she might earn another recreation session in the lounge, before dinner, where she'd be allowed to socialize with the other patients, do an art project, play board games, or watch television. It was telling of how small her world had become that the possibility of the lounge held such an exotic mystique.

At least Vera was kind. Took as much time as she could with Loretta during her rounds. Brought her books. Listened when Loretta talked about her children and reassured her that Dr. Hansen was trying his best to get her released. He had filed an appeal to the board of directors on her behalf—an appeal requesting a full psychological evaluation with himself present as a consulting psychologist. But even if Loretta passed the evaluation, she would be released into Pete's custody. The thought filled her with visceral fear. He'd put her here once. He could do it again. Over and over. And even if she managed to leave him, with a psychiatric stay on record, her chances of gaining full custody of the children were tenuous at best.

A shrill whistle interrupted Loretta's thoughts. "All right, ladies. Time's up." Nurse Fletcher stood in the middle of the yard like a prison matron, her robust arms crossed over her uniform, glaring at Loretta. "Come along, Davenport."

Loretta drank in one last dose of open sky, watching the starlings swoop and turn in formation as sunset shredded the clouds with deep fuchsia and scarlet. It was Christmas Eve. She thought of Charlotte and Luke, alone with Pete. She imagined how different things would have been if she'd refused to go to the Christmas gala. She might have gathered the children and left that very night. Might have started their new life in time for the New Year. Instead, she'd ignored her gut. Just like she did with Mama on the day of the accident. And look what happened.

But she would get out. Eventually. And once she was out, she'd find a way to leave Pete and start a new life. She would hire an attorney, the best her money could buy, and fight for her children, no matter how long it took.

As Loretta joined the other patients, she thought of her manuscripts. Her next story was due this week, by her calculations. It was in the safe-deposit box at the bank, with the rest, but she'd miss her deadline with the *Star*. Unless . . . unless she could send a message to Dr. Hansen, through Vera.

"Is Vera working tonight?" Loretta asked Nurse Fletcher as she marched the line of patients into the manor's barren, green-tinged central hall.

"No. She's off for the holiday," Fletcher barked. "You're fond of her, aren't you?"

"Not especially," Loretta lied. "I was just curious."

"She'll be back again on Monday night."

Monday night would be too late. By the time Vera got a message to Dr. Hansen, the post office would be closed, and the mail, even at its fastest, took two days to get from here to Kansas City. She'd miss her Wednesday deadline. As a new columnist, missing a deadline would probably be enough to get her feature canceled. And without the money from her writing, she'd never be able to hire an attorney to fight Pete. Without an attorney, Pete would take the children.

Loretta's shoulders sank.

"Look lively, Davenport. Dinner's in an hour," Nurse Fletcher said, nudging her up the stairs to the second-floor ward. "Sisters will be here, giving out gifts. They're bringing fruitcake this year."

Fruitcake. Loretta grimaced at the irony of the nuns' gift.

"Is there any way I might have a phone call tonight? Just one? Perhaps after dinner."

Fletcher narrowed her eyes. "You haven't earned that privilege yet. You know I can't do that."

"Are you a mother, Nurse?"

"Yes. I am. Not that it's any of your business."

"I have a little boy and a little girl. This is the first Christmas I've ever been away from them. I haven't seen them or spoken to them for two weeks. Might I call them? I'll keep it short."

For the first time, she saw a softening in Nurse Fletcher's manner. "I see." She pulled Loretta to the side, away from the nurses' station. "I could get fired for letting you do something like that. You understand?"

"I know. But we women—we mothers—we have to watch out for one another. And I've been good, haven't I?" Loretta offered a gentle smile.

Nurse Fletcher huffed a breath. "Yes. But good isn't enough to get you a phone call. Not until Dr. England approves. Outside phone calls can interfere with your treatment. Set you back."

"I understand." Loretta lowered her eyes. "But my children won't understand what happened. Why I'm not there."

Nurse Fletcher scratched beneath her cap, huffed again. "Fine," she said in a harsh whisper, looming over Loretta. "When I make my rounds before shift change, I'll take you to my office. You'll have two minutes. I'll do a full-body cavity search after, so no funny business. You try to pull anything on me, and you're over, Davenport. I'll have you in restraints and a veil bed faster than you can blink."

Loretta blanched. "All right. I understand."

"And if you ever tell another soul I did this for you, I'll make sure you never leave this place. Understand that?"

"Yes, ma'am."

Nurse Fletcher stalked down the hall and unlocked Loretta's door, then ushered her inside brusquely. "I'll come for you after dinner."

The thought of being beholden to Nurse Fletcher frightened her. She'd have to watch her every move. And what the cavity search might entail sickened her. But she would endure whatever it took, for her children.

❧

Nurse Fletcher made true on her word. At fifteen minutes to seven, she came into Loretta's room, took her vitals, and then motioned with her head for Loretta to follow. "Hurry up. The other nurses are with their patients. We have to be quick."

"Thank you," Loretta whispered.

Nurse Fletcher merely grunted and steered Loretta around the corner. Her office was just ahead, a plain brass placard on the outside of the door: EMILY FLETCHER, RN.

She unlocked the door and pushed Loretta inside. The room was spare and undecorated, a spotless desk at its center, with only a gooseneck lamp, a blotter, and a black telephone on its surface. An unpleasant sense of déjà vu flickered through Loretta's mind. She'd been in a room like this before, and something terrible had happened to her. She shook her head, trying to remember. The daily shock treatments had done a number on her mind.

"I took out anything you might try to use as a weapon, earlier. Like I said, no funny business. I find anything on you, that'll be the last time you see the outside of your room. No more exercise yard. No more dining hall. Got it?"

"Yes, ma'am," Loretta said.

"Two minutes."

Nurse Fletcher closed the door, and Loretta hurried to the phone, dialing Dr. Hansen's number. It rang four times. Five. "Please, please answer," she whispered, watching the seconds tick by on the clock above the door.

Finally, on the sixth ring, he answered. "Hello?"

"Dr. Hansen. It's Loretta."

"Loretta! How were you able to manage a phone call?"

"I don't have much time. I need you to go to the bank. Open my safe-deposit box. My manuscripts are there. I need you to send all of them to the *Kansas City Star* as soon as you can. Address them to Hal Lorenz. And my post box key is there, too. The *Star* sends my checks there now, instead of the house. It's box 1129. If you could keep them for me until I'm out."

"All right. I will. And I'm working on getting you out, Loretta. Until then, try to listen to the doctors and nurses and do what they say. I'm so sorry this has happened."

Loretta eyed the clock. She had one minute left. "I have to go. I . . ."
Her words hung in the air. She *what?*

She hung up, just as Dr. Hansen echoed her with an "I . . ." of his own. She wondered what he was going to say. Wondered if the ghost of his own unspoken words haunted the space where he stood, just as they haunted her. But she didn't have time to think about that right now. Loretta quickly dialed her own phone number. It rang twice. Charlotte answered, and Loretta wilted against the desk at the sound of her little voice.

"Char, it's Mommy."

"Mommy! When are you coming home?"

Loretta squeezed her eyes shut as tears gathered and spilled over. "I'll be home as soon as I can. I love and miss you and Luke very much."

"Where are you?"

"I'm . . . I'm in the hospital."

"Are you hurt?"

She heard a garbled female voice in the background.

"Who is that?" Loretta asked.

"It's Miss Susan," Charlotte whispered. "She watches us when Daddy is at work. Sometimes she spends the night."

Loretta froze. "Is that so?"

She heard a frantic crackling on the line, as if someone had wrested the phone away from Charlotte.

The door to the office creaked open, just as the clock's second hand approached ten. Nurse Fletcher glared at Loretta and made a motion with her hand across her throat.

"Mommy has to go. Merry Christmas, honey. I love—"

The dial tone sounded. Loretta replaced the receiver in the cradle, her heart sinking.

Susan. Why was that name so familiar? She'd heard it somewhere before. Other names without faces flitted through her consciousness: Dora. Joan. Paula. Darcy. Susan. Loretta repeated the names to herself quietly, like an incantation. Who were these girls? And why was this Susan in their home, with *her* children?

"Take off your smock," Nurse Fletcher said.

"Pardon?"

"Take it off, Davenport. I have to search you."

"Here and now?"

"Yes. Now take it off before I take it off myself."

Loretta shrugged out of the scratchy cotton dress. She crossed her arms over her chest, covering her nakedness as best she could. Nurse Fletcher scanned her body with her eyes, pausing on the scars on Loretta's lower belly. She pulled on a pair of gloves. "Open your mouth. Don't you dare bite me." Fletcher swabbed a finger deep inside Loretta's mouth. Loretta gagged.

"Good. Now turn around."

Loretta did as she was told, wincing as Nurse Fletcher wrenched her arms behind her back and forced her to bend over the desk. Cold metal kissed Loretta's bare skin. Another vague memory crowded into her psyche—of being held down by strange hands, her screams a distant echo in her mind.

Vomit rose in her throat as Nurse Fletcher kicked her feet apart. "I'll try to be as gentle as I can."

But there was nothing gentle about what happened next.

Chapter 28

Loretta sat in her bed, staring at the wall, knees drawn to her chest. The moon cast flickering shadows on the pale-green plaster. Clawlike tree limbs scratched against the hospital window as the wind howled outside. It was New Year's Eve.

Down the hall, she could hear Cloris Wray singing. Cloris always sang the same lullaby, over and over. Something about pretty little horses. The older woman had a lovely voice, but the repetition grated on Loretta's nerves. She'd learned from one of the other patients that Cloris had fallen into madness after the death of her only daughter, more than twenty years ago. She'd been at Agape Manor ever since. Loretta clapped her hands over her ears as the woman began the song again.

"Please stop," she whispered.

Even though she'd been "leveled up" the week before, and now had her longed-for lounge privileges, and her daily ECT treatments had been replaced by insulin therapy, Dr. England showed no signs of letting her go free. There were days when she wondered if she'd end up just like Cloris, here indefinitely, never to taste freedom again. She had a feeling Pete might want it that way.

A soft tapping came at her door. Vera entered, carrying a tray. She switched on the overhead lights, and Loretta blinked at the brightness. "I brought you something. They already had ham and black-eyed peas in the kitchen, for tomorrow. Got you a slice of buttered cornbread, too."

"I'm not hungry," Loretta said, turning away.

"Loretta, you have to eat. If you don't, they'll take you to the shock room again. You don't want that."

"I don't care anymore."

"You don't mean that."

Loretta looked at Vera's kind face. "I'm never getting out of here, am I? You can tell me the truth."

Vera sighed and set the tray on the foot of the bed. "Well, there's good news. And bad. Since you have no documented history of mental problems, the hospital board and Dr. England agreed to another evaluation by an outside psychologist, followed by an interview with the board, but it won't be Dr. Hansen doing the evaluation. Your husband told Dr. England that you and Dr. Hansen know one another. He even implied the two of you were having an affair." Vera bit her lip. "I'm sorry."

"And Dr. England believed that?"

"I'm not sure how much he believed. But your husband presented hospital discharge papers showing that an emergency physician had referred you to Dr. Hansen a few months ago. That was all the proof they needed to show that Dr. Hansen is not a disinterested third party. So he can't evaluate you. It will have to be someone else."

Despair flooded Loretta. "Do you know who the psychologist will be?"

"Not yet. But the evaluation will take place this month."

"So there's still a chance I might be released?"

Vera covered Loretta's hand with her own. "There's always a chance. Now, will you please eat something?"

"All right."

Vera lifted the tray and brought it to Loretta. The scent of the food curled up Loretta's nostrils, rousing her appetite. "I brought you something else. From Dr. Hansen. He thought you'd like to see it." Vera motioned to the tray, where a folded newspaper sat under the bowl of beans. Since her last shock treatment, Loretta's memories were beginning to return, and she now remembered some of the things that had happened before her hospitalization. She wondered if there had been any news about Paula Buckley, the murdered girl in the cave at Dearing Park. Perhaps the paper held news of George Buckley's arrest.

Loretta unfolded the paper. It wasn't the *Myrna Grove Focus*. It was last Friday's edition of the *Kansas City Star*. Loretta's pulse quickened. Could it be?

"Your story's toward the middle."

Loretta thumbed through the pages until she found it, nestled next to an ad for Russell Stover candies. She read through the familiar lines—the lines she had written—and smiled when she saw the byline with her pseudonym: Daphne Harrington. She could hardly believe it was real—that her stories were good enough to print. Unexpected tears clouded her vision.

"Thank you, Vera."

"Of course. Dr. Hansen wanted me to let you know he sent your other manuscripts and he's collecting your mail so he can deposit your checks."

Loretta's heart lifted. "He's really doing that?"

"Yes. I think that man would do anything for you, Loretta. I truly do. It's terribly romantic."

"He's very kind, isn't he?" Loretta looked down bashfully.

"He is. Now, please eat, so they won't take you to be shocked again."

Loretta dutifully tucked into the meal, thinking of Vera's words about Dr. Hansen. He had proven his friendship and devotion to her, time and again. But why? Although nothing improper had ever occurred between them, Loretta was tempted to believe his feelings for her went beyond the platonic.

She nearly laughed at the thought. A man like Dr. Hansen would never see her as his equal. She was homely. Uneducated. An object of pity. That must be it. He pitied her, like some poor, witless creature. Just like Pete had, all those years ago.

But why, then, would he go to such extremes to tell her how remarkable she was? *Could* there be something there, beyond friendship?

Not that it mattered. She was married. Even if she did get free of the hospital, and then Pete, Dr. Hansen deserved better than her. And it was obvious he was still in love with his wife and still grieved for her. It would be foolish to think she could ever replace Esther Hansen. Loretta imagined Esther as lovely and regal as her biblical namesake, her beauty and well-heeled upbringing the perfect match for Dr. Hansen's lifestyle. She could never compete. Not in her wildest dreams.

Loretta finished her dinner and pushed the tray aside. The food sat heavily in her belly, like a stone. She'd eaten much too quickly.

Vera looked up from her romance novel, smiling. "All done?"

"Yes. It was delicious. Thank you."

Vera rose and took the tray from Loretta's bed. "I'll leave the paper with you. I'll bring next week's edition, too. Barb always brings them home from the office."

"How did you and Barbara meet?" Loretta asked.

"Oh. We met at a charity drive for the hospital when I was a student nurse. Barbara was one of our sponsors. She and Cur—Dr. Hansen both."

So, Vera called him Curt as well. The three of them seemed rather cozy and familiar.

"Did you ever meet Dr. Hansen's wife?"

"Esther? Oh yes. She used to come to our events, too." Vera smiled tightly. "It's a shame about what happened. Dr. Hansen sent her to France for her health. She had tuberculosis, and the Mediterranean air helped. We were all devastated when we got the news about the accident."

"I can only imagine."

"Well, I'd better be making the rest of my rounds. I'll be back later, before my shift ends. Would you like me to turn off the light?"

"Yes, please."

After Vera had gone, Loretta nestled under her covers and listened to the sounds of the other patients winding down for the night, many of them in a drug-induced stupor. Her curiosity about Esther Hansen was hardly diminished by Vera's revelations. Tuberculosis. So, Esther had been sickly. And then died tragically, along with their son. She marveled at Dr. Hansen's resilience in the face of such a terrible loss. At his strength. Loretta wasn't sure she could survive such a thing.

As she was drifting off to sleep, Loretta imagined Charlotte and Lucas, asleep in their beds, and how she'd never gone a night without tucking them in and reading them a bedside story.

She wondered if *Susan* was doing that now. Loretta remembered where she'd heard her name before. A Susan had answered the telephone at Ashley House when she'd called, looking for Joan. Pete had a history of taking young female students, especially those from out of state, under his wing. She'd fed several of them at her table, and even hired them as babysitters, now and again. But she had her suspicions that Susan was much more than a babysitter. If Pete thought he could lock her up and replace her with this girl, he was mistaken.

The thought made her even more determined to fight.

That much more determined to win.

Another week passed. Loretta stared at the bleak January sky through the gothic pickets in the exercise yard, her hospital-issue coveralls doing little to cut the cold. Her hands itched to write. But there were no pencils or pens allowed in the wards. They were too easily converted into weapons.

She shoved her hands in her pockets and walked the fence, back and forth, then back again, like an anxious circus panther pacing its pen. On days like this, when winter's hopelessness lay over her like a gray, damp blanket, Loretta took to counting her blessings with each picket she passed.

1. Unlike many of the other patients, who had to share rooms, she had her own room, tiny though it was.
2. She could get outside, see the sky during the thirty minutes of exercise they allowed her each day.
3. She could go to the rec lounge and the dining hall. Watch television and play cards with the other patients.
4. Thanks to Vera, she had the *Star* to look forward to, and seeing her stories in print.
5. Most of all, she was grateful for Dr. Hansen.

By her calculations, she should have well over a hundred dollars in the bank by now, thanks to him. Money that would someday provide her and the kids with a new life. The ten articles Dr. Hansen had sent her editor would help buy her some time. Perhaps, if she leveled up to the unlocked first-floor ward, where the transitional patients lived, she would ask for a typewriter for her room. Those patients even got day privileges outside hospital grounds.

Nurse Fletcher blew her whistle, putting an end to Loretta's musings. Loretta turned with a sigh to go back inside. As they were filing through the doors, Loretta noticed a new patient, sitting alone in the lounge, her back to the empty fireplace. Even though her halo of hair had been shorn to a scrubby fuzz of copper, Loretta recognized her immediately. Joan Everly—Darcy's soprano friend. Loretta remembered some of the Christmas gala—listening to the choral performance, then meeting Joan in the bathroom. But everything that happened after was still a mess of static in her mind.

If Joan was here, it wasn't a good sign. But at least she was alive.

"Nurse Fletcher?"

"What is it, Davenport?"

"Might I have a few moments in the lounge, instead of going back upstairs?"

Fletcher sighed. "If you'd like. But you'll have to stay down there until after dinner. I'm not running up and down these stairs again."

"I understand."

Loretta approached Joan slowly, from the side. She was rocking gently back and forth in her chair. Loretta noticed, as she neared the girl, that her forearms were covered in scabbed-over marks. She was injuring herself. Just as Loretta used to.

"Joan?" Loretta asked softly.

The girl looked up at her, her eyes widening.

"Do you remember me?"

"Yes. You're Professor Davenport's wife, aren't you?"

"I am. Mind if I sit next to you?"

"No."

Loretta pulled a chair in front of Joan's and sat. "Why are you here?"

"Lots of reasons," Joan said, smirking. She gestured to her arms. "This." Then her shorn hair. "This. My parents didn't know what to make of it when I came home for Christmas a mess. I've always been their perfect daughter." She laughed bitterly.

"I used to do that, you know. The cutting. When I was a girl."

Joan looked incredulous.

"I didn't do it on my arms, though. I did it on my belly. So no one else would see."

"Did anyone ever find out?"

"No."

"Well, they found out with me. So now I'm stuck here. Sometimes I do it because I want to crawl out of my own skin, you know?"

"I do know."

"So, why are you here?" Joan asked.

"Pete—Mr. Davenport—had me committed."

"I'm not really surprised. He was always telling us you were crazy."

Loretta stilled. "What did you say?"

"Professor Davenport. That's what he tells all of us. That you're crazy."

"All of you?"

"Oh my God. You really don't know, do you?"

Loretta felt the blood drain from her face. "Know what, Joan?"

"It's practically a joke at Bethel. Professor Davenport always chooses a girl from the freshman class. It starts out innocent enough. He pretends to be looking out for them. He mentors them and gives them free tutoring. Tells them how brilliant they are. Then he starts complaining about you—trying to gain their sympathy. The next thing they know, he's convinced them to sleep with him. That it's God's will for them to be together." Joan laughed, shook her head. "I was foolish enough to believe him. I was last year's girl. Susan is this year's. She must really be special, since he's actually doing what he promised, for once."

"What he promised?"

"Yes. Getting rid of you."

The room seemed to spin around Loretta, even though Joan wasn't telling her anything she didn't already know in her gut. She gripped the arms of the metal chair, trying to stay calm. "Susan is his . . ." She couldn't bring herself to say the words "lover" or "mistress." Not for a woman who was little more than a child.

"Disgusting, isn't it? I can't believe I ever slept with him. He's not even that good-looking."

"No, but he can be very charming. He was with me, once," Loretta said, thinking back to her sixteenth year, when she thought Pete hung the moon and the stars. He'd told her they were fated by God, too.

"He always told me you were plain. That you'd let yourself go. But you're not plain at all. And you seem nice." Joan shook her head again.

"So many times, I've found myself wishing I could go back and change things. I don't think I'd be here right now if I hadn't slept with him."

"It's not your fault. I was once your age. I know how vulnerable a girl can be." Loretta reached out, covering Joan's hand with her own. "It's his—"

Suddenly, the floor fell out from under her feet. Loretta cried out as she fell, tumbling through space, into a white room with harsh, bright lights. Fear raced through her as she realized she was strapped to a gurney. She struggled to free herself, thrashing her head from side to side. A doctor leaned over her, his face half-covered by a surgical mask.

"No! This isn't what I want! Help! Pete!" Not her voice. Joan's voice.

"Hold her legs."

HoldherlegsHoldherlegsHoldherlegs

Her legs were wrenched apart by unseen hands, her feet placed in cold stirrups and held there. There was a brief prick of pain inside her elbow. Warmth trailed up her arms. "You won't feel a thing. This will all be over with soon, Joan."

Blackness descended as Loretta's eyes opened. She was still clutching Joan's hand. Felt the loss emanating from her core. The pain.

"They took your baby, didn't they?" Loretta said quietly. "You were pregnant."

Joan's eyes widened. "How . . . h-how did you know about the baby? Did he tell you?"

"No. I saw it, just now. When I touched you. That's the real reason I'm here. Pete thinks I'm crazy, but I see things sometimes when I touch people. When I touch their things."

"Wow . . . I-I don't know what to say."

"I know." Loretta shook her head. "It's a lot for me to wrap my head around, too. Believe me."

Joan's lip trembled. Tears brimmed in her eyes. "He made me do it. The abortion."

"Pete made you?"

"Yes. There's a doctor, in Saint Louis."

Loretta's breath escaped in a rush. "He took you there after Thanksgiving, didn't he?"

"Yes. He tricked me. When I told him about the baby, he said he'd break things off with Susan. He told me we were going to Saint Louis to pick out rings, for when he divorced you." Joan began to sob, burying her face in her hands. "He lied."

Loretta stood and wrapped her arms around the girl, trying to comfort her as she wept. Anger thrilled through her. A righteous, horrific anger that set every nerve in her body to tingling. Pete would pay for this. He'd pay for what he did to her, and to every other young girl he'd warped and manipulated through the years.

"Hey! Davenport! No physical contact." The nurse in charge of the rec lounge stormed toward them, her face set in a scowl. "Back off."

Loretta tried to let go of Joan, but the girl clung to her, as if she were a life buoy in the middle of the ocean. A rush of disjointed images filled Loretta's head, like a slideshow reel gone wild. Screeching tires. Darcy's face, caught in the glare of headlights. A piercing scream.

"You were there," Loretta said breathlessly. "The night Darcy died. You know what happened. Were you with Pete? Did he have anything to do with it? Joan, please tell me."

Joan suddenly pushed away from her, her body grown rigid. "Get away from me! Help! Somebody, help! She's hurting me!"

"Joan, no! I can help you. Is Pete the one you're afraid of?"

The charge nurse bear-hugged Loretta from behind, lifting her off her feet and wrenching her away from Joan. "What the hell do you think you're doing, Davenport?"

"Let me go!" Loretta tried to get free, her hands digging into the nurse's arms. Orderlies swarmed into the room. Panic thrummed through her at being forcefully handled. "I was only talking to her!"

The nurse wrestled her to the floor, planting a knee in her lower back. "Wilson! Bring a straitjacket. I need a sedative!"

A volley of footsteps echoed on the linoleum floor. Hands assailed her from all directions, gripping and grasping. Loretta was rolled onto one side and then the other as her arms were encased in thick canvas. She screamed and kicked as hard as she could, to no avail.

The straitjacket tightened around her like a corset, stilling her movements. A needle slid beneath the skin at the back of her neck. She was placed on a gurney and wheeled into another white room, this one all too familiar. Nurse Fletcher's face swam in front of her. "Dammit, Davenport. You were doing so well." She swabbed the conducting salve on Loretta's temples and placed the leather bit in her mouth. "Bite down."

"Full charge, nurse."

The crackle of electricity. A blue lash of light, like a whip. Panic. Pain. Fire running through her skull, every muscle in her body clenching at once. Then darkness. Over and over. Days without end. Bleeding one into the next, stealing her memories. Stealing her mind.

PSYCHIATRIC REPORT
January 15, 1956

Patient: Loretta May Davenport
Case No: 26531
Admission Date: December 10, 1955
Age: 27

Informant: The informant is the patient's husband. The informant appears to be reliable in his documentation of patient's history. There is no apparent reason to question the reliability of the account as given.

Main Complaint: The patient was admitted due to repeated psychotic episodes, in which she purportedly hears disembodied voices and becomes hysterical. Patient presented at admission with postconcussive amnesia and evidence of severe psychological trauma. Evidence of self-mutilation was encountered upon full-body examination by staff physician.

Present Illness and Evaluation Findings: Patient suffers from delusional psychotic episodes, occasionally becoming violent and combative with staff and other patients or, conversely, becomes catatonic and unresponsive. Patient reports feelings of hopelessness and despair. It is almost impossible for the patient to identify the onset of symptoms, although she mentioned a brief viral illness in September. Patient is insistent that she speaks to "spirits" of the dead, and her psychotic episodes are visions given to her by "the other side." Evidence of visual and auditory hallucinations. Patient often requires sedation.

Family History: Patient is the only child of a farmer and a homemaker. Patient's mother died in a car accident when patient was twelve years old. Father died of stroke in 1952. Patient is a married homemaker and mother of two children.

Current Course of Treatment: Sedatives, Insulin Therapy, Electroconvulsive Therapy. Restraints when necessary.

Prescribed Course of Treatment: Trans-orbital lobotomy and continued inpatient care.

Summary: Patient is unable to function effectively in society. Evidence supports an intractable schizophrenic condition. Continued inpatient care advised.

Chapter 29

"Loretta. You need to wake up. Please."

Loretta blinked awake, her eyes adjusting to the darkness. Every bone and muscle in her body ached. The days had become an endless blur of pain and confusion. The last thing she remembered was being wheeled into the electrotherapy room, in a straitjacket. Everything before and after was lost to her. Nothing remained of her psychic abilities. She'd tried to read various objects. Tried to open the door in her mind. It was futile. The ECT and the drugs had stolen everything. Had made her someone else.

"Loretta. Wake up." Vera was silhouetted outside the veil bed's mesh curtain, her lemon verbena perfume wafting into Loretta's nose. "You must listen to me."

"What . . . what's wrong?"

"I've just seen the notes from your psychiatric evaluation."

"What do they say, Vera?" Loretta snapped to full attention, sitting up. Her head pounded like a kettledrum.

"They're going to give you a lobotomy."

"What is that?"

"Do you remember hearing about the Kennedy girl? Rosemary?"

Loretta scoured her befuddled memory. "Yes, somewhat."

"Well, that's what they did to her. They take an instrument and puncture the frontal lobe of the brain, by going through a space at the corner of the eye. They do it a lot here. Sometimes it works. It helps. But mostly, it makes people worse. You have no way of knowing until after." Vera pointed to the ceiling. "Some of those people up there, on three? They've had lobotomies."

Loretta's mouth went dry. The third-floor ward was where they kept the lost causes. The people who would never be allowed to leave. Loretta often heard their screams through the ceiling.

"When is the surgery?"

"On Wednesday. I saw your name on the OR schedule."

"What day is it now?"

"Sunday."

"Only three days!"

"Yes. Dr. Hansen is trying to file an emergency injunction to stop the surgery, but it's no use. He has no legal right to do so. Not in a private hospital, with your husband as informant. I'm sorry to say, Mr. Davenport signed off on the surgery. We have to get you out of here."

"How?"

Vera stilled, looking down. "I'll help. I'm working on a plan to help you escape. It's the only way."

"They'll fire you, if they find out."

"I know. So we can't let them find out."

"How?" Loretta whispered again.

"I've been thinking things through. The window washers come every other Tuesday, in the early afternoon. I've put in to work a double shift. One of the other nurses needed Tuesday off. The washers take the outside grates off the windows to wash them. One of the window washers is sweet on me. I could distract him. Give you time to climb out the window. You should be able to hang from your hands and drop to the kitchen roof, below you, and then climb down to the ground. There's a loose picket in the side fence, near the kitchen. It's almost rusted through. If you kick it, it'll come loose. You can slip through, into the alley. But you'll need clothes. A wig. You can't go looking like this. You need to look like a visitor. Or better yet, a nurse." Vera clapped. "That's it! I'll steal a uniform for you."

"My goodness, Vera. You're a genius."

"It's all those tawdry novels I read," Vera said, with a soft laugh. "The heroine is always trying to escape some castle or haunted manor."

"I'm not sure I can pull this off. I've never done something so brave."

Vera sighed. "I know. But they're never going to let you out of here unless you can find a way to legally challenge your husband's rights as informant, Loretta. I saw it on the report. It said your condition is intractable. And since you were unable to speak for yourself, they railroaded you. It happens all the time."

Loretta clenched her fists. "This is exactly what Pete wants. To make me into some kind of zombie."

"I'm sure you're right. It's mostly women who get lobotomies. Their husbands often ask for them, specifically. It's terrible."

Pete wanted her completely witless, so that he could take away everything without a fight while she rotted in here, destitute and forgotten.

"But what about if I manage to escape? Where would I go? If they find me, Pete will put me right back in here."

"You'll stay with Barbara and me, of course. We have a spare bedroom. I'll get it aired out for you tomorrow. You'll have to go into hiding. Your husband will likely report you missing, and the police will be looking for you."

Loretta's mind spun, thinking of all the ways an escape might go wrong. What if she got caught? What if Pete found out where she was hiding and came after her? And even if she escaped, Pete would surely have the upper hand when it came to custody, since she'd been institutionalized. She might never see her children again. The thought chilled her. Perhaps it might be better to submit to the surgery.

"I don't know if I can do this. Escape."

"You have to try, Loretta. You have nothing to lose by trying. And a lot to lose if you don't."

"But you said yourself the surgery helps some people. What if I'm one of them?"

"The odds aren't good. You may not be able to speak, feed yourself, or even toilet properly afterward. You'd be permanently institutionalized at that point, and your husband would have complete control over you. I've seen grown women reduced to an infantile state by lobotomy. It's terrible."

Loretta squeezed her eyes shut. Down the hall, she heard Cloris start up her mournful lullaby. "All right. I'll try."

⚜

On Tuesday, when the other patients on the second-floor ward went down for lunch, Loretta waited for Vera. The floor was quiet, almost unnaturally so. Loretta had been a bundle of nerves ever since she and Vera spoke about the escape. She'd tried her best to hide her anxiety from the other nurses, to prevent another round of ECT, but her body shook with agitation. Everything hinged on today. Her future. The kids. Perhaps even her life.

A few minutes before one o'clock, Vera came in, carrying a bundle beneath her arms. "The window washers just got here. I brought your disguise."

Vera hurried to the veil bed and unzipped the mesh side. Loretta slipped out, her pulse beating hot behind her ears. "What will happen when the next nurse comes on duty and finds me gone? They'll know I had help, getting out of this bed. I don't want you to lose your job. I'd never forgive myself."

"I've thought of that. I made something for them to find, to make it look like it was all you."

Vera rummaged in her pocket, pulled on a pair of gloves, then produced a metal hair comb. She went to the other side of the veil bed and slashed at the mesh side with the comb's teeth, tearing it open, then handed it to Loretta. "Get your fingerprints all over it. There. Now leave it on the floor. As to how you happened to have such a thing, I'll suggest you found it during your exercise session. People who walk by the hospital occasionally drop things outside the fence—sometimes on accident, sometimes on purpose. We always have to watch out for stuff like this."

"You are so brilliant, Vera."

"Crafty, at least," Vera said, smiling, as she rezipped the other side of the veil bed. "Now, let's get you dressed. I'll take your gown and throw it in the incinerator bin. That way they won't know you're not still wearing it, out there. They'll be looking for an escaped patient, not a nurse."

A few minutes later, Loretta stood ready, dressed almost identically to Vera, down to a brunette wig that resembled the pert, young nurse's short hair.

"Wait for my signal. You'll hear me call out 'Charlie' to get the window washer's attention. I'll make sure the grate is completely off your window before I call out. I'll lead him around the side of the building and flirt with him to keep him occupied while you escape. Once you're on the ground, you should be fine. Barbara will be right around the corner, parked on Locust and Sherman. You'll look like any nurse, out for a lunchtime stroll."

"I won't ever be able to repay you for this, Vera. Or Barbara." Tears sprang to Loretta's eyes. "The chance to be free of this place—to hopefully see my children again—I can't thank you enough. I'm so sorry to be such a bother. But I'm grateful for all your trouble. And your kindness."

Vera blushed, dipping her head. "Well. Don't thank me yet. Wait until you're out."

A muted thud came from outside, and Loretta watched as the upper rungs of a ladder came to rest against her window frame.

"I need to go. Remember, wait until you hear my signal and I go around the corner before you open the window. You'll have to work pretty hard to open it—they don't get opened very often and the wood swells, but I think the adrenaline surge you're about to have will work wonders." Vera winked. "See you at dinner. I'll be home by seven thirty."

As soon as the door snicked shut behind Vera, Loretta's legs went weak as Jell-O and her belly turned with anticipation. She paced the floor in the borrowed, soft-soled shoes, watching as the young man outside began unlocking the grate on her window. She stilled, listening for Vera's voice.

"Charlie! Is that you?"

"Oh, hello, Miss Vera," the young man answered. "I was hoping you'd be working today."

"Say, could you come down here? I have something I need to show you on the grounds."

"Sure thing! Be right down."

The window washer fumbled with the window grate for a moment, and Loretta momentarily panicked. What if he secured it before descending? She'd be stuck here. But thankfully, he gave up with an exasperated sigh and let it drop against the window frame.

Loretta crept to the window, peering out. She watched as Vera led Charlie to the corner of the hospital, then disappeared. She warred within herself for a moment, then quickly climbed up onto the windowsill and reached for the window latch. Paint flaked off as she turned the lock, her fingers aching as the dull metal cut into her skin. She prayed the window itself wasn't paint-locked. She hopped back down to the floor and pushed upward. The heavy ballast-weight window inched open, slowly, the wood protesting, cold air seeping into the room. Thank heavens it was winter and not a sultry, humid summer day; otherwise the wood might have been too swollen to budge. After working at things for a minute or so, Loretta was able to wedge her forearm beneath the bottom of the window and wrench it open enough to slip out.

She lingered on the window frame for a long moment, straddling the windowsill, half-in and half-out of her room, until thoughts of Charlotte and Lucas drove her the rest of the way out. Sheer, dizzying terror struck as she worked her way off the sill and lowered herself over the edge until she hung by her elbows. The window grate banged against the bricks with her movement. She closed her eyes before straightening her arms and dropping onto the kitchen roof below. Her knees bore the brunt of the drop. Loretta winced as her kneecaps rolled on the slate roof, drawing a sharp hiss of pain.

She crouched there, catching her breath, and peered through the bare limbs of the sweetgum tree shrouding the yard from view. She couldn't see Vera or her beau, but could hear Vera's girlish giggle nearby, followed by the muffled sounds of kissing.

Loretta crawled to the side of the kitchen roof and, checking her surroundings once more, climbed from the low roof using the sweetgum tree as leverage. She smoothed the skirt of her uniform, wiped the dirt from her white nylons, and casually crossed the yard. She'd almost made it to the fence when a sharp whistle bounced off the sides of the building.

"Hey, Charlie!" A man's gruff voice sounded behind her. "Somebody opened this window. Charlie! Where the hell'd you go?"

Loretta froze, her blood running cold.

"Hey, miss?"

She slowly turned. The man was older than Charlie, dressed in overalls, a smile quirking his lips as he looked her up and down. "You must be a new hire. Never seen you here before."

Inwardly, Loretta screamed, but she tried her best not to let her fear show. She smiled as becomingly as she could at the man. "Yes, I just started this week."

"You see a young fella over here? He's one of my guys. Got a wandering eye for one of the nurses." The man gestured toward her open window. "You know if there's a patient in that room?"

"I don't know, sir. I work on the third-floor ward."

"Oh," he said, nodding sagely. "That's where they keep the screamers and the vegetables."

Loretta flinched, desperately trying to stay calm. "The severe cases, yes."

"Well," he said, lifting his cap. "I better find that boy. Get his mind back on his work. Maybe I'll see you around sometime?"

"Sure thing. That'd be swell." Loretta smiled at him again, her heart slamming against her rib cage.

"What's your name?"

"Daphne," she said, turning away. She waited, pretending to be interested in the shrubbery, until the man had disappeared around the corner. She darted for the fence. After testing four pickets, she found the one Vera had mentioned, rusted nearly all the way through beneath its spiked finial. She twisted and pushed, until the picket snapped loose, falling to the ground. Loretta wedged herself through the narrow opening. As she did, she caught a glimpse of Vera pressed against the brick wall at the side of the building, half-hidden in shadow, her eyes closed as she necked with Charlie.

Gratitude flowed through Loretta, but there was no time for thank-yous now. She pushed through the hedges lining the fence and disappeared.

Chapter 30

Loretta sighed, lying back in the tubful of warm water, luxuriating as her sore muscles uncoiled. She sipped from the glass of red wine perched on the tub's edge, enjoying the complex explosion of flavors on her tongue. She'd never had wine before. The aroma of delicious food wafted from the kitchen and through the bathroom door. Her belly rumbled with hunger.

Though her newfound freedom was intoxicating, Loretta's mind wheeled with a plethora of worries. What happened next? How would she protect herself, or her friends, if Pete came looking for her? And then there were the children . . .

Loretta took a big swallow of wine to quell her tears. She had to keep her head.

She heard the front door open and then close, laughter filtering in from the other room. Vera must be home from her double shift. Loretta stood, soap bubbles dripping from her body. She looked at her naked form in the mirror. She'd lost weight while in the hospital. She could see her hip bones, just barely, and her clavicle seemed sharper than she remembered.

As she toweled off, a soft knock came at the door. "Loretta? Dr. Hansen brought something for you to wear. It's a little much, for dinner, but perhaps tomorrow we can go shopping for something more casual," Barbara said.

Loretta cast an eye to the discarded nurse's uniform on the floor. It had served her well, and was all the clothing she had, but she certainly didn't want to wear it again.

"Are you decent? Can I hand this in to you?"

"Yes." Loretta wrapped the towel around herself and opened the door a crack. Barbara passed one garment bag through the door, and then another. Loretta took them, her curiosity piqued.

"I'll leave the shoes outside the door."

Loretta hung the garment bags on the shower bar and slowly unzipped the first. Her breath caught in her throat when she saw the sliver of olive-green taffeta emerge. It was the dress from Savage Juliet. He'd bought the dress. Loretta choked back a sob. It was the most thoughtful thing anyone had ever done for her.

The other garment bag held the underthings that went with it. A few minutes later, Loretta emerged into the hall, silently slipping into the delicate, metallic-gold kitten heels sitting on the plush carpet outside the bathroom door. She could hear Dr. Hansen in the living room, his rich baritone voice rumbling as he chatted with Barbara and Vera.

She made her way through the cozy, immaculate house, admiring the soft floral tones in the wallpaper and the array of charming knick-knacks and crocheted doilies scattered about on shelves. This was a woman's house, with womanly things, and inside it, Loretta felt safe. When she rounded the corner, she encountered Vera lying on the couch, still in her uniform, her bare feet in Barbara's lap. Barbara rubbed Vera's arches in slow, circular motions, their conversation muted and personal.

Dr. Hansen sat across from them, his back to Loretta, his suit coat folded over the arm of his chair. She could only see him in profile, but the anticipation of his eyes meeting hers set her pulse racing. If she wasn't careful, she'd make a fool of herself tonight. The wine and the warm bath had already gone to her head . . . and then the dress. Why had he done such a touching thing?

Loretta cleared her throat, fluffing the full skirt with her hands. Vera swung her feet from Barbara's lap and hastily sat up, tucking her legs beneath her.

"Goodness. You're certainly a sight for sore eyes," Barbara said, smiling. "Curt . . ."

Dr. Hansen rose, slowly turning. Loretta's eyes skipped, danced, skittered from his gaze, her cheeks heating as he looked at her. "Loretta."

"Dr. Hansen." She crossed the room. Every step felt as slow as molasses. He took her hands in his, one thumb tracing the delicate line of her wrist.

"I'm so glad you're here." He leaned forward, and Loretta imagined she felt the brush of his lips against her cheek. "I've missed you."

Loretta stepped back, dropping his hands, embarrassed. "Why did you do this?" she asked, motioning to the dress.

"I went back that day, after I took you to the boutique. The shopgirl said you'd tried it on. If you don't like it, we can take it back. Get something else."

We. The word hung in the air, replete with meaning.

Loretta's lip quivered. "Of course I like it. It's perfect . . ." Her eyes spilled over, and she wiped at them, annoyed. "I promise, I'm very happy. I'm . . ."

Dr. Hansen smiled at her. "Don't say anything else, then. There'll be time for words later." He touched her waist, gently guiding her to the dining room. "Barb's prepared a lovely dinner for us. I hope you like to eat. There's enough food for an army."

He pulled out a chair, and Loretta sat, thankful for the glass of water sitting next to her plate. She swallowed quickly, chasing away the damning tears. Dr. Hansen sat next to her, and Barbara and Vera came in soon after, taking their places across the table.

"What a day!" Vera said, sighing. "But we pulled it off!"

"I couldn't have done it without you," Loretta said, touching Vera's hand. "Everything feels like a dream right now. I'm not sure what's real and what isn't." The aftereffects of the ECT still had her mind in a muddle. Shards of disjointed memories came and then went again before she could make any sense of them. A girl with shorn red hair. Something about a baby . . .

Loretta pushed her fingers against her temple, rubbing the skin there. "I don't know what I should do next. About the kids . . . Pete. He'll certainly call the police if the hospital hasn't already."

"Oh, they already have. Fletcher went right to the phone when she found you missing. The place was in an uproar before I left," Vera said. "There'll likely be a news story or two. You'll need to lay low. You should keep the wig. It suits you." She winked.

"Did they suspect you?"

"Not at all," Vera said, shrugging. "Fletcher gave me a dressing down about the comb, but I'm one of her best nurses. She won't fire me."

"Vera's a spectacular actress," Barbara said, nudging Vera with her shoulder. "It's her true calling. Nursing just pays the bills."

Vera laughed. "Perhaps, but poor Charlie was my alibi. He's the one who might lose his job over this. His boss was furious."

"He caught me as I was crossing the yard. Charlie's boss. But I think I fooled him."

"If he's the only one who saw you, and that appears to be the case, I don't think he'll put two and two together. You looked like any other nurse."

Loretta turned to Dr. Hansen, who'd been quietly listening to their conversation. "Pete will go to your office when he finds out I've gone missing. I'm afraid of him. Of what he might do."

"I've already thought of that," Dr. Hansen said. "Which is why it might be best for us to meet here for the time being. I'll need to get my guest cottage in order, in any case. It's much too cold and drafty as it is. Together, we'll come up with a plan to get you free of Pete and get custody of your children. But for now, you're safe, and warm, and here with us. So let's toast the present." Dr. Hansen lifted his glass, regarding her warmly. "To Loretta, and her great escape."

❧

Loretta stared at the dancing flames in the fireplace, her eyes glazing over with tiredness. Barbara and Vera had gone to bed, leaving her and Dr. Hansen to bank the fire. The wine settled in her limbs, making them heavy and limp. She needed to tell him.

"I think it's gone," Loretta said, softly.

"Pardon?"

"My ESP."

"Why do you say that?"

"The electroshock treatments. They changed me. There's nothing there now. I can't remember anything that happened after the Christmas gala." Loretta shook her head. "Just bits and pieces, and none of it makes sense. I've tried to read things. People. Tried to open the door in my mind. There's nothing there, Doctor. Only scraps of memory and hints of something dark, but I couldn't tell you what it is. It makes me wonder if the psychiatrists at the hospital were right. That it was all a schizophrenic delusion."

He was quiet for a moment, looking down thoughtfully, the firelight limning his silhouette with scarlet. "It wasn't a delusion, Loretta. I've treated many schizophrenics. You aren't one of them."

"How can you be so sure?"

"The police found Paula Buckley. Right where you said she would be. They gathered enough evidence to arrest George Buckley three days later."

"Oh," Loretta said.

"Yes," Dr. Hansen said, turning to look at her. He removed his glasses and polished them with his tie. "You're Detective Pierce's new darling. He can't stop talking about you."

Loretta laughed. "How silly."

"He could help protect you from Pete. He could even be a valuable witness for you in a competency hearing, if it comes to it. We'll have to wrestle with the legal ramifications of your hospitalization and elopement. Eventually."

"But even if Detective Pierce tries to protect me, won't the police make me go back to Pete? Maybe I should. At least I'd be with the children."

"And he'd put you right back in the hospital, Loretta. You and I both know that. He'll want to maintain control over you. You escaped from a psychiatric hospital in which he had you committed as informant. He's your legal next of kin."

Loretta shook her head. "Everything is so complicated now. I wonder if it might have been better to let them lobotomize me."

"No. It's a barbaric surgery."

"But what am I to do about Luke and Charlotte? They won't understand any of this."

"You'll need to speak with an attorney. Do you have any cause for a divorce, apart from his drinking and abuse?"

"Isn't that enough?"

Dr. Hansen smiled sadly. "It should be. Unfortunately, I've seen far too many women in my practice denied a divorce on those grounds. The burden is on you, to prove fault on his part. Has he ever been unfaithful?"

"I . . . I have my suspicions." Everything was still so muddy. "Something happened in the hospital. I met someone. She told me something about Pete." Loretta pinched her eyes shut and squeezed the back of her neck. "Oh, why can't I remember anything?"

"It's all right. It's only the aftereffects of the ECT, Loretta. It's temporary. Things will begin coming back. And if you like, when I come again, we can put you under hypnosis to try to bring things back."

"I want to try. I need to. There's something important missing. I know it. Something that might help my cause." Hopelessness flooded Loretta with regret. If only she'd never gone to the Christmas gala. If only she'd left Pete weeks before, when the bad feeling first started. When would she learn to trust her intuition?

Dr. Hansen leaned forward, his blue eyes level with hers. "Loretta, try not to despair. We'll put one foot in front of the other. First, a consultation with an attorney. And then, whatever it takes after that. I'm here to help you, in whatever way I can. But *you must c*hoose to fight."

"I want to be free of Pete. I do. But I don't want my children to think I've abandoned them. That I've given them up without a fight."

"They know you would never do that. You're a good mother, Loretta. And you *will get* your children back."

Loretta went quiet for a long moment, considering everything Dr. Hansen had said, watching the fire die down to embers. She was emboldened, just enough, by the wine to change the subject.

"Barbara told me about what happened to your wife and son. I'm so sorry. It must have been terrible."

Dr. Hansen sighed. "It was. We'd been apart for months when it happened. I blamed myself."

"It wasn't your fault."

"No, but I sent her and Gregory away."

"Gregory?"

"My son."

Loretta's heart sank. "I'm so sorry."

"He was only five, when it happened. He'd be your Lucas's age now."

Loretta couldn't find the right words to say, so she reached out a hand, tentatively, and rested it on Dr. Hansen's arm. He covered her hand with his own, and they sat looking at the fire together for a long moment, in silence.

"I'd better be going," he said abruptly, rising from his chair. "I'm sure you're awfully tired, after today's excitement."

Her hand dropped back to her side and her spirits sank. The clipped finality of his words jarred her. She'd gone too far. Gotten too familiar, in bringing up his family. Shame flooded her face with heat. "I apologize for being forward."

"You've nothing to apologize for." He crossed the room, and Loretta followed him, wringing her hands uselessly. "I'll come over again on Thursday, after I've seen my last patient. We'll do some exercises to test your abilities. Your memory. I'm positive the amnesia will fade with time. In the meantime, try to rest as much as possible. Let Barb and Vera take care of you."

As she walked Dr. Hansen to the door, she wondered at this enigmatic man who was her sometime friend, her sometime mentor. He plucked his hat from the coat-tree, shrugged on his overcoat, then walked out onto the porch, his breath fogging the air. "Good night, my dear."

"Good night, Dr. Hansen."

"You know, I'd give my kingdom for your calling me Curt." A mischievous grin played across his lips as he gently pinched her chin with his fingertips. He gazed at her for a long moment. "You do look lovely in that dress, Loretta."

Loretta closed the door behind him and pressed her cheek against it. Her skin tingled where Dr. Hansen had touched her.

It was no use fantasizing about something that would never be. Though his wife was gone, his lingering love for her was obvious in the way he always wore his wedding ring and in the sad, distant manner in which he'd spoken of her and their son tonight. Loretta was jealous of Esther Hansen. It was true. But she was even more jealous of the kind of love that could endure beyond death.

Dr. Hansen probably suspected her affection for him. Especially after tonight, when she'd been a bumbling idiot in his presence. He knew he could have her if he wanted. If he ever kissed her, she would come undone. But at what cost? Pete already suspected her of having an affair. If he had proof, her chances of ever seeing the children again would disappear. And if that happened . . .

No. It wasn't worth it. She'd rather maintain Dr. Hansen's friendship and her integrity, even though being near him tempted her in ways that warred against her better nature.

She had to think about her children. Her future. Not tie herself to futile romantic fantasies that would only result in ruin and shame. For almost twelve years, she'd lived with a man who had lied and abused and tricked her. Pete had taken a lonely girl of sixteen, charmed her with pretty words, and molded her into what he wanted, and then destroyed his creation with indifference and neglect. She would never let another man do that to her again.

She had to put up her walls before she completely lost her head. It was time to find out who she really was. To take the cold, bracing plunge into reality, and come out the other side a changed woman. The woman she was meant to be.

Chapter 31

The next morning, Loretta sat watching Barbara and Vera work in tandem as they cooked breakfast together, dressed in their robes. Their movements were so in tune with one another it almost resembled a dance.

The reality of her escape evaded Loretta's logic. She still expected to see Nurse Fletcher coming down the hall, armed with her syringes. While life at the asylum had been horrible, the order and structure had at least been predictable. Now she was adrift, floating unanchored and rudderless on a sea of questions without answers. She briefly wondered if prisoners felt the same way, after leaving jail.

At Barbara's insistence, Loretta took her coffee and sat in the breakfast nook, where the sunshine streamed through the windows and two lazy tabby cats named Abelard and Heloise dozed on the cushions. As Vera made Loretta's eggs to order (over easy, just like Barb's), Loretta tried her best to relax and be gracious, although she was unused to being waited on in such a way—and despite the women's cheerful protestations to her offers of help, she felt guilty all the same.

After they'd finished breakfast, Barbara excused herself to get dressed for work. Loretta rose and began clearing the table with Vera.

"I'm sorry if I've taken your room," Loretta said. She'd gathered, from the size of the house, that there were only two bedrooms. "I don't want to be a bother."

"You're not a bother at all, Loretta. We're happy you're here. You're welcome to stay as long as you need to."

"I'm very grateful."

"Barb usually leaves the car for me, on my days off, and takes the bus to work. So we'll be able to go and get you some new clothes and whatever else you might need later. I think I have a few sweaters and skirts that might fit you, for now."

"Could we go by my house, while we're out?"

"Do you think that's wise? What if your husband is home?"

It was a harrowing thought. But she needed her typewriter. Her next round of articles for the *Star* would be due soon. She also needed to gather the rest of her secret money—all the cash she had hidden around the house over the years. She had neglected to put all of it in the safe-deposit box, just in case she might need it before she left Pete. She now saw the folly in that.

"I'll be careful," Loretta said, running warm water over the dirty dishes. "I'll go in through the back door. Pete will be at work and the kids will be at school. I'll be quick. In and out. I just need my typewriter and a few other things."

Vera nodded. "All right. It makes me a little nervous. But I'll take you."

Barbara rounded the corner, dressed in a gray suit that complemented her elegant, long-limbed frame. "I'm headed to work."

"Tell Dr. Hansen I said hello," Loretta said. "I'm still speechless over the dress. He shouldn't have done that. It was too dear."

Barbara smiled. "Well, Curt cares about you a great deal. He wants to see you happy."

"I'm very fond of him as well," she said quietly. Loretta felt the maddening blush creep up her neck and began scrubbing dishes to distract herself.

"Did he talk to you last night?" Barbara asked. "After we went to bed?"

"Yes. He told me about Paula Buckley. That they found her. I'm so glad. He said we'll work on some exercises to recover my ESP when he comes on Thursday."

"And that's all you talked about? ESP?"

"Well, we talked about Pete and the kids. We agreed that I need to consult with an attorney."

"I can give you the name of the attorney I used for my divorce. He's still in practice. He does free consultations." Barbara took a pen from her pocketbook and scribbled a name on the notepad on the counter. "I was hoping you and Curt would . . . oh, never mind." Barbara pursed her lips and shook her head. "I'm sure yesterday was a lot for you both. I should be going. I'll see you tonight."

"I'll walk you out," Vera said.

Loretta peeked around the corner as the two women went out onto the porch. Through the picture window, she saw Barbara hug Vera goodbye. How wonderful it must be to have such a close friendship. Loretta envied their easy way with one another. She thought about Gladys, and how close they'd become. Loretta was tempted to call her. But if she did, Gladys would ask too many questions. It was too risky. Perhaps someday they'd be able to reunite.

After she and Vera finished the breakfast dishes, Loretta took a quick shower and dressed in Vera's borrowed clothes and the wig. As they drove to Loretta's neighborhood in Vera's sporty little Fiat, a nervous tickle ran through Loretta's belly. What if Phyllis saw her, sneaking through the back door? In her disguise, Phyllis might not recognize her, but that could be good and bad. Phyllis might think Loretta was trespassing and call the police. She'd need to be careful.

Vera turned onto State Street a few moments later. "I'm at 2531. Drive past the house, then go around the corner," Loretta said. "There's a one-lane alley behind the house. You can wait for me there."

As they passed the house, Loretta gasped. The corner of the house nearest the garage had sunk into the ground. A jagged crack fractured the roof. The chimney had toppled to the side and bricks were strewn across the driveway. She'd been right about the foundation. Orange utility tape encircled the porch railing—a warning to keep out. It looked almost exactly as Luke had drawn it, months before. "Oh my."

"Is that your house, Loretta?"

"Yes. I'd been telling Pete for weeks that there was something wrong with the foundation. He wouldn't listen to me. And now look."

"I don't think you should go in there. What if it falls in on you?"

"I have to. I need my typewriter to do my work, and I want photos of the children. Please, Vera. I'll be quick and careful. I promise."

"All right." Vera sighed. "But I don't like this. Not one bit. If something happens to you, I'll have to call an ambulance. They'll see your records and put you right back in the hospital. Please be careful."

"I will."

Loretta was jumping with anticipation by the time Vera pulled into the hedge-cloistered alley behind the house. She hurried across the yard and went to the birdbath in the middle of her lily garden, where the spare house key was hidden. She lifted the concrete basin with one hand, tipping ice-cold water onto the ground, and snatched the key from the top of the pedestal with the other. She cast a furtive glance at Phyllis's house. The curtains were drawn. Good.

A yellow condemnation notice was pasted on the back door, dated January second. Inside, the house was eerily quiet as she crept down the hall. The floors had warped and tilted like a fun house. Rainwater stood in puddles in the living room. The couch was mildewed. She could see a patch of sky through the ceiling. All the repairs they'd just done were for nothing. An overwhelming sadness descended on her. These rooms held so many memories of her children. Charlotte's first steps, Luke's crayon scribbles on the staircase wall, birthday parties and Christmases. As if it felt her sadness, the house groaned in commiseration. Loretta wiped her eyes. She needed to hurry. She had no time to mourn all she had lost right now.

In the kitchen, trash and dirty dishes lay everywhere—glasses encrusted with filth, restaurant containers, and empty milk bottles. The smell was noxious.

Loretta placed a hand over her mouth to block out the odor and went to the basement door, flicking on the flashlight. Pete hadn't been down here, thank goodness. The typewriter was still perched on the broken bar cart, a half-written page from her new, dark story still in the carrier. She lugged it up from the basement and placed it on the kitchen table, then went upstairs, tentatively testing each step before continuing.

When she got to the top, she went to her old bedroom and found women's clothing strewn throughout the room—none of it hers. A pair of nylons draped over her vanity mirror. A white lace brassiere lay on the floor. A name floated into her consciousness, and Loretta scraped at it, like a fingernail scraping over a scab. Susan. Susan. Who was Susan? That name . . . someone had told her that name. But who? She couldn't remember. She still couldn't access all her memories, thanks to the electroshock treatments.

Loretta rummaged under the rumpled bed for the box where she kept Luke's and Charlotte's baby pictures, then found the picture of Charlotte in the broken frame atop her dresser and placed it on the box. Angry tears threatened as she remembered their fight the day the frame had broken—the burning books, Pete shoving her to the floor. His assault in the kitchen. With a desperate cry, she took their wedding portrait off the wall and flung it to the floor. She carefully removed the twenty dollars she'd hidden behind the backing and pocketed it. There. That was better. Next, she picked up the Wedgwood vase Pete gave her for their first anniversary—the only anniversary he'd remembered, until this year. It would be their last. She took the money from the vase, then threw it at the wall. It, too, shattered. Next she threw his mother's Hummel figurines, one by one, at the vanity mirror. It cracked, right down the middle. When she finished, Loretta coolly surveyed her damage, wiped her trembling hands on her skirt, and walked away. She left the back door hanging open, not bothering to lock it, and went to Vera's car, carrying the typewriter and box of photographs. Vera unlocked the Fiat's trunk, and Loretta carefully placed everything inside.

"Are you all right?" Vera asked.

"No. But I will be. Eventually. Could you take me to the school, Vera? I want to see my children."

"Are you su—"

"Please."

When they reached the school, Vera parked along the curb and took off her sunglasses. She offered them to Loretta. "Just to be on the safe side."

Loretta put them on, her hands shaking.

"Are you sure you want to do this, honey?"

"It might be the last time I see my babies for a very long time. I need to make sure they're okay."

"I understand." Vera smiled sympathetically.

Loretta opened the door and went to the fence surrounding the playground. Thankfully, they'd timed things right. It was recess. In the distance, she spotted Luke. He sat in one of the swings, arms crossed over the chains, rocking back and forth.

"Luke!" Loretta called. She waved recklessly, all her love and fear colliding at once.

His head snapped toward the fence. He sat there for a moment, looking, and then jogged toward her, his face reddened by the cold. He broke into a grin. "Mom! I didn't recognize you."

"Luke, oh, my darling." Loretta pushed her fingers through the fence, and Luke wound his through hers. "I've missed you so much."

"Where have you been? Dad told us you were sick. You don't look sick."

"I'm not. Listen to me very carefully. I've been in the hospital. I'm all better now. But I can't come home." Loretta's voice cracked. Tears brimmed over and edged from her eyes. "I'm so sorry. I should have left, and taken both of you with me, a long time ago."

"Can't you take us with you now?"

"I can't. Your father has custody of you. Do you know what that means?"

"Yes, I think so."

"If I take you and Charlotte now, he could have me arrested. For kidnapping. And then I'd never see you again. I'm going to do my best to get you back—the right way, through the courts. But I promise, I won't give up until you're with me, Luke. Please know that."

Luke's jaw clenched. "I hate him. This is all his fault. He told us you have a boyfriend, and that you left us for him, but I don't believe him. He says Susan is just a babysitter, but I caught them kissing one day."

"Susan."

Ohmygodyoureallydon'tknowdoyou?

Loretta shook her head. Confusion tangled her thoughts at first, but then she remembered the fleeting phone call she'd made to Charlotte on Christmas Eve. Someone named Susan had been in the background. Had taken the phone from Charlotte and hung it up. Loretta's sense of déjà vu rose. There was something else about Susan. Loretta vaguely remembered another girl, one with red hair and scabs running up and down her arms. They'd had a conversation, at Agape Manor. But they'd met somewhere else, before then.

Why couldn't she remember?

"Is Susan nice?" Loretta asked. "Is she good to you?"

"She's not mean. But I don't like her. She tries to act like she's our mom. I told her I already have a mom. That made Dad real mad. She lives in the new apartment with us. I hate it. It's too small."

Loretta pushed a finger to her forehead, to quell the throb of anger brewing between her brows. "I went by the house. What happened?"

"There's a sinkhole underneath. The firefighters made us leave. They said it's not safe." Luke frowned, toeing the ground with his shoe.

"They're tearing it down next week. I want to go get my art supplies, but Dad won't let us."

"I'm so sorry, honey. I promise you, I'll buy you all the art supplies you could ever want once you're with me." Loretta scanned the playground, looking for Charlotte's blonde pigtails. "Is Char out here, too?"

"No. She's sick today."

"So she's with this Susan?"

"Yes."

Loretta imagined Charlotte, feverish and weak, being cared for by a faceless woman who favored lace brassieres and silk nylons. A woman Pete thought better than her. More suited. But what if she was? What if Pete had been right about her, and she was the selfish, unfit mother he'd always accused her of being? The thought sickened her. "Where is the apartment?"

"It's close to Dad's work. It's a brick building."

There were lots of brick apartment buildings clustered around Bethel. Finding the right one would be like trying to find a needle in a haystack.

"Do you know the address? Or even the street name?"

"No."

A whistle pierced the air, announcing the end of recess. The kids started gathering in a loose formation. Luke let go of her fingers. Loretta's heart clenched. "I have to go, Mom."

"I know, honey. I'll try to come see you, like this, as often as I can. Please don't tell Dad or Susan I was here. It's very important."

"I won't." Luke's lip began to tremble. "I love you."

"I love you, too, sweetheart. And I promise, I'll come back for you. I will."

Luke turned to go, jogging to join his classmates, but not before she saw him swipe at his eyes with his coat sleeve. She stood there, watching, until he'd gone into the school, a tiny blue dot in a sea of other children.

Chapter 32

Loretta looked at the name Barbara had scribbled down that morning and picked up the telephone. She dialed "0" and waited for the operator.

"Operator speaking, how may I assist your call?"

"Yes, hello. I'm looking for Barnaby Quinn. He's an attorney."

The operator chuckled. "Just a moment, hon. With a name like that, it shouldn't take long."

Loretta waited, tapping her toe on the linoleum. Her visit with Luke had steeled her resolve. She was ready to fight. Ready to do whatever it took to get her children back.

"I have Mr. Quinn's number, ma'am. Would you like to be connected?"

"Yes, please."

Loretta listened to the familiar clicks as the call went through. On the fourth ring, a woman answered. "Quinn, Gage, and McDowell. Peggy speaking."

"Hi, Peggy. I was referred to Mr. Quinn by a friend of mine. Would he be available for a consultation?"

"Is this for divorce and family law or for estate law? He does both."

"Divorce." The word dropped from her lips with terse finality.

"You've called at the right time. He's just back from lunch. Hold on and I'll connect you. Unless you'd rather come to our office for your consultation."

"No. No," Loretta said hastily. "Over the phone is perfect." She'd seen her picture in the local paper just yesterday. With her name and picture in the news, she was likely to be recognized by someone eventually, even wearing Vera's wig.

"Very well. I'll connect you."

Loretta eyed the list of questions she had written down in preparation.

"Hello? This is Quinn." The attorney's voice was cool and clipped, with the hint of an East Coast accent.

"Hello, Mr. Quinn. I was given your number by a friend of mine. My name is Daphne Harrington, and I'd like to divorce my husband."

⚜

Half an hour later, Loretta sat heavily at Barb and Vera's kitchen table, her head in her hands. She eyed the mess of notes she'd made during the phone call with the attorney. Most of the notes made no sense to her addled mind, but she knew enough now to realize her dreams of getting custody of the children seemed impossible.

Mr. Quinn had told her that no judge would grant her a divorce, as petitioner, without just cause. She must prove Pete guilty of at least one infraction: infidelity, persistent drunkenness, abandonment, prolonged separation, or spousal assault. Admissible proof included photographs, police reports, or notarized documentation of his infractions. Mr. Quinn had advised her to document everything she could and, if money allowed, hire a private investigator to follow Pete.

Worst of all, just as she feared, her hospitalization compromised her fitness as custodial parent. She'd need several character witnesses willing to make statements on her behalf as well as proof of mental competency to be awarded custody. Mr. Quinn had recommended a voluntary committal at another hospital for an evaluation as a rebuttal to the records from her stay at Agape Manor. Records that Pete would undoubtedly supply the judge.

The only good news was that Lucas, once he reached twelve this summer, would hold significant sway in the court's decision. He'd be old enough to speak for himself, and for Charlotte. If he said he wanted to live with Loretta, it would go far toward a favorable decision.

"No judge wants to take children from their mother," Mr. Quinn had reassured her. "But the children's welfare must be paramount. The burden of proof will be on you, Mrs. Harrington. To prove your husband's guilt, and your competency as their mother. Call me when you're ready to move forward."

Vera swept into the kitchen, lightly touching Loretta's back. "One step at a time, Loretta. I know it all seems overwhelming right now. But nothing is impossible."

Loretta wiped at her eyes and tried to smile. "Everything feels impossible today."

Vera offered Loretta a cup of coffee. "Coffee helps. And so does spite. Think of every hateful, terrible thing he's ever done to you, and that'll have you back in the ring fighting in no time at all."

"I know he's guilty of infidelity. The rest, I might not be able to prove. But if this Susan person is one of his students, and I have a feeling that's the case, Pete would be in heaps of trouble at Bethel, being married and dating a student. He might even lose his job." Loretta pressed the heel of her hand against her forehead. "And there's something else. Something right on the edge of my memory. A name. Joan. She's important. I just have to remember *why*."

❧

Loretta closed her eyes and lay down on Barbara's couch, clutching Mama's brooch. Somehow Vera had been able to recover Loretta's personal belongings from the hospital and had brought Loretta's purse, the awful pinching shoes, and the gray dress she'd worn to the Christmas gala. Loretta threw the shoes and the dress in the trash but kept the brooch and her pocketbook. The bag still held the lipstick case from Savage Juliet and the change from the twenty-dollar bill she'd used to buy it.

"Go back, Loretta. To a time before the hospital, before the ECT, to the night of the Christmas gala. When you're ready, tell me what you see." Dr. Hansen's calm, soothing voice rolled over her, raising goose bumps on her flesh.

Loretta focused on her breathing, on the bursts of color blooming behind her eyes. She couldn't remember a thing from that night, starting from the moment she'd left the table to go to the bathroom. She remembered arriving, talking to Gladys, but everything after had become a blank. It had been Dr. Hansen's idea to hypnotize her—to clear the cobwebs of amnesia from her mind. Then perhaps her abilities would return and she'd remember everything she had forgotten in the weeks between then and now. There was still something missing, some vital piece of information from that night that she couldn't put her finger on.

"I remember getting dressed. Pinning on this brooch."

"Yes. Focus on that. The brooch was with you all night. It remembers what happened, too."

"I wasn't feeling well. I'd been sick to my stomach all day. When I got to the party, my friend Gladys was there."

"Good. What happened next?"

Loretta wrinkled her brow, pushing herself back deeper. A flash of copper hair. Joan. Joanie. That name again. "There was a girl. A singer. Her name was Joan."

Suddenly, a flash of terrible memories crowded into Loretta's head, all at once, like someone had thrown open Pandora's box. "Those men. That night. Pete let them hurt me. He was there."

Loretta arched her back, pushing against unseen hands. "No. Stop."

"You're safe, Loretta. No one can hurt you now. Tell me what you see."

"They're praying. Shouting. Holding me down. And Darcy is there . . . Darcy's spirit. She says she wants in."

"Darcy Hayes? The missing girl?"

"Yes. She said she could make them stop. But they didn't stop."

Loretta whimpered, remembering. Remembering being herself but not herself, as she was carried into a back room, her hands and ankles bound, her face clenched between hands that hurt and punished. And she remembered voices that hurled foul words at her as her head was lifted and brought down on the metal desk, again and again. Pete's breath, hot on her skin, his words sharp in her ears.

ShutupShutupShutup!

"*He* told me to shut up. But it wasn't me speaking at that point. It was Darcy."

"You channeled her spirit?"

"Yes. She wanted in. I let her in."

"What did she say?"

"'Riverside,' over and over."

"The restaurant? In Ozark? The Riverside Inn?"

"I don't know. I don't know."

"And what about Joan? Who is she?"

Loretta clenched her teeth as another memory came hurtling from the nether reaches of her consciousness. A memory from the hospital, of a beautiful, broken girl who had told her the truth about Pete.

"Joan." Loretta's eyes popped open. "Joan is the key to *everything*."

❦

Loretta sat on the couch, her head in her hands, shaking. She felt as if she'd just returned from battle, all her wounds laid bare, raw, bleeding. Not remembering had been better. She'd do anything to escape the memories. The horror. Pete had wanted to kill her.

Dr. Hansen reached out to her, and she flinched away. "Don't touch me," she hissed.

"I'm so sorry."

"Are you?"

"I can give you something if you'd like. It will calm you."

"I don't want any more pills!" she shouted, standing. She paced around the room like a caged animal and pounded the heels of her hands against her head, trying to excise the memories.

Dr. Hansen regarded her calmly. "I didn't know what they'd done to you. I had no idea, Loretta. I'm so sorry."

Loretta immediately regretted her harsh words. Yes, Dr. Hansen had brought the memories to the surface. But she'd asked him to. It wasn't his fault.

"Didn't Gladys McAndrews call you? My friend?"

"No. I didn't know what had happened until you missed our session the next week. Barbara called around to all the hospitals, looking for you. She and Vera put two and two together and realized you were at Agape Manor because Vera recognized your name."

Loretta's heart sank. She felt betrayed by Gladys, but the truth was, Earl had probably prevented her from calling Dr. Hansen. She could see him saying it was none of their business, especially if Pete had bullied him into silence. Men like Earl were followers.

"Pete tried to kill me that night. He wanted to."

"I believe you."

Loretta sat, stood, paced. Sat, stood, paced. Sat, stood, paced. The light changed, grew warm and red. Then went away altogether. Tiredness settled in Loretta's bones. She finally sat in a heap on the floor at Dr. Hansen's feet, her skirt pooling around her.

"Loretta," Dr. Hansen, said, gently. "I'm going to get you a glass of water and a sedative. And then I want you to go lie down. I'll sit with you if you'd like. While you sleep."

"Please don't leave me."

"I won't. Barbara will be home soon. I'll tell her not to disturb you. Are you hungry?"

"No." Loretta swiped at her eyes.

"Can I help you up?"

"Yes."

Dr. Hansen offered his hand, and Loretta took it. Clung to it. "I'm sorry."

"You have nothing to be sorry about."

He led her down the hall, and when they reached the yellow bedroom, he turned on the lamp next to the bed. "Can I take off your shoes?"

"Yes," Loretta said, lying back on the pillows.

Dr. Hansen gently removed her shoes and placed them next to the bed. "I'll be right back."

As soon as he left, Loretta drew her knees to her chest and sobbed like a child, the nightmarish memories overwhelming her. She wished she could go back to that night. Start over. She thought of Charlotte and Luke, their trusting faces lit by the Christmas tree lights. She should have listened to her gut. Should have stayed home. There were so many things she would have done differently if she had the chance.

Dr. Hansen came back a few moments later. He sat down on the edge of the bed, waiting until her sobbing died down. "Here, Loretta. Take this. Just this once. It's a Miltown. It won't take long for it to work. It's not like the Thorazine they gave you at Agape."

Loretta sat up, wiping her eyes. Dr. Hansen handed her the tiny white pill and a glass of water. She swallowed the pill and lay back on the mattress. Dr. Hansen gathered the folded quilt from the end of the bed and covered her up, tucking it around her, then sat in the wicker chair in the corner.

Loretta blinked slowly, watching him through heavy eyes. The medicine curled through her, easing her anxiety and fear, but she longed for something that medication alone couldn't give her.

"Curt," she said, testing out his name. It felt right, suddenly, to call him that when it never had before. "Would you do something for me?"

"Anything, Loretta."

"Will you come lie next to me? Just until I fall asleep?"

"Are you sure?"

"Yes."

He cleared his throat, loosened his tie, and took off his shoes, placing them next to the chair, then stood, removing his suit jacket, then his tie. He carefully approached the bed and eased onto the mattress, lying atop the covers next to her. On his back. Ever the gentleman.

Loretta sighed and turned to face him, inhaling the scent of his cologne. "I feel so safe with you," she murmured, nestling close to him.

He stiffened at first, as her hand came to rest on his chest, and then relaxed. "You *are* safe with me, Loretta."

"You always say the right things, Dr. Hansen. Do you know that?"

He laughed gently, a low rumble. "Oh, we're back to Dr. Hansen again?"

The medicine wrapped her in gentle warmth, bringing a sensation of goodwill. As she drifted off to sleep, Loretta thought she felt a soft kiss land on the top of her head. But she couldn't be sure. Perhaps it had only been a dream.

Chapter 33

Loretta spent the next week wrestling with herself. With her choices. With her past. With her memories and the facts. After the hypnosis session with Dr. Hansen, the floodgates of her memory had opened. And so she wrote everything down on one of her yellow legal pads, just in case she forgot again:

1. Pete had tried to kill her during the deliverance. He wanted her dead.
2. Joan knew what had happened the night Darcy died. She was there.
3. Joan had been sleeping with her husband and had gotten pregnant by him.
4. Pete had forced Joan to get an illegal abortion from a doctor in Saint Louis.
5. There were other girls. Other mistresses. Susan was the latest.
6. Pete had been sleeping with his students for some time. This was in violation of school policy. He could get fired. Possibly charged with statutory rape if any of the girls were underage. If one of the girls went to the dean to report Pete's misconduct, she'd have the record of his infidelity she needed for the courts.

7. Pete may have killed Darcy. Accidentally or on purpose. Or he knew who did.
8. If Pete went to jail for either of the reasons above, she could get her children back. As long as she was deemed mentally sound and Lucas testified that he wished to remain with her. She would need to designate a guardian, just in case. Someone trustworthy.
9. She couldn't testify against her husband, but Joan could.

Loretta sat looking at the list, chewing on her pencil eraser. It was near the end of January, and a shroud of snow covered the ground. Classes would be back in session at Bethel by now. Pete would be busy with teaching. If she could find Joan—prevail upon her to report Pete and perhaps convince her to testify against him—she would have a case for divorce. And Detective Pierce might have a suspect in Darcy's homicide.

As soon as her divorce was granted, she'd never have to worry about Pete having the authority to lock her up in an asylum again. She would be free.

Her psychic abilities were coming back, slowly. For a fleeting moment the other day, when she'd touched Vera's hand, she'd seen the true nature of her relationship with Barbara. She understood, now, why they were so close. They were in love. But when it came to channeling the dead, the veil would not part, and the door inside her mind remained locked and dark.

Conjecture wouldn't be enough to have Pete investigated. She needed something concrete.

That afternoon, Loretta picked up the phone and dialed the number she'd found at the bottom of her pocketbook. Dora Hayes answered on the third ring.

"Hello? Dora? This is Loretta Davenport."

"Oh. Hi." Dora's tone sounded flat, unaffected. "I haven't heard from you in a while. Saw your picture in the paper, though. What happened?"

"It's . . . too much to tell you over the phone. I've had a time of things lately. How are you?"

"Not great." The girl sighed. "Why are you calling?"

"Listen, I know this may sound strange, but did you hear about Paula Buckley?"

"The girl in the cave?"

"Yes. There's a detective there, at the police department, who believes in my abilities. Detective Pierce. He overheard us that day, talking to Detective Eames."

"Okay? What does this have to do with me or my sister?"

"Well, Detective Pierce asked for my help. I'm the reason they found Paula's body. We went to the park where she disappeared, and I put on the hat she was wearing the night she went missing. My impressions were much stronger as a result, having something that belonged to her. I'm wondering, if I had something that belonged to Darcy, if it might help. Do you think you could meet me, tomorrow, after school, with something of Darcy's?"

"I don't know. This is all so hard. My mom is really sick."

"Oh my. I'm so sorry."

"Yeah." Loretta heard a muted snuffling. "What kind of thing do you need?"

"Anything that she wore often. Especially if she wore it that night."

"I can give you her locket. She was wearing it when they found her."

"That would be perfect. Where's your school?"

"I go to Myrna Grove High. Across the street from Bethel."

"Could I meet you there tomorrow? And please, don't tell anyone else you saw me or spoke to me over the phone. It's very important, Dora."

"Okay. School's over at three o'clock. I'll meet you out front, by the sign."

꧁꧂

The next day, a frigid rain sluiced heavy through the streets of Myrna Grove, rinsing away the dirty piles of snow lining the gutters. Loretta climbed aboard the city bus, in her wig and Vera's borrowed sunglasses. Her nerves ratcheted higher the closer they got to Bethel. She was wary of running into Pete. But Joan might be there, too. As the bus swung around the corner, Loretta lifted her head and looked out the window, watching for a bright torch of short red hair. Since recovering her memories, thoughts of Joan haunted her. They were kindred in many ways—in Pete's lies, in his rejection, in his mistreatment.

Vera had checked Agape Manor's records, on Loretta's insistence. Joan had been released in the middle of January. Loretta wondered if she'd returned to classes at Bethel, or gone home instead.

The bus pulled up to the curb in front of Myrna Grove High. Loretta stepped off the bus, gathering her new wool peacoat around herself. The school loomed in front of her, like a great gothic castle, three stories tall and made of red brick, with turrets and windows perched in its pointed eaves. Dora stood near the sign, huddled beneath a hooded yellow raincoat. Loretta looked around furtively, ducking her head as she rushed across the lawn.

Dora looked up at Loretta's approach and nodded in greeting. "Hi. You've changed your hair."

Loretta patted the wig, the synthetic hair springy and foreign beneath her fingertips. "Yes. I'm hiding out. Staying with a friend."

"The mental hospital, huh?" Dora smirked. "How was that?"

"Horrid. My husband put me there. He's dangerous. No one can know where I am. Do you understand? If they put me away again, I won't be able to help you."

Dora nodded. "Yep. I won't say anything. Promise."

"How's your mother? Is she feeling any better?"

"It's cancer. She had surgery last week. We'll know more in a few months."

"I'm so sorry."

"Thanks." The girl thrust her hand in her coat pocket and withdrew a small, oval pendant on a gold chain. "Here you go. This was Darcy's."

Loretta took the locket in her gloved hand. "Hopefully I'll get some impressions from this. Do you remember Darcy talking about anyone named Joan? A friend?"

"Oh yeah. Joanie. They met at Riverside. Darcy worked there. Joan started a few months before Darcy disappeared. Darcy really liked her. They had a lot in common."

Loretta blanched. "Riverside?"

"Yeah, the restaurant? It's right by the Finley River, in Ozark. When Darcy worked the late shift, she'd walk to my aunt's house to spend the night, since she lived nearby."

It all came latching together, in Loretta's mind, like puzzle pieces. Joan truly was the connection.

"Thank you, Dora. Do you happen to know how to get hold of Joan?"

Dora shrugged. "I don't know. Her phone number might be in Darcy's address book. I can look. I think she lived at Bethel, though. In Ashley House. Darcy would go there sometimes for parties."

"If you could find a number, I'd appreciate it. Do you know anything else? Anything at all that Darcy might have mentioned about Joan might help."

"I do know she was dating an older guy. Darcy didn't much care for him. He was always coming to Riverside late at night, before close, and running up a bar tab."

Loretta's hands clenched at her side. That sounded like Pete. "Did she ever mention his name?"

"No. Not that I remember." Dora shivered. "Hey, I'd better go. I have a ton of homework. I'm trying to get caught up."

"All right." Loretta smiled. "You're going to be okay, Dora. You know that, don't you?"

Dora shrugged, gave a halfhearted smile. "I guess."

Loretta told Dora goodbye and went back to the bus stop to wait for the next bus. It was only a few minutes late. Once she settled in her seat, she opened the locket. Inside, there was a photo of Mrs. Hayes on one side and a man in uniform on the other. Darcy and Dora's father. Both girls had his expressive, brown eyes. She closed the locket and put it in her coat pocket. As they passed Bethel's gymnasium on the way south, Loretta startled. She saw Pete coming out of the building, dressed in gym clothes. He'd let his hair grow. It now brushed his collar. He was unshaven, with a scruffy beard. He had grown so thin he looked gaunt. Sickly. When the bus came to a stop at the corner, Pete caught up to them. His head swiveled toward her, as if he'd felt her looking at him. Loretta gasped and sank low in the seat, her heart racing. She cowered there, afraid to look again, thankful for the dark wig and sunglasses.

A moment later, the light changed and the bus crept forward with a rumble. When Loretta looked out the window again, Pete was gone.

Chapter 34

Loretta sat cross-legged in the middle of the bed, holding Darcy's locket, her skirt tucked under her knees. She listened to the steady thrum of the rain outside the window and slowed her breathing. Dr. Hansen sat in the wicker chair, watching her. "Nice and easy, Loretta. Don't push things. Don't rush them."

Loretta closed her eyes and focused. A few moments later, the locket began to tingle in her hand, as if it held a buzz of electricity, just as Paula's ring had when they'd tested her abilities with Detective Pierce. She tightened her grip around it, emptying her mind of all thought. The door inside her consciousness opened, just a crack, white light seeping around the edges.

Come on. Show me what you need me to see, Darcy.

The familiar taste of wet leaves crowded Loretta's tongue. "She's here," she managed to say, just before Darcy's spirit slammed into her like a one-ton truck.

She was suddenly in a restaurant, carrying a stack of dirty plates. Just like with Paula, Loretta realized she was seeing the world through Darcy's eyes.

The loud clatter of a kitchen greeted her as she bumped a swinging door open with her hip. The cooks and servers were wiping down the grill, prepping raw vegetables for the next day's menu, and sweeping the tiled floor. Loretta placed the stack of dirty dishes on the counter next to the sink. Her limbs ached, and she felt feverish. She put a hand to her forehead and wiped away sweat.

When she turned, Joan was there, an exasperated look on her face. "I'm sorry, Darce. I know you're mad."

"He's not making me late again. Tell him to close out his tab. He's had too much to drink, anyway. So has his buddy. I don't feel good. I want to go home."

"They're giving me a ride. They have to wait until I get off."

"Joanie. Come *on*. Neither one of them's in any shape to drive. You can spend the night with me at Aunt Sally's. She'll take you back to town tomorrow morning, when she goes to work."

"He'll be mad if I do that."

"Who cares? He's too old for you, Joanie. He's married. It's not gonna go anywhere, anyway."

"I'm late, Darce."

"Yeah? We're both gonna be late, on his account."

"No. I don't mean that way. I'm *late*."

"You've been stressed with midterms. It's probably just that."

"No. I'm never late."

Loretta felt Darcy's frustration, rising like heartburn. Her belly rumbled, sugar sick. "You can't have a baby. Remember your scholarship? If you drop out, you won't get your degree. Think!"

"So you think I should get rid of it?"

"I don't know. But you should get rid of *him*. He scares me."

"He loves me." Joan's face was florid. Tears gathered in the corner of her eyes.

"He's just saying that, Joanie. Telling you what you want to hear."

She turned away and began scrubbing the pots in the deep-welled sink. God, she hurt. Everything hurt. "I'm gonna finish these dishes, and then I'm leaving. Come with me. We can slip out the back. He won't know."

"I can't." Joan wiped her eyes with the corner of her apron and went back through the swinging doors. Raucous, drunken laughter filled Loretta's ears.

Suddenly, the scene changed. It was dark, and she was walking along a curving stretch of pitch-black road. She was alone, with nothing but the distant swish of traffic on the highway in her ears. Loretta looked down at her feet and saw white Chuck Taylors, their once-pristine soles muddied by the damp soil on the shoulder. She hummed to herself to cut her fear and ignored the feeling in her gut that told her something bad was about to happen. Something terrible.

Less than a mile up the road, Aunt Sally's house gleamed through the darkness, windows lit up yellow. She picked up her pace. She'd be in bed soon, tucked under the covers in Aunt Sally's guest room, with a glass of ginger ale to cut the nauseous feeling in her belly and aspirin to soothe the ache in her joints. It was September, and next week was her nineteenth birthday. Maybe, if she got brave, she'd ask Tommy Little out for—

A horn blared. Loretta turned. Headlights swung around the curve, illuminating a deer as it ran from the trees into the road. The car swerved, brakes squealing. And then Loretta was flying, the ground whipped out from under her feet. She screamed as she fell, and met the earth once more, her body limp as a rag doll. She tried to move, tried to get up. She couldn't. She lay there helpless, her leg twisted behind her. Pain radiated from her core.

A car door slammed. Two shadows approached, made long by the headlights.

"Kill the damned headlights, Joan!"

Loretta knew that voice. Had known it for almost twelve years. Pete.

The world plunged into darkness. Footsteps swished through the tall grass. Her heart thu-thumped inside her chest.

In the distance, a high-pitched wail pierced the night.

"Joan," Loretta tried to whisper. But no sound came from her mouth.

"Shut the hell up, Joanie! Get back in the fucking car." Pete squatted next to Loretta. Picked up her hand, let it drop. Loretta tried to wiggle a finger, tried to speak. Nothing came out. "Fuck. She's dead. Fuckfuckfuck!"

"I don't think so, Pete." Another familiar voice. Earl McAndrews. "I saw her move. Just a little. I think she's breathing. We should take her to the hospital."

"And then what, Earl? How the hell you gonna explain this? We're in *your car*. You didn't think about that, did you?"

"We can't just leave her here," Earl slurred. "That ain't right."

"Help me load her up, then. Put her in the back seat."

Hands lifted her, wrenching her leg to the side, then carried her. Her aunt's tiny kitchen window beckoned through the gloom. She prayed that somehow Aunt Sally had heard the commotion. That she might step out onto the porch. And then she remembered. Fridays were Aunt Sally's bridge night. She would have left the key under the mat, as she always did. But everything was going to be all right. They would take her to the hospital. They would get her help. Doctors.

The men opened up the car door and roughly shoved her inside.

"Darcy!" Joan was crying as she moved to the back seat and cradled Loretta's head in her hands, her white hands shaking as she clumsily stroked her hair. Tears dripdripdripped onto Loretta's face.

It's okay, Joanie. Everything is going to be okay.

She tried to move. Couldn't. Something wasn't right. She couldn't feel her toes or fingers anymore.

Outside the car, the men were arguing, their voices frantic.

". . . lose our goddam jobs, our wives, all of it . . ."

"I've been worried about your tail-chasing for a long time. Knew it would come up bad. We gotta get that girl to the hospital."

"Get in the goddam car, Earl. Now!"

Car doors slammed. Tires squealed on asphalt. They flew down the road. The stars twinkled outside the window above the whizzing trees.

"Please, God, please, Jesus, please!" Joanie lifted her hands, palms up as she prayed.

"Shut up, Joanie!" Pete glared over his shoulder. "I can't drive with you carrying on back there."

The car wrenched right, then left, onto a gravel road. Not the highway. If they were taking her to the hospital, they'd be on the highway. Fear clawed through Loretta's mind.

The car came to an abrupt stop. "What are you doing?" Joan asked, her voice spindle-sharp and high. "Aren't we going to the hospital?"

"Shut up, Joan! We have to take care of this. Now."

"I don't know about this." Earl groaned. "What if—"

"You want to lose your job, Earl?" Pete smacked the dash.

"No, but—"

"Then get the hell out of the car and help me. You got anything in the trunk we can dig with?"

"Just a snow shovel I keep for winter."

"Get it. Come on."

The car doors opened, letting in the sound of running water. The mill. They were by the old mill. Loretta tried to move, tried to scream, tried to do anything. She could only blink. Joan wept, prayed, apologized, over and over, in a loop. "I'm so sorry, I'm so sorry. I didn't mean to. I'm so sorry."

Time ticked by, undercut by a muted scraping in the distance. The door to the back seat suddenly flew open. Someone grabbed her ankles and hauled her out into the cold night air. The back of her head hit the fender as they dragged her from the car, sending sparks flying behind her eyes like fireworks. She wanted to fight. Wanted to scream. Wanted to plead for her life. Instead, she cried. Thought about her mother. Dora. Her little white cat curled up on her pillow, waiting for her at home.

When the first damp shovelful of dirt landed on her face, Loretta flung the locket from her hand. "Get out!" she wailed, clutching her heart and gasping for breath. Loretta felt the familiar, muted *whoosh* as Darcy's spirit left her body.

Loretta collapsed into Dr. Hansen's waiting arms. He knelt on the bed with her, holding her as she cried. For Darcy. For Joan. For herself.

"It was Pete. He's the killer. We have to tell Detective Pierce."

"You're sure, Loretta?"

"Yes. I saw it all. He and Earl McAndrews. They buried her alive."

వ్య

Loretta startled awake, her heart leaping into her throat. She looked at the fluorescent alarm clock, glowing next to the bed—3:38 in the morning. What had woken her at such an ungodly hour?

Bangbangbangbangbang.

She sat up, listening. The banging started up again. Someone was at the door. Someone angry. Panic choked Loretta, stealing her breath. She shoved her feet into her slippers and, without turning on a light, went out into the hall. Barbara met her in the hallway, her eyes wide and her corn silk hair down around her shoulders. Vera was at work. They were alone in the house.

"It's a man," Barbara whispered. "I saw him through the window."

"It's Pete. I just know it."

"How did he find out where you were?"

"I don't know."

Barb squeezed Loretta's hand. "There's a telephone in my room. Go in, lock the door behind you. Call the police. After you do, stay there. No matter what you hear, don't come out. If you hear him inside the house, go out the window and run, Loretta. Run to the neighbors, as fast as you can."

"But what if he hurts you?"

"Don't even think about me. I'll be all right."

Another knock shook the tiny house, rattling the doorframe. "Open this door, Loretta! I know you're in there!"

"Go!" Barbara whispered.

Loretta nodded and rushed down the hall to the bedroom at the back of the house, guilt over leaving Barb alone warring with her fear. She picked up the phone receiver and dialed 0, her hands shaking as she knelt on the floor, out of sight of the windows. "I need the police. This is an emergency."

She hurriedly gave the dispatching officer the address and then hung up, rushing to Barbara's closet. From inside the closet, she could hear Pete cursing, the brush of his feet through the wet grass as he went behind the house. She whimpered softly, remembering what he had done to Darcy. His brutality. If he'd done that to a stranger—a child who had never crossed him—what would he do to her? Or Barbara? Hot tears tracked down Loretta's face. The back doorknob rattled.

"Let me in, Retta! So help me God, I'll break down this door if I have to!"

Please, God. Please don't let him come in.

Loretta felt around herself, for anything she might use as a weapon. The best she could find was one of Barbara's high-heeled shoes. She picked it up, the leather sliding in her sweat-slicked hand. If it came to it, she wouldn't run. She would fight. For herself. For Barbara.

Suddenly, the bedroom door creaked open. She cursed under her breath. In her hurry to get to the phone, she'd forgotten to lock it. Her heartbeat ratcheted higher as she heard the sound of a gun being cocked. A shadow crossed the moonlight beneath the closet door. Loretta's muscles tensed as she readied herself. A shoe would be little use against a gun, but she would claw Pete's eyes out with her bare hands, if she had to. And if she died, at least she would die brave.

"Loretta!" Barb's whisper cut through the room. "It's me. I think he's gone."

Loretta eased the closet door open, just a crack. Barbara was crouched on the floor, a silver pistol in her hands. She was shaking, her eyes gleaming with frightened tears.

"Are you sure?"

"I think so. The police are almost here. Can you hear the sirens? I think he heard them, too. He must have run."

Loretta stilled, willing the th-thump of her heart to quiet. Sure enough, a high whine rang in the near distance. "I hope they find him. I hope they throw him in jail."

A sudden crash reverberated through the house. Glass, shattering. Barb whimpered. "That was the kitchen window. I'll go out. Try to hold him at gunpoint until the police get here. Go through the bedroom window, Loretta. Please. Hurry!"

"But . . ."

"Go!" Tears rolled down Barbara's cheeks. "Think of your children."

Loretta rushed from the closet as Barb ran out into the hall. She climbed atop the bed, noticing the picture of Barbara and Vera on the nightstand, their arms entwined. A Ferris wheel stood behind them. In the photo, Vera held a cone of frothy cotton candy. Dearing Park. Loretta choked back her tears and cranked open the casement window.

She'd just gotten one leg through the window when she heard the gunshot. The sirens wailed. Closer now, but not close enough. Loretta almost lost her resolve, thinking of Barb—brave, dear Barb—but then she remembered what Barbara had said. *Think of your children.* With a silent prayer, Loretta flung herself out the window.

Chapter 35

Lights flashed all around Loretta, a blue-and-red kaleidoscope amid the early-morning gray. She huddled next to Barb on the front porch. Barb leaned her head against Loretta's. "It's all right," Barb whispered. "You're all right."

Detective Pierce approached, removing his hat. "We've searched the neighborhood. We can't find him. He must have run when he heard your gunshot, Miss Miller. And you're sure you didn't hit him?"

"No. I fired well above his head. To scare him off."

Pierce nodded. "That's for the best. If he'd been inside the house, you'd have been within your rights to shoot him." He scratched his head. "It's cold out here. Why don't the two of you go inside? We have everything we need. I'll be in after we've wrapped up. I want to talk to Mrs. Davenport. Off the record."

He replaced his hat, then went to speak to the other officers gathered in the driveway.

"I don't want them to put me back in the hospital," Loretta said, clinging to Barbara as they rose as one. "Please don't let them take me."

"I don't think that will happen, dear. Now, let's go in. I'll make some tea. Curt will be here soon."

Loretta curled up on the couch, her nerves so brittle she felt the slightest touch might break her into pieces. Barbara emerged with a steaming cup of tea a few minutes later. "I added loads of sugar. My Irish aunt always said it was good for the shock."

"So did my grandmother." Loretta smiled and took the proffered cup. Barbara settled next to her with her own cup and Loretta turned to her friend. "You were very brave tonight. Protecting me."

"I don't know about that. My instincts took over, that's all. I used to have nightmares about Thad—that was my husband—doing the same sort of thing. It's why I have the gun."

"Well, all the same. Thank you." Loretta placed her hand over Barbara's. "There's something I've been meaning to ask you."

Barbara set her cup down and gazed at Loretta through her thick blonde lashes. "What is it, dear?"

"If something happens to me—if Pete gets to me—I need to know the children will be taken care of."

"Oh, Loretta. Don't think like that."

"I have to." Loretta trembled. "He found me here. He'll find me again, eventually, no matter where I go. And when he does, he'll kill me. I know he will."

"I understand why you're afraid." Barbara took Loretta's hand. "Do you have any relatives, who could look after Luke and Charlotte, if anything does happen?"

"Only aunts and a distant uncle. My mother's kin. They're all in Illinois and Michigan now, though. They moved up north to work. And I don't want Pete's sister taking them. She's cold. She doesn't like children. I want them to stay here, in Myrna Grove. Where things are familiar." Loretta bit her lip. "Do you think . . . you and Vera might take them? I-I know it's a lot to ask. And you can say no. I'll understand."

"I don't know what to say. You'd really want *us*?"

"Of course I would. You and Vera are the warmest, kindest people I have ever known. I know I could trust you to raise Luke and Charlotte with love."

"Then, if it makes you feel better, let's write this down. Like a will."
Barbara wiped at her eyes. "We won't need it, of course, but if it gives
you peace of mind . . ."

"Yes. It would. Please."

Barbara fetched a tablet of lined paper from her rolltop desk, and a
pen. Loretta hastily wrote down her wishes and then signed her name
at the bottom. "I think," Barbara said, "that if two witnesses sign and
date a handwritten will in the presence of a notary, it's legally binding."

"I've heard the same."

"We'll go to a notary later today, then. After you've had some rest."

A gentle tap came at the front door, and Dr. Hansen entered, trailed
by Detective Pierce. He rushed to embrace Barbara and then turned
to Loretta. She practically fell into his arms, the unshaven scruff along
his jaw brushing against her forehead. "I'm so sorry I wasn't here," he
murmured into her hair. "Are you all right?"

"Yes. I'm a little scratched up from my dive into Vera's rosebushes,
but Barbara did a marvelous job protecting us," Loretta said, smiling at
Barbara over his shoulder. "She was very brave."

"Dr. Hansen filled me in outside, Mrs. Davenport," Detective Pierce
said. "He told me your suspicions about Pete and Darcy's murder."

Loretta pulled back from Dr. Hansen and sat on the couch, bracketed by Barb and Dr. Hansen. "Yes. I had one of the strongest visions
I've ever had when I held her locket. It was him. I'm sure of it. Have
you been able to track down Joan?"

Detective Pierce shook his head. "Without her last name, I've had
no luck. I went to Ashley House, at Bethel. Spoke to two young women
named Joan. Neither one of them had ever met Darcy."

"Oh. I have her full name now. It's Everly. Joan Everly." Loretta
glanced down at her bare feet and curled her toes into the plush carpet.
"We met. At the Christmas gala. And again when I was hospitalized.
She had an affair with my husband."

"I see."

"She was there, the night Darcy died. She knows what happened."

"I'll do my best to find her. In the meantime, I recommend you find another place to stay. I didn't put your name on the police report, since there's a missing person notice out for you. I'll do my best, off record, to help protect you from your husband, but these things can get complicated without a court order."

"But if you end up arresting him, I can let the authorities know where I am, and they won't make me go back to Agape Manor, will they?"

"That's right, since you were a private patient."

"Then, please, Detective, please find Joan."

❧

Loretta picked up the hotel telephone and dialed the number once more. "Joan, this is Mrs. Davenport . . ."

The line clicked. Went silent. "She hung up on me again."

Loretta picked up the receiver, dialed again. This time the line rang and rang, with no answer.

"Are you sure you have the right number?" Barbara asked when Loretta hung up, her brow furrowing.

"It's the only one Dora had."

"She's no longer living at Ashley House," Detective Pierce said, stretching. "I know that, for certain."

"I'd bet she's hiding from Pete. Just like I am." Loretta looked at the hotel room's plain gray walls, with heavy, woven curtains over the windows and dismal art above the bed. "I'm sure he's threatened her."

"She's probably very frightened," Dr. Hansen said. "Give her time to think about things, then call again."

"If we have to, we can subpoena her. Bring her in for questioning," Detective Pierce said.

"I don't think that's a good idea. She's just gotten out of the hospital," Vera said. "She's very fragile."

They sat around the chipped kitchenette table, drinking stale coffee and watching the time tick by. At six o'clock, Loretta picked up the receiver and dialed again.

Joan answered this time, her breath a soft rasp on the line. "Hello?"

"Please don't hang up again, Joan. I want to help you."

There was silence at first, then quiet sobbing. "How?"

"Could we meet somewhere, just you and I? So we can talk?"

"Just you?"

"Yes, just me."

"Okay."

"Meet me at Anton's on Glenstone? Around eleven?"

"Tonight?"

"I think the sooner we meet, the better."

"Okay. I can't sleep anymore, anyway."

Loretta gave a thumbs-up to the rapt audience around the table. Vera and Barbara made excited faces at one another. Dr. Hansen squeezed Loretta's shoulder.

"I'll see you soon."

She hung up the phone and let out her breath in a shaky rush.

"We should go with you, Loretta. Wait outside. Just in case," Detective Pierce said.

"I don't think that's a good idea. This is such a delicate situation. If I can talk to her, one to one, and get her to trust me, she's more likely to want to help instead of feeling like she's being forced. She's so young." Loretta sighed. "I remember being that age. She won't trust adults, especially men, after what Pete put her through."

"You're right. It's for the best if Loretta talks to her alone." Dr. Hansen stood, and Loretta stood with him.

"But what if Pete shows up?" Barbara said. "Can I or Vera go with you, Loretta? Wait in the car? That way if there's trouble, we can call the police."

"We'll be in a public place. Pete would be foolish to start anything."

"Once we have a sworn statement from Joan, we should call the FBI. Let them handle his arrest," Detective Pierce said. "Go above the local law. They'll be able to get things done more quickly. I found out today, after you called me, that Earl McAndrews is out of state. He might go on the run once he finds out Joan squawked."

"There's no guarantee she'll cooperate. She might not tell me anything," Loretta said.

"For her sake, I hope she does," Detective Pierce said, his face stern. "Because either way, if your impressions are accurate, and I have a feeling they are, she's just as culpable in this as your husband and McAndrews. If she cooperates, I'll do everything in my power to make sure the prosecution grants her a plea bargain."

"All right." Loretta felt as if a fifty-pound boulder hung around her shoulders. "I'll do my best."

Chapter 36

For the first time since she'd escaped Agape Manor, Loretta left Barbara's without wearing her disguise. Before going to meet Joan, she made herself look as harmless and unintimidating as possible, wearing a simple dress and woolen stockings beneath her coat, her hair tied back in her usual tidy bun.

As Loretta drove down the quiet streets, the windshield wipers on Vera's Fiat swept the falling snow from the glass in a graceful arc. It was a lovely night. The kind of scene that belonged on a Currier and Ives plate, with the silent snow banking along the roads, and swathing the houses in gingerbread delight. But all Loretta could think about was her children, and how they were in the custody of a murderer. Out of curiosity, she turned onto her old street. The house was gone. All that remained was a snow-covered pile of rubble. Loretta's heart sank. Even though she hated Pete now, he'd given her two beautiful children. Children she would do anything for. Absolutely anything.

She thought of everything she and Detective Pierce had discussed, concerning the kids. If Luke and Charlotte couldn't be returned to her, in the event of Pete's arrest, she'd made her wishes clear—Barbara was the only person she trusted as a guardian. The rest would be up to Child Welfare and the courts. No matter how long it took, Loretta would find a way to get them back.

When she got to Anton's, only one other car was parked in the lot. From outside the diner, she could see Joan's bright-red hair through the windows, her curls grown out just enough to frame her face in soft waves.

Loretta cut the engine. She took a moment to center her thoughts. She needed to choose her words carefully. Joan was a frightened rabbit. If Loretta came on too strongly, the girl would bolt. She stepped out of the car and entered the diner. The same waitress who had been working the night she and Pete came here, months ago, looked up from the counter and rolled her eyes.

"You eatin' tonight?" she barked. "Kitchen's about to close."

"I don't think so," Loretta said, approaching Joan's booth. "Do you want anything to eat, Joan?"

Joan turned. Her face was pale, dark circles etched behind the delicate wire-framed glasses perched on her nose. "No. No food."

"Could we just have some coffee, please?" Loretta eased into the booth across from Joan. "Hello."

"Hi. You were the talk of Agape Manor after you escaped." A wry smile twisted one corner of Joan's mouth, but Loretta took note of the tremor in the girl's voice. She was nervous. "How'd you do it?"

"The window washer left the grate off my window. It wasn't locked. I lifted it and climbed out."

"Like a cat burglar."

"I suppose." Loretta laughed, softly. "How are you?"

"How do I look to you?"

Loretta smiled. "Tired. Lonely. Afraid."

"Yeah. I'm all that and more."

The waitress brought their coffee, and Loretta added cream and sugar to her cup, stirring it. Joan did the same.

"We even drink our coffee the same way." Joan smirked.

"I think Pete has a type. Young, vulnerable, and naive."

"How did you meet him?"

"At a revival, one summer. He was lit up with a fire for God. Filled my head full of pretty things. What he offered was miles better than my daddy's farm. I couldn't resist." Loretta shrugged. "I was sixteen. Didn't have my mama anymore, to talk sense into my head."

"I know the feeling. My mom died when I was twelve. Dad remarried, but . . . she's not my mom. You know?"

"He really does have a type." Loretta propped her cheek on her hand, looking at Joan. "You deserve better than Pete. So did I. I just hope you've learned that now, instead of at twenty-seven like I did."

"Yeah. Still hope the right one's out there, someday, though."

"You got any plans, after college? Besides getting married?"

"There's a conservatory, up in the Catskills. New York. I have a scholarship for this summer. I want to study to be an opera singer. I'm done with Bethel. My choir director says Juilliard recruits from that workshop. I might have a chance."

"Oh, that's wonderful. I always wanted to be a writer, myself. Always wanted to go to New York, too."

Loretta paused, running her thumb along the rim of the cup. "It'd be a shame if Pete stole your dreams away, Joan."

Joan bit her lip, looked out the window. "You know, don't you? About Darcy. I don't know how you do, but you do."

"I do. I saw it all. In a vision. Do you believe in visions?"

Joan shrugged. "I guess. My mom named me Joan because she liked the story of Joan of Arc."

"Such a sad story. They burned her. For cross-dressing, of all things. Called her a heretic. Said her gifts were from the Devil, not from God. Wasn't right, was it?"

Joan shook her head. "No."

Loretta sighed, leaned back in her banquette. "If you go to the police, they can help you. They can make sure you won't lose your future. The music program. Any of that. If you don't . . ." She shrugged.

"They might charge you as harshly as Pete or Earl. I don't think you deserve that, and I don't think Darcy would want that. Do you?"

"No. She was a good friend. The best person I've ever known." Joan's voice cracked. "I'm tired of this. Of the sleepless nights. The guilt. She haunts me. Darcy. I hear her crying, all night long. And *he* keeps threatening me. Tells me he'll kill me if I ever tell anyone what happened. I'm afraid of him." Tears built and rolled down Joan's sallow cheeks. "I'm always looking over my shoulder. He could be anywhere." She took off her glasses and swiped at them with her hand. "I just want my life back. I want to be happy again."

"I believe it. And you deserve to be happy."

"What would I have to do?"

Loretta smiled, her mind spinning the perfect net for Pete to fall into. "I'll tell you. But first, you have to tell me the truth about everything that happened that night."

Chapter 37

Joan sat, stiff-backed and nervous, hidden behind a curtained alcove inside Dr. Hansen's study. Loretta gave her shoulder a gentle squeeze. "You're going to do fine, Joan. Just stay hidden until we tell you to come out."

It had been a week since Loretta's meeting with Joan at the diner. The police had put Joan in protective custody and taken her statement the following morning. She'd delivered it in a calm and steady voice, holding Loretta's hand as they recorded it on reel-to-reel tape in the interrogation room.

Now Detectives Pierce and Eames were stationed in the connected parlor with Dr. Hansen, hidden behind the pocket doors, sidearms at the ready. Two blocks away, parked on a side street, another patrol car waited, as backup.

Two o'clock came. Loretta heard the doorbell ring, right on the nose. Adrenaline surged through her. She heard the click, click of Barbara's high heels on the hardwood floor. Then the creak of the door. "Good afternoon, Mr. Davenport."

"Where is she?" Pete demanded, his voice ragged with anger. Loretta's heartbeat responded. What if Pete had a gun? What if he killed her, before the officers had a chance to intervene? She glanced at the parlor doors and prayed they were ready.

"She's in Dr. Hansen's study. Right here."

Barbara opened the door as Loretta slowly turned, her emotions a wild, violent sea. Pete stood there in the doorway, swaying slightly.

His rumpled clothing hung from his frame. A scent like rotten onions rolled off him. "Retta."

"Hello, Peter."

"I've missed you. The kids miss you."

"I saw the house." Loretta pursed her lips. "How's Susan?"

"Susan." He laughed, tilting his head back. "She left. Just like you."

"I didn't leave. Remember? I was going to. Someday. But you didn't give me the chance." Loretta sighed, remembering Detective Pierce's instructions. *Provoke him.* "What did Susan get tired of? Your drinking? Your temper? Your lies?"

"Goddammit, Loretta." Pete smacked the doorframe. "You made me lose my job."

"It wasn't me. How many of them were there over the years? Susan, Joan . . . how many more?"

"Joan?" Pete blanched.

"Yes. Joan. She's the one who went to Dean Matthews. Not me. But that's not all. Joan told me what you did to Darcy Hayes. I'm going to the police."

"The hell you are!" Pete charged across the room and stumbled into her, clumsily knocking her to the floor. Loretta held in her scream as he covered her with his body, his rank, disgusting odor filling her nostrils. Not yet. She had to wait. Had to wait until his malice was undeniable. Criminal.

"I should have killed you, you little whore," Pete growled. "You and your rich doctor friend."

Loretta bucked her hips as his hands closed around her neck. Panic threaded through her like a cold knife. "Help!" she screamed, clawing at Pete's hands. His fingers tightened around her neck, closing off her air and her words. Loretta closed her eyes and, for an instant, saw Darcy's spirit, flickering at the edges of her consciousness.

The pocket doors slid open. "Get off of her, and put your hands up!" Loretta heard a click as Detective Pierce leveled his gun. Eames circled from the other direction, his pistol cocked as he pulled Pete off her by his collar. Dr. Hansen rushed in and helped Loretta to her feet, guiding her to the corner of the room.

"You're under arrest for the murder of Darcy Hayes, Mr. Davenport," Detective Eames intoned. "As well as aggravated assault against Mrs. Davenport." He slid a pair of handcuffs onto Pete's wrists and wrestled him to his knees at gunpoint.

As the detective led Pete away, Dr. Hansen helped Loretta to a chair. She gasped for air, her throat burning where Pete's hands had choked her. Ollie butted her leg gently with his head, meowing plaintively. She scratched him behind the ears to reassure him. He curled at her feet, purring.

"Are you all right?" Dr. Hansen asked, his eyes filled with concern.

"I think so," Loretta said. Her voice was raw. Raspy. Every word hurt her throat. If they'd waited much longer . . .

She leaned against Dr. Hansen, a fog of disbelief hanging over her. She was alive. She was safe now.

"That was the hardest thing I've ever done," he murmured, "staying in that room while he attacked you."

"I can take care of myself, Doctor," she said, looking up at him with a tenuous smile.

"I've never had a doubt."

"Joan, you can come out now," Detective Pierce called.

Joan opened the curtain and stepped out, shy and awkward as a baby deer. Detective Pierce handcuffed her. Loretta met Joan's scared eyes across the room and tried to smile in a reassuring way. "The prosecuting attorney is expecting you, Joan," Pierce said. "He and the judge will set bond. Dr. Hansen has generously offered to post your bail. You should only be in jail for a few hours while we get the paperwork drawn up."

"And Pete? Will the judge set bond for him?" Loretta asked, holding her throat.

"It's doubtful. Given Joan's statement, the prosecutor will likely charge him with first-degree murder."

"And my children?" Loretta thought of Luke and Charlotte, at school, completely oblivious that their world had been turned inside out.

"One of our best juvenile officers is on her way to the school," Pierce said. "As we discussed, Child Health and Welfare will take them into custody, they'll be examined by a doctor and a psychiatrist, and the temporary guardianship order will go into effect. A social worker will be assigned. She'll transport them to Miss Miller's house this evening and visit periodically to check in on them. Once you've had your psychological workup and appear before the judge, it's very likely the children will be returned to your custody, Mrs. Davenport, although it may be weeks or even months before that happens."

"I understand," she rasped. "And I'll be able to see them?"

"Of course. I'd recommend you hire an attorney, to represent your best interests."

"I already have one in mind."

"Loretta?" Barbara stepped into the room. "Vera and I will do everything we can to make the children comfortable and happy. You can see them as often as the court allows." She took Loretta's hand. "Your trust means the world to me. I don't take this lightly."

Loretta's eyes filled with tears. "Oh, Barbara. I couldn't trust anyone more. You saved my life, after all."

"Oh, I don't know about that." Barbara smiled. "If it's all right with you, I can go down to the welfare office now. Maybe meet the kids, tell them you and I are friends, so I seem less like a stranger when they arrive tonight."

"I'd like that," Loretta said.

"I'd better be getting Joan to her appointment with the prosecutor," Detective Pierce said. "We'll be in touch once we have a court date. And Mrs. Davenport, even though your testimony won't be admissible in court for your husband's case, the defense will likely subpoena you as a witness for Joan."

"I'd be happy to help, in whatever way I can." Loretta shared a long look with Joan. "Thank you, Joan. You were very brave today. Soon, this will all be over, and I look forward to seeing you on a stage someday."

"You will, Mrs. Davenport," Joan said with a shy smile. "Someday."

Chapter 38

May 1956

Loretta sat in Dr. Hansen's gardens, sipping a frothy drink next to Barbara and Vera while Charlotte and Luke played with the new puppy. It was a beautiful spring day, and the children had been home with her for just over a week. They'd enjoyed choosing their rooms in Dr. Hansen's guest cottage. Luke had decided he wanted to paint a mural on his walls, and Charlotte wanted pink curtains, a pink bedspread, and pink carpet.

Life had taken on a languorous rhythm after their ordeal in family court. The hearings had been tedious and filled with paperwork that Loretta knew only half the meaning of, but she'd regained custody of the children, in full, and her divorce was underway. Pete was in jail, awaiting trial. Only time would tell whether he'd be convicted. If he ever got out of jail . . .

Loretta did her best to put her worries aside. Her children were with her, where they belonged, although they'd grown very close to their "aunts" Barb and Vera during their time with them. Loretta had even reconnected with Gladys, who'd been completely blindsided by Earl's arrest. She often came to visit, with baby Katie in tow.

As for Loretta, she and Dr. Hansen had begun working on a book together, and Loretta's weekly column for the *Star* was still going strong.

"Dinner's ready," Vera called from the grill. She brandished a hot dog in a pair of tongs. "Kids, go wash up."

"Where did Curt go?" Barbara asked, craning her elegant neck to look for him.

"He's probably buried in his work, knowing him," Loretta said. "I'll go look." She rose, slipped her sandals on, then crossed the terrace to the house.

"Curt?" Loretta called, entering the cool darkness of the house. "Vera's finished with dinner. Won't you come eat with us?"

When no answer came, Loretta went into the study. Only Oliver was there, lying in a puddle of sunlight. She searched the rest of the downstairs and saw no sign of him. She glanced up the stairs. She'd never been to the second floor. Those were Curt's living quarters, his private rooms. But she'd had just enough of Barbara's rum cocktail to make her brave, and so she slipped off her shoes and crept up the stairs on bare feet.

When she got to the landing, an open door at the end of the hall beckoned. Soft light leaked out. She padded to the door and knocked softly. "Curt?"

When he didn't answer, she pushed open the door and went inside, her curiosity getting the best of her. The room was handsomely furnished, with a massive four-poster bed and tasteful, classic art on the walls. There was evidence of Curt everywhere—his dressing gown and slippers at the foot of the bed, his cuff links in a crystal dish. The room smelled like him—warm and masculine and comforting. She heard water running. He was in the shower.

She should have left, but Loretta paused before his bookshelves, running her fingers over the leather spines. A photograph caught her eye, on the top shelf. Loretta took the silver frame down and looked at it.

It was a family portrait. In it, a younger Curt stood behind a beautiful woman with pale-blonde curls cascading over her shoulders. A little boy perched on her lap, a toy train in his hand. The same toy train Loretta had picked up once, months ago, on the day she demonstrated her abilities to Detective Pierce.

Someone cleared their throat.

Loretta nearly jumped out of her skin. She turned to see Curt standing in the doorway, dressed in only his undershirt and trousers. He was toweling his hair dry. Her eyes jumped from his bare arms, to his muscled chest, to the way his trousers rode low on his hip bones. "You startled me," she said.

"I'm sorry. But I must say, even though I never expected to find you in my bedroom, it's not at all unpleasant." He smiled, the dimple in his chin deepening.

Loretta suddenly felt light-headed. Her face blazed with embarrassment. "The food . . . the food is ready. Vera. Um. I was just . . . I was just coming to tell you."

"What's that, in your hands?"

Loretta turned the picture toward him. Her face was surely a thousand shades of red by then. "Is this your family? Esther?"

"Yes. And Gregory."

Loretta's stomach dropped as she looked at the photograph in her hands—at the pretty blonde woman she'd been jealous of all these months, and the sweet little boy smiling up at his handsome father. "She was beautiful. And your son favored you. You must miss them terribly."

"I do." He sighed, his shoulders rising and falling. He was silhouetted against the window, his face hidden in shadow. "It's easier if I don't talk about them. I don't really talk about that part of my life with anyone, Loretta. It's easier to imagine Esther as she was the last time I saw her, with Gregory, playing on a beach in Cannes. Not the best thing for a psychologist to admit, I'm afraid. But the women who come to me are vulnerable. I find they trust me more if they believe me to be married. Sometimes they get romantic ideas about their doctors, especially if they're unhappy. It's more common than you might realize."

Barbara had said the same thing. Loretta crossed her arms in front of herself, as if she were shielding her very heart from view, the photograph dangling from her hand. "I suppose that would complicate things . . . if a patient were to get the wrong sort of idea."

"Yes. It would." He came toward her, his eyes soft in the low light. "But you're not my patient, Loretta. Remember?" He gently took the silver-framed picture from her hands and replaced it on the shelf where she'd found it. "I have a confession to make."

Loretta's pulse roared in her ears. She made herself meet his gaze, though the warmth she saw there made her tremble. Whatever he said next—whether it broke her heart or sent it soaring—she would hear him out. She would listen to what he had to say.

"When I first met you, I was attracted to you, certainly, but also . . . if your abilities proved to be real, I thought perhaps you might be able to help me. Not only with my research. But with Esther. I thought you might be able to bridge the gap. Bring her or Gregory back to me, in some small way." Curtis smiled sadly. "When they died, it was as if a part of myself had been forever lost. That day, in my office with Detective Pierce, when you held Esther's pearls, I was hoping she would come through."

"We should try again. She might come through, yet. Now that I know who wore them and how much she meant to you . . ."

Curt reached out and brushed a hand gently across Loretta's cheek. "No, Loretta. She won't come through. And even if she did, I must learn to let go of the past. Because I've realized I'm quite in love with someone else."

"Oh. Curt . . . I . . ."

He silenced her with a kiss, pressing her back against the wall. Loretta's knees nearly buckled as his warmth surrounded her. She wound her arms around his neck, returning his ardor. This was happening. It was really happening. Her Dr. Hansen—her beloved friend—wanted her just as much as she wanted him. He moved to kiss the soft skin below her jaw, his hands roving over her body as her deepest forbidden fantasy became reality. She closed her eyes, desire blooming low in her belly.

She would give him the world, in this moment, if he asked. But she wanted it to be right.

"I love you," she whispered, gently pushing against his chest. "I *do* love you. But I need time."

"Of course you do," he said, stepping back to gaze at her with heavy-lidded eyes. "I'm sorry. I shouldn't have been so rash."

"Don't be silly. I've been wanting you to do that to me for months. And more." She laughed and toed the soft carpet with her bare foot. "I just need to find out who I really am first, Curt. I've been lost for so long, in someone else's desires, in someone else's needs. I *think* I have an idea of who I am. Finally, after twenty-eight years. But I need to be sure. For your sake, as well as mine. I want to take the kids and travel. Meet new people and see what's beyond Myrna Grove. I need a sense of what freedom really tastes like. That way I'll appreciate having it all the more."

"I understand." Curt gently lifted her chin, gazing into her eyes. "Take all the time you need, Loretta."

Chapter 39

Loretta blinked slowly, watching Curt as he slept. Her nerves still hummed from his touch, from the delicious things they'd done together. She wrapped her leg around him, molding her naked body to his. He stirred slightly, drawing her close.

When they'd finally come together, after the long summer months filled with longing, he had wanted to see her. All of her. And she'd let him.

At first, she'd flinched away when his fingers grazed the scars on her belly. When he looked up at her, his eyes filled with love and concern, she merely shook her head. "Not now," she whispered. "I don't want to talk about that right now." And so, he bent his head and kissed her there, and then he made her fall apart. With his hands. With his mouth. With his body.

As he made love to her, Loretta knew she was beautiful. Desirable. Complete. Accepted as she was and respected for it. But most of all, she knew she was loved.

Curt opened his eyes. "What are you thinking about, Loretta?"

"How content I am. Here, with you. I saw lots of places on my travels. Experienced things I never imagined. But all I could think about was how much I wished you were with us. You are my home, Curt. My sanctuary. You have been, from the very first day I came here."

He lifted her hand to his mouth and kissed it. "I'll always be your home."

"You always say the right things, Dr. Hansen." Loretta tucked her head beneath his chin, listened to the steady thrum of his heart. "Has anyone ever told you that?"

"Perhaps. A time or two."

EPILOGUE

Loretta finished dressing the turkey and put it in the oven to roast long and slow. Charlotte was in the living room with the grandkids, their fair hair tinged with morning light from the floor-to-ceiling windows. "Looks like a big crowd," Charlotte said. "We'd better go down soon, find a spot, so the kids can see."

"You say that every year, Char. We won't miss anything." Loretta smiled, pausing to rest her hand on Sylvie's head. The child looked up at her grandmother and smiled, then went back to playing with her sister and the wooden puzzles Curt had given them upon their arrival the day before. "Are Luke and his friend ready? Dale, isn't it?"

"This one is David," Charlotte said, tossing her mane of blonde hair. "Dale was last year. I can't keep them straight, either."

"I heard that," Luke said, from down the hall. He emerged, yawning, his long hair mussed becomingly around his shoulders. He was already dressed, in green velvet pants with flared legs that emphasized his height, and a peasant top half-open at the chest, a leather jacket thrown casually over his shoulders. There was something of Pete in the way he walked, cocky and self-assured, but he held none of his father's worst traits, much to Loretta's relief. He went into the kitchen, plucked an apple from the fruit basket, and leaned against the pillars separating the kitchen from the living room. "I think Dave and I might go to a party in the Village this weekend. Check things out. You want to go with us, Char?"

Charlotte waved her hand. "You know that's not my scene."

Loretta listened as her children bantered good-naturedly, opposites in many ways, yet the same in many others, as they'd always been. With Loretta's guidance, Charlotte had come to embrace her inherited gifts of clairvoyance. She hosted discreet readings for highbrow clients in Philadelphia, where she lived with the children and her husband, Brian, who was a trauma surgeon, on call during the holiday.

Luke had managed to evade the draft—much to Loretta's relief—and now lived in Chicago among the burgeoning arts community, where he had a roster of patrons who regularly commissioned his fantastical, dreamlike paintings. Loretta was proud of both of her children's accomplishments. But mostly, she was glad that they were happy.

She wandered into her and Curt's shared study and paused to gaze out the window at the Manhattan skyline and the parade beginning to come to life below. She and Curt had moved to New York ten years before, after the kids had flown the nest and Myrna Grove became too quiet and small for their ambitions. She found it easier, being here, where something was always happening. She and Curt were often asked to speak at events, and he was in high demand as a lecturer. They had coauthored several books on parapsychology, and Loretta still occasionally used her abilities to aid in missing persons and murder investigations. But it was Loretta's fiction that had brought them here. The popularity of her novels had eventually made it possible for Curt to close his practice so they might focus on the metaphysical work that brought them together in the first place.

She went to the shelves lining the walls and chose a slim volume, holding it in her hands before opening it. She still remembered the day she'd begun the story, in a dark, cold basement, on an ancient typewriter with keys that stuck, when hopelessness and depression ruled her days.

The Girl in the Shadows had gone on to become a bestseller and had opened the door to all the books that followed—haunting novels about troubled young women with sly, quick minds. But Rachel, the protagonist of *Girl*, would always be Loretta's favorite, because she was based on someone Loretta once knew.

"You're ever saving Ophelia in all your books, darling." That's what Curt had told her, just last night, when she'd shown him her latest draft.

"That's because Ophelia *needs* saving," she'd answered. "From all sorts of monsters. Even the monsters within."

Loretta opened the book and took out the letter she'd tucked between the pages, long ago. The ink had smeared slightly over the years, but it was still legible.

Dear Loretta,

I'll always be grateful for what you did for me. There's so much I would change if I could. I've replayed that night over and over, in my mind. I should have left with Darcy. Should have been wearing my glasses. Should have hit the deer, instead of swerving. I should have never slept with Pete. If I hadn't, none of this would have happened. But Darcy doesn't haunt me anymore. I feel like she's at peace now.

The music program is going well. The director says I infuse all my work with deep meaning and a sense of melancholy. He thinks I'll even make it to the Met, someday. Here's hoping.

Please write back when you have the chance.
Joan

"Ah, there you are."

Loretta turned at the sound of Curt's voice. She slid the book back onto the shelf and went to greet her husband with a kiss.

"The kids are ready to go down, if you are," he said. "Sylvie and Sophie are very excited."

"I'm sure they are!"

Loretta followed Curt into the foyer and pulled on her coat. They all trundled onto the elevator, Luke's friend still wiping the sleep from his eyes. When they joined the crowd lining Central Park West, the parade was just beginning. Loretta remembered a time when she and the kids had only watched the parade on television, and she'd promised to someday take them to see it in real life. For the past decade, it had been their tradition. She hoped it always would be.

Curt hoisted little Sophie onto his shoulders as Tom Turkey passed by on his long trek to Herald Square, animatronic eyes slowly blinking. Loretta leaned against Curt with a contented sigh, a paper mug of hot chocolate in her hands. Their marriage was a partnership of equals. They had made one another happy, in every way. Surrounded by her family, Loretta thought of the lost girl she once was, and smiled, knowing she had found herself, at long last.

AUTHOR'S NOTE

This novel was born of three things: my appreciation and respect for homemakers, my love of Shirley Jackson . . . and groceries. When this idea came to me, on an ordinary spring afternoon, I was putting away the latest grocery delivery, sorting through the refrigerator to find room for the new additions. The title popped into my head first, which led me to ask several questions: Who was this mysterious Mrs. Davenport? What did her world look like? Was she happy? What did she want most? And who was the "devil" in this story? Later that day, I had crafted a bare-bones plot about a midcentury psychic housewife. At the time, I was twenty thousand words into another novel, which I quickly put to the side in order to chase this new idea. It has been my experience that the very best ideas hit like this—out of the blue, during times when your mind isn't even on writing.

During the COVID-19 lockdown and after, when I served as my mother's live-in caregiver, my life was steeped in domesticity. I cooked. I cleaned. I washed endless sinks full of dishes. By necessity, my writing was mostly relegated to the wee hours of the morning. This deep dive into domestic life got me to thinking about women like my grandmother, and how they must have felt as lifelong homemakers. I soon came to realize that their (often thankless) work must have been all-consuming, without any breaks in either the monotony or the workload.

And so, this novel initially came about as my homage to homemakers—a difficult job that is often maligned through the scope of modern feminism. While sweeping changes in the 1960s and '70s brought much-needed reform and helped establish equal rights for women, women such as Loretta, who had married young and had no workforce experience, often found themselves unemployable. Even if they wanted to escape their lives of domesticity, they felt trapped—and many of them were. Abusive, controlling marriages, such as Loretta's, were all too common. In the United States, women could not take out a loan, or sign up for a line of credit, and they were often unable to open their own bank accounts without their husband's or another male family member's permission until the 1970s. No-fault divorce did not exist before then in most states, either. For the majority of married women at midcentury, joining the workforce was an impossible feat. If a woman was granted a divorce and custody of her children, entry-level, nonprofessional jobs rarely yielded enough income to support a family, and alimony wasn't always guaranteed.

Even if a woman was happily married and her husband supported her career aspirations, if she had children (and this was the Baby Boom, so large families were common), who would watch the children while she worked? Like Loretta, women had to employ creative means in order to pave their way and assert their independence within the confines of midcentury marriage.

No writer did this better than Shirley Jackson, who successfully juggled the demands of domesticity with her writing career. She cheekily wrote in *Life Among the Savages* that when she went to the hospital to deliver her third child, the desk clerk asked her to name her profession. When she answered with "writer," the clerk wrote down "housewife" instead! By the time *Life Among the Savages* was published, Shirley was at the height of her career and squarely the main breadwinner of her household. While Loretta isn't a fictionalized version of Jackson, Shirley Jackson's influence can be seen throughout this novel, and in my work in general. Along with Daphne du Maurier, from whom Loretta takes her pen name, these iconic female authors helped till the ground in which modern, feminist gothic fiction took root.

Jackson's brand of quiet horror, as well as her humorous domestic memoirs, with their small-town, provincial characters, work as wry social commentary and offer a glimpse into the lives of women at midcentury. In Jackson's horror novels, women disappear, run away, and often encounter malevolent, misogynistic characters that feel all too familiar. If you'd like to know more about Shirley Jackson and the inspiration behind her work, I highly recommend Ruth Franklin's phenomenal biography, *Shirley Jackson: A Rather Haunted Life.* While writing this novel, I reread most of Shirley Jackson's catalog, including her lesser-known work: *Hangsaman, The Road Through the Wall,* and *Life Among the Savages,* all of which helped inform my chosen dialogue, details of the Davenport family's daily life, and aspects of culture specific to the era, through a gothic lens.

Hangsaman, in particular, served as the primary inspiration for my novel and the characters of Paula Buckley and Darcy Hayes. This short, quietly horrific novel stars a precocious and impulsive college student, Natalie Waite, who was rumored to be based on Paula Jean Welden—a student at the women's college, Bennington, where Jackson's husband later became a professor. At the time of Paula's disappearance, however, the Jacksons were living in Connecticut, so any inspiration Shirley may have taken from this news story is purely conjecture, although the similarities between fact and fiction are fascinating to consider. Paula Jean Welden disappeared from North Bennington one fall afternoon, while taking a walk in the woods. She was never found. Over the years, several other young women vanished from the same largely rural corner of Vermont, causing the media to dub it the "Bennington Triangle." While far from Vermont, the Ozarks (the setting for this novel) have also had their share of unsolved murders and disappearances—most of them young women.

In 1992, the summer before my senior year of high school, three local women went missing under mysterious circumstances. Called "The Springfield Three," Sherill Levitt, her daughter, Suzie Streeter, and Suzie's best friend, Stacy McCall, disappeared one afternoon from Levitt's home, leaving all their personal belongings behind. The only evidence of a struggle was a broken porch light globe. Over the years, many theories surfaced concerning what might have happened to these women, but all investigations (including those of a psychic nature) have turned up no new leads, and the case remains unsolved. If you have any information about the Springfield Three, please contact the Springfield, Missouri, Police Department; the Missouri Highway Patrol; or the Federal Bureau of Investigations.

And there are others—Shirley Jane Rose. Tina Sue Spencer. Gloria Jean Barnes. Angie Hammond. All Missouri women whose unsolved murders and abductions deserve justice and answers.

It bears repeating that any historical inaccuracies or errors found within this novel are my own, although I made every attempt to portray the era with accuracy. During my research for this novel, I consulted several resources. For a general overview of American history during the Eisenhower era, I read *The Age of Eisenhower: America and the World in the 1950s* by William I. Hitchcock. I also gleaned much about day-to-day life in the 1950s from reading Honor Moore's wonderful biographical memoir, *Our Revolution: A Mother and Daughter at Midcentury*, as well as works of contemporary fiction from the era. During the course of writing and revising this novel, I reread Sylvia Plath's *The Bell Jar* and *One Flew Over the Cuckoo's Nest* by Ken Kesey to help inform my portrayal of Loretta's struggle with mental illness and her institutionalization at Agape Manor, as well *Desperate Remedies: Psychiatry's Turbulent Quest to Cure Mental Illness*, by Andrew Scull to provide a historical overview of the psychiatric protocol and treatments that would have been in place during Loretta's lifetime. I also consulted with attorney and fellow author Mansi Shah, who provided articles from the *Missouri Law Review* concerning the laws governing involuntary psychiatric hospitalization during the era, as well as divorce and family law in the midfifties.

Finally, regarding Dr. Hansen and Loretta's studies in parapsychology, I consulted *Unbelievable: Investigations into Ghosts, Poltergeists, Telepathy, and Other Unseen Phenomena, From the Duke Parapsychology Laboratory* by Stacy Horn. The Duke parapsychology lab, directed by Dr. J. B. Rhine, and housed within the university's psychology department, was the first time that parapsychology was studied in a scientific setting. Rhine's work was initially mocked by establishment-trained scientists and academics alike, but Rhine's research successfully helped demonstrate the existence of telepathy and other paranormal phenomena, such as psychokinesis. The lab eventually garnered the attention of several respected scientists of the era, among them Carl Jung, who was considerably more open than his compatriots to the value of studying the metaphysical. The anecdote about the medium who developed psychic abilities after falling off a ladder, as mentioned by my fictional Dr. Hansen, is real: he was Peter Hurkos, a former house painter from the Netherlands, who contacted Rhine after his mind-altering accident. The twins Dr. Hansen mentions in his lecture were also real case studies from Dr. Rhine's lab. While I took some minor liberties with Dr. Hansen's characterization as both psychologist and parapsychologist, his professional interests and investigative curiosity about the unknown, as well as his charisma, have much in common with J. B. Rhine.

One of Rhine's contemporaries, Hans Holzer, was also an avid student of parapsychology and the metaphysical. During his lifetime, he authored well over a hundred books on the paranormal. During my research, I read *Are You Psychic? Unlocking the Power Within* and *Psychic: True Paranormal Experiences*, which gave perspective on the varying types of psychic phenomena and abilities a person might possess. I also studied *The Law of Psychic Phenomena*, by Thomson Jay Hudson, which is one of the books Dr. Hansen loans Loretta. While outdated by modern standards, the episodes of psychic phenomena described in the book added depth and historical value to my research. With its emphasis on hypnosis and mesmerism, Hudson's work would have definitely held a place in Dr. Hansen's library!

Myrna Grove itself is a fictionalized version of my hometown: Springfield, Missouri. While I took liberties with some place-names, longtime citizens of Springfield will remember many of the businesses I mention with a sense of nostalgia. Consumers Market, the Shady Inn, Savage Juliet (spelled Juliette), the Riverside Inn, and Anton's were all landmark businesses in the Ozarks, which would have been around during the time in which this novel is set, apart from Anton's Coffee Shop, which did not open until 1974. Dearing Park is Doling Park in real life, and did indeed once house an amusement park—although no murdered women were ever found in its cave, that I'm aware of.

Bethel University is fictional, although Springfield is very much a university town, having several colleges, many of them with an ecumenical/evangelical foundation. I loosely based the campus of Bethel on the Drury University campus, which has all the beauty and charm of an Ivy League college. Although Drury is not a Bible college, it was originally founded as an "independent church-related" college. Bethel's academic philosophy more closely resembles that of Evangel University, which was founded by the Assemblies of God—Loretta's denomination.

Like Loretta, I was once a member of the Assemblies of God— one of the largest Pentecostal denominations in the world. Founded in America in 1914, Assemblies' churches believe in two baptisms: the Baptism of Salvation, and the Baptism of the Holy Spirit, with the evidence of speaking in tongues. Pentecostalism also carries a strong belief in faith healing and deliverance (which is akin to exorcism). At best, deliverance might look like a gentle laying on of hands and prayer; at worst, it can result in a theatrical explosion of emotion and violence. While the deliverance scene in this book may seem extreme, there are many accounts of deliverance and exorcism attempts that have gone too far, resulting in injury or death. In 2022, a three-year-old child, Arely Naomi Proctor, was killed by her family during a deliverance session at their small church in California. Her parents were thoroughly convinced she was possessed by demons and that they were saving her. The cognitive dissonance required to justify such actions may seem astounding, but to adherents of charismatic faith healing, demonic oppression is all too real and a threat to the eternal soul as well as the temporal body.

My hope, dear reader, is that you will examine Loretta's story, measure it against today's issues, and come to your own conclusions. Whether you are a person of faith or not, violence and a general lack of understanding, undercut by fear, are as rife today as they were in the 1950s and '60s, during the Civil Rights Movement and Women's Rights Movement. With new draconian laws and policies targeting women, minorities, and those of us in the LGBTQ+ community being established almost daily, it takes all of us who are willing to listen and take action to make a difference. The biggest threat to liberty is our own hypocrisy and indifference.

Thank you so much for reading.

ACKNOWLEDGMENTS

In many ways, writing this novel proved incredibly difficult. After the death of my mother in late 2022, I found myself unable to write for many, many weeks. During this fallow period, the encouragement of friends and family gave me the strength to move forward and find the words I needed, despite my grief. While this novel isn't dedicated to my mother, there is so much of her in it. Like Loretta, she suffered in abusive, controlling marriages, and I bore witness to the insidious nature of domestic abuse as a result. My mom didn't live long enough to see me finish this novel, but she knew about the premise, and told me she wished she'd read a book like mine when she was younger. So, Mom, I hope you're proud, wherever you are. Loretta would have never existed without you.

If you or someone you love is suffering from domestic violence and abuse, please reach out. Talk to a friend or contact the National Domestic Violence Hotline at 1-800-799-SAFE (7233). Help is out there, no matter how helpless you may feel.

I'm eternally grateful to my own husband, Ryan, for not being like the husbands in my novels. And to Avery, who challenges me to be stronger than the roots I grew from. I am a better mother because of who you are.

I am filled with gratitude to my agent, Jill Marr, who is an ever-present source of encouragement and belief in my work. I am so lucky to have you in my corner.

And by extension, a huge thank-you to the entire team at Sandra Dijkstra Literary Agency, who work tirelessly behind the scenes with rights, royalties, and all the other important things that help ensure my success as an author.

And to my editors: Firstly, Erin Adair-Hodges, whose wisdom and sparkling wit serve to both educate and inspire. You are an absolute pleasure to work with, and I'm so thrilled to have your support and guidance.

To Jodi Warshaw, my developmental editor for this novel, and the novels before it. You were the first editor to believe in me, and always a joy to work with. I'm so glad we got to work together again.

To Danielle Marshall and Melissa Valentine—thank you deeply for championing *The Witch of Tin Mountain* and my career. I'm honored to be part of the Lake Union family.

Special thanks to the rest of the Lake Union crew: Gabriella Dumpit, Kellie Osborne, Jill Schoenhaut, and Kimberly Glyder for a remarkable cover. A book doesn't become a book without an amazing team of professionals. I'm thankful for each and every one of you.

To my steadfast critique partner, Thuy M. Nguyen, for your insights and your unflappable support and friendship. I'd be lost without you.

To my #RevPit and Writer in Motion family: Maria Tureaud, Jessica Lewis, S. Kaeth, Megan Van Dyke, Alex Gotay, Belinda Grant, Kathryn Hewitt, Justine Manzano, Melissa Bergum, Sheryl Stein, Susan Burdorf, Jessie Braverman, Kristen Howe, Jenna Mandarino, and Jeni Chappell: you all *carried* me through 2022. Thank you for checking in on me. Thank you for your cards and letters. Thank you for the love. I felt it. Immensely. And I love all of you right back.

To the brilliant and witty Sara Goodman Confino—your texts and encouragement kept me afloat, even when I felt like I could not write one more word. You knew I could finish this book, and I did. I love you!

Thank you to Mansi Shah, who offered advice on the legal matters in this novel, as well as a listening ear. You make Los Angeles seem a lot smaller because of your friendship. I can't wait for our next author lunch!

To my APub sisters Jennifer Bardsley, Eden Appiah-Kubi, and Elissa Grossell Dickey—thanks for everything you have done to show your support. I can't believe it's been more than three years since our debut novels launched, and I'm so happy our friendship has endured beyond.

To Agatha Andrews of the *She Wore Black* podcast, whose support of the gothic, mystery, and horror community shines like a beacon, especially for marginalized and underrepresented writers.

To Hester Fox and the other Gothic and Dark Fiction chat authors—thank you so much for everything you have done to demonstrate your friendship. Hester, you write the most beautiful blurbs, and I'm grateful to share a genre with someone who is so unfailingly gracious and talented.

To my fellow Blue Sky Book Chat authors, Barbara Davis, Thelma Adams, Marilyn Simon Rothstein, Christine Nolfi, Susan Walter, Joy Jordan-Lake, Patricia Sands, Lainey Cameron, Bette Lee Crosby, and Alison Ragsdale: thank you for providing a platform to interact with our readers and to celebrate all our wins. Special thanks to Kerry Anne King / Kerry Schafer for all the admin work you do to keep things running smoothly!

Big thanks to Suzanne Leopold of Suzy Approved Book Tours for your continued support!

Special thanks to author friends Piper Huguley, Aimie K. Runyan-Vetter, Allison Epstein, Nicole Eigener, Andie Newton, Louisa Morgan, Libbie Grant / Olivia Hawker, Nancy Bilyeau, Kris Waldherr, Olesya Salnikova Gilmore, Jane Healey, Rochelle Weinstein, Tif Marcelo, Constance Sayers, Robert Gwaltney, Erin Litteken, Alyssa Palombo, and so many others . . . Your camaraderie, advice, and support mean more than you know!

To the reviewers, Bookstagram influencers, and podcasters who have taken the time to have me as a guest, to feature my work in any way, and to show your interest in my writing: thank you, from the bottom of my heart.

And finally, to my readers: thank you for being the living, breathing soul behind my words. Without readers, these books would be nothing more than the musings of a socially awkward Gen Xer. Knowing you want more books is the reason I pull myself out of bed every day at five a.m. to write. I wouldn't be able to do any of this without you.

DISCUSSION QUESTIONS

1. When Loretta first develops her psychic abilities, she believes them to be a gift from God. How did you interpret this, within the scope of your own beliefs? Were her powers real or a figment of her imagination?

2. Domestic abuse is a major theme throughout the novel. At first, the reader might be fooled into thinking Pete is a good husband. How did you find your feelings shifting concerning Loretta and Pete as the abuse became more obvious? Does this mirror any relationships you've witnessed or experienced in real life?

3. From the #MeToo movement to the scandalous and criminal behavior of many of today's evangelical leaders, Pete's serial manipulation of young women might seem familiar. What are some of the ways the events of this novel mirror modern examples of misogyny, sexism, and abuses of power?

4. Loretta's relationship with Dr. Hansen is a central component of this novel. Did you find their eventual romance gratifying? Do you feel he overstepped professional boundaries with Loretta, given the era? Why or why not?

5. When the cracks begin appearing inside the Davenport home, did you feel the destruction of the house had ties to Loretta's psychic abilities? Or was it simply a natural consequence of the sinkhole beneath the house?

6. The titular "Devil" might be interpreted in many ways. Loretta faces many devils throughout this novel: depression, abuse, infidelity, institutionalization. How did you interpret the symbolism of the devil in this novel?

7. Did you find Joan to be a sympathetic character? Why or why not?

8. At the end of the book, we see Loretta nearly twenty years later. Were you satisfied by the ending? Were any of your questions left unanswered?

ABOUT THE AUTHOR

Paulette Kennedy is the bestselling author of *The Witch of Tin Mountain* and *Parting the Veil*, which received the prestigious HNS Review Editor's Choice Award. She has had a lifelong obsession with the gothic. As a young girl, she spent her summers among the gravestones in her neighborhood cemetery, imagining all sorts of romantic stories for the people buried there. After her mother introduced her to the Brontës as a teenager, her affinity for fog-covered landscapes and haunted heroines only grew, inspiring her to become a writer. Originally from the Missouri Ozarks, she now lives with her family and a menagerie of rescue pets in sunny Southern California, where sometimes, on the very best days, the mountains are wreathed in fog. For more information, visit www.paulettekennedy.com.